T0196614

Entangled Secrets

ALSO BY PAT ESDEN

The Northern Circle Coven series
His Dark Magic
Things She's Seen
Entangled Secrets

The Dark Heart series
A Hold on Me
Beyond Your Touch
Reach for You

Published by Kensington Publishing Corp.

Entangled Secrets

A Northern Circle Coven Novel

Pat Esden

LYRICAL PRESS
Kensington Publishing Corp.
www.kensingtonbooks.com

LYRICAL PRESS BOOKS are published by

Kensington Publishing Corp.
119 West 40th Street
New York, NY 10018

All Kensington titles, imprints, and distributed lines are available at special quantity discounts for bulk purchases for sales promotion, premiums, fund-raising, educational, or institutional use.

Special book excerpts or customized printings can also be created to fit specific needs. For details, write or phone the office of the Kensington Sales Manager: Kensington Publishing Corp., 119 West 40th Street, New York, NY 10018. Attn. Sales Department. Phone: 1-800-221-2647.

Lyrical Press and Lyrical Press logo Reg. US Pat. & TM Off.

First Electronic Edition: July 2020
ISBN-13: 978-1-5161-0634-9 (ebook)
ISBN-10: 1-5161-0634-2 (ebook)

First Print Edition: July 2020
ISBN-13: 978-1-5161-0635-6
ISBN-10: 1-5161-0635-0

Printed in the United States of America

For my sisters, Robin and Ruby:
because they too cast spells woven from
the power and beauty of the imagination.

Acknowledgments

First and foremost, I'd like to thank all the readers, reviewers, and bloggers who have supported my novels. There is no greater joy than to be cruising social media and discover a review or kind mention. Seriously, you bring joy to my heart and make future books possible.

To my first readers, Casey Griffin and Jaye Robin Brown, you rate my undying gratitude and a massive number of hugs. Both of you are pure magic. I'd also like to thank Suzanne Warr and Lily Black for your ongoing astute suggestions.

Sincerest thanks to my brilliant editor Elizabeth Trout for your support, wisdom, and for inspiring me and giving me freedom. And to Selena James; without you, the Northern Circle Coven series would be nothing more than a crazy dream.

I'd also like to thank all the wonderful people at Kensington Publishing and Lyrical Press. A special nod to Alexandra Kenney. Thank you for all the time, work, and thought you put into the Northern Circle Coven series.

Chapter 1

*Burlington's flying monkeys. The originals
were crafted out of steel decades ago.
I created mine out of car parts and garden
tools as a gift to my son on his third birthday.
Truly, if I could have made them fly, I would have.*
—WPZI interview with artist Chandler Parrish

Chandler set the hand grinder aside and flipped up the visor of her welding helmet. She studied the fist-size heart on the workbench in front of her and smiled, pleased with the results. If she could just find the perfect strands of wire to use for the arteries and veins, the heart would be ready to install.

She glanced across the workshop to where her latest flying monkey sculpture crouched on a rusty oil drum. It was crafted from scrap metal like its predecessors. But this one was going to be an updated model with a trapdoor in its chest and a heart—a cross between the Tin Man and the flying monkeys of Oz fame.

"Mama?" Her son's voice came from behind her.

"Yeah?" She turned to see what he wanted.

Peregrine stood in the workshop's open doorway, silhouetted against the autumn-orange leaves of a maple that sheltered the entry. Dirt smeared his jeans. His wild blond hair was tangled. Her chest swelled with joy. If she could ask the Gods and Goddesses for anything, it would be for his life to remain as carefree as that of the eight-year-old he was right now.

"Devlin sent me to get you. Some guy's waiting in the main house."

"Who is it?" Chandler asked.

He shrugged. "I don't know. The guy saw a shapeshifter turn into a loup-garou. Wish I'd seen it."

Chandler pulled off her welding helmet and thumped it down on the workbench. *Damn it.* Their mystery visitor had to be the journalist. His spotting a shapeshifter transforming in public—illegally, of course—wasn't that recent of news, but his dogged interest in the event, and his intrusion into the Northern Circle coven's ongoing issues in general, was proving to be a major pain. Actually, she was shocked he'd showed up here at the coven's complex. A couple of days ago, two coven members had paid him a not-so-friendly visit at the fleabag motel where he'd been staying to discover if he truly was a threat to the witching world's anonymity, or if he'd only come across as crazy to the average person.

"Devlin thinks the guy's lying," Peregrine added.

"Even if Devlin did believe him, he couldn't tell the journalist what he saw was real, right?"

"I don't think Devlin likes him."

"That's because the journalist is a troublemaker." She walked over to Peregrine and smoothed her hand down his cheek. At twenty-five, Devlin was younger than she by almost four years, but that made him no less wise. He was Ivy League smart, a powerful witch with polished good looks and a kind heart that made him perfect for the Circle's high priest position. She gentled her voice. "Do you know where Brooklyn is?"

Peregrine nodded. "She and Midas are making dinner."

"I need you to go help them until the visitor leaves. Okay?"

Peregrine stuck out his bottom lip in a pout. "Can't I just listen? I wanna hear about the loup-garou. Please?"

"Not this time." She crouched, looked him in the eyes, and turned on her mama-dragon voice. "You need to stay away from this man. He's dangerous. Understand?"

"He didn't look dangerous to me. He just talked kinda funny."

"No arguing. I want you to hang out with Brooklyn and Midas. I'll tell you all about it later."

Peregrine glanced over his shoulder toward the yard, then his gaze whipped back to her. "What do redcaps really look like?"

Chandler shook her head. Peregrine's ability to shift seamlessly from one topic to another never ceased to amaze her. "Where in the Goddesses' name did that question come from?"

He tucked his hands into his pockets and shrugged. "Just wonderin'." He stole another glance behind him. His voice trembled a little. "Do they really dip their hats in blood?"

Chandler straightened to her full height. Hands on her hips, she followed his gaze. There was nothing unfamiliar or strange in their yard or in the parking lot beyond it, except for an old, lime-green Volkswagen Beetle in front of the main house, undoubtedly the journalist's ride.

A spark of fear flickered to life inside her, a fear she'd prayed she'd never have to face. "Did you see something strange?"

"There was this creepy person-thing next to that guy's car."

In two swift motions, she pulled him all the way inside and slammed the door shut. Heat and the thrum of protective magic blazed up the dragon and monkey tattoos on her arms and across her shoulders. She studied the yard again through the door's window, hoping to spot a fox or a mangy racoon. Something. Anything.

Peregrine wriggled in beside her, his breath fogging the windowpane. "It kinda looked like the drawings of redcaps I've seen in books."

She scrubbed her fingers over the soft bristle of her close-cropped hair. *Shit. Shit. Shit.* Not this. Anything but this. Peregrine was the age when most witches' abilities manifested. And—though she rarely thought of him—Peregrine's biological father possessed the gift of faery sight, an ability to see through the glamour faeries used to make themselves invisible; fae such as redcaps. The gift was rare nowadays because the gene pool of witches with the ability had shrunk to a handful, after eons of them being murdered or blinded by the fae, who preferred to remain concealed. It was an extraordinarily dangerous gift for the few adults who possessed it. But for an eight-year-old boy? For her boy?

She wrapped an arm around Peregrine's shoulder, snugging him closer. "Are you a hundred percent sure you saw something?"

"Yeah. Uh—maybe."

Maybe? Her tension eased a fraction. In truth, it could have been nothing more than wishful thinking on Peregrine's part, combined with an imagination as active as hers. Even if he had seen a faery, it could have been a benign and unglamoured one that Brooklyn had invited into the complex to help with her herbs and concoctions.

A movement caught Chandler's eye. Something coyote-size and hunched low to the ground was creeping out from behind the Volkswagen. It slunk along, dragging something—

Chandler shrieked. A body! A child.

She pushed Peregrine behind her, then eased the door open just far enough to get a better view. She had to have been mistaken. It couldn't be carrying a child.

The creature swiveled to look at her. It dropped the body. Tufts of straw trailed from where the child was missing an arm.

Chandler let out a relieved breath. She recognized the child and the creature now. "There's nothing to worry about," she said. "It's just Henry with Brooklyn's scarecrow." Well, there wasn't anything to worry about as long as Brooklyn didn't see Henry, Devlin's golden retriever, making off with her straw man. If she did, there'd be hell to pay.

Peregrine wiggled past her to look. "I wasn't afraid of nothin'. And that isn't what I saw. What I saw was bigger. A lot bigger." He fanned his arms, indicating something twice as tall and large as the scrap-metal rhinoceros that she'd sold to a client last month, impossibly larger than a redcap.

She gave him a side-eye look. Now he was fibbing, except...

A chill traveled up her arms, prickling against the magic in her tattoos. But what if—other than the size—it wasn't a fib? What if he did have the sight like his father?

Chapter 2

*Some say the duplicity comes from demons vying for man's soul
or the fae seeking sovereignty over this realm.
Many believe it's witches tainted by a lust for power.
It is all these things and more.*
—Rafael Mastroianni, High Chancellor
Eastern Coast High Council of Witches

"Do redcaps leave footprints?" Peregrine asked as they passed the journalist's Volkswagen on their way to the main house.

"Can we not talk about redcaps anymore?" Chandler said.

He scuffed his feet against the walk. "If their hats are all bloody, why don't they leave a gooey trail wherever they go?"

"That's disgusting."

"I wish I'd see someone shift into a loup-garou. I wonder if Gar can shift. His father's a loup-garou…"

Chandler tuned out Peregrine's chatter, focusing instead on the soothing energy wheeling off the main house. The brick building that served as the heart of the coven's complex had been an abandoned factory before Devlin and his sister, Athena—who had served as high priestess beside him—had taken over the project of revitalizing it from their mother. Chandler had loved the place from the first moment she'd arrived, well over eight years ago now. There was something about its psychic energy. Perhaps it was the memories imprinted into its scarred floorboards by the factory workers who'd traveled over them for decades, or the emotions crackling off the graffiti that still slashed its brick-walled hallways, tags left behind by people who had claimed the factory during the years it stood forsaken.

Chandler couldn't help wondering if their current confrontation with the journalist would also fuse itself to the building's soul.

Of course it will, she answered her own question. If the journalist hadn't attempted to infiltrate the coven, things might not have gotten to the point where the Circle couldn't ignore him. But he had—and, unfortunately, it had happened after a witch by the name of Rhianna had murdered Athena and used dark magic to impersonate her. Every single member of the coven felt ashamed that they had failed to realize Rhianna wasn't Athena. However, the journalist most likely still believed that Athena, and not Rhianna, had performed the ghastly spell that left his brain scrambled.

Chandler opened the building's front door and let Peregrine race into the foyer ahead of her. He spread his arms out as if transforming into the falcon he was named after. Then he screamed into the hallway, his birdlike shrieks echoing off the brick walls as he made for the stairwell down to the first floor.

She rushed after him. But by the time she reached the open stairwell, he was already in the living room below. He made a loop around Chloe, who was setting a bottle of wine on the coffee table, then beelined into the lounge before vanishing into the dining room hallway. Hopefully, Brooklyn and Midas would be able to keep him occupied for at least a few minutes.

Chandler hurried down the stairs. "Where is everyone? I thought the journalist was here?"

Chloe was in her early twenties, willowy, blonde and bound-for-med-school brilliant. She was one of the most recent initiates to the coven, but she and Devlin had already formed a close relationship. That was a good thing; coping with the fallout from Athena's murder hadn't been easy for any of them, especially not for Devlin. He loved his sister deeply and needed the support—and distraction—of a vivacious witch like Chloe.

Sadness tightened Chandler's chest. She missed Athena so much. Sure, Athena's spirit was still present. But that wasn't the same as having her longtime friend around, not at all the same.

"Unfortunately," Chloe said, "the journalist is most definitely here. Devlin and Gar are giving him a tour of the teahouse right now. They should be back any second."

Chandler frowned. "A tour seems a little friendly, all things considered."

"I imagine they're testing to see how much he remembers about the stuff that happened here with Rhianna. Not to mention trying to figure out if he really witnessed a loup-garou transforming."

"That does sound smart." Chandler eyed the wine bottle, weighed the idea of having a glass, and decided against it. "I wish I'd met the journalist that night and stopped Rhianna before she cast the spell on him. I can't believe I missed everything."

"Rhianna probably went out of her way to keep you in the dark."

"I suppose." She still felt awful about not noticing what was going on right under her nose. "How much damage do you think her magic did to him?"

"Something's wrong with him for sure. He stumbles over his words as if he can't get his thoughts to come together. If Brooklyn hadn't told me that he was fine before Rhianna's spell and worse as it went on, I'd assume he was recovering from aphasia."

An ache pulled at the back of Chandler's throat. A few years ago, when her adoptive mom had the stroke that put her in the High Council's palliative care infirmary, she'd suffered from aphasia. It had been heart-wrenching to watch such a dynamic woman struggle to form even a single word.

The glass-and-steel industrial doors that formed the back wall of the living room glided open. Devlin and the journalist strolled in, shadowed by Gar's broad-shouldered outline.

Though Chandler hadn't met the journalist before, she had seen him on TV. It had been a rebroadcast of him ranting to a reporter that witchcraft was responsible for a club fire and a ton of crazy incidents around the city. He'd come across as irrational, but he'd been a hundred percent right about everything. At the time, she'd registered only that he was a slim, determined black man in his mid to late twenties with haphazardly chopped-off hair. Now, in real life, his loose-jointed stride and crazy hair made her think of Ichabod Crane from "The Legend of Sleepy Hollow." The fact that he wore slightly twisted librarian-style glasses only added to the unconventional vibe.

Chandler pressed her lips together to hide an amused smile. If she were to create a sculpture of him, she'd start with pipes from a child's swing set for his long legs and wild curls of dark chain for his hair. She wasn't sure what she'd use for his lips. He had beautiful lips.

She clenched her hands, squeezing them tight to stop the sculpture from coming to life in her head. She couldn't afford to let his quirky appeal convince her he was harmless. He was dangerous. If they couldn't convince him he was wrong about everything he'd witnessed and keep him quiet, the High Council would rescind the reprieve they'd given the coven. The Circle would once again be accused of being responsible for breaches in the witching world's anonymity. For sure, they'd get disbanded. Worse than that, the Council could even have the members' abilities to work magic removed. Their sacred objects and all their assets could be seized, including the complex. They could lose everything.

The journalist's gaze zeroed in on her. He smiled broadly, hesitated as if gathering his thoughts, then spoke in a tone that was measured but as warm as earth in summertime. "You—are Chandler Parrish?"

She extended her hand as he walked up to her. "You're Lionel, right?"

"Lionel Parker." He took her hand, his long fingers wrapping hers in an earnest grip. "I am—a huge fan. Your sculptures are remarkable."

"Thank you." She kept hold of his hand and met his gaze full-on, buying herself time to assess his energy. He had a creative fire, kindness, empathy... His energy warped, wringing so tight she couldn't read it anymore. Whatever spell Rhianna had worked on him, it was powerful, multilayered, and fiercely debilitating. It was a miracle that Lionel was able to hold a somewhat normal conversation, let alone survive day to day with an upheaval like that going on inside him. How brilliant had he been before the spell?

As bright as the light from a welding torch, her instincts whispered.

His smile widened and his lips parted. A spark twinkled in the depths of his dark eyes.

Chandler released his hand as fast as if it were a greased cobra. Heat flushed up her cheeks. She knew that twinkle. He'd mistaken her lingering touch for romantic interest, and he wasn't rejecting it. She wouldn't have been as certain or taken aback, except she rarely saw that spark in a man's eyes. Women, yes—though she had no interest beyond friendship with them.

Gar cleared his throat. "Well, Lionel, what do you say we drop the pretenses and get to the point of this visit?"

Chandler moved away from Lionel, retreating to stand behind the coffee table with Chloe. It made sense to let Gar lead the conversation. Lionel didn't know it, but Gar was more than just a tough-looking guy in worn jeans and a camo baseball cap. He worked as a special investigator for the High Council of Witches. In fact, the coven had first met Gar when he'd been sent to assess them for possible disbandment after Lionel's rant on TV—not to mention that the Circle had awakened Merlin's Shade while under Rhianna's influence, and in turn the Shade had brought a bunch of her flying monkey sculptures to life. The important thing was, when push came to shove, Gar had proven to be the Circle's staunch ally.

Lionel's voice quieted. "I—I am not fond of games. I would prefer to get to the point."

Gar glanced toward Chandler and Chloe. "When we were touring the teahouse, Lionel admitted he isn't certain he saw a loup-garou."

"He thinks he might have seen a dog," Devlin added.

Lionel straightened to his full height, a good several inches over six feet. He spoke slowly, enunciating each word with care. "That is not right. I said I wasn't sure I saw a person transform into a loup-garou. But I did see a person—a street performer, posing as a statue of *The Thinker*—change into a wolflike animal. Um—I know shapeshifters and magic are real. I am not mistaken. And you all know it."

"What makes you so sure?" Chloe said, before Lionel could take a breath.

Chandler hated the idea of ganging up on anyone. She'd told Peregrine a million times that bullying was wrong. But browbeating Lionel into thinking things like magic, powerful witches, and shifters didn't exist was vital for the coven's welfare, and for Lionel's safety, too. Why did he have to be so determined to expose them? For that matter, what made him so willing to believe things other people dismissed as unreal?

She narrowed her eyes and took over the badgering where Chloe had left off. "Did you get a photograph of this street performer changing? A video? What proof do you have that it wasn't just part of the performer's act?"

Lionel's voice went as taut as brass strings on a harp. "Why—why are all of you so interested in convincing me that I am wrong?" His gaze darted around the room. "Where—where is your high priestess? I expected to talk to her."

Chloe stepped toward him, skirting the coffee table. "First of all, let me clarify that we aren't the Grimm's fairy tale coven you're imagining." She gave him a second to mull that over. "That said, I'm the coven's high priestess." It wasn't a lie. Chloe had agreed to temporarily take the position after they discovered Athena's murder.

"Bullshit." Lionel raised his hand, showing his wrist. The outline of a barely healed cut stood out against his skin. "The real high priestess slashed my wrist with a dagger. She took my blood. She chopped off my hair and cut my fingernails. She cast a spell on me. In this room." He shoved his misshapen glasses up higher on his nose, preparing to add an important detail. His expression pinched, like he'd lost his train of thought. Then it brightened again. "She said, 'Sacrifice willingly given. Hair and blood...'"

As he continued repeating the words of the spell, the air in the room began to vibrate with energy. It prickled against the nape of Chandler's neck and made her tattoos tingle. Lionel wasn't a witch. He didn't have any ability to work magic. But the spell Rhianna had worked on him had imprinted itself on the room.

"That's enough," Devlin snapped.

Lionel stopped reciting. "I—I am right, aren't I? You are more than Wiccan or Pagan."

"What *you* are is confused," Gar said flatly.

Chandler nodded in agreement. She slanted a look at Devlin. As high priest, he technically was the one in charge of dealing with things like this along with Chloe.

Devlin folded his arms across his chest. He rocked back on his heels. "What if you are right about us? How could you expect us to be honest with you? It's no secret that you stole an invitation in order to infiltrate one of our parties. You pretended to be a potential coven initiate. Who did you steal the invitation from? What happened to that person?"

Lionel swiveled away. He paced toward the door to the gardens. Staring out, he rubbed his hands down his arms as if the question had given him the chills. He turned around and paced back to them. "You have to understand. All my life, I've sensed magic was real. I need to prove it. I have to."

Chloe harrumphed. "You stole the invitation and lied to us in order to write an article that would expose our personal lives and whatever you think our coven does to the entire world."

"Yes," he admitted. "I was going to do that. But that's not how it went down. A clairvoyant gave me the invitation. He said my life is as entwined with witches as his was with death."

Cold dread crept over Chandler. *A clairvoyant.* She had a suspicion who this person was and where this conversation was about to go, and the darkness of it was something she'd hoped never to revisit.

Chloe hugged herself. "What did this clairvoyant look like?"

"He was a goth. I met him in a bar. He was reciting poetry." Lionel's voice became almost too low to hear. "S-someone killed him. The police called it a suicide. They said he cut strips of skin from his own body. But that is not the truth, is it?" His gaze pinned Chloe, as if he were a psychic capable of compelling the truth from her.

She paled. Her mouth opened. Finally, she relented. "No, it isn't."

A sick feeling lodged in Chandler's stomach. She'd never met the clairvoyant goth, like Chloe had. But she knew the fake story the police believed and the more gruesome truth about the missing skin.

Lionel tapped a finger against his temple. "That spell may have screwed with my head. To be honest, I have never been totally normal. But I know I saw other things, too."

"Like what?" Gar asked.

"I found the clairvoyant's body in the cemetery. I am the one who called the police." Lionel's voice was as solid as bedrock, not the slightest hint of hesitation or confusion. "I wrote the article about him skinning himself that went viral online, but it wasn't the truth. I saw who really killed the goth and cut the skin from his body. Your high priestess. She made a charm from it in the shape of a bracelet. It looked a lot like the necklace she wore to make herself appear younger. Your high priestess wrote the goth's suicide note, too. I saw her do it."

Chandler bit her tongue to keep from correcting him. What he'd seen and confessed to doing answered a lot of questions. But he was wrong about the purpose of the gruesome charms. The necklace he'd seen her wearing wasn't designed to make her look younger. It was designed to allow Rhianna to impersonate Athena—and was made from Athena's skin.

Devlin's tone hardened. "Maybe that's what you think you saw. But you're wrong."

Gar chuckled. "Lionel, you do realize how crazy you sound?"

"Th-that is what I saw."

"Maybe you should speak to a psychiatrist," Chloe said quietly.

Lionel punched a fist against his thigh. "I'm telling the truth."

As Gar and Devlin continued to gang up on Lionel, Chandler's shoulder muscles pinched so tight that she winced from the tension. She couldn't stand this. The coven and the witching world's anonymity had to be protected at all costs. But messing with Lionel's head like this wasn't right. It was painful for him. And painful for Chloe, Devlin, and Gar, she was certain of it. She had to stop this, for everyone's sake.

Chandler rested her hands on her hips. There was only one way out of this stalemate as far as she could see. She needed to give Lionel the full truth and then make him believe it was a lie. It was a technique—used along with sarcasm—that had served her well on many occasions, like when potential customers walked in on her using magic to weld sculptures. Hopefully, everyone else would get what she was up to and play along.

She raised her voice above everyone else's. "You're right, Lionel. We are real witches. *Heritage witches* is the term we prefer. Magic is real. It's also true that the woman who cast the spell on you was not our high priestess…" She went on, revealing the entire truth about Rhianna, Athena, and the necklace charm, and ended by saying they hadn't known for sure until now who killed the goth.

Lionel blinked at her, openmouthed like an archeologist struck dumb by unearthing the Holy Grail.

Chandler raised a hand to keep everyone else silent. Then she tilted her head to one side, then the other, as if weighing what she'd said. "The question is: was what I said the truth or a lie?" She fixed her gaze on Lionel. "You believed me, didn't you? There are people out there who will try to take advantage of trusting people like you. We aren't that way.

The Northern Circle coven is nothing more than a group of people who live together because we share similar spiritual beliefs and an interest in discovering truths that remain unproven—that is the real story. In some respects, we aren't much different from you. We aren't the fantastical, magic-wielding witches or bloodthirsty evildoers you believe us to be."

His gaze remained on hers, unflinching. When he spoke it was with unobstructed clarity. "If that's so, then explain one thing to me. What makes me so willing to believe things others dismiss as unreal?"

Chandler's mouth went dry. Word for word, that was the same thing she'd asked herself only a few moments ago. She covered her surprise with a nonchalant smile and shrugged. "That would be a good question to ask the psychiatrist that Chloe recommended."

Chapter 3

Take me, sweet slumber.
Give my flesh to the Shade. Give my breath to the sky.
I have no use for either. I crave neither thorns nor rose.
—Suicide note found on clairvoyant goth's body

What makes me so willing to believe things others dismiss as unreal?
Chandler couldn't get the question out of her mind. She also had a sneaking
suspicion the Circle wasn't going to be able to shake Lionel until they
knew the answer.

Mostly, she was just glad when Devlin called the impromptu meeting
finished and escorted Lionel out to his car. She was also glad that no one
jumped down her throat about the technique she'd used to tell Lionel the
truth. Both Gar and Chloe agreed it was a good move, though it had taken
them by surprise at first. She was even happier when Peregrine raced into
the living room with a big smile on his face and a trio of squirming kittens
squished against his chest. Em followed in his wake.

The kittens technically belonged to Em, though the coven had adopted
them. Like Chloe, Em was a recent initiate to the coven. She was a slight
woman in her early twenties, an alcoholic recovering from her addiction
and a horribly abusive past as a legendary psychic medium. The coven had
offered Em sanctuary at the complex, similar to the way Em had rescued
the tiny kittens and given them a second chance at life. And, very much
like the way Athena had given Chandler a safe haven when she'd discovered
she was pregnant with Peregrine.

Peregrine released the kittens onto the floor and grinned up at her. "Did
the shapeshifter turn into a gigantic loup-garou?"

"We aren't even sure he saw a loup-garou," Chandler said, hoping to put an end to his interest.

He scowled at her answer and turned toward Gar. "Why don't you change? You're part wolf."

"Peregrine," Chandler said sharply. "It's not polite to ask personal things."

Gar brushed off her concern with a flip of his hand. He smiled at Peregrine. "Not everyone with loup-garou blood chooses to change."

"Why would anyone not want to be a wolf? I'd be a big gray one with yellow eyes."

"Believe me, there are better ways to unleash your inner beast." Gar winked at Em. "Right?"

Her cheeks reddened. She hooked a length of mousy brown hair behind one ear and gave him a coy smile. "By other ways, you mean like jogging or playing frisbee? Or poisoned darts?"

Chandler smothered a laugh. Of course, the unleashing Gar was referring to happened in Em's bed and didn't involve shifting or the outdoors, at least that she knew of. A week ago, when Gar had arrived to investigate the coven for the High Council, she wouldn't have believed him capable of joking around, let alone that he'd hook up with an introvert like Em. But in truth, their lives were interconnected in a myriad of ways. They'd met briefly years earlier when Em had first escaped from her abusive aunt and mother. Saille Webster—the ghost of a Northern Circle high priestess—had been influential in Em's bottoming out and entering recovery. Later, Saille's spirit had attached herself to Gar in hopes of having him solve her murder, a haunting that Em noticed when he'd arrived to investigate the coven.

Peregrine gaped at Gar. "You have poisoned darts? Can I see 'em?"

"No darts for you, young man," Chandler said. Then the earlier redcap scare slipped into her mind. Just because Peregrine didn't have faery sight now, that didn't mean the ability wouldn't manifest at some point, making him a target for the fae. Gar had top-notch skills when it came to weapons, skills that would be a nice addition to the martial arts Peregrine was learning from Devlin. "Unless—maybe Gar would be willing to coach you in weapon use and safety?"

Gar grinned. "I'd be happy to. I'm headed back to Council headquarters the day after tomorrow. When I come back, I can bring something appropriate to start with. Maybe a boomerang."

"Really?" Peregrine turned to her. "Please, Mom. Can I really?"

"You have to do everything Gar says and be very careful." The thought of Peregrine growing up and the imminent onset of his abilities made her heart heavy. She understood better now why her biological mother had freaked when she'd learned Chandler shared her father's gift for working with fire. Not only the fear of the possible danger the ability presented, but also the hard inevitability of your little one creeping away from childhood. Still...

Chandler clenched her teeth, anger boiling to the surface as it always did when she thought of her biological mother. Neither fear nor the hard sense of a child growing up made her mother's withdrawal after the death of Chandler's father or her eventual suicide any more understandable. Mental illness or not, how could any mother turn her back on her child?

She looked at Peregrine. Her sweetheart. Her little imp. Being cast aside by a parent was one thing he'd never have to worry about. She'd be there for him always, and beyond.

Chloe picked up the open wine bottle from the coffee table and waggled it at Chandler. "You want a glass?"

"Very much, thank you." After Chloe poured, she took the glass. The wine was deep red and semisweet on her tongue, a heady flavor and soothing relief. "I feel awful about the things we said to Lionel. When I shook his hand, I sensed only kindness."

"I totally agree," Chloe said. "Also, I didn't think about it until he mentioned The Thinker. But when I saw that same performer that night, I did notice he had the energy of a shifter."

Gar took off his cap and raked a hand over his rumpled black curls. "Did you think he was a loup-garou?"

"All I know is that we need to talk to this guy and make sure his transforming in public was a one-time mistake."

Em's quiet voice broke into the conversation. "It's effing awful that the Circle is responsible for the actions of people who aren't even members of their coven."

"Like it or not, it's the law," Gar said. "Shapeshifter. Fae. Full demon. Or half-demon cambions, like Merlin's Shade and his half brother, Magus Dux... It doesn't matter what kind of being they are, if they pose a threat to the anonymity of the witching world, it's the local coven's responsibility to police the situation."

Em picked up one of the kittens, stroking it. "I get the need for anonymity. Still, it's not right for a coven or anyone to police other peoples' or beings' lives."

"The law is law. It's not up for philosophical debate," Gar said.

"Unless you're standing in front of the Council, right?" Chandler added.

Gar dipped his head, an admission that she was correct. He cocked an eyebrow. "However, in this case, we may have a third option. If this street performer is indeed a wayward loup-garou, I'll call my dad and ask him to have his pack come down from Quebec and take care of the situation. The Circle's had enough problems lately without dealing with this."

"You can say that again." Chandler smiled to herself. She'd never have believed a day would come when she'd hope someone would turn out to be a wayward loup-garou, so a bunch of French Canadians could come straighten him out.

Ten minutes later, Chandler stood at the kitchen island putting together a plate of tacos. Midas and Brooklyn had outdone themselves creating the dinner spread. There were bowls of grated cheese, spiced beef and black beans, tomatoes, and lettuce from the coven's greenhouse, chopped herbs, and ripe olives soaked in wine. All the delicious aromas made her mouth water and she had a hard time choosing what to take. Thank goodness putting together Peregrine's plate had been straightforward.

With plate in hand, Chandler settled down on a stool between Peregrine and Midas. She was about to take her first bite when the kitchen door swung open and Devlin walked in, returning from seeing Lionel off.

"I'm glad that's over," he said. "But I'm afraid it's not the last we'll see of Lionel."

Gar looked up from his spot beside Em at the end of the island. "We should try to track down The Thinker first thing tomorrow. See for ourselves if he's a loup-garou."

"I agree," Chloe said. "Do you think just a couple of us should go? Would too many of us frighten him off?"

Midas set his taco in the middle of his plate. "I can't go. I've got to make some headway on my thesis."

Chandler viewed Midas as both an exciting new coven member and a mystery. As a person who worked in frayed sweatshirts and welder's pants and rarely made it past 9:00 a.m. before being covered in grime, she could hardly fathom how Midas managed to always look impeccable. Even the layers of his tacos were as neat as his bead-studded dreadlocks and button-down shirts. Then again, Midas approached everything, including his geomancy, with scientific precision.

"How about if Gar and I go," Devlin said. "And maybe you too, Chandler. Does that sound good to everyone?"

"I'd like to go," Chandler said.

As Chloe reiterated where she'd previously seen The Thinker, Chandler got up and fetched an extra napkin for Peregrine. When she returned to her stool, Devlin tapped his knife against his wineglass. "If we can forget about the shapeshifter for a second," he said, "there's something else I'd like to discuss while we're all together. I was going to wait until we finished eating. But, frankly, I can't keep it to myself any longer."

"Sounds serious," Midas said. His attention whipped back to his taco as Brooklyn pinched a ribbon of cheese off the top of it. He playfully swatted her hand. "No stealing."

She popped the cheese into her mouth. "If you're not nice, I won't tell you what Devlin's talking about."

Midas frowned. "You know?"

"Uh-huh. I saw it in the cards this morning." Brooklyn licked her lips, drawing out the suspense. Today, she was dressed in turquois and dark purple. An embroidered talisman bag and shells dangled from her beaded necklace. Of all of the coven members, Brooklyn always looked the most like the mainstream concept of a witch—albeit, a young Haitian version. Chandler liked Brooklyn and trusted her, though she did have lingering mixed feelings about how Brooklyn had continued to support Rhianna even after the rest of them had realized something was horrifically wrong with her. Still, when it came down to it, Brooklyn had turned her back on Rhianna. An act that was admirable and took a lot of courage.

"Want to give us a clue?" Chandler said to her.

Brooklyn smiled smugly. "No. But I know exactly what Devlin has in mind. And I vote *yes*."

Chandler rubbed her upper chest, sensing the warmth of her most recent dragon tattoo. "I'm guessing this doesn't have anything to do with Lionel?"

Devlin lifted his wineglass, toasting her.

Chandler forced a smile, totally confused by the gesture.

Lowering the glass, Devlin continued. "Gar wisely advised us last week to appoint a temporary high priestess. Chloe hoped to fill the position until the situation with the High Council was completely squared away. However, she's worried about keeping up with her classes."

"It'll be a miracle if I pass organic chem," Chloe said.

Chandler nodded. Actually, she couldn't see how Chloe kept up at all, let alone achieving the grades she needed to get into medical school.

"At any rate," Devlin said. "We've been talking about who should take Chloe's place as the coven's high priestess. I think the choice is obvious."

As his gaze came her way, Chandler's breath stalled in her throat. Her? The Northern Circle's high priestess? She was an adept witch, not a new initiate like Chloe and Em. She'd helped Athena with the day-to-day running of the coven for years. Maybe the choice was obvious, but she'd never considered doing anything other than serving at the right hand of the

Circle's high priestess. "If you're thinking of me, I'm not the only choice. You need to at least consider Brooklyn."

Brooklyn held her hands out, like she was fending off the plague. "No way. Without even mentioning how I screwed up with Rhianna, there's too much garbage that comes with being a high priestess, like dealing with High Council assholes." She shot a look at Gar. "Sorry, kind of."

"No insult taken. I pride myself on my asshole ability." Gar's expression grew serious. "You want to remember—every coven's high priest and priestess are automatically eligible to be included on the High Council election ballot. With all the duplicity and political maneuvering currently going on, the possibility of election makes choosing a self-confident and smart high priest and priestess even more vital, and it makes serving more hazardous to those who are chosen." His voice lightened. "That said, if I were a Northern Circle member, I'd vote for Chandler."

Midas waved his hand. "I second Chandler's nomination."

Chandler could barely think as everyone else raised their hands. She certainly hadn't seen this coming.

Devlin looked at her steadily. "What do you say, Chandler? I've already got absentee votes for you from everyone at the vineyard and from the coven's other auxiliary members."

Peregrine gripped her arm. "Do it, Mom. It would be the best thing ever."

"Ah—" She swallowed hard. Since Devlin had a full-time job as a landscape architect, the high priestess position included managing the complex and overseeing the coven's businesses. With Brooklyn's and Em's help, she could accomplish that as well as her art commissions. Of course, another set of problems could arise if Peregrine did develop the sight and had to be homeschooled.

"You handled the situation with Lionel perfectly," Devlin said. "I was bordering on trying the same truth-telling technique myself."

Chandler let her thoughts go deeper. Athena had worked hard to make the coven profitable after her and Devlin's mother had embezzled from the Circle and run off. But that wasn't all Athena had done. Athena had seen to it that the coven supported local charities and organizations.

"I can't think of anyone better." Em's voice drifted in the room's silence. "You've supported me, encouraged me to go to AA meetings and driven me to them countless times. You made me feel welcome."

"You'd be high priestess right away," Devlin said. "But we could hold off and have the official swearing-in next week on Samhain."

Sadness swelled in Chandler's throat. Athena wasn't coming back, at least not physically. Thanks to Rhianna and the cambion, Magus Dux,

Athena was a spirit bound to a diamond that was attached to the key that opened Merlin's Book of Shadow and Light, a book that had been given to Em by Merlin himself. Athena was now capable of only a fleeting manifestation or a few words. If the book was close by, she could conjoin her magic with the coven, but only briefly.

Chandler looked at them all, one at a time. She wanted more than anything to honor Athena's memory, to carry on her best friend's dreams and legacy of charitable works.

"I'll do it," she said. It felt terrifying, and beyond right. It felt as if she'd stepped out of a dark forest and into a future she'd been walking toward forever.

Chapter 4

Oak for sovereignty, power, and protection.
Willow rules emotion, cycles and inspiration.
The hawthorn is a tree of the fae,
love, fertility, and forgiveness belong to her.
—From *An Apprentice's Guide to Woods and Fire*
By J. L. Hansel, Professor Emeritus, Greylock Academy

A short time later, Chandler headed home. Her apartment was in the same renovated 1940s concrete-block garage as her workshop. Comfy and energy efficient, it appealed to both her artsy and practical natures.

Once Peregrine was in bed asleep, she grabbed a bundle of dried rosemary from the kitchen and went out to her terrace. Going down the steps, she beelined for a well-worn trail that led through an overgrown field. Hip-high spires of goldenrod and asters brushed the sides of her caftan. She passed a group of scrap-metal dragons and griffins glistening under the moon's light, which was one day short of full.

After a few more yards, the field gave way to a circular space of mowed grass. In the middle of it was a coiled path outlined by ankle-high rocks. Her walking labyrinth.

A few days before Chandler had given birth to Peregrine, she'd been drawn to build the labyrinth. She'd tamped down the snow by torchlight to mark its classic outline. In the spring, she'd bundled Peregrine against her chest and walked the labyrinth every day, packing the earth and creating the winding trail one bare footstep at a time. Rather than creating a traditional labyrinth, she'd left a large open area at its center. There, she'd built a firepit in honor of the Great Fire Salamander, her personal guide and guardian, who'd always been there for her, even in the dark days after her father's death. It was where her magic was the strongest. It was also the spot she'd told Peregrine to go if he ever was alone and needed protection, his *safe place*.

When Chandler reached the beginning of the labyrinth's path, she took a deep breath, quieting her mind and opening her heart. As she moved forward, she surrendered her conscious self to the rhythm of her steps and the sense of the earth against her feet. She said a prayer that she was right in believing that the redcap was nothing more than a figment of Peregrine's imagination—and another prayer that when his gift did develop, it would be anything other than faery sight. She released those thoughts, then asked for guidance and strength on her new journey as the coven's high priestess.

At the entry to the labyrinth's heart, she stopped beside the tarp-covered rack that held a supply of firewood and kindling, sorted by size and variety. Her father had always said maple was best for cooking and roasting marshmallows. Oak, birch, and hawthorn were for calling the Great Salamander, the Serpent of the Embers.

She carried an armload of mixed woods to the firepit and assembled a small pyre. The bundled rosemary was the last thing she added. With that done, she knelt. The ley lines hummed in the earth beneath her knees. In front of her, the pyre begged for her to call forth fire. She held out her hands, visualized the rosemary bursting into flame. "Ignis ignite." *Fire ignite.*

Using Latin—or even speaking aloud—was technically unnecessary. But it was the way her adoptive mom had taught her the Craft.

Sparks *crackle-snapped* across the rosemary, responding to her command. They ignited the birch twigs and flared upward to encircle the oak and hawthorn. Sweet smoke filled the air, whirling off into the moonlight.

She focused her magic where the burning wood met the firepit's fieldstone lining. Fire and earth. Her elements. Her abilities. The gifts that allowed her to work metal with her inborn energy as well as with traditional tools.

"Evigilare faciatis." *Awaken*, she called out to the Great Salamander.

Blistering energy whipped from the flames. The surging power seared and curled the hawthorn's bark. Sap boiled from the logs' raw ends. Embers formed in the blink of an eye, red and gold brightened by the dance of flames. Within the embers, Chandler spotted the Great Salamander uncoiling his glowing body from the heat, expanding, growing larger as the sense of energy seethed in the air.

"Great spirit, Serpent of the Embers," she intoned. "Fill me with understanding and wisdom. Guide me."

His magic blazed hot against her face and arms. His voice resonated in her ears. "Daughter of fire and earth. Open your mind. See with your soul and understand, understand... and see..."

Her skin tingled. Her mind whirled and filled with sparks of ember-colored lights. Darkness descended. Not the darkness of a dream; she was in her own body and watching herself at the same time. A vision, that's what it was. A gift from the Great Fire Salamander.

Chandler stands beside a different fire. Flames whip-crackle as tall as the distant treetops. Music echoes in the air. Flutes. Drums. Harps. People laugh. People dance. Streamers of white and yellow ribbons flutter in the firelight.

She holds her arms out, looking at the flowing white trumpets of her sleeves. She touches her head and finds waves of long hair encircled by a wreath of hawthorn branches and flowers. This could be only one night. One fire from her past. Over nine years ago now.

Beltane.

An eager hand slides around her waist. In the other hand is a bottle of wine. His touch makes her heart quiver. Wildness twirls in her belly. She smiles at him. He's perfect. The handsomest May King to ever grace a Council Beltane celebration. Chandler knows who he is, and he knows her, a stand-in May Queen appointed by the celebration committee after the original queen missed the last train from the city. She knows him and takes the bottle from his hand. May wine flavored with sweet woodruff. Potent. Perfect.

She moves with him, away from the fire and noise. The Maiden and the Greenwood Lord falling into the shelter of the forest. New leaves unfurl on twigs. White blooms of the shadberry trees shatter and drift through the moonlight, down onto a glimmering stream.

His mouth is eager against hers, hot and moist, and she urgently needs to feel the mossy earth against her bare skin, to feel him inside her. Naked, he is as gorgeous as she fantasized, with the muscled body of a man who captained the sculling team at Yale. A young witch of notorious powers, from a family of power, a guy so out of her league she'd never dared do more than daydream about being with him.

She closes her eyes, lost in the sensation of his kisses, his lips against her skin. Her dress comes off. Her body arches in response, her moans echoed by others coming from the forest. May Day. Beltane. The night of greenwood marriages. The budding of summer. Of wine, and communal baskets of foil-wrapped condoms—not like ancient times, when the heightened fertility level of the night went unchecked.

He moans as she takes his cock in her hand, exploring the hard silk. She uses her mouth and lips to slide the condom down his shaft. "Chandler." He groans her name. That's something she never thought she'd hear from his lips. Beltane. She's the Queen, and he's her May King. He smooths back her hair and looks at her for a long moment. Moonlight slants down, lustrous on his blond hair and the leaves of his wildwood crown. The light catches on a deep scar that stripes his forehead, missing his left eye by inches before marking his cheek. She knows the story behind the scar, about the fae attack and him fighting them off. His prowess. His skill with magic. His faery sight, which allowed him to see through his attackers' glamour. The sight the fae fear.

When he enters her, she screams from the pleasure. It's Beltane. A night for unbridled passion. No questions. No worries. Let the Gods and Goddesses predict the future. Crazy. Wanton. Greenwood sex. As it's always been for the single and married, for the free and not so free—or at least that's what she tells herself as they scramble to find condoms strewn on the forest floor, before making love for a second and third time.

Chandler jolts awake. Something is wrong.

She rises, pulling on her dress and leaving him behind as she runs toward the edge of the forest and the brightening horizon. A delicious ache from lovemaking in the greenwood lingers in her body... then again, it's as if it happened years ago.

Confusion comes over her. Chandler holds out her arms. Sleeves of dragon and monkey tattoos color her skin. She touches her head. No hawthorn wreath. Soft bristles of close-cropped hair instead of long curls. But she senses the May King rising from the moss in the forest. And she senses Peregrine growing in her womb.

She blinks and she's in a different, older forest, an oak forest where the ground is snarled with roots. The Isle of Anglesey. Castle Aberlleiniog. The sacred grove on Summer Solstice. She knows for certain that's where she's standing. She was there only five months ago with Rhianna, though she believed her to be Athena at the time.

Ahead, purple mist rises from the ground. Chandler's fingers itch to dig in that spot, to unearth the amethyst crystal that she knows waits there, the peach-size stone that once crowned the head of Merlin's staff. But there is no need to dig. The crystal now lays in her cupped hands.

Light from the rising sun slices through the forest and catches in the stone's facets, sending rays of purple light shooting up onto her face. But that's not important. Something is wrong. She needs to get out of the forest, has to before the sun inches any higher.

The oaks part, making way for her as she runs. She reaches the edge of the oak forest and comes out on the top of a grassy hill. Below is the coven's vineyard. Devlin, Chloe, Em, Brooklyn, Midas... even the auxiliary members of the Northern Circle wait by the remains of the Beltane bonfire, looking toward her. There are others there too, Gar and Lionel.

She quivers at the sight of Lionel and wildness twirls in her belly, like when the May King took her into the forest. But the sensation fades as Em walks up the hill toward her with Merlin's Book of Shadow and Light in her extended hands. It's closed, and the triangle-shaped gold key that opens it is affixed to its cover, the key that Athena's spirit is bound to.

When Em reaches her, Chandler sets Merlin's crystal into the center of the triangle-shaped key. As she lets go of the crystal, pain streaks across her chest. She groans and falls to her knees. Her head rolls back in agony as the red dragon on her chest claws its way free from her skin and soars into the sky. Its eyes are red and gold, like the coals in a fire. Its wings are razor sharp and shade everything below it bloodred, as crimson as a redcap's hat.

Chandler clutches at her chest, expecting to discover a gaping wound. But her skin has already healed.

"Be wise. Be strong." Peregrine's voice comes from inside her.

Another child calls from the greenwood, echoing him. "Wise. Strong."

Her instincts scream for her to search for that child, a boy-child lost in the forest. A sad child whose voice she doesn't know. But her gaze catches the outline of a second dragon rising against the red horizon. Rising fast, razor wings spread, tail lashing in anger as it turns to face her dragon.

"Daughter." The Great Fire Salamander's commanding voice yanked Chandler from the vision.

"Yes," she replied, bowing her head. Her body still tingled as if she'd just left a lover's bed. She rested a hand on her belly and sensed a phantom quickening, the memory of Peregrine's first heartbeats.

"Daughter of earth and fire," the Great Salamander said. "Be wise. Be strong. Listen to the quiver of your heart and the shiver of your soul. Be your dragon when you must."

She opened her mouth to ask what it all meant, but another flood of memories brought on by the vision sent her thoughts reeling in a different direction: The May King. After that Beltane night in the forest.

"It was fun," he'd said. "Maybe some time we can get together again."

"I'd like that."

A week or two later, she called.

"I'm going to be in town," she said. Some things need to be discussed in person.

He hesitated. "I'm going to be away."

She tried two weeks later. He didn't answer. She didn't leave a message. She called the next day. No luck.

A month later, or maybe two, another call.

He answered. "Chandler?"

"I need to tell you something," she said.

His voice hushed. "It was fun. But you can't keep calling." He hesitated. "I'm getting married. I don't need you messing it up. The marriage is important to me, to my family."

"I didn't realize."

"I haven't known her that long. Things just came together."

"Oh. Ah—congratulations."

"Yeah. Goodbye." He hung up.

Her anger came. It passed. Guilt grew and faded, ebbing like the ocean as her belly widened and Peregrine arrived. Hard emotions returned every year on Beltane, and when she saw photos of him and his family in the witching newsletters. But those feelings calmed and wore away over time. Her adoptive mother had been a fantastic parent without the help of a man, a far better mother than her biological one had ever been. It was better for Peregrine if he and his father never knew each other, healthier than being cast aside by a parent whose flame of love had gone out, or perhaps had never been there to start with.

Chandler squeezed her eyes shut, pushing back the memories and the sting of tears. The afterglow was gone from her body. Her thoughts were settling back to normal.

The Great Salamander's words returned to her.

"Be wise. Be strong. Listen to the quiver of your heart and the shiver of your soul. Be your dragon when you must."

She glanced toward the firepit, ready to ask what the vision meant and why it required her to be strong and listen to the quiver of her heart.

The flames were gone, coals and embers already turned to gray ash.

Panic seized her. "Please! What does it mean?"

A breeze rose. The ash tumbled across the firepit, scattering into the air, thin scraps edged with sparks of red. The sparks blinked out as the ash fell onto the grass and frostbitten weeds.

Chapter 5

Two yellow diamonds sit in the corners of the triangle-shaped key: the power of witches' spirits separated from their bodies. The Crone and the Mother, Saille Webster and Athena Marsh. The third diamond still lives, a witch named Emily Adams, the so-called Maiden that Merlin gifted his book to.
—Transcript of interview with prisoner Magus Dux. Interrogation cell, EC-HCW headquarters

First thing the next morning, Chandler sent Peregrine to find Devlin and Gar and tell them that she'd meet them in the coven office. It was an unnecessary task; she could have simply texted the guys and told them she was ready to go track down the loup-garou. But it had turned out that Brooklyn couldn't babysit Peregrine and it would be easier to ask Chloe and Em in person if they'd be willing to take over the job. It would be even easier without Peregrine around. He already wanted desperately to go with her on the hunt for the shifter.

With Peregrine headed to Devlin's apartment, Chandler took off for the office on the second floor of the main house.

As usual, the office was dimly lit and warm. The scent of leather-bound books and coffee hung in the air. Chloe was hunched behind the enormous desk, scribbling intently in a journal. In front of her, an assortment of fountain pens and ink, crystals, and a large bowl of pink salt were carefully laid out. Clearly, she and Em were in the middle of something important.

Chloe glanced up. "I thought you and the guys were going to Church Street to look for The Thinker."

"We are." Chandler gave the things on the desk another look, then abandoned her idea of asking them to babysit. Concentration and eight-year-old boys didn't mix well. "I wanted to make sure you two didn't need anything while we were downtown."

Em's voice came from off to her left. "I'd kill for a bag of cheese puffs and a ginger ale."

Em emerged from a panel in the wall next to the grandfather clock, also known as the secret entrance to the coven's walk-in vault. As she strolled across the room, a sense of déjà vu washed over Chandler. Merlin's Book of Shadow and Light rested in Em's extended hands, exactly the way it had in her vision. The only difference was that this time Merlin's crystal already glowed in the center of the triangle on the book's cover.

Em set the book on the desk next to Chloe's open journal. When Magus Dux had been captured and imprisoned, largely due to the Circle's efforts, the High Council had claimed the enormous inventory of stolen and long-lost arcane books that had been in Dux's lair. However, even the Council hadn't dared lay claim to Merlin's Book, not when the great magician himself had given it to Em. And, since Em was part of the coven, that technically made the entire Northern Circle responsible for its safekeeping.

"What are you doing?" Chandler stepped closer to the desk and glanced at Chloe's journal.

Chloe snapped it shut. "We're researching."

"Ah—that's cool." What had Chloe not wanted her to see?

Em brushed her hand along the edge of the book. "When we were in Magus Dux's lair, he claimed he had a spell that could heal the Vice-Chancellor's son. We know that's what he used to bribe the Vice-Chancellor's wife into doing his dirty work."

Chloe jumped in, her voice tart. "We're not sure Dux really knew what or where the spell was, but I'm convinced he believed it was somewhere in Merlin's Book—and Em and Devlin agree."

"Could be," Chandler said. She bit her tongue to keep from adding anything that Chloe might take wrong. Finding a cure for the Vice-Chancellor's son, Aidan, was an understandably touchy subject with her. Five years ago, Chloe had been babysitting for the Vice-Chancellor of the High Council and his wife when Aiden had fallen into the family pool. Aiden survived, but the near drowning left him in a vegetative state. Chloe felt responsible for the tragedy and longed to right her wrong. In fact, shortly after the accident, she'd been caught in the boy's hospital room in the middle of an unsuccessful healing attempt, involving a spell from an ancient book she'd stolen from her father's office. No doubt, Chloe's defensiveness was because she expected Chandler to question the timing of this research—or perhaps even if they should get involved with it at all.

"I feel really bad for the boy," Em said.

Chandler nodded. "I do too. It's strange to think that Aidan and Peregrine might have gotten to know each other at the Council's junior events. There isn't that much difference in their ages." She let the subject drop as a pained expression came over Chloe's face. "Sorry, I can't help comparing the two of them."

Chloe pressed her hands over her eyes. "This whole thing just makes me feel so helpless. I need to do something—and I think we can. It's not as if the Council doctors have been able to find a cure. All they do is keep Aidan stabilized. It's nothing more than a living death..."

Chloe's voice faded into the background as Chandler's thoughts jumped back to what she'd just said: *I can't help comparing the two of them.*

Two of them. Last night, in her vision. The second child. The boy-child lost in the forest, echoing Peregrine's words. She knew the voice now, though she'd never heard him speak. It had been Aidan. The vision had predicted that Chloe—that the Northern Circle—would take this path toward helping him. That's why she'd also felt a sense of déjà vu a few moments ago when she saw Em holding Merlin's Book.

"Are you all right?" Em asked.

Chandler pasted on a smile. "Yeah, fine. It's just overwhelming to think about." She wasn't ready to mention the vision to anyone, at least not until she had time to think it through and remember it all. The last thing they needed was for her to get something wrong and for it to send the coven spiraling into a worse situation than they were already in. She folded her arms across her chest. "It would be amazing if there were a cure for Aidan in the book. But we can't afford to forget that Merlin has a dark side."

Chloe scoffed. "If you think after everything that's happened, I'm not aware of the danger, think again. Merlin's a cambion, just like his half brother. I get that."

"I'm just playing devil's advocate." Chandler gentled her voice. "You should look into this. But there are issues to consider—like the fact that Merlin's Book is written in Archaic Welsh, right?"

"Em and I were just talking about that," Chloe said.

Em nodded. "When I was in Dux's lair, I performed a spell from the book. I couldn't read the words, but Athena and Saille's spirits helped me understand. One or both of them must know Archaic Welsh." She slid a finger along the book's key, touching one yellow diamond and then the other, as if to include Athena and Saille in the conversation.

Chandler thought for a second. "I know Athena could read it, at least to a degree. If I'm remembering right, she mentioned once that Saille was fluent."

Chloe's face brightened. "We'll have to start at the beginning of the book and work our way through the spells one at a time, but maybe we can find it."

"Why not just ask Athena or Saille if they've seen a ritual or spell in the book that would work on Aidan?" Chandler asked.

Em stared at her in amazement. "I can't believe we didn't think of that."

"It certainly can't hurt to try," Chandler said. Sadness weighed in her chest as she looked back at the diamonds. "Do you mind if I try to contact them? I'd love to hear Athena's voice."

Em stepped back, giving Chandler room to move closer to the book. "Sure. I can't think of a reason why they wouldn't speak to you."

Chandler splayed her hand on the book's cover and rested her fingertips against the key and its two diamonds. Even with her eyes open, she could sense Athena's energy rippling from the nearest diamond, warm and sunflower-scented. "Sweet friend." She closed her eyes and focused on the sensations. "Is there a spell within this book that can heal the brain damage caused by a near drowning?"

The warmth transformed into a rhythmic heartbeat, murmuring against her fingertips.

After a moment, Athena's voice whispered, "I have not seen all the spells, sweet coven-sister... all the words and incantations. I can translate for the voice of the dead, for Emily. I can help her understand the old language as she turns the pages..." Her voice floated in the air, faded and then returned. "The line is fine between dark and light. Work the great wizard's magic with care. Blessed be, Chandler, new high priestess of the Northern Circle."

A crushing sense of sorrow overwhelmed Chandler. She hugged herself and rocked forward to ease the ache. Athena. Her dear friend. Her best friend. The friend she'd admired since they'd first met at Greylock Academy. The woman who had supported her decision to not tell Peregrine's father about his child. The woman who had offered her a place to start her life over. The witch she'd gladly called her high priestess, had just called her by that very same title.

Chapter 6

According to Isobel Lapin—an herbalist with an extensive knowledge of the arcane, having descended from both Isobel Gowdie and Compere Lapin—the spores of the fungi Calvatia caeus can be treated with Hyoscyamus niger to efficiently deliver and induce twilight sleep.
—Journal of Athena Marsh

Less than an hour later, Chandler pulled her Subaru into a parking space around the corner from Church Street. Gar was riding shotgun with his camo cap tugged low over his eyes. Devlin and Peregrine were in the back. She really hadn't wanted to bring Peregrine with them, but Chloe and Em wouldn't have made any progress with him around. Plus, Gar and Devlin thought having Peregrine come would be a good learning experience for him.

"This is the photo I took last Sunday." Devlin held his phone over the seat so Gar could look. "It shows The Thinker in front of City Hall."

Gar frowned. "I can't believe you didn't sense he was a shapeshifter."

"At the time, I was busy trying to resist the Shade's magic and leave a trail of photos online so Chloe could follow us." His voice toughened. "The last thing I was paying attention to was the vibe of a seemingly innocuous street performer."

Peregrine scooched across the seat toward the phone. "Let me see."

Chandler gave him the evil eye. "Remember, young man, you need to behave and stay close to us. Tell us if you see The Thinker but do it quietly. He could be dangerous."

Peregrine huffed. "The shapeshifter's dangerous. The journalist's dangerous. Everything fun is dangerous."

"Peregrine," she said warningly. "I'm not kidding."

Devlin handed the phone to Peregrine. "Listen to your mom. We don't know anything about this guy."

Peregrine nibbled his lip, studying the photo. "He doesn't look scary to me. He looks like a woman."

Devlin snatched the phone back. He squinted at the screen. His forehead wrinkled. "You're right. It could be a woman."

"Not all women are skinny." Peregrine tsked. "My mom isn't. She's strong, like a grizzly bear."

Despite the admiration in her son's voice, self-consciousness swept a prickle of discomfort through Chandler. She'd never been petite or as thin as a fashion model. And she'd gotten only more broad-shouldered and muscular from hauling around scrap metal and creating her sculptures, but she was hardly a grizzly bear. Still, there was another issue here. "Peregrine, just because a woman is small, it doesn't mean she isn't muscular. Strong comes in all shapes and sizes and isn't just about being able to fight or lift a lot of weight."

Gar chuckled. "You can say that again. Em's no bigger than a flea and she's as fierce as a T. rex."

"If everyone's ready we should get going," Chandler said, pocketing her car keys. It was better to put an end to this conversation before Peregrine started his usual stream of questions and it morphed into an extended lesson about appearances, shapeshifting, and gender.

She got out and waited by the parking meter. The sidewalk teemed with people headed into restaurants and stores. Sunshine gleamed off the car windshields. Overhead, a plastic FALL FESTIVAL banner snapped as a breeze whipped down the street. It was a truly glorious Indian summer day. A welcome change after the cool weather they'd been having, including a round of slushy snow last week.

Peregrine wiggled his hand into her grip and whispered, "Don't worry, Mom. I'll be careful."

She squeezed his fingers. "Love you."

"Love you more than chocolate chip cookies and ice cream," he said.

She let go of his hand and slipped her fingers inside her sweater jacket to make sure her wand was still safely tucked into the waist of her wraparound pants. Hopefully it was an unnecessary precaution. The wand could magnify her energy tenfold, but the last thing the coven needed was to have one of them seen using magic in public, and worse yet in the presence of a Council investigator. Gar might not want to say anything that could hurt the coven. But the Council didn't hold back when it came to interrogating employees. And an hour in one of the Council's infamous interrogation cells was reputed to crack even the toughest resistance.

Gar caught her eye and nodded approvingly toward where her wand lay hidden. He patted his forearm, indicating that he was armed as well. Most likely with his dart gun and a supply of potion-tipped darts.

Her worry about Peregrine's safety deepened. Clearly, Gar was also concerned that they might be walking into trouble.

Devlin stepped close to Gar. "Smell anything?"

Gar took off his cap and put it on backward. He lifted his head and sniffed, like a wolf scenting the air. "Hotdogs. French fries with cheese, poutine, my favorite… patchouli with an undertone of pot, not my favorite."

"No loup-garou?"

"Not a trace."

With Peregrine beside her, Chandler followed Devlin and Gar to the end of the block and out onto Church Street. The term "street" was a misnomer. Decades ago, the street had been closed to car traffic and transformed into a wide pedestrian space flanked with businesses and dotted with street vendors. Music from a flute and harp drifted in the air from somewhere up the street. Close by, laughter and the clank of dishes echoed from a sidewalk café.

Chandler drew up her magic, then released it slowly, letting it fan out as she searched for any trace of uncanny energy. She sensed a nearby pulse, but it emanated from a display of geodes in the window of a jewelry store.

"Mama." Peregrine tugged her sleeve. He pointed past a coffee stand. "Is that him—I mean her?"

Chandler craned her neck, looking between the stand and the people waiting in line for drinks. Sure enough, a hundred or so yards beyond that, The Thinker sat in front of City Hall as motionless as the statue she depicted, exactly like in Devlin's photo. Metallic shades of teal and black paint covered every inch of her muscular and seemingly naked body. It was impressive how closely she resembled the original statue, though Chandler did pick up on a hint of bound breasts instead of defined male pecs.

"Not a loup-garou," Gar stated bluntly.

Chandler studied the shapeshifter again, this time using her artistic eye to see creative possibilities. She took in the elongated lines of the shifter's spine and skull. The negative space between her hunched shoulders and belly. The distance between her dark eyes. The curl at the sides of her nostrils. Thin lips. Chandler had no trouble envisioning the feminine skeleton beneath the masculine shape of The Thinker. And she took those lines and shapes and shifted them into something very different, and very real.

"I know what she is," Chandler whispered.

"I smell rodent," Gar said.

"You're close. She's a hedge-hare. I'm certain of it." Hedge-hares were solitary, shapeshifting witches, highly skilled and often tricksters with a folklore legacy that encompassed cultures around the world. Four or maybe five years ago, Athena had invited one to join the coven. But the older teenage girl had turned her down flat, claiming she preferred to remain independent.

Peregrine went up on his tiptoes, staring toward the shifter. "Like a bunny?"

"Definitely not." Chandler rested her hand heavily on his shoulder, easing him back onto the flats of his feet. "Come on, let's go talk to her. But no running."

Devlin lowered his voice. "What was the name of that hedge-hare Athena knew? Isobel something or other?"

Chandler nodded. "Isobel Lapin. I'm not sure this is her, though."

"How could Lionel have ever mistaken a rabbit for a loup-garou?" Devlin said. "It doesn't make sense."

Gar chuckled. "That would be one vicious-looking rabbit."

"Either way, we need to talk to her." Chandler took a firm grip on Peregrine's hand and led the way down the street. A couple of tourists were snapping photos while their friends lined up next to The Thinker, posing like her with their fists under their chins.

Chandler hung back a few steps, waiting. Finally, the tourists shoved cash into the shifter's donation box and moved on.

She stepped up close to the shifter and whispered, "I'm Chandler Parrish. From the Northern Circle. Are you Isobel?"

The shifter remained frozen, like a snowshoe hare under the eye of a soaring hawk.

"I believe you knew my sister, Athena," Devlin added.

The shifter still didn't move, but a vibration of coiled energy built in the air around her as if she were readying to bolt.

"Please. We just want to ask a couple of questions." Chandler kept her tone friendly. Whether The Thinker was guilty of careless shifting or not, it seemed likely that Lionel had witnessed it. If he hadn't, then how else would he have known she was a shifter of any sort? That wasn't something a person without magic could detect.

Peregrine poked Chandler in the ribs, yanking her attention away from The Thinker. "Mom, look!"

She glanced in the direction he was pointing. Up the street, a familiar long-legged silhouette emerged from under the shade of the coffee stand's striped awning. Lionel.

As he waved and jogged toward them, excitement shivered inside Chandler, like it had when she'd seen him in her vision. She hadn't stopped to think about that detail. It seemed so unimportant compared to battling dragons and Peregrine's conception. But here it was again, that same quiver in her heart and wild twirl spinning low in her body. It made no sense for her to be even slightly drawn to him. He was a threat to the coven. But no one had ever said attraction belonged in the same box with rational behavior. Her life certainly was a good example of that.

Gar grumbled under his breath, "Maybe we can get some answers now."

Chandler nodded. "I'm with you there."

When Lionel reached them, his smile widened even further. "I—um, see you've decided I'm not totally crazy?"

"Actually, we're more convinced you were wrong," Devlin said.

Chandler tilted her head at the shifter, still maintaining her *The Thinker* pose. "Is this the person you saw change into a wolfish something?" Whether the hedge-hare was Isobel or not, she was a witch, so it didn't matter if she overheard. Insinuating that she'd turned into a carnivore might piss her off enough to make her speak up about what happened.

"I'm sure of it." Lionel turned away, gesturing at an alleyway between city hall and the building just north of it. "It happened over there. One minute there was The Thinker, then—" He abruptly stopped talking. He straightened his glasses and glanced back at The Thinker, then at the alley again as if confused. "What the hell?"

"What's wrong?" Chandler followed his line of sight. Two white-haired old ladies toddled out from the darkness of the alleyway, arm in arm.

Lionel's voice turned firm. "Don't you see it? The loup-garou. It's watching us. It's not The Thinker."

Chandler looked again. No wolves. No dogs. Nothing except for old ladies.

"I don't see it," Gar snarled.

"It's leaving!" Lionel took off, racing toward the alleyway.

Gar sprinted after him, zigzagging between the ladies and leaping over a bicycle rack. Chandler started to follow, but Devlin caught her sleeve. "Stay here with Peregrine. I'll see what's going on."

The authority in his voice made her blood boil, but the mama dragon inside her agreed with him. It was safer to stay put and not get Peregrine involved.

She reached for Peregrine's hand—

He wasn't there.

She caught a glimpse of him, a second behind Gar and Lionel, moving impossibly fast and vanishing into the alleyway.

"Shit." Chandler bolted after him with Devlin beside her. The old ladies scurried out of the way as they flew past them. Hopefully, Lionel had seen a shadow. Something wolf-shaped. Maybe a hunched person. An optical illusion, like how she'd mistaken Devlin's dog with a scarecrow for a redcap and its victim.

The alley was dark, even darker than Chandler had expected. There was nothing in it. Nothing at all. Not Lionel. Not Gar. Not Peregrine! Not a single person.

She reached the other end of the alley, where it opened into a small park. Her pulse hammered in her ears as she scanned the walkways and between the maple trees. Where were they? They couldn't have gotten far.

She spotted Peregrine beyond the maples, near where a line of parked cars edged the greenspace. Gar had a grip on the back of Peregrine's hoodie. Lionel stood next to them, hand shading his eyes as he looked up the street and between the cars. But there were no people gawking or pointing at anything. No one screaming about a wolf. No shrieks of terror. Nothing to indicate that something strange had run through the park ahead of them. As a matter of fact, only a few yards from them a man was calmly feeding a parking meter. A woman did eye Lionel suspiciously for a second as she pushed a baby stroller past him.

Devlin let out a sigh of relief. "Looks like another false alarm."

"Thankfully," Chandler said, though her pulse still wasn't ready to calm down.

Devlin smiled. "One thing's for sure, Gar can confidently testify in front of the Council that Lionel isn't a threat to the witching world's anonymity. No one in their right mind would believe Lionel about anything."

"I suppose you're right," Chandler said.

While she watched, Gar released his grip on Peregrine's hoodie. Peregrine turned, saying something to Lionel.

Chandler exhaled sadly. "I feel bad for Lionel. He seems like a good person."

"That might be," Devlin said. "But it's time to put this problem to rest and move on."

Chandler kept pace with Devlin as they jogged across the park. When they reached them, Lionel's expression tightened. "I—I really thought I saw…"

A deep scowl darkened Devlin's face. "*Thought*—as in imagined—seems to be the key word here."

"It had red eyes," Lionel said firmly. "Loup-garou's eyes glow, right?"

Gar huffed. "You've got your myths confused."

"It was oily black and twice the size of a St. Bernard," Lionel insisted.

Chandler went cold. Real or imagined, he was perfectly describing a *black dog*. A type of hellhound. A portent of death. A fae creature.

"There it is again!" Peregrine screeched. He waved toward where a city bus was pulled up across the street. Then he took off like a sprinter from a starting gate, flying past the man still standing beside the parking meter. He darted between parked cars and into traffic.

"Stop!" Chandler shrieked. She raced after him, dodging around the man at the meter and squeezing between two pickup trucks parked far too close together.

Ahead of her, a car squealed to a stop, inches from Peregrine. He dodged around it and reached the other side of the street, vanishing from view behind the city bus.

The traffic started moving again, blocking Chandler's way.

"Watch where you're going!" a driver shouted at her.

Lionel was beside her, holding up his hand to stop traffic. Cars squealed to a stop, but the city bus took advantage of the break in traffic and pulled away from the curb, blocking her way and leaving her trapped in the middle of the street.

One long second passed, then another as the bus chugged by. People stared at her through the bus's smudged windows. Finally, the rear of the bus slid past. She dashed behind it and reached the far side of the street.

She looked up the sidewalk, along the line of buildings. Peregrine wasn't there.

"Do you see him?" she shouted to Lionel.

Lionel scanned the opposite direction. "He can't have gotten far."

Bang! Crash! The clatter of metal hitting pavement echoed from a wide alley that served as a bistro's outdoor seating area. Someone yelled, "Fucking kid!"

Chandler took off toward the bistro. Lionel was beside her. Gar and Devlin were a second behind, their footsteps pounding. As she rounded the corner, she spotted Peregrine zinging through the outdoor seating area. Ahead of him an empty table crashed over, chairs flew into the air though nothing appeared to have bumped into them. A customer swore. A waiter shouted.

Lionel followed Peregrine's path. Gar and Devlin trailed him. But Chandler veered to one side, picking up speed as she raced down a walkway that edged the seating area. At the end of the walkway, she swerved right. If she was lucky, she could cut off whatever Peregrine was chasing before he caught up with it.

The rope that formed the back boundary of the seating area swayed as if something big had jumped over it. Peregrine leapt the same rope. Chandler pushed her legs harder as Peregrine winged by a parked delivery truck and careened around a corner, passing dumpsters.

Adrenaline screamed in Chandler's legs. Protective magic throbbed in her tattoos. She was gaining on them. Almost there.

Peregrine froze midstride. She couldn't see the creature, but its wild energy wailed in the air a half dozen yards ahead of Peregrine, stalking toward him. A low and very audible growl reverberated.

"Back off, hellhound." Gar's voice echoed close by. He had a way with animals and his dart gun. But she wasn't about to leave Peregrine's safety to anyone else, especially someone who could no more see the creature than she could.

In one swift motion, Chandler drew her wand and flung herself forward, between the creature and Peregrine. If it wanted to get to him, it was going to have to go through her first. This hellhound was going to learn he'd messed with the wrong boy.

"Holy shit," Devlin screeched.

Two yards ahead of Chandler, the crouched dog materialized. It was enormous. As black as oil with ruby embers for eyes and teeth like switchblades. Its spiny hackles were raised. It crouched even lower, readying to spring.

"Get down!" Lionel raced toward her. She felt the sudden weight of his body as he flung himself over top of her and Peregrine, pushing them to the pavement and covering them.

"Mama, I'm scared," Peregrine whimpered close to her ear.

Chandler glanced up in time to glimpse the hellish dog sailing over all three of them with the effortless power of a gigantic tiger bounding a fence.

Chapter 7

Species: *Black dog. Known by a variety of nicknames. A type of solitary hellhound.*
Characteristics: *Wolflike. Shaggy black hair. Glowing red eyes. Vanishes at will.*
Location: *Crossroads, execution sites, and ancient byways. May appear elsewhere or be attached to a person or be associated with an object such as treasure.*
Threat Level: *Feral by nature. May be affiliated with any fae or fae court.*

—From *Book of Good Folk*
by B. Remillard

The black dog landed, then charged off in the direction it had come from, disappearing into thin air before he made it past the delivery truck.

Chandler grabbed hold of Lionel's extended hand and let him pull her to her feet. Her back was soaked with sweat. Her legs were as shaky as a boneless giraffe.

She took a deep breath to steady herself, then rested her hands on her hips and narrowed her eyes on Peregrine. "You do realize you're in big trouble, young man?"

"But, Mom, the dog... Lionel wasn't imagining it. It just wasn't a loup-garou."

"Don't 'but Mom' me. We're going to have a long talk about this later. Disobeying. Running across a street. Not to mention chasing a dangerous creature."

Chandler's head spun from the enormity of what had just happened. Not just that Lionel had seen through the black dog's glamour, but that Peregrine had as well. A black dog. A fae creature. Sure, the Northern Circle had at one time worked closely with the fae. But not anymore. Not for eons. Even Brooklyn's benign fae helpers were far from trustworthy.

She pressed her hand against her upper chest, drawing strength from her dragon. She'd prayed this day would never come. She'd begged the Gods and Goddesses to give him any gift but this one. Still, she'd known deep in her heart there was no escaping it. And there was no denying it now. Her son. Her beautiful, carefree boy had inherited faery sight from his father. And she wasn't the only one who knew. Devlin and Gar had witnessed it as well.

Devlin cleared his throat. "We should get out of here."

He motioned for everyone to follow, then he hurried deeper into the alley. As they started through a narrow passage between two buildings, Chandler hung back. She wasn't worried that Peregrine would run off again. But there was a strong possibility that the city police might come running up behind them. After all, they had caused quite a disturbance at the bistro. If they needed to talk their way out of this one, she wanted it to be her.

Gar slowed his pace, falling in step with her. He caught hold of her shoulder, slowing her further until they were out of everyone else's earshot.

"Is this the first time Peregrine's seen through glamour?" he asked.

"I'm not sure. Yesterday he mentioned something. But I didn't think it was real."

"You're not gifted with faery sight, are you."

It was a statement, not a question. Still, she shook her head in denial while scenes from that Beltane night flashed in her mind: The moonlight gleaming on the May King's face. His scar glistening against his beautiful tan skin, a mark left from when the fae had attacked him because he could see through their glamour. The same ability that had led to his grandfather's torture and death at the hands of the fae.

She looked at Gar. He pressed his lips together, sealing his thoughts away. But the firm set of his jaw told her that he'd guessed the name of Peregrine's father. That didn't shock her. Gar had researched every Northern Circle member before he'd come to the complex to interrogate them in his capacity as Council investigator. He knew about her birth parents and the single woman who had adopted her after their deaths. He also undoubtedly knew she'd attended prep school at Greylock Academy during the same time span as one of the few witches known to have faery sight, a guy that Athena and her friends had hung out with. Gar could make only an educated guess who she'd had sex with and when. But faery sight was a rare, practically unique gift.

"Well," Gar finally said, "this is an interesting complication."

She nodded. "And terrifying."

"I assume Peregrine's father doesn't know?"

She nodded again. "I tried to tell him."

"You know I'll respect your right to privacy," Gar said. "But I'd want to be told."

They fell silent as they came out the other end of the passageway and onto a side street.

Devlin motioned them into a huddle. "It would be smart to get off the streets for at least a few minutes, avoid any chance of running into the police." He slanted a look at a nearby Tibetan restaurant. "Anyone want lunch?"

"Good idea," Lionel said.

Chandler noticed Devlin and Gar glance sharply at Lionel, as if to question when he'd become a voting member of the group. But if either of them had objected, she would have demanded he be included. Like it or not, they'd passed the point where hiding everything from Lionel made sense. He'd seen the same creature they had and seen it before them. Besides, he'd risked his life to protect her and Peregrine from the dog.

As they settled in around a table at the back of the room, Peregrine poked her in the arm.

"Now do you believe me about the redcap?" he said.

Devlin's gaze winged to her. "What?"

Chandler frowned at Peregrine. It would have been nice if he could have kept that to himself until the two of them were alone. "Didn't we already decide that was Henry dragging around one of Brooklyn's scarecrows?"

"I told you that wasn't what I saw," Peregrine insisted.

"You also said it was as big as a rhinoceros."

He folded his arms across his chest, slumped in his chair, and kicked his sneakered feet against its legs.

As a waiter sauntered up to the table to take their orders, Chandler pointed at something on the menu. She really didn't care what she ate. Mostly she wanted a cold drink. Iced tea. Lemonade. A tall glass of something cool, at home in her living room, alone with Peregrine where she could give him a good talking-to in private.

Once the waiter left, Devlin fixed his gaze on Lionel. "Are we right in assuming you've never had any supernatural experiences besides seeing this dog?"

"Never. And I—I've only seen the dog twice. This time and when I mistakenly thought I saw The Thinker shift into a loup-garou." He scrubbed a hand over his uneven hair. "I told you the truth yesterday. All my life, I believed magic was real. That's why I borrowed the invitation to the coven's party. My goal wasn't to hurt anyone."

"But if you'd found proof you would have exposed the Circle to the world by writing an article?" Gar asked.

"Um—I don't know. I might not have." A pained expression furrowed Lionel's forehead. He closed his eyes. "You don't know what it's like to never have people believe you. You don't know how good it felt when I met the goth and he told me about the Circle. Suddenly, someone believed me. I wasn't alone. It was the same today when Peregrine and the rest of you saw the dog."

Devlin leaned back in his chair. He rested his hands on the tabletop. "So, you never saw any weird or unexplainable creatures until very recently?"

Lionel closed his eyes, carefully summoning the right words. "I suppose I did see things, when I was half asleep. Out of the corner of my eye. But, *no,* not fully formed creatures in broad daylight."

Chandler's thoughts went back to when she'd shook Lionel's hand. She'd sensed a creative fire in him, like that of an artist. It wasn't unusual for highly creative people to construct ghosts out of moonlight or imagine faery faces in the wrinkled bark of trees. He was right, too: creative imagination was not the same as seeing through glamour.

Lionel nudged his glasses up higher on his nose and stared steadily over the lenses at Devlin. "Where are you going with this?"

"It doesn't make any sense for an adult person who lacks any supernatural ability to suddenly develop one." Devlin didn't say it aloud, but Chandler knew by "adult person" he was referring to non-witches.

Lionel leaned forward. "What if a spell messed with someone's brain? Could that give them the sight? Um—like the spell your high priestess"—he corrected himself—"like Rhianna performed on me when she was impersonating your sister." He turned to Chandler and smiled warmly. "Yesterday, I believed you when you told me the truth and then claimed it was a lie to demonstrate my naivete. At least, I believed you for a few minutes. I—I don't blame you for trying to protect the coven."

She let herself look deeper into his eyes and saw nothing but kindness and honesty. There had to be a way to at least begin to resolve this stalemate, a way through this maze of Lionel's astute guesses and their uncomfortable but necessary lies.

Peregrine nudged her foot with his. "Mom?"

"What?" she said sharply, followed by a warning side-eye.

He shoved his hands into his pants pockets and looked down as if rethinking before getting in trouble again. "I was just thinkin' about what Gar said last night—about laws and people being responsible for things even if they didn't do them."

"I was talking about a different situation," Gar said quickly.

Peregrine crumpled deeper in his chair. "Yeah, I guess."

A lump formed in Chandler's throat. She swept her hand over her head, feeling the soft bristle of her hair. Peregrine was onto something. Along with covering up threats to the witching world's anonymity, covens were responsible for policing illegal magic. There was nothing legal about the spell Rhianna had used on Lionel. Plus, just because they weren't aware of a spell that could cause a non-witch to have abilities, it didn't mean one didn't exist. In this case, it was the only logical answer for Lionel having the sight. He didn't have it before the spell affected his mind, but he did afterward.

Chandler rested her elbows on the table. Then she steepled her fingers and looked from Devlin to Gar and lastly to Lionel. She was the Circle's high priestess now, and she knew in her heart the first step Athena would have taken toward resolving the situation. There was only one right choice, morally and by High Council law.

She lowered her voice and mustered an Athena-like tone. "It seems clear to me that the spell performed on Lionel affected his thought processes and somehow gave him the sight. As the current acting high priestess of the Circle, I feel we are obligated to find a way to reverse the damage done by someone illegally presenting themselves as a member of our coven."

"I told you—" Peregrine started to say.

Chandler put a hand on his arm. "Quiet."

"I tend to agree that helping Lionel is only fair," Devlin said. "But we need to have a way to ensure his future silence."

"Um"—Lionel blinked uneasily—"I don't blame you, if you don't trust me after what I did. But if you can straighten out my head, I promise I won't ever tell anyone or write about the coven or heritage witches."

"You'll also need to sever all contact with our world," Gar said. "And simply giving your word won't be good enough."

Chandler wasn't sure she liked the sound of that. The type of pledges the High Council required came with major risks attached for violations—like deadly consequences.

Devlin shot a hard look at Gar. "As high priest of the Northern Circle, I say his word is good enough for now. We'll figure something else out later." He focused on Lionel. "I'm sorry about what Rhianna did to you. I promise, no one will force you into anything this time."

"Thank you." Lionel bowed his head, then looked back up at Devlin. "I'm sorry about your sister. That's got to be rough. What Rhianna did to her was... I can't even think of a word for it."

"It hasn't been easy," Devlin said.

Gar chuckled. "At least Rhianna's one thing we don't have to worry about. She's dead, gone, and never coming back."

"Shh..." Chandler silenced everyone as a boisterous group of customers swarmed across the restaurant toward the table next to theirs. A second later, the waiter arrived with their drinks and the mountain of appetizers Chandler had unwittingly ordered.

Devlin frowned. "Maybe we should focus on eating for now and finish this conversation at the complex?"

Lionel nodded. "I would like that."

"I agree," Chandler said. Something else occurred to her, but she bit her tongue until the waiter left to get their meals. Then she leaned toward Lionel and whispered, "You should have a protection charm. A triskelion. Peregrine wears one. It doesn't work against all fae and, judging by what's happened lately, it may be less effective than I was led to believe. But it's supposed to make the fae—things like the black dog—less inclined to attack the wearer. It wouldn't take long for me to make one for you."

He reached across the table and brushed her wrist with his fingertips. "I'd appreciate it."

The warmth of his touch and wholehearted smile sent a ripple of joy threading through her. If only something as simple as a triskelion could keep him permanently safe from the fae. It might help, but unfortunately it was still a long way from a real solution.

Chapter 8

The triskelion, like the number 3, is sacred and powerful. Its root is ancient, appearing in cultures and religions around the world. It is a symbol of the never-ending cycle. It represents the aspects of the Goddess: Maiden, Mother, Crone…
—S. Jocelyn, "Numbers & Symbols" (lecture 2, Greylock Academy)

On the way back to the complex, Chandler took Peregrine and Devlin in her car, and Gar rode in Lionel's cluttered VW Beetle.

Rather than waiting until later, she took advantage of the ride to give Peregrine a lecture on how his actions had endangered himself as well as the rest of the group. Devlin stayed out of it for the most part, but he agreed when she suggested Peregrine's martial arts lessons should be preceded by an additional ten minutes of quiet time focused on learning self-control. Peregrine scowled at that, which made Chandler happy.

"Also"—she glanced at him as they stopped for a red light—"today's TV time is going to be replaced by reading in the *Book of Good Folk* about the dangers of fae encounters."

He didn't scowl at that, which was good as well. The *Good Folk* textbook wasn't easy reading. Chandler hadn't tackled it until she was several years older than Peregrine. But he seemed to enjoy the challenge, the same way he enjoyed school in general more than she ever had.

Once they got back to the complex, they discussed with Chloe and Em the idea of looking in Merlin's Book for a spell that would reverse the damage Rhianna had done to Lionel at the same time as they were hunting for one to heal Aidan.

As everyone started talking in more depth about the two issues, Chandler got to her feet. "If nobody minds, it's time for Peregrine and me to head home." She looked at Lionel. "I'm going to work on that triskelion."

"I'd appreciate that," he said.

It took only a minute for her and Peregrine to get back to their apartment. She hauled the *Book of Good Folk* from the cabinet under their altar and opened it to the section that gave an overview of hazards. "I want you to make a list of the top ten places you're likely to run into dangerous fae. Before tonight's full-moon ritual, we'll go over the list. Tomorrow, I'll have you do some reading on detection and protection."

"Okay, Mom. I'll be an expert like you in no time."

She smiled. If only the expert part were true. She knew a fair amount about the fae, more than many witches. Between her and Brooklyn, they'd have no trouble getting through the basic and intermediate levels. Still, she wished they had more than book knowledge to rely on. Peregrine's father was the obvious choice when it came to hands-on experience with the fae, but he was a Pandora's box of trouble they were better off leaving firmly closed.

As Peregrine headed for his room with the book, Chandler snagged a Switchback from the fridge, put on her favorite do-rag, its sides embroidered with flaming salamanders, and went out to her workshop.

Once there, she took a refreshing sip of beer, then got out a miniature cauldron and set it near where the iron monkey heart still lay on her workbench. The cauldron was the size of an orange, perfect for bespelling charms.

Next, she retrieved three extralong horseshoe nails from their storage bin. The nails would form the physical portion of the triskelion charm. The iron wouldn't repel all fae, but it would ward off some, and the protective magic she'd imbue them with would, at a minimum, be a signal that Lionel was under the protection of those with abilities, namely a witch who worked with fire and earth.

She put on her safety glasses and settled down, half-sitting on a barstool up close to her vise with the nails and her tools within reach. She secured one of the nails into the vise's jaws, then alternated applying magic to heat the nail's center to red-hot and using pliers to slowly work it into a hook shape. Sometimes—like when she'd created the monkey heart—she used standard equipment and safety gear. Other times, like now, she used her magic to protect her hands and work the metal. It was totally a matter of her mood and if she had extra, pent-up magic from lack of use or keyed-up emotions.

She heated and bent a second nail, falling into a rhythm as she finished that one and started to shape the third into a hook. Her mind wandered to thoughts of when she was Peregrine's age and her abilities first emerged, a gift for working with fire that she'd shared with her father. She remembered every moment of the night when he'd first showed her how to build a bonfire and call the Great Salamander. She also recalled every moment of the horrific day not long after that, when her father burned to death saving a family from a house fire.

Tears prickled in Chandler's eyes. She stopped working and took a deep breath. She couldn't have prevented her father's death, any more than she could have done anything other than witness her mother fall apart afterward, piece by piece, like a glacier giving way to the crash of the ocean. She didn't remember anything from the day her mother killed herself. But she clearly recalled the funeral and her mother's best friend holding her, the first time anyone had held her since her father's death. Holding her and choosing to adopt her. A strong, single woman not afraid to love fiercely and never let go, even when life wasn't easy.

Chandler wiped her eyes on her sleeve. She missed her adoptive mom with every inch of her being. But they'd had a lot of good years together. And Chandler had been there two years ago in the Council's palliative care unit when her adoptive mom had passed. She and Peregrine had kissed her mom and held her hand as she took her last breath and left this life.

Blinking back another round of tears, Chandler returned to work. She secured one of the hook-shaped nails in the vise. With her magic, she fused another hooked nail onto that one and then added the last, joining them together to create the shape of a triskelion. Nails reformed into something new, like a little girl's shattered life reinvented into something even more powerful by the unwavering love of a witch who had chosen to be her mom.

Chandler set the triskelion into the miniature cauldron, then sprinkled a layer of salt and blessed earth over it. On top of that, she placed a cone of Brooklyn's protection incense.

"Ignis ignite," she said, lighting the incense with her magic. As the heady scent of sage and sandalwood drifted into the air, she closed her eyes, cleared her mind, and envisioned the triskelion. "Shield of light surround you," she intoned. "Protect the wearer from those with dark intent. Spirits of the wood. Spirits of the air. Spirits of earth and fire. Only the good come close. Scuto circumdabit te de lumine…" She repeated the spell in Latin, letting her power flow into the cauldron, bathing the salt and earth, coating and imbuing the triskelion with a force-field-like shield of energy.

Somewhere in the back of her mind, she sensed someone enter the workshop, waiting off to one side as still as one of her sculptures. Peregrine? Devlin? Lionel, maybe? She wasn't sure. But their energy felt familiar and right now she couldn't afford to pay attention to them, not with the triskelion nearing completion and her wavering between consciousness and the euphoria of a peaking spell.

A glow radiated up from the cauldron. Bright gold explosions flashed. Once. Twice. Three times. Light as bright as the eyes of the red dragon in her vision. The glow fizzled downward, sucking into the earth and salt, then vanishing.

Chandler bowed her head. "Thank you, Great Salamander, Serpent of the Embers. Blessed be your wisdom and strength," she prayed. Then she turned to see who was watching.

Lionel stood next to the oil drum with one hand resting on the flying monkey's shoulder. His gaze shifted abruptly to the workbench, like he didn't want her to know just how intently he'd been looking at her. His smile turned playful and he nodded at the monkey heart. "Um—I hope charm making didn't interrupt vital surgery?"

She laughed. "It's for the monkey. But I need to find the perfect veins and arteries before I can contemplate surgery. However, your charm's all set." She smiled to herself. *His* personal charm certainly was all set, and working overtime to make her heart stumble. She took a deep breath and turned back to the workbench. Using the end of a screwdriver, she pushed aside the incense ash, salt, and earth, then retrieved the still-steaming charm with a pair of pliers. She waved it in the air for a moment to cool it down. "Hold out your hand. The protection magic will bond with you even better if you're the first one to touch it."

As she placed the triskelion on his outstretched palm, the witch in her took note of what lay before her eyes. His fate line was unusually distinct, with a hard break above his heart line. Palm reading was only a passing interest of hers, something that came with a general artist's awareness of anatomy. Still, she felt drawn to comment. "You had a difficult childhood."

He shrugged. "No more so than most." His expression closed off. Then his dark eyes opened wider, their depths welcoming her in with unabashed candidness. "I never knew my birth parents, at least I don't remember them. I was adopted by an amazing woman when I was five."

His mention of being happily adopted sent a warm feeling of connection flickering through her. She smiled. "I was raised by an amazing adoptive mom, too."

His fingers folded around the charm, squeezing it tight. "Um—I actually came to Burlington because of my adoptive mom. But I'm glad I did. If I hadn't, I wouldn't have met any of you."

As he opened his hand and looked at the charm, her thoughts returned to the job at hand. "Why don't you give that back to me? I'll fix it so you can wear it around your neck. Is leather cord okay or would you prefer hemp?"

"Leather would be great, thank you."

She opened a drawer in her workbench and took out a precut length of deerskin cord. As she started to attach the charm to it, she returned to their previous conversation. "So, your mom lives in Burlington? I assumed you weren't local, since you're staying in a motel."

"My—my mom's in Massachusetts. I came here because of the ferries— ferryboats, that is."

"Really?" She stopped threading the cord through the charm to look at him. There were several ferries on Lake Champlain, the lake that stretched between Vermont and Upstate New York, and up to Canada. She and Peregrine often walked to Oakledge Park to watch the ferries cross. She could think of only one reason someone would come to Burlington because of the ferries. "You work on one of the boats? I thought you were a full-time journalist?"

"I am a journalist, freelance. I grew up in Boston." He hesitated, jiggling his fingers at his side as he thought through what to say next. "My adoptive mom claimed she found me on a ferry. Wh-when I was little, I thought it was a made-up story like parents saying they found a baby under a cabbage leaf. Except, I wasn't a baby when she found me. Later, I realized her story was true."

For a long moment, Chandler was too stunned to speak. "You're kidding? On a ferryboat in Burlington?"

He nodded. "She's never actually told me it was here. But I know it's true." He looked down. "When I was a kid, I liked to pretend my adoptive mom worked for the FBI, that I was a famous child who got handed off to her on a boat and sent into hiding. Or, I was an alien child, a black Superman."

Chandler would have laughed, except Lionel's tone was dead serious. Besides, maybe he wasn't a witch and didn't have magic in his blood, but this foundling story was strange. In fact, it qualified as uncanny, especially when combined with him developing the sight from being bespelled by Rhianna. "What makes you so sure it's true?"

"I vaguely remember the ferry," he said. "For a long time, I thought it came from hearing my mom repeatedly tell the story of finding me on the wet deck and hiding me under a blanket." He stared past her toward the monkey heart. His voice quieted, barely above a whisper. "In my heart, I always knew the memory of the ferry was real. Um—I lived a lot of places, but that ferry was always in the back of my mind. Finally, I decided to write a travel article to justify searching for it. "Car Ferries of New England." I thought, if I visited all the ferries in New England, I might recognize one. If that didn't work, then I'd expand my search westward until I found the boat."

"But aren't all ferries pretty much identical—other than size?"

"Some are on fresh water. Some ocean... Different smells. Different vibes."

Different vibes. Chandler rubbed the triskelion's cord between her fingers. Now he was sounding like a witch. "And you found the ferry. Here. In Burlington?"

He nodded. "My birth certificate says Boston, Massachusetts. I started my search there, then I went to Connecticut and Maine."

Chandler thought for a second. "Does your mom know you're here now?"

"She thinks I'm in Stowe working on an article about tourism." He hesitated. "But there's something about Burlington that speaks to me, beyond the ferries..."

She handed Lionel the necklace. "Like black dogs?" she said it jokingly, to clear the tension from the air. But she'd noticed something else. His speech was smoother, and his thought process faster than it had been earlier. "Are you feeling better?"

"Very much so. It's from being around all of you. I felt this way with the goth, too. And when I came here to the complex last night, and the other time, before the high priestess—I mean, before Rhianna put the spell on me."

Before she put the spell on him? "I didn't think you had a hard time putting your thoughts together until after the spell?"

"I didn't. But I've always daydreamed a lot, zoned out. But not with the goth or here." He slipped the leather cord over his neck and tucked the triskelion under his shirt. "It's the magic. It keeps me in the moment. Totally present." He rested his hand against his chest, pressing the triskelion over his heart. "This feels wonderful, like the chime of grasshoppers on my skin and in my head. It is like yoga without the work."

She did laugh at that. "That's the strangest way anyone's ever described my energy."

His eyes met hers. And in the soft light of the workshop, she could see what a truly beautiful man he was. Everything about him was long and narrow, but all the proportions worked. The smoothness and tone of his skin was more stunning than the darkest brushed bronze she'd ever seen. His lips were satiny. If she'd drawn a likeness of his face in college, her art professors would have criticized the bone structure for being too impossibly flawless.

A gleam sparked in his eyes and his lips twitched into a goofy smile. "Um—sometime, would you like to go out for dinner?"

She stared at him, shocked. Okay, she liked him. Physically he was more than a little appealing. But where had that come from? "Ah—no."

He raised a hand to ward off the words. "Sorry. I thought… I am an idiot. I completely get it. I am not exactly—"

"It's not you. I just—" *Shit.* It was her fault. He'd misinterpreted the way she looked at him, again. "I couldn't even consider going out with anyone right now, not with everything that's going on. I need to focus on Peregrine." That was politely general and true. But it also wasn't the answer her body wanted to give. It whispered that spending alone time with Lionel could be a lot of fun. She liked tall men. She liked thin men. He made her smile. She'd dated black men before, and guys with energy that hadn't been anywhere near as tempting as his. For Goddess's sake, the guy had thrown himself over her and Peregrine in the alley to protect them from a hellhound. Peregrine even seemed to like him.

However, there was a huge issue. Once they corrected the damage Rhianna's spell had caused and were satisfied that Lionel would remain quiet about magic and the witching world, then he'd have to go back to Boston or even farther away—somewhere his connection to them would be permanently severed, like Gar had suggested. Severed so completely that the Council could never catch wind of any involvement between him and their world. It wasn't fair to encourage Lionel into thinking there could ever be a place for him here, by agreeing to a date or even a one-time fling.

"Hey," Devlin said, walking into the workshop.

Chandler let out a relieved breath. "Perfect timing. I was about to call you."

Devlin frowned as if he sensed he'd intruded on something. "What's going on?"

Chandler glanced toward Lionel, careful to not let her eyes linger this time. Now that she thought about it, Lionel wasn't so much a good-looking version of Ichabod Crane as a wild-haired version of a taller and younger John Legend. Really nice.

She clenched her teeth, driving that thought from her head, and instead focused on Devlin. "I finished the charm. It should help until Chloe and Em find the spell."

"That's great." Devlin turned to Lionel. "I'm not sure if you're fully aware of the extent of the danger the sight poses. Fae don't like it when people can see them. They don't just attack. They'll aim to kill, or at a minimum, blind you."

Lionel's Adam's apple bobbed as he swallowed hard. "More like a horror movie than Disney?"

"Exactly." Devlin rested back on his heels. "After you left to come out here, we discussed your situation a bit more. If it's okay with Chandler, we'd like to invite you to stay at the complex until we find the spell and perform it. No charge. Free food and wi-fi. We're worried about your safety. Wearing a triskelion is smart. But it's not a guarantee."

"Good idea," Chandler said. After the "want to go to dinner" thing, him staying at the complex would be a little awkward. But they were adults and she didn't want to see Lionel in danger. Besides, last week when Brooklyn and Midas had paid Lionel a visit to discover if he truly was a threat to the witching world's anonymity, they'd said the motel he was staying at was a cockroach pit.

Lionel shook his head. "I appreciate the offer. But I have to say no." He hugged his arms close to his chest. "I want to go through with whatever it takes to right the damage from the spell. But a lot has happened in the last few hours. I need space and time to think everything through."

A sick feeling tugged at Chandler. "Before—when I said no to your offer—I didn't intend to make you feel unwelcome."

Devlin jumped in. "I meant what I said about not forcing you into anything."

Lionel smiled at Devlin, then met Chandler's eyes. "It's not you. Not either of you. It's me. I didn't just see the black dog. I saw the skin cut from my friend's body. I saw it made into a charm. I know Rhianna was responsible for those things. But my head is reeling. I don't trust myself or my instincts right now. I need to step back and think before I make any more decisions." His smile widened. "I'm assuming if I change my mind, the offer will still stand?"

"Of course, you're welcome anytime. Day or night," Chandler said.

But a horrible feeling twisted deep inside her chest. As much as he denied it, she couldn't believe her refusing his advances hadn't played a role in this incredibly unwise decision.

Chapter 9

Hang in there. It's better to be the witch with one true friend
than part of the popular crowd because of your wealth and family name.
Hugs and kisses, Mom
—Note scribbled on Greylock Academy's Guidance Office letterhead

After Lionel left and she was finished reviewing Peregrine's dangerous fae location list, Chandler put on a white caftan and the moonstone rings that she'd inherited from her adoptive mom. Then she and Peregrine headed up the driveway toward the back entry to the coven's garden. Tonight, for the first time as a high priestess, she'd lead the full-moon ritual. She'd also decided it was time to give Peregrine the added responsibility of carrying the lighter he'd use at the end of the ritual, as part of his expanding role as a witch with abilities.

She was mulling over the wisdom of the lighter decision when Peregrine came to an abrupt halt in front of where Devlin's apartment was attached to the coven's garage. He looked up at her. "Mama, are you going to take me out of school?"

It took a second for what he'd said to register. It was something she'd contemplated earlier. How else could she keep him safe now that he had the sight? Fending off fae attacks wasn't exactly something the average public-school teacher was prepared for.

"I'm not scared of faeries." He pouted. "Please. I don't want to be homeschooled."

It broke her heart, but she had to be honest. "I'm not sure we have a choice anymore."

His voice edged upward. "Schools aren't on the dangerous place list. I have my triskelion. We could make some spray like Keshari has for demons."

"The spray is a great suggestion," she said, hoping to soothe his frustration before it turned into a tantrum. Truly, it was a good thought. Though demons and the fae were old adversaries—both forever vying for domination over humans and witches—the spray Chloe's friend Keshari had made, based on Tibetan shamanism, probably could be tweaked to work on faeries as well. She stashed the idea in the back of her mind, then gave Peregrine's cheek a light stroke, infused with comforting energy.

His eyes widened. "You really think the spray would work?"

"We can talk to Keshari about it. But no matter what, you're going to have to stay home until we get everything figured out."

"All right, I guess." His voice took on a sly tone. "When I was reading the *Good Folk* book, I looked at some extra stuff."

"You did?" She was surprised he'd had time for that.

"Did you know black dogs aren't always bad? It said so in the addendum." He sounded out the last word with special care. "Some black dogs are benevolent. That means they are nice. Some even guard treasures."

"No, I didn't realize that," Chandler said. She actually hadn't had time to think about the black dog in depth at all. "But you're still going to have to stay home for a few days."

"The faeries wouldn't dare attack me. You're Mama Dragon. You work with iron."

"That's exactly my point. You need to stay close to me."

"Oh, yeah."

As they reached the garden, blue light wavered up from the solar-lit path, gleaming brighter as the sun quickly settled into twilight. Chandler wanted to hurry Peregrine along. Most likely everyone was already waiting for them in the teahouse. Still, she felt bad for him. "How about if we talk to everyone tomorrow? No promises, but maybe we can figure out a way to keep you in school."

He perked up. His voice once again turned sly as he skipped a few steps ahead, then swiveled to face her. "I wouldn't mind being homeschooled *if* it was with other witch kids. Like boys my age that are getting their powers. We'd have fun doin' stuff. It would be like going to the Council's summer camp. They have one, right?"

Chandler scrubbed a hand over her face. Dear Goddess, he'd just given her the same argument her mom had used years ago to convince Chandler to accept the scholarship to Greylock Academy. And her mom's argument had proven to be spot-on. That was, once she'd settled in at school and made friends with Athena. Life certainly did run in cycles

Peregrine dashed ahead of her, racing past where a griffin sculpture peered from a grotto of trees. Devlin had designed the gardens: the stone archways, paths, waterfalls, and pools. It was essentially a life-size portfolio of his style as a landscape architect. But all the coven members had added plants and features that strengthened the garden's energy. Some of the features even helped protect the complex from uninvited guests, like redcaps. But no magic was infallible, and all of it came with limits. Unfortunately.

She hurried after Peregrine, over a small arched footbridge and up the teahouse steps. Its sliding translucent doors stood fully open, ready to welcome the light of the hunter's moon when it rose.

Inside, coals glimmered in the brazier that sat in the center of the room, bathing everything in a warm red glow. Everyone—Devlin, Chloe, Em, Midas, Brooklyn and even Gar, who wasn't technically a coven member— had already gathered around an ankle-high altar draped in white cloth.

"Thank you for getting everything ready." Chandler smiled at the layout on the altar: white candles representing the four cardinal directions, plus scraps of birch bark, white feather quills, and a bowl of oak-gall ink. She breathed in through her nose, enjoying the heady aroma of the sage smudge.

"I made the banishing herbs extra potent," Brooklyn said, placing a bowl filled with roots and crumpled leaves next to the quills. "It seemed smart with hellhounds and perhaps even redcaps lurking around."

Midas folded his arms across his chest. "I wish I'd seen the dog. They aren't all evil, you know."

"So, I've been told." Chandler resisted the urge to glance at Peregrine and turned to Devlin instead. "Ready to get started?"

He smiled. "Lead the way, high priestess."

Chandler began the ritual by using her wand to cast a circle with the altar and brazier in the center. With each step, she opened herself up to the Gods and Goddesses. "I give myself as your tool to lead my coven at the end of this lunar cycle," she murmured the words she'd heard Athena say so many times, "to release and cleanse, to open up to renewal. Let your guidance and words fall from my lips. Let me cast aside self and speak through your wisdom."

After that, she and Devlin jointly welcomed everyone into the circle. Once he withdrew to stand next to Chloe, Chandler took the bowl of Brooklyn's banishing herbs from the altar and sprinkled them into the brazier's glowing coals.

Magic tingled on her skin as the aroma of burning mint, bay, thyme, and the tang of... other things she couldn't quite distinguish smoked the air. She waited a moment, then continued, "As Summer wanes and the night of the crone awakens, I call to the direction of north, element earth. I call to the direction of east, element air..."

Em, Chloe, and Brooklyn's voices formed a soft chorus, echoing her words as Chandler called the rest of the directions. Devlin's, Midas's, and Gar's deeper tones thrummed liked bass drums. Peregrine's careful intonations went right to her heart.

With that done, Chandler released her magic into the universe, sending it out to the Great Fire Salamander and everyone else's guides and guardians as well. "Tonight, as the full moon rises," she said. "I'm ready to cast out, to release those things that hold me back."

She selected a white quill from the altar and a scrap of birch bark, tools she'd use to write down what she needed to let go of in order to start the next lunar cycle with renewed peace, energy, and determination. "I welcome you all to join me. Meditate as the full moon rises. Put into words what holds you back."

She let her attention slide long enough to make sure Peregrine was selecting his quill and birch, then sitting back down with them in his lap like everyone else.

Satisfied he was all set, she closed her eyes and let her mind turn inward. But she didn't have to meditate for more than a second before she knew what she needed to release.

She dipped her quill into the ink and scratched words onto her scrap of birch bark. Gar, Chloe, and Midas finished a second after she did. Moonlight flooded into the teahouse, brightening the entire room as Devlin and Em, then Brooklyn and Peregrine inked their quills and scratched their words.

Chandler rose to her feet. "If you will all follow me, we'll finish the ritual by doing the burn and release outdoors, closer to the moon herself."

The night air cooled Chandler's face as she led the way out of the teahouse and down the steps. The hem of her caftan swished against the path. Behind her, everyone else's footsteps murmured in the quiet air, like the shush of owls' wings moving through the forest.

When they reached the peak of the footbridge, she faced east, perfectly aligned with where the light of the rising moon reflected onto the stream. Devlin came to stand on her left. She signaled Peregrine to come up close to her on the right. The rest of the Circle took up positions on either side of them, heads bowed as they waited for her to speak.

"We give words to flame." She sent her energy and voice out to the gardens and sky. "We release. We turn to ash. We let go. We move forward, leaving behind the past, renewed like the moon, like the earth, the flow of the elements and magic made manifest by this act."

Devlin held his scrap of bark out over the bridge's railing. It burst into flames, ignited by his magic. He let go of it. As it drifted toward the water he murmured, "I accept and release my grief anger."

"I cast aside my self-doubt." Chloe let go of her bark. It sparked and crackled and drifted upward in a lifting breeze before settling at the edge of the stream in a clump of cattails.

Em set her glowing bark free without a word.

"Ouch!" Peregrine tossed his flaming piece into the air as if he'd nearly scorched his fingers. Chandler cringed at that thought, but mostly she was happy that he'd turned around his behavior from earlier in the day and had performed the ritual without aid.

"Selfishness," Midas said succinctly.

Brooklyn smirked at him, then lit her bark and let it go.

"Selfishness and impatience," Gar grumbled.

Chandler pushed her magic slowly into one edge of her scrap, willing it to light. The bark curled, smoked, then flames licked upward. As she watched the blaze grow, she thought about the words everyone had spoken and the unspoken ones as well. She wondered about her own words, scratched onto the now burning bark.

Clouds passed over the moon, first hiding its light and then returning it brighter than ever.

"Fear and sorrow," she said. She didn't share the third word she'd written. Guilt.

Guilt over hiding things. A guilt she shouldn't feel, because some secrets needed to stay hidden for everyone's benefit. Like who Peregrine's father was. No good would come from sharing it at this point, not for Peregrine or her—or his father:

Evan Lewis.

Aidan Lewis's father.

The Vice-Chancellor of the High Council.

Chapter 10

The next morning, Chandler left Peregrine studying the *Book of Good Folk* and went out to her workshop. She was pleased he'd taken it upon himself to keep reading. Doubly so because she needed to put some time into work, despite everything that was going on. Her sculptures didn't make themselves and she had a commissioned piece she'd promised to finish before December. Not to mention the winged monkey waiting for its heart.

She went into the storage area where she kept smaller odds and ends of scrap metal. There were bins piled with coils of cable, wire, lengths of various types of rusty chain. She dug through them, selected a piece of tubing and carried it back to the workshop. But when she held it against the heart, the colors were too similar to give the effect she wanted, and its diameter was wider than she'd have preferred.

"Damn it," she grumbled.

"Trouble in the jungle?" Gar's voice asked.

Startled, she turned to find him striding across the workshop toward her. "More like frustrated." She rubbed her hands down the sides of her welding pants, wiping grime from her fingers. "I thought you had to head back to High Council headquarters this morning?"

"I got a message from Ignatius that I wanted to pass on to you and Devlin before I left."

"Oh." She stood up taller, attempting to look businesslike. Ignatius Jones was a High Council member. He also was Gar's mentor and direct boss. He was one of the few people at headquarters—other than Gar—who had proven an ally to the Circle, or at least he wasn't on their suspect list of witches determined to have the Northern Circle disbanded. Clearly, this wasn't a casual message. "Did you tell Devlin already?"

"He's not around. Brooklyn said he took Henry for a walk. I forwarded Ignatius's email to both of you, but I wanted to talk to one of you in person." He took out his phone and swiped his finger across it, bringing up the message for her to read.

"Just tell me what it says," she said, anxious for him to go on.

"The Council is hosting a gala reception to show off the books recovered from Dux's lair. They want—expect—representatives from the Northern Circle to be there, since technically you're the heroes being honored."

She laughed. "More like they want an excuse to brag and pat each other on the back."

"Exactly. Anyway, it's this Thursday. Cocktails at 5:00 p.m. followed by"—he flapped his hand, dismissing the details—"all the usual bullshit. Devlin will get an official phone call eventually. Ignatius just wanted you forewarned, since it's happening so soon."

"I'm sure Devlin will be happy to go. Chloe will jump at the chance too."

Gar frowned. "Chloe's welcome to go, as are all the Circle members. But you're the high priestess. Your presence isn't a choice."

Dread knotted in her chest. It was an ego boost to think of all the social-climbing witches she'd gone to Greylock with who'd be there in hopes of rubbing elbows with the powers that be—and she'd be there as a high priestess and guest of honor. But among those alumni there was one very specific person who'd be there for sure. Evan Lewis. "That might be expected, but I'm not going to leave Peregrine alone right now."

Gar raised an eyebrow. "You sure that's your only reason? You can't avoid his father forever."

Heat rushed across her skin. She clamped her lips together. In the alley, after the terrifying incident with the hellhound, Gar had made it clear he'd guessed who Peregrine's father was. But keeping private information to himself was part of his job. He'd respect her right to stay silent. And it wasn't like she owed him any further explanation.

He smiled knowingly, then shrugged. "I better get going. Take care of that boy of yours. Who knows, when Vice-Chancellor Lewis retires from being Special Envoy to the Good Courts, Peregrine might be the perfect replacement."

Chandler gawked at him. "Are you kidding me? I never figured out why Evan agreed to act as ambassador to the fae. Being the envoy is dangerous, especially considering his gift. Wasn't the vice-chancellorship enough for him?"

He chuckled. "I knew that would get you to open up." His tone gentled, like a brother offering a special insight to a younger sibling. "I suspect Evan's reasons for accepting the envoy position go beyond his ability to literally see through the fae's disguises and to his own duplicity—most likely involving allegiances and demons, considering his wife's association with Magus Dux."

"You really think so?" In the past Gar had said he thought "something fishy" was going on at the Council. She'd suspected he was referring to Council members having secret pacts and allegiances with the fae or demons; so had everyone else in the Circle. To a degree, under-the-table agreements like that had been a fact of Council politics forever. But to hear Gar say it straight-out and in connection with Evan's political positions as well as his wife, was more than a little unsettling.

"There are also built-in benefits to being a special envoy, such as no-harm clauses." Gar turned and headed for the door, then turned back. "Don't poison Peregrine against the idea. What the witching world needs is less of the old guard and more independent thinkers at its top ranks."

"I get that. But not my son," Chandler said with finality. Still, for a heartbeat she visualized herself in a chancellor's robe, Peregrine standing beside her with a fae envoy's insignia on his cloak, she and her son working together to restore the kinship between the witching world and that of the fae. It would be amazing. And, certainly more appealing than having the demons and cambions like Dux gain the upper hand.

She smiled to herself at that ridiculous thought. There were so many powerful witches and witching families who would destroy the Northern Circle long before they let them gain any real political power. And it really was a long way from the peaceful life she'd envisioned for herself and Peregrine, a very long way.

Not long after Gar left, Chandler gave up the idea of doing something creative and headed for the main house with Peregrine to see how Em and Chloe's hunt for the spells was going. As she opened the front door, Peregrine winged inside first with his arms spread in his usual falcon imitation.

He came to an abrupt halt. "Yikes!"

Right in the middle of his flyway—also known as the foyer—stacks of boxes were piled. Brooklyn was just adding a neatly labeled carton to the mound.

Peregrine peered into the box. "Pickles? You can't get rid of them. They're my favorites."

"Don't worry. There's plenty more," Brooklyn said.

"What's going on?" Chandler asked. The coven sold pickles, jams, and honey at the same stores that carried their wine, but generally it was delivered directly from the vineyard.

"Laura brought this stuff down from the vineyard a few weeks ago for the city food bank. I thought… Athena usually—" Brooklyn's voice choked. "I added a box of my lip balms and salves, and there's more boxes of paper supplies in the kitchen."

Chandler's chest tightened. How could she have forgotten? Four times a year Athena put together extra-large donations for the food bank, October being the largest. "It's not a matter of getting back threefold what you give," Athena had always said. "It's about gratitude and being a decent human."

As thoughts of Athena's death and related things that needed to be addressed rushed into Chandler's mind, the tension in her chest settled into her belly, as weighty as melted lead.

Dampness shone in the corners of Brooklyn's eyes.

"Mom?" Peregrine nudged her hip. "Can I go downstairs and play with the kittens?"

"Of course," she said, without looking away from Brooklyn.

Once he was out of earshot, Brooklyn said, "We need to talk to Devlin about what to do with Athena's personal things. She'd want some of them donated."

Chandler nodded. "Em has hardly any clothes. She's smaller than Athena was, but Athena had so many beautiful things. Devlin should have all her jewelry." She touched Brooklyn's hand. "You should keep a couple of things, too. Athena would want you to have something special."

"I'd like that." Brooklyn took a deep breath. "Devlin said Zeus wanted to have a celebration of Athena's life this coming weekend, something small but open to the public." Her voice faltered. "I'm not sure we can do that with everything else going on."

Chandler's throat squeezed. Zeus was Devlin and Athena's grandfather. When Devlin and Athena's parents had divorced, Zeus bought the complex property to give their mother a place to raise his grandchildren and continue as high priestess of the Northern Circle. After their mom took to embezzling from the coven to pay for extravagant vacations and partying, Athena and Devlin had taken over ownership of the complex.

Chandler flipped through her mental calendar. The gala at the Council headquarters was in a few days. Then there was the weekend… "We could have a public service next week on the morning before Samhain." She cringed. "It feels really strange even talking about this when Athena's spirit is still with us."

"The whole thing is bizarre. I can't believe I didn't realize Rhianna had murdered her. That—that she was impersonating…"

Chandler held out her arms. "Hug?"

"Yeah." Tears choked Brooklyn's voice as she stepped into the embrace. She rested her head on Chandler's shoulder. "I feel so horrible. And I miss Athena so much."

"Me too." She squeezed Brooklyn close, rubbing her back and letting her magic offer comfort. She'd never doubted that Brooklyn felt remorse for remaining a victim of Rhianna's subterfuge longer than the rest of them. But she hadn't stopped to think just how much pain and shame still lingered beneath Brooklyn's blithe exterior.

"Would you mind if I organized the service?" Brooklyn said. "I'd ask Devlin first, of course. We'd want to make sure it didn't interfere with the Samhain celebration itself, and your official swearing-in."

Chandler released Brooklyn. "I'm good with whatever you decide."

"I could ask Zeus to contact Devlin's parents. I'm sure they'll want to come, despite everything."

Chandler laughed, hoping to lighten the mood. "That will be interesting, especially if his dad brings one of his girlfriends."

Brooklyn sniffed back tears. "You can say that again. I don't think his parents have been in the same room since the divorce."

"They're not all bad. His mom's the most self-centered woman I've ever met. But when I came here pregnant, she was good to me."

"Self-centered sounds pretty much like the opposite of Athena."

"And Devlin."

Brooklyn wiped the corners of her eyes and smiled. "Thanks. It felt good to talk things over out loud."

"It's not like we can pretend nothing's happened." Chandler glanced toward the hallway. "I should get going and talk to Em and Chloe. Are they in the office?"

"Em went upstairs to nap." Brooklyn rolled her eyes. "I don't think she or Gar got much sleep last night. Besides, Chloe had class this morning, so she couldn't help Em look for the spells."

"Shit. I should have offered to come over."

"You have a lot going on already," Brooklyn said.

Chandler rubbed her arms, her energy waning as she thought about Em lacking the help she needed to look for the spells, other than Athena and Saille's spirits. She glanced at the pile of boxes Brooklyn had assembled to take to the food bank. She'd been high priestess for all of two days and already she'd started her day searching for veins for a nonessential monkey heart when coven members and business should have been her priority.

She nodded at the boxes. "If you want, I'd be happy to load everything in my car and take it to the food bank."

Brooklyn let out a relieved breath. "That would really help me. If you want, I can keep an eye on Peregrine while you're gone."

It took Chandler about an hour to get all the boxes up from the kitchen and organized in her Subaru. She drove away from the complex and straight out onto the main road, focused solely on the job at hand.

She lowered her window, the tension easing from her shoulder and neck muscles as she took in the fresh air and sunshine. This really had been a great idea.

When she reached the food bank parking area, she pulled into an empty space near the main entry and headed for the door with one of the boxes.

A lanky woman in a glittery Halloween sweatshirt rushed to hold the door open for her. "My heavens. This looks like goodies from Athena Marsh."

"It is. I hope you don't mind that I didn't call first." Chandler set the box just inside the door.

"No problem. You're Athena's friend who makes the flying monkeys, aren't you? I recognize you from the article last month in *Seven Days*." She frowned slightly. "Athena's all right, isn't she? We expected to see her weeks ago."

A wave of deep sorrow crashed over Chandler. She shook her head and spoke with measured precision, afraid that the wave might be followed by tears if she wasn't careful. "Actually, Athena passed away."

The woman paled. "Oh, I'm sorry. I didn't realize."

"It was sudden." Chandler swallowed a fresh swell of emotion and took a breath before continuing. "I have a lot more boxes in my car."

"Let me help you get them."

"Thanks. That would be great."

The woman trailed her back to the car. "I can't believe Athena's gone. She did so much for everyone..." She continued, telling a story about

Athena dropping off cases of much-needed tampons and toilet paper in the middle of a snowstorm.

"I never heard that one." Chandler handed the woman a small box that contained Brooklyn's healing lip balm.

"Did she ever tell you about the carrot soup?"

"No."

The woman went on, talking nonstop about Athena as they went back and forth, hauling boxes inside. The only time she stopped helping was when she dashed off to talk with a growing line of people gathered by a side door. One of the guys was older with a scruffy beard. A skinny woman with two toddlers stood just in front of him. They had backpacks and bags and were shifting restlessly, like they were anxious to get inside.

The woman returned. "Looks like it's going to be a busy afternoon," she said, taking hold of the box of pickles that Peregrine had eyed earlier.

Once the car was empty, Chandler pulled a business card from her wallet and handed it to the woman. "Give me a call if there's ever anything special you're looking for. If it's possible, I'll try to get it for you."

"Thank you, so much." The woman blinked back tears. "And again, I'm so sorry for your loss. Athena was a wonderful woman."

Chandler nodded. She started to leave before her own tears could surge, but she turned back. "We're going to have a public celebration of her life next week. If you'd like, I can send you the details once they're finalized."

"I'd appreciate that. Send it through the food bank email. I know there's lots of other people who'd like to be there."

Chandler nodded again like a bobblehead, then hurried away. But when she reached the Subaru, she was surprised to find herself overcome by a sense of joy rather than sadness.

She slid into the driver's seat, rested back with her hands splayed on the steering wheel and stared across the parking area. She felt truly happy. It was as if by delivering the food and talking to a stranger about their shared connection, she'd released herself from inside the walls of a box she hadn't even realized she'd built. She'd always felt like a part of the local community the way Athena was, but that was a delusion. A wish devoid of real actions, until now.

A few cars away, a delivery van backed out of a parking space, giving her a better view of the hardscrabble people waiting by the side door. A couple of more people joined the group. A guy with a knit cap pulled low and—

Chandler sat bolt upright. She leaned forward, squinting at one of the newcomers. It was Lionel, huddled with a couple of the guys like they were best buddies.

Brooklyn and Midas had told her that the motel Lionel was staying in was a fleabag. That pretty much said he wasn't rolling in cash. But if he was so hard up that he needed to use a food bank to eat, it seemed like he would have taken them up on their offer and stayed at the complex. He'd have had plenty to eat. A nice bed. A private bath. Safety. This was awful. And not necessary.

Chandler started her car and sped out of the parking space. The last thing she wanted was for Lionel to catch her staring at him. She didn't want to push him further away by making him feel embarrassed or awkward. What he needed was the time and space he'd asked for. He'd said he might change his mind about staying at the complex. He'd come around. He'd get past her turning down his dinner offer, too. He had to realize the whole date thing felt to her like it had come out of left field. Besides, it was an offer he clearly couldn't afford to make.

As she turned into traffic and headed for home, she rubbed her fingers over her upper chest, feeling the dragon tattoo warm beneath her touch. She felt bad for Lionel, but in a way, she understood why he hadn't mentioned his personal difficulties to them. After all, she'd kept her own secret for a very long time.

Chapter 11

Heart of the Sun. Desire. Passion.
Creative energy. The seed that is fire.
The beginning that is all.
—The Ace of Wands
Tarot card drawn for Chandler on Beltane Eve.

No sooner had Chandler got home from the food bank and started up the walkway toward her workshop than she noticed a watermelon-size mound of sand on the grass next to her front door. What the heck had Peregrine been up to?

She beelined toward it, her curiosity growing with every step. It was sand for sure. Not loose sand, though. It was mounded and tightly packed, like a sandcastle he might have built on a beach.

She stopped. She blinked, unable to believe her eyes. It was a sand sculpture. But not something Peregrine could possibly have made by himself.

Pure, molten joy tumbled through Chandler as she hurried to it.

It was a sand sculpture of a baby dragon emerging from an egg. There even was a ring of autumn leaves sprinkled around it to look like a nest.

The carefully handprinted note that sat next to it simply said:

For Chandler

☺

She took out her phone and snapped a photo of it. Well, maybe a dozen photos. Not only was it the sweetest surprise anyone could have made, the timing was perfect—yet another reminder of the power of small acts of kindness.

Chandler put on her artist's eye and studied the sculpture more closely: a perfectly rendered 3-D egg with carved cracks and a lifelike dragon half emerged. Tiny clawed paws. Wrinkly unfolding wings. Its eyes were so detailed that they even had slit pupils, like the red dragon on her chest. It was remarkably well done.

Plus, there was the matter of the sand. It wasn't from the yard. Most likely it had come from the park. Even if Peregrine had come up with the idea, he'd had a partner in crime, most likely Brooklyn. She did have neat handwriting.

Smiling, Chandler changed course and headed for the main house. She needed to find both of them and give them big hugs. She couldn't believe they'd even thought to surprise her with something like this, especially with everything that was going on.

She found them in the kitchen eating peanut butter-and-honey sandwiches. Before she could get a word out, Brooklyn excitedly waved her into silence, washed down her mouthful of sandwich with a gulp of milk, then blurted, "Chloe had a great idea and Em agrees—about the journalist. The spell. I think they're right."

Chandler stared at her in surprise. "Are you trying to say they found a way to help Lionel? I didn't even think Chloe was around."

"She got back right after you left." Brooklyn went on, talking even faster. "They came across a section in Merlin's Book about reversals. That gave Chloe an idea. Lionel's damage was caused by Rhianna's spell, not by something external like the energy ball that hit Keshari or the near drowning like in the case of the Vice-Chancellor's son. Or, in Em's case, from years of alcohol and mental abuse."

"But if they don't know what spell Rhianna used on him, how can they reverse it?"

Brooklyn grimaced. "I gather Lionel recited part of it the other night? Well, I remember quite a bit of it too."

Peregrine's mouth fell open. "You were there? I thought the spell was evil."

Chandler would have preferred to shelter him from the ugliness of what had happened, for his sake and to spare Brooklyn the pain of embarrassment. But, at the moment, being open about things felt wiser. She looked at Peregrine. "Brooklyn was under Rhianna's influence. It was powerful magic, like the kind the fae use to confuse people."

"I was stupid and pretty screwed up at the time," Brooklyn added. She finished the last sip of milk in her glass, then wiped her mouth with a napkin. "They already called Lionel. He's coming by later this afternoon to talk about what reversing the spell would entail. They're hoping to do it tomorrow."

"That soon?" Chandler said. "That's fantastic. But I can't believe so much happened. I wasn't gone that long." She thought for a second. "I need to head up to the office and make sure Lionel told them about his strange childhood. It's probably nothing, but they should know about it."

"Devlin didn't text you about the reversal?"

"He might have. I haven't checked my phone in a while." The reason she hadn't done it as soon as she'd got home came back to her. She pressed her lips together to hide a smile and put on a stern mama-dragon frown. Peregrine deserved a bit of ribbing, considering how good of a job he was doing not spilling about the sand sculpture. She toughened her voice. "Is there something you want to tell me, young man? Like maybe something someone did in the yard?"

His eyes bulged. "I didn't do nothin'."

"Well, I love your nothing," she said, releasing her smile.

Peregrine scowled. "What are you talking about?"

"The baby dragon?" She turned to Brooklyn. "It's fantastic. I've seen what you can do with frosting and cake, but this is a whole new level of art."

Brooklyn side-eyed Peregrine. "Your mom's gone nuts."

"Stop it, both of you. I'm talking about the sand sculpture. You did make it, right?"

Peregrine leapt off his stool. "Cool! How big is it? Humongous, like the one we saw at the fair?"

"It's nowhere near that big," Chandler said. Her mind spun. Devlin could have used his earth magic to sculpt it. But he had too much going on to waste time on something like that. Besides, he'd been in the office with Em and Chloe. Not Midas, for sure. Not Laura from the vineyard. She had one heck of a green thumb, but she wasn't artistic at all.

Artistic. Chandler's thoughts froze as someone else occurred to her. Someone whose energy had tons of creative fire. A determined and increasingly mysterious guy who didn't have money but had enough heart to realize something like a sand sculpture—especially a dragon—would mean more to her than dinner at any restaurant or ten dozen roses from a florist.

Lionel. But he'd been at the food bank.

Brooklyn waggled her eyebrows suggestively. "Chloe thinks tall, dark and journalistic has a crush on you. She also thought she saw his VW out on the road when she came back from the university. Maybe he made it."

Chandler swallowed hard, surprised that Brooklyn had the same thought as she'd had—let alone that Chloe had picked up on Lionel's interest. She shook her head in denial. "Now Chloe's the one seeing things."

"Yeah, right." Brooklyn snickered.

Peregrine poked her. "I wanna see the dragon."

"First, I need to go to the office, then I'll show it to you." Chandler glanced at Brooklyn. "Thanks for taking care of him. I appreciate it, even if you didn't make the dragon."

"No problem. He and I are buddies."

Chandler started for the kitchen door with Peregrine. But the door swung open before they got to it. Chloe sailed into the room with Devlin and Em.

"There you are!" Chloe beamed.

Chandler smiled back. "I was just coming to see you. Brooklyn told me you want to do a reversal on Lionel."

"That's not all." Her grin grew impossibly wide.

"You're not saying you found a cure for the Vice-Chancellor's son?" *Dear Goddess, please make it so.*

"We did," Em said softly. "Us and Athena."

Devlin cleared his throat. "You should clarify there's still more work to do."

"The spell's complicated and we just scanned it quickly," Chloe said. "It involves Merlin's crystal and centers on the same theory that's been in medical journals recently, involving air pressure as a tool to repair the damage done by near drowning."

"Air pressure?" Brooklyn cringed. "That's way out of my area of expertise."

Chandler tucked her hands into her pockets. "That sounds more than just complicated. Maybe we need to discuss our options." This did involve a child's life. A child who wasn't theirs or even a Northern Circle member. "We could give the spell to the Vice-Chancellor. Then he and his wife could decide for themselves if they want to risk doing it."

Em's hushed voice stilled the air. "Gar and I talked about that. He says there are powerful witches who might sabotage the healing attempt, then claim we provided the Vice-Chancellor with a corrupt spell. It would be a way for them to destroy the Northern Circle. Those same witches would be delighted to see Aidan die as the result of sabotage. Killing Aidan would weaken the Vice-Chancellor and his wife's dynasty of power."

"That's exactly what I'm worried about," Chloe said. "The only way to guarantee that the spell won't be tampered with is to keep it a secret, make sure we have every detail perfect, and then perform it ourselves. This isn't about being fair or unfair to Aidan's parents. This is about making sure a little boy is healed safely by eliminating the chance of anything going wrong."

Chandler nodded hesitantly. She wasn't sure she was sold on the idea. But a child's life being forfeited for political gain was alarmingly possible. If it were Peregrine laying there in a vegetative state—which was easy to imagine since he and Aidan were technically half brothers—she'd want as few witches involved in his cure as possible. Keeping it a secret made sense, as long as they were positive the spell would work and no word would leak out.

"The Vice-Chancellor's wife hates me," Chloe added. "If we gave them the spell and she somehow screwed it up without it even being sabotaged, she'd blame me for it failing. That won't happen if we do the spell ourselves."

Em folded her arms across her chest. "The spell also requires the presence of Merlin's Book and its attending spirits. I'm the book's protector. And I'm not willing to loan it to the Vice-Chancellor and risk it being claimed by the High Council."

"We're not making any final decisions yet," Chloe said. "Em and I need to go through everything more closely. But, right now, it looks workable." Chloe's gaze settled on Chandler. "However, we do have a question for you."

"Sure. What is it?"

"The spell requires a summoner's bowl. The last time I remember ours being used was just before we did the psyche spell on Em. Did you put it away afterward?"

The anxious tone of Chloe's voice worried Chandler. "The last time I saw it Athena—I mean, Rhianna—was carrying it upstairs. I assumed she was taking it to the vault."

"It's not in there?" Brooklyn said, clearly surprised.

Devlin shook his head. "We checked and double-checked."

Chandler thought back again. But she couldn't remember anything more. She looked at Chloe. "Have you tried to locate it with your pendulum?"

"No. But that's a good idea," Chloe said. "I've handled the bowl and know what its energy feels like. I should be all set, as long as Rhianna didn't cloak it." She took her charm bracelet off, holding it so the crystal pendulum dangled down. "Can someone get me a pad of paper and a pen?"

Chandler headed for the kitchen's junk drawer. "Let's hope Rhianna hid the bowl somewhere in the house. If she did, then she wouldn't have had time to reclaim it before she fled."

"There's lots of old stuff in the potting shed," Peregrine said. "What does it look like?"

Brooklyn cupped her hands to indicate the bowl's size. "It's gray and rough with little ridges."

"It's the crown of a wizard's skull," Chandler explained. She hated being blunt about what the bowl was as much as she loathed the dark edge of magic the bowl represented. But being straightforward seemed the best way to turn this into a teaching moment rather than a treasure hunt.

Excitement lit Peregrine's face. "Cool! Is it really old?"

Devlin nodded. "Old and priceless. It dates to Merlin's time, when the Northern Circle worshipped in oak groves and worked closely with the fae."

Peregrine scowled. "If the faeries liked us then, how come they hate us now?"

"Hate isn't exactly the right word." Devlin's voice turned firm, not an ounce of give to it. "Some of the Good Folk are more trustworthy than others. But they all take pleasure in outsmarting witches. Even back when our coven aligned with them, great care was taken, and costs paid. Bad things happened. Trust was broken. That's why we only associate with the most benign now, like Brooklyn's garden fae. It's also why you need to pretend you can't see any of them until you learn how to protect yourself."

"The black dog's not bad. I think he's guardin' a treasure at city hall. Maybe that's where the summoner's bowl is!"

"Could be," Chandler said to placate him. "Now what do you say we sit really still and let Chloe try to locate it?"

Devlin sketched a floor plan of the main house's first story on the notepad, then Chloe held the crystal pendulum over it and closed her eyes. As she blew out a quiet breath, a barely perceptible hum of magic vibrated in the air, moving down her fingers and into the crystal.

"Show me where the summoner's bowl is," Chloe murmured. "Guide me to it."

The crystal quivered and then swung back and forth across the drawing. Back and forth, back and forth, like the pendulum of the grandfather clock in the office.

Chandler leaned forward, watching intently and praying that the crystal would stop swinging and start circling to indicate the bowl's location.

"Not on this floor," Chloe murmured. Devlin replaced the first sketch with one of the second story. She shut her eyes, her magic humming even louder. "Show me where the summoner's bowl is."

The pendulum swung, back and forth across the sketch. But it didn't circle.

Devlin tried another floor plan, then one of the entire complex.

"Dear Hecate, please help me find the bowl," Chloe intoned as Devlin slid a sketch of the North American continent in front of her.

The crystal swung once, wide across the entire outline, then it hung lifeless over the sketch as if to say the bowl was nowhere to be found.

"Fuck," Brooklyn grumbled.

Chandler glared at her. She didn't blame Brooklyn for feeling that way, but Peregrine was standing right beside her.

"Sorry," Brooklyn said. "But it does suck."

"It sure does." Devlin shoved the notepad aside.

Chandler scrubbed a hand over her head. The more she connected the dots between the upsetting things that had happened and were happening—the missing summoner's bowl, Peregrine's sudden onset of the sight, Merlin's Shade, Rhianna and Athena's murders, not to mention her not exactly untarnished past and everyone else's mistakes—the more she wondered if there was a preeminent power at work, dealing out just deserts to them.

Cold sweat slid down her spine, chilling her to the core as her thoughts moved beyond the Northern Circle. She'd heard rumors that trickery and underhanded magic were involved in Evan Lewis gaining the vice-chancellorship at a younger age than any of his predecessors. His wife was tangled up with Magus Dux. It was unsettling to even think about it, but could Aidan's accident have been less about Chloe's negligence and more about negative blowback from Evan's actions over the years? All witches understood: *What you put out into the universe, so you receive back times three.*

Chandler pressed her hand over her chest, feeling the stirring of the red dragon's magic and the slow throb of her heart. Had this same blowback of negative energy been the seed of her belief that keeping Peregrine's existence from his father was for the best? In her soul—early on, when she'd tried to tell him about the pregnancy and again as the years passed—she'd felt regret and sadness over her choice.

Devlin's voice deepened. "Besides ours, I know of only one other summoner's bowl."

"The one on display at High Council headquarters?" Em asked.

He nodded.

"That's perfect," Chloe said.

Chandler froze, worried by the eagerness in Chloe's voice. "What are you suggesting?"

"We're expected to be there for the reception on Thursday," she said. "Aiden's in the palliative care infirmary on the seventh floor. That's only a few floors up from the gala. We wouldn't have to steal the bowl. We could use it and then return it when we're done."

Devlin drummed his fingers on the kitchen island. "The guards will be protecting the entrances, the High Chancellor, Council members... important people. It's unlikely the staff of the infirmary will change. No matter what, Gar will be privy to that information."

The chill pervading Chandler deepened. "I have a bad feeling about this."

"I'm with you," Em said. She bit down on her bottom lip. "But if we can help a child, then not doing so would be wrong."

Brooklyn's voice grew taut. "I'll help with whatever. But don't expect me to go to headquarters with you. I've never been there, and I don't intend to start now."

"Well, Chandler?" Devlin asked. "You're the Circle's high priestess. I recommended you because everyone respects your opinion. If you vote this down, we won't move forward with the idea. Like we said, nothing's set in stone yet."

Chandler glanced at Peregrine. He'd claimed the paper with the sketch of North America on it and was drawing the likeness of two kids playing with a gigantic dog. Considering what they were talking about, it didn't take much imagination to know one of the kids was him and the other was most likely Aidan. Aidan Lewis, a little boy who had lost years of his life that could have been spent playing with other kids, enjoying the sunshine, and learning about magic. For the love of everything, stealing the summoner's bowl and performing an untried healing spell under the nose of the entire High Council and countless other witches was ludicrous. If they got caught, not only would the coven be disbanded, but everyone involved would undoubtedly have their ability to work magic stripped. She, Peregrine, and all of her closest friends would lose everything and most likely end up in a cell next to Magus Dux.

She rubbed her arms. The risks to the coven from performing the ritual in secret were essentially the same as giving the spell to the Vice-Chancellor. Except, if they did it themselves, then the chance of anyone sabotaging the spell was nonexistent. In other words, the chance of Aidan dying vanished and the chance of success was a great deal higher.

And if they succeeded, Aidan—a witch boy who possessed the same blood as Peregrine, a boy who'd spent the last five years confined to a hospital room—would have a chance to live.

Chandler nodded. "I don't like it. But I agree, it's the safest route."

Chapter 12

Twas arrogance that wrought the rift.
A queen offended, the reason forgotten in a day.
But one day in Her eyes is eons to mankind.
—Sibile, Fair Priestess of the Outer Isles

"It's better than the best!" Peregrine raced up the walkway toward the sand sculpture.

It was just after three o'clock and Chandler was more than ready for some downtime before Lionel stopped by to talk to her and Devlin about the reversal. As impossible as it seemed, the little dragon had slipped her mind.

She lengthened her strides. "I really thought you and Brooklyn had made it."

Peregrine pointed at something on the ground near the dragon. "What's that?"

She stepped closer. A massive dog footprint sat in the middle of a stray puddle of sand.

"That's not from Henry," Peregrine said excitedly.

"It certainly isn't." Maybe she should have been, but Chandler wasn't surprised she hadn't noticed the footprint earlier. It was about a yard away from the sculpture itself, and she'd been totally fixated on it at the time. It also was impossible to tell for sure when the track had been made, but it wasn't incredibly recent. One side of it was a tiny bit windblown, the same as the edge of the dragon's egg. Most likely the dog had either been with the person who created the sculpture or passed through shortly after it was finished.

"I'm gonna go get Brooklyn's game camera!" Peregrine shouted.

"Wait a minute." Chandler latched on to his arm. "A camera won't do any good. If it was the black dog, it's gone now."

"Dogs have territories. He probably peed on the dragon. When he comes back to pee again, the game camera's motion detector will take a picture."

His logic was astoundingly sound, and Chandler was tempted to let it go at that. Creating a trap with the camera would keep Peregrine busy for a while. Except she hated to see him disappointed. "Are you forgetting the dog wouldn't show up on a photo? He's invisible."

"Like you know anything." Peregrine smiled mischievously. "Brooklyn's camera is special. When the motion sensor goes off, so does a grenade."

"A grenade. Really?" This was moving away from logical and starting to sound like his rhinoceros-size redcap story.

"Not a real grenade. It's a balloon filled with flour." He rolled his eyes like she was the densest person in the universe. "Somethin' was knocking over plants in the greenhouse. Brooklyn thought it was pixies. Midas rigged a camera, so when the motion sensor went off it shot a photo and a flour grenade. The flour covered the invisible thing and made it show up in the photo."

"Let me guess, instead of something invisible, you got a photo of a kitten?"

"No. A gigantic rabbit!"

Chandler laughed. That made sense, there were lots of cottontails in the neighborhood. She bit her lip as the hedge-hare, Isobel Lapin, flashed into her mind. But Brooklyn would have mentioned if there was something odd about the creature or the incident. "All right, go ask Brooklyn if you can borrow her camera-grenade launcher gizmo. Don't take it without permission."

"Okay, Mom." He took off at a run, speeding back toward the main house.

No sooner was he out of sight than the grumble of an approaching car engine caught her ear. A second later, Lionel's Volkswagen chugged into sight.

She rested her hands on her hips, watching as the car drove under the arch of the coven's gateway. A small troop of her flying monkeys peered down from the gate's peak, seeming to watch him pass. She smiled, wondering if the monkeys had also noticed how unpredictable his arrivals and departures were. In this case, hours early for his scheduled meeting.

Lionel parked by the main house, got out and started toward her. He had on a black T-shirt beneath a faded jean jacket. His hair was as uneven as before, but his previously crooked librarian glasses now sat square on his nose. He smiled at her and lengthened his strides. He looked so happy that she couldn't help but smile back.

When he got close, he glanced at the dragon. "Um, I guess, I should—"

"Confess? You made it, didn't you?" She'd intended to say it teasingly, but her tone had turned sharp in the end. And she didn't fully regret the bite. Sure, she loved the sculpture and liked Lionel. But down deep it was unsettling to have a man she barely knew doing things in her yard on the sly.

"Honest. I—um"—he rapped a fist against the side of his head as if to knock the words free—"I am not a stalker. I was not planning on making it."

His struggle to explain went straight to her heart, soothing her uneasiness. She might not have been an empath or a mind reader, but she felt nothing other than good intentions coming from him. She also couldn't forget that he'd risked his life in the alleyway, protecting her and Peregrine from the dog. Still, there were other questions. "When did you have time to do it? I wasn't gone that long." On top of that, she'd seen him at the food bank.

His grin was joined by a gleam in his eyes. "Earlier, I stopped by to ask if you wanted to go for a coffee. I thought, maybe dinner was too big for a first step." He took a breath. "Your Subaru was parked in front of the main house. Its tailgate was open, but you weren't around. I had several buckets of sand in my car. I was going to use them for something else."

"So, you just decided to create a dragon?" she said with force. But as the spark in his eyes faded, she gentled her tone. "I'm not saying I don't like it. It's incredible, actually."

He pushed his glasses way up on his nose, then nudged them back down. "I—um—"

"You dropped off the sand and then...?"

He looked down at the dragon. When he spoke his voice was steadier, as if by sheer force of will he had pushed through the confusion caused by Rhianna's spell. "I picked up the sand at Oakledge Park. It was for a little girl who lives at the motel where I'm staying. She's never made a sandcastle. I wanted to give her the chance. I plan on getting some more for her later."

"Oh," Chandler said. That didn't explain everything, but it wasn't the sort of excuse a person could make up on the fly. And it was an amazingly sweet thing to do.

Lionel continued, "I hid my car on the main road and walked back. I was just finishing making the sculpture when you left. Honestly, I was surprised you drove past without even glancing this way." He met her eyes. "When I was young, my adoptive mom took me to India. There was a sand sculptor there. He inspired me. I went back a few years ago and interviewed him. His name is Sudarshan Patnaik. Have you heard of him?"

"He's a sculptor?" She took a step closer to Lionel, out of the shadow of her house and into the dappled sunlight. Sand sculpting was something she knew nothing about, other than beach castles like the one Lionel intended to help the girl make.

"He started the Sand Art Institute in Puri. His work is astonishing. You would love it." He took out his phone, played with it for a second, then held it out to her.

Images of sand sculptures with captions underneath them spanned the screen. One was a tribute to tsunami victims, an emotional piece, especially silhouetted against the waves of the Indian Ocean. Another was dedicated to world peace. It had won first prize at an international competition in Berlin. There were other sand sculptures too, brilliant works of art, heartfelt and finely rendered.

"They're stunning. You said his name is Sudarshan Patnaik?" Chandler committed the name to memory, so she could look him up later.

"I learned basic techniques. I'm not an artist, like you. But I work fast." His voice hushed. "Sometimes the sand calls to me. When I create with it—it feels like I have magic." He smiled down at the dragon in its nest of leaves. "I saw this one in a dream. I knew it was for you. Something wise and strong, and new. Born from sand and fire."

Chandler blinked at him, unable for a moment to connect the dubious journalist who had infiltrated their coven with the remarkable man standing in front of her. She studied him as she'd done before, but this time unabashedly. He wasn't just a long-limbed black guy with perfect bone structure and skin like brushed bronze. He was beautiful, deeply sweet, and thoughtful on the outside and the inside.

"I don't mean to move too fast," he said. "Seriously, I planned on taking the sand to the motel. But it was meant to be yours, at least these first bucketsful."

Her throat clenched, so tightened by emotion that she could barely talk. "It's too late to go for coffee. But would you like to come inside for a beer?"

The joy on his face stole what little reluctance she had left. "I'd love to."

She opened the door and motioned for him to go in first. As he passed by her, she touched his arm. "Thank you. I love the dragon. And don't worry, I don't think you're a stalker. I hoped you'd made it."

He glanced down self-consciously. Then he smiled and his voice turned playful. "That's a relief. I was starting to wonder if Devlin had used the reversal as an excuse to lure me back here, so he could permanently get me out of your hair."

"If I wanted you permanently gone, I wouldn't need Devlin's help," she said, deadpan.

He did a double take, then laughed. "I imagine you wouldn't."

Warmth radiated through her body. She looked at the dragon. It was adorable.

The dog's footprint caught her eye. *Shit.* She'd almost forgotten about that. "Did you happen to see the black dog when you were here?"

"No. Why?" He followed her line of sight. "That wasn't there when I left. I—I'm not kidding."

Chandler could feel his honesty in the air. Honesty and fear. And she certainly didn't blame him for being afraid of a gigantic supernatural dog with glowing eyes and teeth like switchblades. In fact, his current fear made his act of throwing himself over her and Peregrine seem even more selfless.

She shuddered. Maybe, in the end, the dog had fled rather than attacking them, but they still couldn't afford to assume it was harmless. It also made absolutely no sense for Lionel to sleep in a shitty motel with paper-thin walls and probably no form of security at all, especially not with a fae dog trailing him.

She wet her lips. "The invitation to stay here is still open. You don't need to pay us anything. Besides, once we do the reversal, you're going to need a place to recover for a few days."

"I'm fine," he said. He hesitated. "I'm used to being on my own."

Chandler rested a hand on her hip. That wasn't much of an excuse and it wasn't the same as the one he'd given yesterday, about wanting time and space to think.

An image of Lionel standing in line outside the food bank swept into her mind and a voice whispered that there was more to this. One of the things she'd learned driving Em to AA meetings was just how hard it was for some people to admit defeat and reach out for help. Perhaps, in Lionel's head, not taking their offer wasn't as much about his personal comfort and safety as about him accepting that he was nearing rock-bottom financially. Perhaps, even the thought of staying at the complex made him feel like a failure. Her rejecting him probably only added to his sinking sense of self-worth.

She gathered her nerve. "When you saw me leave here, I was on my way to the food bank. I saw you waiting by the side door."

He frowned. "I didn't see you."

"It makes me uncomfortable to think of you being hungry or sleeping in a horrible motel when it isn't necessary." There, she'd put it all on the line.

He clamped his lips together, but a laugh tugged at the corners of his lips. "You think I went there to get food?"

"Brooklyn and Midas said the motel they found you at was... wasn't exactly—"

"It is a dump. But I'm not there because of the cost. I'm there for the same reason I was at the food bank. I'm working on an article about poverty."

Heat washed Chandler's neck and across her cheeks. She hid her face in her hands, totally mortified. "I'm such an idiot. I'm sorry."

Of course, whether Rhianna had messed with Lionel's head or not, he was a journalist. He'd traveled to India to interview a famous sculptor. He'd crisscrossed New England researching ferryboats, and become entangled with the Circle in the hope of uncovering real magic and witches. He wasn't a failing wannabe. He was a professional who submerged himself in his research. He was the real deal and working on a subject that was incredibly important.

"I—I haven't found the heart of the article yet." Lionel went on without seeming to notice her embarrassment. "I'm thinking, it's not so much about poverty as about people who are hungry. I'm not talking about just a hunger for food. I'm talking about people who lack things they crave: a safe place to sleep, love, family... and the hunger for destructive things like drugs. Hunger drives and destroys lives. It sucks people dry." His voice became quieter, self-reflective and shadowed with despair. "If I hadn't found the goth and the Northern Circle, I'm not sure what I wouldn't have done to satisfy my hunger to be close to magic. I was—I feel obsessed sometimes."

Fear rushed through Chandler. Her magic. His obsession. That explained why he was attracted to her. She shrank away from him, covering her panic with a laugh. "Not sure what you wouldn't do? Like make a deal with a demon—or perhaps hook up with a witch?"

Lionel grabbed her shoulders, a firm grip. "Don't even joke about that. My obsession might have led me to the coven. But that's not why I'm standing here. It's not why I asked you out for dinner or made the dragon."

The force of the conviction in his voice replaced her fear with regret. "I'm sorry. I shouldn't have said that."

His grip gentled. His gaze locked on hers and his voice went husky. "I like *you*, Chandler. I want to know *you* better."

He released her shoulders and gently swept his fingers along her jawline. Her breath faltered. She raised her hand and tentatively touched his lips. Plush. Warm.

His lips parted, waiting for her to say "yes" to the question glistening in his eyes. Would she let this go further? Would she kiss him?

She moistened her lips and tilted her head back—

"I got it!" Peregrine's voice sounded in the distance.

Chandler stepped away from Lionel just as Peregrine winged into sight, running full tilt across the parking lot toward them.

She gave Lionel an apologetic grimace, then explained, "He saw the black dog's footprint. Now he's determined to get a photograph of the dog."

Peregrine reached them. He glanced at Lionel. "You got here just in time. This is going to be fun."

He held out the camera contraption for them to see, a MacGyvered combination of boxlike game camera and PVC pipe all bound together with what looked like a mile of camo-colored duct tape.

Lionel crouched to get a closer look. "How does it work?"

Peregrine gleefully thrust the device into Lionel's hands. Then he pointed at its various parts and explained how the flour grenade and firing mechanism were already inside the pipe. How the motion sensor would set them off and cause the invisible dog to get covered in flour just as the camera snapped a photo.

"Where are you going to set it up?" Lionel asked.

"I wanna tape it to the tree." Peregrine flagged his hand at the maple directly across the walkway from the dragon. He pulled a roll of duct tape from his hip pocket. "Brooklyn gave me this to use."

Lionel looked up at Chandler. "Do you mind if we cover your tree with duct tape?"

"Be my guest." A laugh burbled up inside her. "I have more tape in the workshop if you need it."

Lionel winked at her. "If we need more, I'll let you know."

Peregrine let out a falcon screech and ran to the tree. As he began to explain to Lionel how the dog would return to pee on the dragon, Chandler decided to leave them alone and get drinks for everyone. When she returned, Peregrine was holding the camera in place while Lionel struggled to wrap tape around the tree.

Smothering a laugh, she dropped down on the steps and popped open a beer. For a minute, she listened to Peregrine give Lionel instructions. Then she moved on to admiring Lionel's butt when he shifted positions. He did have a nice butt, more muscular than bony.

Lionel glanced over his shoulder and grinned at her.

She blushed, embarrassed to have been caught staring.

"I hope that other beer is mine." He nodded at the unopened Switchback on the step beside her.

She smiled. "I brought juice too, if you prefer."

"Hmm... you decide." A spark brightened his eyes. "I'm just glad to be here."

As he went back to work, Chandler took a deeper, longer sip of her beer. *Dear Gods and Goddesses, of fire, earth, water, and air.* This felt too easy. Too perfect and right. Lionel was great with Peregrine. Peregrine seemed to like him. She liked Lionel too.

But in less than a half hour, they'd be in the main house discussing the reversal with Devlin. Tomorrow it would happen. It might take Lionel a few days to recover. But after that, all his ties to the Circle and the witching world would have to be severed. It would be part of a promise that Lionel would need to make. A deal that she'd have to stand behind as a high priestess speaking for the welfare of her coven.

She couldn't surrender to her and Lionel's attraction—to their hungers, as Lionel would probably call it. It made no sense to let anything grow between them. For his sake. For her sake—and for Peregrine's emotional well-being.

Chapter 13

The ink was made from galls,
harvested centuries ago from the Charter Oak.
The needle was forged from meteor steel.
The art was my creation: Dragons for protection. Monkeys for cleverness.
—Jon Sebastian. Tattoo mage. Savoy, Massachusetts

Once Lionel finished helping set up the camera, Chandler went with him to the main house to meet with Devlin.

The three of them discussed what Lionel remembered from Rhianna's original spell and a general outline of what the reversal would entail. She also talked Lionel into sharing the story about the ferryboat and him being a foundling. Devlin agreed the story was strange. But the fact that Lionel didn't have magic in his blood also made it insignificant, at least as far as the reversal went. As the conversation continued, Chandler silently asked Athena for the strength to ignore her attraction to Lionel and instead approach the situation as an unbiased high priestess.

Still, as the meeting neared its conclusion without the necessary subject of Lionel's promise to stay silent and sever all ties with them coming up, Chandler decided to not point it out. Instead she agreed to meet again with Devlin at the teahouse first thing in the morning to go over the last-minute details. Then she used Peregrine as an excuse to duck out of the meeting.

But instead of going home, she took Peregrine to play with Em's kittens in the greenhouse. She figured it was smarter to stay out of sight until she was certain Lionel was gone for the evening. He wasn't the only one who needed space and time to think things through.

"You look beat," Devlin said the next morning when Chandler straggled into the teahouse. The crisp air on the walk from her apartment had helped clear her head. Still, she was grateful to see there were coals already glowing in the brazier.

"I didn't sleep very well." She tugged off her sweater jacket and hung it up. "Thanks for starting the fire. The heat feels really nice."

"No problem. It gave me time to think about the reversal some more."

"That's what kept me awake, along with dreaming about black dogs." She didn't mention Lionel, Evan Lewis, and the dragons from her vision, though they all had played a part in her tossing and turning.

Devlin took a teapot from the brazier and set it on the low table. "I wish Lionel could have filled in more of the blanks for us. If anything sends this reversal sideways, it'll be the details he and Brooklyn forgot."

Chandler took two teacups from the storage cupboard. "Maybe we should come up with a different idea?"

Devlin shrugged. "We could create a likeness of Lionel out of beeswax. His hair, fingernails, and blood would be perfect for a taglock, since Rhianna used them in her original spell."

Chandler thought for a second. It was a good suggestion. Rhianna's spell could be transferred into the beeswax poppet. The taglock would form what amounted to a magical umbilical cord between him and the beeswax likeness, allowing Lionel to function normally while the spell slowly dissipated from the wax figure. But there was a problem.

"That might fix the issue Lionel's having with getting his thoughts out. But what if something happens to the poppet before the spell dissipates?"

"You mean, what if the fae get their hands on it?"

"If the faeries didn't already know that Lionel has acquired the sight, the black dog knows now—and he's no normal dog. The fae could use the poppet to kill or blind Lionel—or worse." As she set the teacups on the low table, another possibility occurred to her. "There's one person who would remember the entire spell: Rhianna."

Devlin laughed. "Are you kidding?"

"Yeah, it was stupid to even suggest that." Dux had used his demonic machine to create a diamond out of Rhianna's body parts and trap her spirit, like he'd done with Athena and Saille. But Rhianna's diamond was most likely in the hands of the High Council. Besides, a sociopath like Rhianna would never feel obliged to help Lionel, even if she'd caused his troubles.

Devlin sat down at the table on a floor cushion. "We should stick with the reversal. We just have to be prepared to act fast if something goes wrong."

Chandler settled down across the table from him. She reached for the teapot. "The whole idea of Rhianna's spell giving Lionel the sight is strange. He's not a witch. He's not a shifter or demon or even a cambion. I get that his brain was affected. But I have a hard time believing there isn't something else going on, especially if you consider his weird childhood." She sighed. "Lionel is special—I like him."

Devlin nodded heavily. "I'm sorry, Chandler. I like him too."

Puzzled, she replayed his answer in her mind. "What do you mean, *I'm sorry?*"

His expression hardened. "The coven's risked a lot by being as open as we have with him—a man who for all practical purposes remains a threat to the witching world's anonymity. Opening ourselves up to him was the morally right thing to do. But it is a violation the Council won't overlook if it leaks out. We need to make sure what Lionel's learned doesn't go any further."

Dread stole over Chandler. "Are you talking about Lionel's promise and Gar's suggestion about severing all ties? I was wondering why you didn't bring up those points to him last night."

"Once Lionel's had time to recover from the reversal, we'll need to remove his memories of everything that happened over the last month. It's the only fail-safe solution."

"What are you saying?" Her head whirled from the implications.

"I was talking with Gar. He mentioned a spell for the treatment of PTSD that my grandfather Zeus has been involved with. It's an experimental forgetting spell designed to pinpoint and eliminate specific memories. It wouldn't leave Lionel's brain muddled like Rhianna's spell did. It's not like the Council's amnesia spell that wipes out a person's entire memory and carries the risk of someone reverting to an infantile state..."

Every ounce of energy drained from Chandler. She heard Devlin stumble on, arguing a point he clearly would rather not have had to make. She saw the sympathy in his eyes. And she understood in her heart that Devlin was right. Lionel not remembering them would be best for everyone. It would wind back time to before he'd become a threat to the witching world, especially when combined with him leaving town.

". . . it sucks," Devlin said. "You deserve to be happy."

Chandler wiped her hands over her face, then gazed past Devlin toward the glow of the brazier. This would have been easier before she'd almost kissed Lionel. Before he'd helped Peregrine with the camera. Before the baby sand dragon. Before he threw himself over them in the alley, before she'd touched his hand that first time and felt his kind energy.

"I'm really sorry." Devlin nudged a full teacup across the table toward her. "It's chamomile. It'll help."

She faked a smile and channeled her inner high priestess. "How I feel or don't feel about Lionel is beside the point. We need to keep the High Council off our backs. It's not like forgetting us will hurt Lionel. It'll keep him safe."

Her chest squeezed, a sharp ache branching outward until every cell in her body trembled from its power. It felt like the red dragon on her chest was retreating from her skin and clawing its way into the hollow cage of her ribs. It was like the day her dad died and her mother withdrew, leaving behind an icy whisper in her head: *I'll always be alone, always cast aside. Deserted.*

There was another issue as well. Zeus's experimental forgetting spell might make Lionel forget the Northern Circle and everything he'd experienced with them. It would no doubt take away the faery sight that Rhianna's spell had caused. But Lionel's hunger to be close to magic would remain. He'd always felt that, long before he met them.

Devlin agreed to let Chandler tell Lionel privately about the forgetting spell before they performed the reversal. But as the hours ticked by and morning turned to early afternoon, she became more and more sickened by the idea of what had to be said and done.

Still, when three o'clock came and she heard the grumble of his VW, she hurried across her workshop to waylay him before he could head for the main house.

"Hey!" She waved from her front steps, signaling for him to come over.

He retrieved a backpack and something that resembled a saucepan lid from his car. With the pack slung over his shoulder and the mystery item in one hand, he hurried toward her, avoiding the sand dragon and camera-grenade launcher.

She nodded at his pack. "Does that mean you've decided to stay at the complex?"

He shrugged. "Devlin called again to offer. He said there are plenty of guest rooms in the main house."

A knot formed in her throat. She didn't doubt that Devlin had worked extra hard this time to make the rooms sound appealing. With Lionel staying here, it would be easier to transition into doing the forgetting spell.

She faked a laugh. "More like an entire floor of extra rooms."

"Um—I hate to admit it, but I am worried about how I will feel after the reversal."

"Well, knowing you'll be here makes me feel better," she said. The knot in her throat tightened.

His smile broadened and he held out the mysterious lid-shaped thing to her. "I hope you can use these."

She took it, only then realizing what it was. A coil of wire. And not just a single gauge of wire or one variety. It was a mixture, all neatly bundled together. "Wow. Thanks."

"Will it work?" he asked.

She frowned, unsure what he meant. For the most part, her thoughts were focused on what she needed to tell him.

"For the monkey's heart."

Her breath stalled. Of course, the arteries and veins. Struck speechless, she let her magic reach out, sensing the composition of the coiled wires: brass, steel, and what was likely a steel-fiber bronze.

"Harp strings," Lionel answered her question before she could ask. "A man at the motel is a harpist. He busks downtown."

She could only stare at him, her entire body numb except for her heart, thundering loud and insistent. She'd had passing relationships with artists who had sketched and painted her likeness in oils and with pencils and pastels, who'd created silver jewelry to decorate her fingers and ears, and goblets out of glass for her to drink from. But this man—this man with a blazing creative fire who claimed to not be an artist—offered her gifts that touched her soul where the others had left her cold.

Before she could stop herself, Chandler wrapped her arms around Lionel in a grateful hug. "They're perfect."

His arms enveloped her, warm and surprisingly strong. "I'm glad."

"It's more than that. I love that you even thought to give them to me." Her already wild heart thumped even more insanely as she pressed her breasts against his chest, moving the hug past a friendly gesture to say she was open to more—even more than the kiss that had almost happened yesterday. Perhaps not right at that very moment in her doorway, with a backpack slung over his shoulder and a coil of wire in her hand. But she couldn't bear the thought of never kissing him like a lover, of not ever being with him, at least once before they wiped her from his mind and he walked away.

His hand brushed up her spine, lingering on the back of her neck. He murmured, "You—you're amazing. Your soul. Your heart."

"Lionel," she said, breathless. "I need to—"

She closed her eyes. She had to tell him about the forgetting spell. It wasn't fair to let him think this heat between them could lead anywhere beyond the briefest fling. She'd offered—*no*—she'd insisted on being the one to tell him. Devlin had said he'd do it if she didn't want to. But she'd wanted to. She had to. But she longed to feel Lionel's lips against hers, to caress his chest and long legs, to feel the heat of his body against her.

She stepped back, out of the embrace.

He smiled. "Um—I should go. Devlin is waiting to show me the guest room."

"Yeah. I guess." She gritted her teeth, readying to tell him. Instead she said, "Peregrine's with Devlin. I hope you don't mind if he helps with the reversal. With the sight coming on, it's time he become more actively involved in the adult aspects of the coven."

Lionel touched her chin, nudging her face upward until their gazes met. "Peregrine is a remarkable boy. If I ever have a child, I hope he—or she—is like him." He stopped talking, waiting expectantly for a response.

"Remarkable," she parroted his word. But that wasn't what she needed to say. She opened her mouth. She closed it.

Lionel's brow wrinkled with concern. "What's wrong?"

She squeezed her eyes shut, hiding in the darkness behind their lids. "After you recover from the reversal, we'll need to do a follow-up spell on you. It'll make you forget everything that's happened over the last month."

His arms fell limp at his sides. "Everything? You've got to be kidding."

"You won't be confused or have speech issues. You'll be fine." She stepped back, bracing herself for his anger. "It's for the best. For everyone."

His hands clenched. The tendons on his neck stood out, as taut as if they might snap. "I—I won't remember the coven? My past? You?"

She nodded. "I don't like the idea either."

His face tightened with emotion, anger or fear—or maybe both.

"I'm sorry. I wish there was another way to keep everyone safe."

He looked down, ran a hand over his head, and muttered, "Damn it to hell."

Unsure what to say, she waited for a heartbeat, sweat icing her spine. Finally, she asked, "You okay?"

He gave a slow, grim bob of his head, then he met her eyes. "All right, I understand. If it's for the best, then so be it."

She stared at him, unable to believe he'd agreed so easily. "Are you sure you're all right with this? The ferry. Magic. Heritage witches. You won't remember any of it."

"I'd expected to leave and never talk about anything." His voice was calm and clear, unbelievably so. "I don't like it. But I know this isn't personal.

It's about the Council and anonymity. I trust you, Chandler. I want what's best for the coven, and you."

She looked deep into his eyes, beautiful brown eyes full of sadness. If only he'd shout at her. If only he'd stayed furious, this would be much easier. But complete trust?

Maybe he was going to forget her, but she would never forget him.

Chapter 14

By this spell, what was real becomes but dream,
wisps forgotten, dew dried by the morning sun.
Be gone. Be dream. Be nevermore.
—High Council of Witches' Amnesia Spell

A short time later, Chandler and Lionel joined everyone else in the teahouse. Brooklyn, Midas, and Devlin were busy arranging candles around the room. Peregrine and Em were smudging the air with sage and rosemary.

"We're almost ready," Chloe said. She gestured for Lionel to take a seat on the yoga mat that lay in the center of the room. A black candle had been placed at its head. She smiled at Lionel. "Peregrine was telling us that you studied sand sculpting in India."

"Yes. It was a remarkable experience..."

As Lionel told Chloe about India, Chandler headed across the room to the supply cabinet. She could barely breathe, thanks to the war of emotions tangling inside her. She was certain the reversal was the right thing to do. But that didn't mean it wasn't dangerous. And then there was the forgetting spell; she wasn't looking forward to that. Not in the least.

She got out the silver high priestess belt and secured it loosely over the low waistline of her wrap pants. Then she headed back.

". . . I plan on returning to India, someday," Lionel finished his story.

Chloe set a bowl of crystals at the foot of the yoga mat. "Did you always feel drawn to make things out of sand?"

"Um—I suppose. I liked making sandcastles when I was little." He folded his legs, sitting akimbo.

"When monks and other practitioners create mandalas out of sand, their prayers saturate the grains." Chloe toyed with her charm bracelet for a second. "Devlin and I healed my friend Keshari's mind using mandala sand instead of just the larger crystals the spell required. Of course, sand is essentially thousands of tiny crystals."

Chandler stood still, listening closely. Why was Chloe bringing that up right now? "What are you thinking?"

"Nothing, really. We need a substitute for something in the healing spell for the Vice-Chancellor's son. Unfortunately, it's not going to be as simple as swapping one crystal for another." She glanced at Em.

Em grimaced, then briskly turned away and went back to smudging.

Chandler frowned. What was going on between the two of them?

She replayed their interaction in her head: Chloe's comment, the glance, and Em's grimace. She shook it off. She was letting her worries about the reversal and Lionel turn casual glances and friendly conversation into something it wasn't. It made no sense for Chloe and Em to hide anything. They'd been totally open about Aidan and the healing spell. Still…

An idea formed in the back of Chandler's mind. *Crystals. Prayers. Sand. Healing.* "Well," she said to Chloe, "you might not have found your answer, but you gave me an idea. We have sand from Oakledge Park in the supply cabinet, right?"

"There's a canister on the bottom shelf," Devlin said. "I collected it where the ley lines run under the beach. It's nice and clean. Already blessed."

"Perfect." Chandler scanned the cupboard until she found the sand, then turned to Peregrine. "If you're done smudging, would you like to do something special for me and Lionel?"

"Sure." He dashed over.

"Sprinkle a circle of this sand around the yoga mat, like we normally do with salt. Send your magic into the grains while you're doing it. Say a prayer or just think good thoughts."

"Great idea," Chloe said.

Devlin nodded. "I'm willing to bet it will strengthen the spell."

Chandler took a ceremonial dagger from the cupboard and sheathed it at her waist. The truth was the sand might not do anything. But if there was a connection between Lionel's personal energy and the crystals that form sand, then it could very well amplify the reversal like Devlin suspected. In turn, amplification might help keep the reversal from going sideways.

She shuddered at the thought of something going horrifically wrong. The reversal could intensify instead of releasing the layers of twists and warps she'd sensed in Lionel's energy. Some unforeseen side effect could crop up.

Rhianna's spell was unlike anything they'd encountered before. Either way, creating the sand circle couldn't hurt and it was a safe way for Peregrine to take charge of a small piece of the ritual. The rest of the time, all he'd be doing was mimicking their actions and repeating their words, the way Devlin had instructed him to do.

Peregrine bounded back to her with the empty canister. "All done!"

She rested a hand on his arm to quiet him. "Thank you. It looks perfect." She swallowed back her fear and smiled at Lionel. "If you'll take off your glasses and lie down, we'll get started."

"Of—of course." His voice was calm, but his fingers trembled as he tucked his glasses into his shirt pocket and stretched out on his back with one of Brooklyn's lavender pillows under his head.

Keeping Peregrine beside her, Chandler went to stand at Lionel's head with the black candle at her feet. As high priest, Devlin positioned himself directly opposite her at the foot of the mat. Everyone else filled in the empty spots between them until they formed a circle around Lionel.

Athena, give me strength that I might lead as you would, Chandler prayed. She wiped her hands down her pant legs, drying off sweat. Then she squared her shoulders and met Devlin's eyes. No more worrying. No more fear. It was time to focus and make sure nothing went wrong.

For a moment, they waited in silence as their energy built in the air. Finally, he nodded that it was time to begin and together they chanted, "Today, we seek to reverse that which was done before."

"Reverse that which was done," everyone echoed them—even Peregrine, hugged in close beside her.

She pushed him from her mind. She had to concentrate on the reversal, nothing else. Not even Peregrine.

She knelt, took her dagger out and set it on the floor beside the black candle. Then she wriggled the candle from its spiked holder. "By my free will with harm to none, I call upon the Gods and Goddesses to reverse what has been done."

Devlin's voice rose. "Turn back. Unwind. Return this man to what he was. Untainted by spell."

"Novis! Reverse!" Chandler shouted, as she picked up the dagger and sliced off the black candle's top.

A seismic wave of energy exploded outward from the candle. She leaned into the surges, heat and magic flaring through her body as the energy pushed against her like a riptide.

Lionel curled into a ball and moaned. She longed to reach out and soothe him. She longed to glance at Peregrine as well. But she couldn't. This was just the beginning.

As the surges of energy subsided, Chandler focused on the magic buzzing in her arms and body. She waited for Lionel to uncurl and lie back down, then she counted to three and shoved the candle onto the holder's spike, this time with its wickless bottom facing upward. "Novis! Reverse!"

A surge of energy sucked toward the candle, the pressure of the waves resounding in the room like a sonic echo rebounding from the ocean's depths. She drew up her magic and forced it into her tattoo sleeves until her skin vibrated from the energy of it pulsing through the monkeys and dragons. She pressed her fingertips against the sides of the candle, released her magic and commanded, "Reverse. Turn back. Remove. I call wick. I call flame."

Lionel groaned as the wax on the bottom of the candle curled away from its center point, revealing the previously hidden bottom of the wick. Sweat gleamed on his forehead and dribbled down his temples.

All around her the coven's energy rang and pulsed, vibrating in the air like a surreal chorus. Brooklyn's head rolled back on her shoulders, the whites of her eyes revealed as she called up every ounce of her power. Midas hunched forward, the gold beads on his dreadlocks glistening as he rocked back and forth like a pendulum.

"Mama," Peregrine murmured, huddling closer to her.

She pulled up all her power, releasing it with her voice. "Flame! I call upon you. Ignite!"

Fire leapt from the candle's newly revealed wick, blazing higher than any natural flame.

"Reverse. Turn back!" she called out. "What was given is now returned."

"Reverse. Turn back." Devlin's voice echoed hers.

Chloe took over, "What was given is now returned."

"Reverse. Turn back," Peregrine said timidly.

Pride swelled in Chandler's chest. She glanced his way, signaling for him and everyone else to kneel.

Once they were all ready, she took the dagger and drew its blade lightly across her short hair, shaving off a sprinkling into her palm. For a second, she wished she still had long curls, and hoped her sacrifice would be enough. But it wasn't quantity that mattered. All that mattered was that their offerings mirrored what Rhianna had taken from Lionel.

Chandler dropped the pinch of hair into the candle flame. The flame *snap-crackled* and the stench of burning hair flooded her sinuses. She wrinkled her nose to block out the smell, then pushed it from her mind and took a fresh grip on the dagger.

"Reverse. Turn back," she said, drawing the dagger lightly across her wrist in the location where Rhianna had cut Lionel.

Blood welled from the wound. She held her arm over the candle, letting droplets sizzle into the sputtering flame. A few drops missed their target and fell into the pool of melted wax that surrounded the wick, spreading out like oil across water. She sliced off a crescent of fingernail and dropped it into the flame as well.

"Reverse, return…" Lionel mumbled. His head lolled to one side. His eyes opened. Black on black with no hint of white. His muscles twitched and spasmed.

"Whoa," Brooklyn gasped. "I don't remember that happening when we did the spell."

Chandler quickly passed the dagger to Peregrine. His eyes were bright and eager.

"Careful," she whispered, sliding the candle closer to him. *Great Fire Salamander, protect him and guide him.*

She clenched her teeth as he cut off a thick curl of hair and sprinkled it into the flame, but she barely noticed the smell as he brought the knife toward his wrist.

"Off to one side where Devlin showed you. Not deep," she instructed. If the Gods didn't like her intrusion into the sanctity of the reversal, then so be it.

Peregrine wielded the bulky dagger with care, only a few droplets rising. His fingernails were longer than hers, so he didn't have a problem shaving off a piece. He passed the candle and dagger to Chloe who knelt to his right. She repeated the offerings and passed the candle on to Devlin…

The odor of burning hair and blood overwhelmed the lingering scent of the sage and rosemary smudge.

Lionel whimpered and twitched. His jaw worked, teeth grinding.

Sweat slicked Chandler's back and stuck her shirt to her armpits. Magic thudded in her head, louder than her pulse. The air became heavy and hot, so hot she could barely breathe.

Lionel let out a shriek and began to thrash, like an animal caught in a leghold trap. Then, as Em slid the candle back to Chandler, his eyelids shut, and he fell utterly still.

Hot wax drizzled over Chandler's fingers as she raised the candle skyward. "As the Northern Circle once chose to take from Lionel, we now willingly return the offerings. Hair, blood, and nails, with these tokens may the spell be reversed, removed, turned back, every trace and shadow gone from Lionel. Gone. Untainted by spell! So mote it be!"

The candle flame shot upward like a bolt of lightning, flashing jagged and hot-white. Magic pulsed in the room. The ceiling shuddered. The floor shook.

"Untainted by spell," Lionel wailed, like a child. His body humped upward, arching like the footbridge in the garden and falling back onto the mat as the flame flickered and went out.

Chandler held her breath, waiting for stillness to settle in the air. Logic said the reversal was over. But her instincts whispered it wasn't. There was something building in the air, something bigger—something unexpected.

"I feel strange," Lionel said, his voice distant. He was sitting on the mat, head in his hands. "It's like I'm floating in darkness. Dizzy."

Chloe scrambled forward with a glass of water. When he lifted his head, she held the glass to his lips so he could take a sip. "Is that better?"

He swallowed, then tilted his head. "Not really. There's a roaring noise in my ears. It's getting louder. The sound of an engine." His nose wrinkled. "I smell exhaust—diesel."

Chandler's eyes widened, fear pulsing inside her. "A ferry?"

"That's it."

"That's—" A wave of dizziness engulfed Chandler. Bursts of light exploded behind her eyes. She collapsed on the floor, barely able to focus her eyes long enough to see Peregrine slump beside her. Chloe sprawled on the other side of him. What was happening? What was happening to all of them?

Her consciousness slipped away, spinning her into darkness, away from the teahouse and toward the roar of an engine and the blare of a ferry's horn. The *slap-slap* of water against a boat's metal hull. The taste and stench of exhaust. A ferryboat...

Her spirit tumbled further away from reality, whirling deeper into the sensation, into Lionel's head and body. Hurtling backward through time and into his past, his reality.

Exhaust. Chandler recognizes the smell and flavor on her tongue. But it's terrifying and strange to the little boy whose body she inhabits. He's curled up on the back seat of a car under the weight of a blanket. Cold. Wet. Shivering.

"Shush, shush." A woman's voice sooths. "Stay still. Stay quiet."

Through the vertigo of her thoughts, Chandler senses something else. Her spirit is not alone inside the boy. Lionel is there—as he should be, since it is his past. The rest of the coven is with them too, even Peregrine. Each of them experiencing Lionel's past in isolation but joined by the unraveling threads of a collapsing spell. Not Rhianna's spell. This is a different spell, which imprisoned Lionel's earliest memories but is now unspooling them in reverse. Retrocognition, that's the name for what they are experiencing. Time unspools again, moving backward. Rain slices down, glistening on the ferry's deck. The rumble of the engines vibrates underfoot. The boy sways, fighting to stand. Cold. Hungry. He's never felt this famished before. Hungry, inside and out.

Time takes another step back.

White hands with long fingers lift him above the water, a woman's hands setting a boy-child on the swaying deck. Her hair's entwined with seaweed. Her eyes are bright and as hard as lightning. The waves murmur her name: Nimue. Lady of the Lake. Her name means magic to the waves, to them and all the creatures below. It means power and protection.

Dizziness swirls. Time retreats and the boy is below the lake's surface, looking up. Three silver coins fall onto the waves, shimmering as they descend. A woman's voice reaches down from the boat, a prayer echoing through the water. "Dear Lady, protector of the innocent. Hear my prayers, let my arms not forever be empty of a child's warmth. Let my life not be forever barren."

Chandler blinks and she's not with Nimue anymore. The boy she inhabits stands in a valley beneath the waves. An apple orchard. The hollow clank-clank of wind chimes sounds in the air. Chimes hung in trees. Chimes made of bones. Stag bones. Man bones. Dragon bones. Beneath the boy's feet the grass is cool and vivid green. White cattle the size of rats scuttle away. Beautiful women and men parade, lean and royal, cloaks and dresses flowing out behind them like gossamer. The glint of armor and jewels. Sandcastles rise from mountains of shells. Chandler knows this place, or at least she's heard of it in stories: the home under the lake where Lancelot and his brothers were raised.

"Hurry. Hurry," a young woman whispers to him. She is blonde and beautiful. Some call her Princess Sibile. Some call her Enchantress of the Outer Isles. She places a kiss on the boy's brow, a kiss as gentle as the stroke of a hawthorn blossom. A kiss that will grow into a spell of forgetting. A fae spell inadvertently broken by the Circle, or so Chandler now realizes.

Sibile's blue eyes darken like twilight. Tears burn. Not in her eyes. They burn in Chandler's eyes. But she knows they aren't really hers, either. They belong to the boy, to Lionel. His little fingers curl around Sibile's necklace, elderberries and acorns. He doesn't want to leave her magic. Her touch. Her beauty. Her fury and power. Her iron and the oil-black dogs that shadow her steps.

"My child," Sibile's voice is as cool as moonlight. "Hurry. Go to Nimue. It's against our laws, but kindness must be repaid threefold. As your mother

does for my child, so I do for hers. I release you, Lionel of the Lake. I return you to your kind. I buy your debt with my blood and tears."

Darkness falls. Time retreats. Back. Back. Hours, days, uncoiling.

The sound of footsteps against wet sand, moving quickly, magic rising all around them like mist and stars made of crystal. The boy is clutched against Sibile's chest. An applewood staff is strapped to her back and a knife of iron is clutched in her hand. The iron makes her powerful. It also makes her an outsider in the otherworld; the child senses this even as they flee. Flee a place where the air leaves the tang of magic on his tongue. Fae magic, seductive and razor-sharp. Beautiful people. Terrifying people. Creatures. Beasts. Other children like him. Dancing. Dancing until their feet are bloody. Harps and flutes. The moon rises. Stars come out. Hawthorn trees bloom. Their petals fall. Fruit ripens. Fruit falls. Snow covers bare branches... Time is swift and endless. An hourglass with sand forever falling. Backward, backward.

Chandler senses that the thread of the retrocognition they're experiencing is reaching its end. The dizziness is fading. She smells the sweetgrass scent of the mats on the teahouse floor. But she wants to see the rest.

She pulls on the last thread of Lionel's memories, letting the retrocognition take her once more. Back... back, back.

Sibile holds the newborn boy up like a prize, a trophy of beauty for the otherworld to behold. The magic of her touch and the place tingles on the boy's skin. He sees them all, glimmering and bright. And he is terrified. He wriggles and wriggles. He wants to go back into the warmth of his mother. He wants to go back.

Time turns.

The final second uncoiling.

A snap of her fingers, and the Enchantress of the Outer Isles, the Princess Sibile, stops time and steps out into a birthing room.

She slides a child into the doctor's waiting hands. A fae child with a cleft palate, three fingers on one hand and four on the other, skin mottled yellow, purple, and blue. A sickling child buzzing with magic. Her child.

She reaches between the woman's legs and claims the perfect boy. Perfect little arms. Perfect fingers. Perfect smile. Lionel, taken in a frozen heartbeat of time, after his mother's tears and groaning—and before the chill of the doctor's hands.

One moment in time. One moment and all is changed.

Chapter 15

They said, if you pray hard enough
in the right place, at the right time,
and with the right offering,
a child would be bestowed.
They did not lie.
—Amanda Parker. Boston, Massachusetts

Lionel hoisted himself up on one elbow. His eyes were a little unfocused, but his voice was unimpeded and as clear as the star-bright sky glimmering beyond the teahouse's translucent doors.

"If you don't mind, I'd rather spend the night here than in the house," he said.

Devlin smiled. "Stay wherever you'd like. Just don't hesitate to call if you need anything."

Chandler didn't blame Lionel for wanting to stay put. The reversal alone had to have exhausted him—add to that the surprise of the retrocognition and the breaking of the forgetting spell that Sibile had cast on him years ago, and Chandler was shocked he had the strength to keep his eyes open at all. Plus, with the cleansing they'd done earlier, the atmosphere in the teahouse was utterly tranquil.

Peregrine tugged on her arm. "I'm as hungry as a rat."

She laughed. "Not a hellhound?"

"Well, yeah." His gaze went to Lionel. "Did that Lady steal you from your mom? Were the black dogs her pets? What did she feed them?"

Chandler tousled Peregrine's hair. "Lionel needs to rest right now. You can talk to him in the morning."

Lionel smiled at Peregrine and jutted his chin to indicate the teahouse door. "I think the dogs are more protectors than pets, don't you?"

Peregrine wheeled, looking toward the doorway. "Holy bananas! I didn't notice him. You think he's protecting us?"

Chandler followed Peregrine's gaze. Soft lights brightened the teahouse doorway and steps. There was a planter filled with frostbitten mum plants, but no dog.

In a heartbeat, a black hellhound materialized, sitting sentinel-straight next to the planter. Its eyes glowed red as it stared back at her. It leapt to its feet, bounded down the steps, and vanished into the darkening garden.

Midas stared at Lionel, mouth open. "You still have the sight?"

"I guess. I mean, I saw the dog as clear as anything." Lionel touched the pocket where his glasses were stashed. "And now I don't seem to need these, which is a whole different type of miracle."

Chandler thought for a second. "Maybe the faery sight was a gift from Sibile rather than part of a spell?"

"Maybe," Devlin said. "It also could have been an ability he acquired from living in their realm."

Brooklyn grumbled. "Lousy faeries never offered me the sight."

"You actually think the sight is a good thing?" Chandler snapped. Instantly, she regretted her tone. She cringed. "Sorry. I know you realize how dangerous it is."

Brooklyn sighed, then whispered as if to keep Peregrine from hearing, "It's one of those fantasies that you wouldn't mind being offered, but don't really want. Like three guys at once. Three is a magic number, but enough is enough."

"On that note"—Chloe took Devlin's arm—"I think it's time to get out of here and let Lionel have some peace and quiet?"

"I'm ready for a beer," Midas said.

As everyone started for the door, Chandler hung back.

"You comin', Mom?" Peregrine asked.

"You go ahead. I'm going to turn on the bathroom light and get Lionel a blanket." She watched as they went out and down the steps toward the footbridge. Then she returned to Lionel.

"Thanks for staying," he said.

She sat down on the floor next to him and rested her hand on his. "That certainly was an unexpected side effect. You okay with it?"

"You mean still having the sight or the stolen and raised by faeries part?"

"It's all pretty crazy, isn't it?" She released his hand and ran her fingers over her head, pausing at the spot where the dagger had bared her scalp.

"Actually, I was thinking about the silver coins in the water and the prayer for a child. Was that your adoptive mom's voice?"

He nodded. Sadness darkened his eyes. "She kept the truth from me. All these years."

"She did tell you part of it," Chandler said.

"Yeah, but she made it sound like fiction."

The sadness in his voice went straight to her heart. But what could she say? The truth was moms kept secrets and became dragons to protect their children. If need be, they buried their hearts and killed their souls for their child. Still, sometimes in the unspooling of days and years, people like her wondered if they'd made the right choices. At some point, his adoptive mom had probably also questioned her decision to stay silent.

Chandler sat motionless, sadness weighing heavy inside her. There were the other moms in Lionel's life, too. And perhaps his faery mom, Sibile, was the strongest mama dragon of them all. She'd given him up and returned him to the human realm out of a sense of justice, something Chandler wasn't sure she could have done.

Lionel's voice hushed even further. "My retaining the sight complicates the upcoming forgetting spell, doesn't it?"

She lowered her gaze to his hand, fingertips an inch from hers. Zeus's experimental spell—she didn't even want to think about that. The thought of stealing a month of Lionel's life from him had been bad enough before, but now that same month included the retrocognition. He'd forget everything he'd just learned about his childhood and the fae. But he'd be left hungry for magic and seeing things that he didn't dare mention out of fear of coming across as crazy. She was certain he'd still go along with having the spell performed. And doing it would protect the coven from the Council's sanctions. But was it still right?

She faked a smile. "Before we do anything, you need to take it easy for a few days. Get your strength back." She thought for a second, then steered the conversation away from the forgetting spell. "I assume you realize that the coven is attempting to help another person?"

"Chloe mentioned something about the Vice-Chancellor's son." Lionel stretched out on his side, head on the small lavender-scented pillow. "I've caught other bits and pieces as well."

"His name's Aidan. We're going to attempt to heal him later this week. On Thursday, during a gala reception at the High Council headquarters in Connecticut." There was no reason to keep the details from him. He wouldn't remember any of it after the forgetting. "Chloe and Em found a spell to use on the boy. But there are things they still need to work out."

"That's nice." Lionel closed his eyes. "Chandler, I'd like to talk some more. But I can barely stay awake."

She touched his arm, enjoying his warmhearted energy for a moment. "That's normal after all you've been through. I'll get a blanket, then you can get some sleep."

She tiptoed to the bathroom, turned on the night-light, and retrieved a larger pillow and soft blanket from the linen cupboard. When she returned, Lionel opened his eyes and let her replace the small lavender pillow with the larger one. His wild-weed crazy hair was dark against the soft white of the pillowcase. She pulled the blanket over him, tucking it under the bottom of the yoga mat to make sure his feet would stay warm.

Once she was done, she stood up, folded her arms across her chest and dared a lingering look at him. Shadows gathered across his cheekbones and in the hollows under his eyes. He was completely spent.

"Sure you'll be all right out here alone?" she asked.

He nodded.

She smiled. She totally got it. The air was still. The only sounds were the trickle of the distant stream and the soft rustle of autumn leaves tumbling across the teahouse steps. The perfectness of the moment was palpable, as perfect as the calm that was settling over Lionel's face... his beautiful face.

He reached out toward her, beckoning for her to come closer. She walked away from the foot of the mat and knelt near his chest, close enough that he could touch her upper arm.

"Kiss me," he whispered. "I want to go to sleep with the taste of you on my lips. I want to remember you tonight."

She leaned in. His fingers swept her jawline, then cupped her face. His lips were moist and warm. The kiss was tender. Slow. As pure as the light from the rising moon that frosted the floor and the walls around them. Innocent. Loving. Unforgettable.

Chapter 16

WILLIAMSTOWN, MA—Bethany Parrish—age 35—was found dead Tuesday evening of a self-inflicted gunshot wound, two years to the day from when her husband, Captain Cade Parrish, lost his life while rescuing a family from a fire that destroyed a South Williamstown home. She leaves behind one child...

—From *West Mass Independent*

Chandler rubbed a finger across her lips, enjoying the memory of the kiss with Lionel. It was an hour later. She'd left him sleeping in the teahouse and joined everyone else in the lounge. Midas and Brooklyn were playing bartender, passing out waters and juices to get everyone rehydrated. Peregrine was on the far side of the room divider, fast asleep on the living room couch. If she listened closely, she could hear his snores.

Chloe slid off her barstool and faced everyone with her hands shoved deep into her pockets. "There's something we need to talk about. It's kind of bad news."

Em corrected her. "More like it puts an end to our plans for Thursday."

A sick feeling dropped into Chandler's stomach. Thursday was the gala and Aidan's healing. This didn't sound good at all.

Her thoughts raced back to the furtive look Em and Chloe had shared just before the reversal, when they'd been talking about sand and substitutions. Had they known something was wrong, even back then?

"You mean, something on top of having to swipe the summoner's bowl?" Brooklyn asked.

Devlin frowned at Chloe. "Why didn't you say something earlier? This can't be something you just discovered."

"Em and I"—Chloe's voice hitched, raw emotion stealing her words— "we thought it was better to not upset everyone before we did the reversal."

Devlin left his stool and pulled her into a hug. "I didn't mean to sound angry. I'm just surprised you didn't tell me."

She buried her face in his shoulder, her body heaving as she let out a long sob. "I thought—I hoped... I thought finally we could help Aidan, but now—"

A chill traveled the length of Chandler's arms. She hugged herself against it. What had happened? No one had expected the cure for Aiden to be easy or simple. The magic would be advanced for sure. But everything had seemed like it was coming together. She felt horrible for Chloe. She felt worse for Aidan. The boy deserved a chance to live. Poor Evan, too. Maybe the Vice-Chancellor wasn't a part of her or Peregrine's life, but she didn't wish this sort of ongoing torture on anyone.

"It might take some experimenting, but I'm sure we can find a solution," Midas suggested with confidence. "Nothing's impossible."

"This is." Chloe slipped from Devlin's arms, wiping her eyes. "We're screwed. Totally, no way out. Screwed."

Chandler ventured a guess. "Did Gar call? Is the Council's summoner's bowl missing too?"

Em sighed heavily. "If only it were that simple—or fixable. We missed one of the healing spell's requirements the first time we read through it. The bowl has to be presented to Aidan's lips by his fraternal brother."

"Fuck," Brooklyn said. "Aidan Lewis is an only child, isn't he?"

Chloe shook her head. "He has a sister. But no brother."

The world around Chandler whirled and then vanished into the background, surreal and unimportant. *A fraternal brother?* It couldn't be. It was too horribly coincidental. Too much like a twist invented by a demented god. Or was it the universe sending her a message, more blowback for her keeping Peregrine's existence to herself?

Her gaze went to the room divider and beyond it to where Peregrine slept curled up on the living room couch under an afghan. Her son. Her love. The brightest fire in her life. Dear Goddess, Chloe and Em were so wrong about Aidan not having a brother. More wrong than they could ever imagine. Thank the Goddess, Gar wasn't here. One glance between the two of them would have clued everyone in for sure.

"The Vice-Chancellor and his wife are young. They have time to have another son," Midas said, his voice sounding distant to Chandler's ears.

"For the spell to work, the brother has to have already come into his magic," Chloe said. "Even with the help of fertility and gender spells, at best it would take another eight or nine years for a baby to be old enough."

Em spoke up. "Aidan doesn't have that long. Gar says they're keeping him under one of those magic bubble things: a life-support pall. But his body is weakening. It's past the time when they should have let his spirit move on."

"Damn it," Devlin said.

Chandler couldn't breathe. She couldn't move. Tears welled in her eyes. If she said nothing, no one would ever know—other than Gar, and Athena's spirit. Even if people noted that Evan and Peregrine had the same rare gift, the whole idea of her and Evan as lovers would most likely strike them as absurd.

But if she said nothing, a child would never walk in the sunshine, never feel grass beneath his feet, laugh and find his magic. If she said nothing, Chloe would never have the chance to right her wrong. If she shared her deepest secret, Chloe could move on with her life. Even if no one outside the Northern Circle ever discovered how Aidan recovered—which would be the best-case scenario—his recovery would allow Evan and his wife to move on as well, and hopefully redirect their anger away from Chloe and the coven.

Chandler clenched her teeth. She couldn't endanger Peregrine by having him involved. Her boy. Her heart and soul. What if they were discovered in the middle of the healing? There would be no way that Evan wouldn't become suspicious and figure out that Peregrine was his child. He could take Peregrine away from her. He had the power and money to do it. Even if Evan demanded only visitation rights, he might cozy up to Peregrine for a while, then change his mind and walk away. She didn't want Peregrine to go through that, the loneliness and heartbreak of having a parent withdraw their love and turn their back. *No,* she wouldn't let that happen.

A voice reached up from deep within her memories. Her adoptive mom's voice, from years ago, the terrifying morning when she was getting ready to walk into Greylock Academy for the first time. *"Honor yourself and those around you by doing what's right, even when it isn't easy. That is love, Chandler. That is friendship. That is true power."*

"Chandler, you're being awfully quiet." Devlin's voice broke through her thoughts. "Something on your mind?"

Sweat gathered between her shoulder blades, chilling her as it slid downward, slicking her spine. Terrifying or not, it was time for her secret to die, so a child could live.

Chandler got up from her stool and looked each of them in the eyes, one at a time. "I owe all of you an enormous apology. Sometimes secrets become so ingrained that telling the truth feels impossible. Lies become easier."

Concern filled Chloe's eyes. "What is it?"

She swallowed hard. "Aidan does have a brother. Peregrine."

Devlin gawked at her in disbelief. Through her pregnancy and for the last eight years, Devlin had never once questioned who Peregrine's father was. But no doubt he'd wondered. "I should have guessed. Evan. The sight."

"For the love of Hecate." Chloe shook her head.

Em gasped. "No way."

"I'm with you there," Midas said. "How did you and the Vice-Chancellor ever hook up?"

Brooklyn laughed. "I can't believe it. Evan Lewis is such a fucking snob."

"We went to Greylock at the same time. A bunch of alumni got together for Beltane. I was a stand-in for the May Queen."

Brooklyn snorted. "Don't tell me. He was the Greenwood Lord, of course."

"Does he know?" Em asked, clearly meaning the Vice-Chancellor, not Peregrine.

"No." Chandler's breath came easier now, the weight beginning to lift from her chest as they asked questions and she revealed the story of her and Evan's night together. How she tried to tell him. How he'd told her to go away and breezed into a sudden marriage. How she told Athena the truth and chose to raise Peregrine as a single mom. She paused, glancing toward where Peregrine slept. Her sleepy little monkey. Her sweetheart.

"So, where do we go from here?" Devlin asked the question she was certain everyone had on their minds.

She pressed a hand over her chest, gathering strength from her dragon's warmth. "I'm not sure. I want to help Aidan, truly I do—but I can't put Peregrine at risk."

"I don't want to see Peregrine hurt either," Chloe said. "But this is his brother we're talking about."

Chandler met Chloe's gaze. She hardened her voice. "Tell me you'd risk your own child."

Chloe's face went red. She closed her eyes. "I want to say *yes*. But... Dear Goddess, I don't know."

"I'm sure of one thing," Midas said. "I'd be pissed if some woman had my child and didn't tell me. Pissed as hell."

Heat flared up Chandler's arms. "I tried to tell him. I was young. I was scared… I didn't want Evan to reject Peregrine. A child's better off with one loving parent than going through something like that."

Tension sang in the air. Everyone fell silent.

Then the pad of small footsteps came from the other side of the room divider.

"Mama?" Peregrine walked into the room, and to her horror she realized he hadn't been asleep the whole time. "Mama, I have a brother?"

She looked down at his upturned face, now only a few feet away from her. Innocent, sweet eyes. "Oh, Peregrine. I—I."

"I wondered if I had a brother or sister. Lots of fathers have other families. I hoped… We have to help my brother, Mommy."

She crouched down to his height, eyes dampening as she looked into his. "It's too dangerous. You could get hurt. I can't risk it."

"His name is Aidan?"

"Yes. Aidan." Tears flooded from her eyes. *Aidan.* It was so much easier when she didn't say his name aloud. Just like when she didn't use or even think his father's name. *Evan Lewis.* The May King. The Greenwood Lord. The Vice-Chancellor of the High Council. Special Envoy to the Good Courts. The father of two little boys—one wasting away and another burning with faery sight just like his dad.

"I'm not afraid," Peregrine said. "I wanna help my brother. I'd like to have a witch-boy for a friend."

Chapter 17

Pregnant; the word was magic to my ears.
My wife was pregnant with a boy,
a witch-child to carry on my name and blood.
A man can have no greater joy.
—Evan Aidan Lewis

The serenity of the moonlit garden eased the tension from Chandler's body as she wandered toward the teahouse, ostensibly to check on Lionel. That was her reason to a degree, but mostly she needed time away from the coven to put herself back together.

Careful to not make a sound, she slid the teahouse door open and tiptoed inside. Lionel slept on his side, head bowed and knees slightly bent. She set the bottle of juice and wrapped snacks she'd brought on the floor next to him. Satisfied that he was asleep and not faking it like Peregrine had done, she sat down cross-legged with her back to him, so she could look out at the view of the gardens and meditate on what had happened.

She smiled, wondering if the black dog was looking back at her. She hadn't heard anything or seen the glow of eyes on her walk from the house. But then again, most likely she wouldn't have.

Chandler took a deep breath, holding it, before releasing it slowly. Down in the gardens, the moonlight shimmered on the stream and the tips of the cattails that clumped along its edge, sparkling like the bark they'd released for the full moon ritual.

Whichever God or Goddess—or perhaps the Great Fire Salamander himself—who'd been listening that night hadn't wasted time in calling her out about the word she hadn't shared or truly released. *Guilt*. Guilt over not telling her coven family about Evan Lewis. A secret she'd justified keeping even when her soul and heart knew the choice was wrong. Now, she had finally let go of it. That was both freeing and imprisoning.

She closed her eyes. Blocking out the view, she brought to mind the sound of Peregrine's voice and the words he'd said on their way to perform the full moon ritual. He'd turned around in the pathway, walking backward with a sly grin on his face. *"I wouldn't mind being homeschooled if it was with some other witch-kids. Like boys my age that are getting their powers. We'd have fun doin' stuff. It would be like going to the Council's summer camp. They have one, right?"*

He'd said a very similar thing in the lounge, when she'd expected him to lash out in anger over her withholding his father's identity. If the tables had been turned, she wasn't sure she'd have reacted as selflessly.

"Is that you, Chandler?" Lionel's voice murmured. It was heavy from sleep, but distinctly more intelligible than when she'd left to go into the house. He wormed out from under the blanket and scooted over to sit beside her. "I thought you'd be home in bed by now."

His hair was as crazy as ever, pressed flat on one side of his head and poufy on the other. At some point, he must have gotten up long enough to take off his jeans. Now all he wore was a T-shirt and long-underwear bottoms with a small orange design on them.

She blinked and gave the underwear bottoms another look. She bit back a smile. "Are those carrots?"

He grinned proudly. "They certainly are. My mom gave them to me for Easter. That is, my adoptive mom. But you know what I mean."

"She's Christian?" Chandler asked. She immediately felt embarrassed. It was an oddly personal question to start a conversation with. Still, she really didn't have any idea what path Lionel or his family followed. All she knew was that he wasn't a heritage witch. And that the woman who had adopted him had prayed and left offerings to the Lady of the Lake, Nimue.

"More like my mom loves holidays. Easter. May Day. Memorial Day. Fourth of July. Halloween. Thanksgiving, she's big on food holidays. December is a month-long celebration—Christmas, Hanukkah, National Cookie Day, Festivus. Gazpacho Day."

"So, lots of food and gifts?"

"Exactly."

Chandler lowered her gaze, studying his long hands and fingers as she worked her way past her apprehension. He wasn't a witch, but he came from a background that was more like hers, in some ways, than any of the coven members'. She steadied her voice. "Now that you've had time to think, how do you feel about your mom keeping secrets from you? About her praying to Nimue and you appearing?"

He moved closer to her and draped a comforting arm over her shoulder. His voice hushed. "Why don't you tell me what's really bothering you?"

She sighed. "Peregrine just found out who his father is, everyone did. Evan Lewis. The Vice-Chancellor of the High Council..." She told him the entire situation, including about Aiden and the healing spell's requirement. "Peregrine didn't react the way I expected. He wasn't upset with me."

Lionel massaged her shoulders, slow, supportive strokes. "You think you deserve his anger?"

"It wasn't fair to keep Peregrine's father from him. I kept telling myself it was my choice to raise him on my own—and it was." Despair overwhelmed her. She slumped forward, covering her face with her hands. "I could have tried harder to tell Evan. I should have."

Lionel bent forward, his voice gentle. "First, you need to stop punishing yourself. The past isn't the issue right now. The question is, are you going to let Peregrine help his brother? What is your heart saying, is it the right thing to do?"

Yes, it was. In her heart and soul, she was certain of that. "But if anything happened to Peregrine, I wouldn't be able to forgive myself."

"Then we'll make sure nothing does." Lionel took his arm off her shoulder and straightened, sitting up taller. "You asked how I felt about my mom keeping secrets from me. I'm not angry. But I can't get the other kids out of my mind—the children I was raised with in the fae realm—the dancing children—and the changeling my biological mother raised." He paused for a moment, quietness settling before he went on. "My adoptive mom loved me. Right or wrong, she would never have hurt me. But those other children—the children tangled up with the fae like I was—I want to know them, help them if I can."

Chandler took her hands from her face, fisting them until her blunt fingernails pressed into her palms. Who was she to think Lionel and Peregrine's lack of anger at their mothers was wrong? Who was she to think they should want to punish the offenders, when what they wanted was to help the other victims of the lies? What was wrong with her? *You're a mother,* a voice deep inside her heart answered.

"There's no guarantee the spell will heal Aidan," she argued weakly. "Plus, we're hoping no one outside the coven will ever know what we've done, including Evan and his wife. That means Peregrine won't suddenly have a new brother and best friend."

"Those are things you do need to tell Peregrine." Lionel touched her chin, turning her face toward him. "You did an amazing job raising Peregrine. He's smart. He's happy. He's not going to suddenly choose his father over you."

She nodded, admitting to him that was one of her fears, and more importantly, to herself.

His voice hushed even more. "But what about you?"

She sat back, confused. "What do you mean? About me?"

"Are you ready to move into a new future? To let Peregrine make some of the difficult choices himself, and to maybe quit trying so hard to not let anyone else into your heart?"

"Ah—" She blinked at him. And, in the back of her mind the Great Salamander's words from the night of the vision whispered: *"Listen to the quiver of your heart and the shiver of your soul..."*

He shifted closer. His hands cupped her face. "You, me—this will be gone in a couple of days, even the memory of it. But you're a special woman. Don't close yourself off from me."

His lips brushed hers, warm and as tender as they had been a few hours ago. She skated her fingertips down his arms, long and lanky, roped with muscle. The kiss deepened, lips opening. He didn't taste like breath mints, mouthwash, or the last thing he'd drank. He didn't taste like anything other than himself. A normal man. No pretenses. No secrets or lies.

Heat flushed her skin, enlivening every inch of her. He kissed the pulse point behind her ear, and her nipples and stomach grew taut, aching for more. She wanted him. Wanted him with every ounce of her shivering being.

His lips moved lower, nibbling her neck.

She slid her hands under his T-shirt, exploring his body as his lips returned to hers. She caressed where the triskelion lay against his skin, then followed the runway of curly hair down his chest to his belly. He groaned as her fingers swept his hip bones and started toward his stiffening erection.

Lionel stopped her hand with his. "I wasn't expecting this. Um—I haven't been involved with anyone for a while, but I did get tested recently. HIV... the whole nine yards. I want you to feel safe."

She touched his lip with her finger, silencing him. "Thank you. Same here: clean bill of health."

"Condoms?" He kissed her finger.

She grimaced. "Not on me."

His hand teased her wrap pants, feather-stroking along the fabric that hugged her inner thigh. She quivered as his fingertips massaged the sweet spot between her legs. "If you want, we could work around that."

She wriggled upward against his chest, bringing her mouth back to his. "I'll take that as a yes?" he murmured.

She shifted aside. "Yes, if I can use my magic on you. Safe sex, witch style." As a rule, she hid her magic from normal men, even when she hungered to let go.

"Please," he moaned. His cock pressed hard against her thigh, more than a little ready. "Chandler, I can't believe any spell will ever make me forget you."

She ignored that and stroked her hand down his underwear bottoms. "Maybe we could lose the carrots?"

He wriggled free from them. "Better?"

"Much." She cupped her hands over his butt, tight and perfect. Little dimples on each cheek.

"Fair is fair." He undid the ties on her pants and helped her out of them. His hands went to her shirt. "This needs to go."

He slid her shirt off over her head. She did the same to his. In a second her panties and bra lay on top of the other clothing. Goose bumps rushed across her skin. She took his hand and pulled him laughing and giggling back to his makeshift bed and under the blanket.

She cuddled against him, her toes stroking his shins as they kissed, long and leisurely. Slowly, she drew up her magic. Then she strummed her fingers up his rib cage, releasing a soft wave of energy across his skin.

He sighed. "Dear God, that's... beyond wonderful."

She increased the level of magic, circling his pecs with her fingers until the energy whirled, blue and bright against his dark skin. He collapsed onto his back, eyes closing. A moan escaped his lips. She brought her magic up again, this time into her breath as she kissed the same trail her fingers had just traveled.

He rolled over on top of her, caging her body with his. One hand moved down, fingers working their own brand of magic between her legs, arousing and weakening her until she gasped. His mouth found hers, taking in the hot magic of her breath.

Withdrawing quickly from her mouth, he slid down her body. Before she realized what he was doing, she felt the moist warmth of his breath between her legs—and the rush of her own magic, surging across her vulva. Spasms of pleasure rippled, thrusting her unimaginably fast toward a peak, closer and higher... but not quite there, not quite. This was something she'd always wanted to try with her non-witch lovers, letting them use her magic as a tool of pleasure, but she'd never dared reveal her powers.

Still, Lionel—crazy, awkward, beautiful Lionel—had thought to do it without prompting.

"What I wouldn't give for a condom," he murmured.

She laughed and pulled him back up to her mouth. He took another mouthful of her magic-infused breath. But instead of traveling downward to use it on her body, he exhaled onto his fingers, coating them with ripples of energy. Dear Goddess, just the thought of what he had in mind sent the pulse between her legs spiraling. His thumb massaged her clit. His fingers moved in unison. And she came, unabashedly and more powerfully than she ever had. Still lost in the sensation, she drew her magic into her tattoo sleeves, then released it into her fingers and pleasured him, long and torturously slow until he came in waves equal to her own.

Exhausted, she curled up with her head on his chest.

He stroked his hands down her arms. "You're so beautiful."

Beautiful. She smiled, the word settling warm and comfortable inside her like a kitten curling up in front of a fire. He wasn't saying that to flatter her or because it was expected. He meant it, she knew that down to the very depths of her soul. She closed her eyes, too tired to say anything or to even think as sleep overcame her. A profoundly deep sleep, that led into a dream.

They rise, the dragons from her vision.

One is red. The other gleams white against the backdrop of the fiery dawn.

She pushes Peregrine behind her, hiding him as she backs toward the forest. They'll be safe there. It was where he was conceived. A special place.

She reaches the edge of the forest, but a wall of magic bars their retreat. The trees murmur, "No going back, no going back."

Overhead, lightning explodes. The dragons entangle, fangs sinking into flesh as they battle. Scales fall like rain. Wings rip. Screams echo.

She finds Peregrine's hand and runs for the shelter of a rowan tree that stands alone out in the open. Not a berry or leaf hangs on its branches. But there is no other refuge.

Peregrine trembles as they crouch. He holds her hand so tight that the ring she wears on her middle finger bites into her flesh. It isn't one of her moonstone rings. It's not any ring she's worn before. But she knows it without looking. It's the ring Athena wore. The Northern Circle's signet ring, stolen by Rhianna. It's on her finger. . . and they're no longer alone under the rowan tree. All the Circle members are there with them. Everyone ducked down, hands over their heads. Lionel and Gar are there too.

Light flashes as the white dragon pivots and soars. The rising sun catches on its scales and the expanse of its wings, stripping away all illusion. It's not white. It's black, the darkest shade of black, deeper than coal and more lustrous than silver—as dark as a demon's eyes. She knows now: these are not the famous red and white dragons from Merlin's prophesies, this is not a reference to that ancient battle. This is now. This is here. This is today.

She touches her chest, the spot where the red dragon ripped free. The red dragon is hers—as glistening and crimson as a redcap's hat. But whose is the black?

"Look." *Peregrine points at the plain below the rowan tree. The embers from the May Day bonfire still glow. There are still tables with bottles of wine and bowls empty of condoms, hawthorn wreaths and stemmed goblets. Beneath the tables, witches sleep on the ground. She knows some of them from the Council and Greylock Academy. But there are many others, sleeping, while overhead the dragons battle.*

Battle over what? she wonders.

"Over them." *The Great Fire Salamander nods toward the sleeping witches, oblivious to the raging battle.*

Chapter 18

It is with deepest sorrow that I inform you
of the passing of our beloved Athena Eliza Marsh.
A celebration of her life will be held at our home
October 31ˢᵗ at 11:00 a.m.
In lieu of flowers, please donate to your favorite local charity.
—Celebration of life invitation
from Devlin Marsh

Chandler set her welding torch aside and brought up her magic, using it to draw a focused line of heat along the harp string. The string's metal glowed red, then edged toward salmon, yellow...

"Veni ad me." She called pliers from the workbench to her hand. She used them to bend the glowing wire, then applied more heat. Her hands and magic worked in practiced unison, twisting, shaping, heating. The harp strings became veins and arteries, branching and gripping the heart like roots, like a source of life. More sparks. More heat.

She let her magic relax, then sat quietly, cradling the heart in protective gloves of energy while the metal cooled. It had come out exactly the way she'd visualized. A heart, with streaks of bright silver and other parts dulled and worn.

Once the heart had cooled enough, she placed it in a wooden box on her workbench for safekeeping. Between last night with Lionel and waking up early to work on the heart, her magic was ebbing. She needed to give it a rest, so it could rebuild before tomorrow when they'd go to headquarters for the gala reception and Aidan's healing. Not to mention that they'd most likely perform the forgetting spell on Lionel the following day.

As her thoughts went back to Aidan's healing, a fresh knot of worry tightened in her chest. But her conviction that doing it was right didn't waver. She also felt good about the lie she'd used to cover Peregrine's absence from school. When it came to chickenpox, they didn't even ask for a doctor's note. That had bought her a week to come up with a permanent solution. She wasn't about to go along with Peregrine's suggestion that she pay the black dog to protect him at school.

Chandler took off her safety glasses and work apron and headed inside for a cup of tea. But as she held the kettle under the faucet, she caught a glimpse of someone through the kitchen window. A tall man striding across the parking lot. Not Lionel, for sure. He'd planned on spending the day in his room resting. Besides, this person was arriving, not leaving.

Setting the kettle down, she took a closer look. It was Gar, hurrying toward the main house with his cap riding low over his eyes. What was he doing here? He hadn't said anything about returning from Council headquarters today.

Her phone pinged. She wiped her hands on a dishtowel, then checked. A text from Devlin.

Can you come to the office? ASAP.

First Gar, now this? Something was wrong. She shot off a text to Peregrine. It was the first place he'd check when he woke up and found her not home.

Cereal and juice for breakfast. I'm at the main house. XOX, Mom.

She headed for the front door, pulling on her sweater jacket as she dashed outside and hurried for the main house. Gar had to have left Connecticut way before dawn to get here this early.

When she reached the front hallway of the house, she ran into Em. She was sprinting up from downstairs. Her hair whipped out behind her, caught in a single braid. Steely determination shone in her eyes. It was astonishing how Em had transformed from timid and withdrawn when she'd joined the coven less than a month ago, into a strong-minded, powerful woman.

"What's going on?" Chandler asked. "I just saw Gar."

"I don't know. Devlin just texted me and asked if I'd come to the office. Chloe and Midas have classes, so they aren't here. Brooklyn's still asleep, I think."

Chandler swept along with Em, rushing toward the office. All things considered, it was doubly odd that Em hadn't known Gar was coming.

When they got to the office doorway Chandler hesitated, surprised to see a pot of coffee steaming on the desk next to a large box of bakery donuts. Devlin might have used the office coffeemaker, but the donuts hinted that he'd had more forewarning about the meeting than her or Em. Devlin waved them forward. "What took you so long?"

"You texted what—three minutes ago?" Chandler said.

Gar shot an embarrassed smile at Em, as if he were apologizing for not telling her he was coming, then he looked at Chandler. "It seemed wiser to discuss updates to our plans for tomorrow in person." He drew a small, purse-size pouch from his pocket and set it on the desk.

"Coffee?" Devlin asked her and Em.

"Sure," Chandler said tentatively. She took the mug from him, ignoring her usual spoonful of sugar. As he started to fix a mug for Em, she eyed the pouch. It was black velvet with a gold drawstring.

Out of the corner of her eye, she spotted someone sitting in the shadows at the far end of the desk. Lionel. This was getting odder by the second.

She smiled at him. He smiled back. But it wasn't his usual broad grin. It was more of a quick twitch of his lips. Nervous? Guilt? Oddly enough, her mama-dragon instincts told her it was more likely the latter. Like the sheepish look Peregrine put on when he did something wrong.

Her gaze whipped back to Gar. He was standing military straight with his hands clasped behind his back and his stance wide. She'd seen that pose before. He'd assumed it when he questioned her in this very room, back when he'd first come to investigate the coven. As a matter of fact, he'd ordered her to sit in the same stiff-backed chair where Lionel was now sitting.

She thumped her mug down on the desk and narrowed her eyes on Gar. "You're not about to interrogate Lionel, are you?"

"Actually, I am." Gar pinned Lionel with a glare. "Give me one solid reason you should be allowed inside Council headquarters."

"Because Zeus is going to perform an experimental PTSD forgetting spell on me in two days. I won't remember any of this," Lionel said firmly.

"You'll still be a journalist after the spell," Gar countered. "What guarantee could you give that your curiosity about magic and witches wouldn't get the best of you in the future?"

"Because I've agreed that the penalty for any future attempt on my part to expose the witching world would result in the Council calling for my assassination. Because I don't want to be killed."

Fear prickled across Chandler's scalp. "I don't know what's going on here, but I don't like the sounds of it."

Gar looked at her, his stance relaxing. "Currently, we're rehearsing the answers Lionel should give if anyone questions his presence at the gala."

"What?" she said, shocked. "Lionel's going? When did we decide that?" Anger bubbled up from deep inside her. This was ludicrous. Not safe for Lionel or them. "We never discussed this as a group."

"I never heard about it either," Em said.

Devlin cleared his throat. "Nothing's set in stone. The three of us were just talking. Testing the waters, so to speak."

Lionel got to his feet. "It was my idea."

Chandler gawked at him. "Why? Even if you could get into headquarters, it doesn't make sense."

"You need someone to watch over Peregrine. Someone who won't be off stealing summoner's bowls or entering trancelike states, like the rest of you will be doing during the healing."

"That's a good point," Em said quietly. "I have to bring Merlin's Book. An extra set of eyes on it would be a relief to me, especially if those eyes can see through fae glamour."

"Exactly," Gar said.

Lionel walked over to Chandler. He gave her shoulder a friendly squeeze. His tone lightened. "Frankly, I feel better than I have in ages. I have today and most of tomorrow to rest." He leaned close. "I could go as your date."

She pushed him away and scowled. "What about the assassination part? Don't think I didn't hear that."

"Gar's going to talk to the High Chancellor for me. He thinks if I formally agree to Zeus's forgetting spell and acknowledge I understand the cost of revealing the witching world's existence in the future, then there will be no reason to not let me attend."

"Why would you ever agree to something like that? Even once you've undergone the forgetting spell, you'll still hunger to be near magic. You'll have the sight. You'll still be a journalist. But you won't remember agreeing to accept death as a punishment for uncovering the very thing you'll be driven to search for."

Devlin interrupted. "That's where the good news comes in. First, Lionel having the sight doesn't matter. No one knows he has it, not the Council or anyone outside of us few—and no one ever needs to know."

Chandler's face went hot. "Where's the good news in that?"

Devlin raised his hand to silence her. "Let me finish. So—hypothetically— what if Lionel made that promise, but Zeus only pretended to do the forgetting spell on him?"

"Zeus would do that?" Chandler's anger ebbed. That possibility hadn't occurred to her.

Devlin nodded. "Lionel would still have to sever all ties with the Circle. But he'd know about the agreement and his need to stay quiet. I can tell Zeus that Lionel's last wish, before he has to leave the witching world behind forever, is to go to the gala and spend the night surrounded by magic. That way we won't have to tell Zeus about Aiden's healing."

Lionel looked at Chandler, his expression as taut and unwavering as darkened bronze. "What you have to understand is that I've been listening to you and everyone talk about Aidan Lewis. You all want to help him, and so do I. If you prevent me from going and something happens to you or Peregrine or any one of you, that would be worse for me than having the faeries carve out my eyes or any death a Council assassin could dream up. A lot worse than having to spend the rest of my life hungering for magic and pretending not to see."

A sick feeling invaded the pit of her stomach. Her mama-dragon instincts said that having Lionel come was smart. But her heart didn't like anything about this, especially the promise that would endanger Lionel for the rest of his life.

Chapter 19

He gave me a hoodie, soft and gray.
He sat beside me. He stood beside me.
Kindness in action. Not just in words.
—"Johnny" by E. A.

Chandler retrieved her mug from the desk and added a spoonful of sugar to the coffee. Then she retreated to where Lionel had moved to stand behind the stiff-backed chair. She had to admit the idea of him going was feeling wiser with each passing second.

Apparently, Devlin hadn't approached Zeus yet about falsifying the forgetting spell, but he was certain Zeus could be talked into it. He also reiterated that he wasn't going to tell Zeus about healing Aidan. It was safer for them and Zeus that way.

"If we're all in agreement," Gar said, "I'll approach the High Chancellor about Lionel attending as Chandler's date and about the death-by-assassination pledge. I don't foresee any problems. In the past, the High Chancellor has invited people to events for no other reason than to irritate his opponents. The death-by-assassination agreement will appeal to his warped sense of humor."

"Do I need to sign something?" Lionel asked.

"No. I can swear that you've been officially warned about the penalty. What you also want to remember is that the High Chancellor has a vested interest in Zeus's experimental PTSD treatments. He'll jump at the chance to test it on a human."

Devlin smiled. "Zeus will agree for similar reasons: success with the spell, fraudulent or not, will bring in more investors and lead to a higher chance of the spell's success in the end."

Chandler nodded. What Devlin and Gar were saying fit with what she'd heard over the years about the wealth and power of Zeus, the High Chancellor, and a handful of other witches being rooted in the spell-development industry—not to mention their mutual involvement in a fraternal skull cult.

Gar's gaze went to Devlin. "Speaking of your grandfather Zeus, are your parents going to be at the gala too? Once we get the timing down for the healing, there won't be any leeway for unexpected interruptions."

"My mom won't be there. My father? Open bar. Single women. A chance to draw attention to himself by being associated with the guests of honor—namely us? Yeah, he could be a problem," Devlin said.

Devlin wasn't exaggerating when he said his dad could be a problem. His parents had been divorced before Chandler met Athena at school. Still, she'd heard enough about Devlin's father and his sugar-daddy girlfriends to know to steer clear of him, and that was without counting his affairs with Rhianna. His dumping Rhianna was a large part of why she had set out to destroy the Circle.

Chandler took a sip of her coffee. Despite the added worry of Devlin's father, she was feeling more comfortable about the changes to their plans. She could see the future: Aidan leaving his hospital bed. Zeus faking the forgetting spell. The sadness she'd feel when Lionel left. And the comfort of knowing he was safe in Boston, building sandcastles and writing about poverty and hunger.

"So, what's in the pouch?" Em's voice brought Chandler from her thoughts.

Gar strode to the desk and picked it up. "It happens to be the excuse I used for driving up here. It's something the High Chancellor felt rightly belonged to the Northern Circle, or more precisely"—he turned toward Chandler and held it out—"to you."

"Me?" Totally mystified, Chandler set her coffee down, walked over and cautiously took the pouch from him. What could the High Chancellor possibly have that belonged to her?

She clutched the bag and used her magic to sense what lay inside. Gold. A crystal. Amethyst. It felt powerful and oddly familiar. Merlin's staff crystal? *No.* That stone was far too large to be held in such a small bag. Besides, it was currently in the coven vault, attached to Merlin's Book of Shadow and Light.

The Northern Circle's signet ring, maybe? The high priest ring sat on Devlin's right hand. But the high priestess ring had been stolen by Rhianna. Last Chandler had heard, Rhianna had been wearing it when Dux's demonic wraiths invaded Council headquarters and killed her, a gruesome attack that at first was blamed on the Circle. In reality, Rhianna's murder had most likely been orchestrated by Magus Dux with the help of Evan's wife.

Chandler opened the bag and took out the cotton-wrapped contents. She pulled the covering aside. The light from the chandelier caught on the outline of a gold ring and sparked against the facets of an amethyst carved with an N surrounded by an etched circle. The high priestess signet ring, no question about it.

Chandler gaped at Gar. "Who—when did they find it?"

"One of the Council guards spotted it in Dux's lair when they were packing up the mountain of books. He turned it over to Ignatius. The assumption is that one of the wraiths involved in Rhianna's murder must have given it to Dux. The Council still has Dux in an interrogation cell at headquarters. We'll know for sure once they get the truth out of him."

Em leaned in, looking closely at the ring. "It's lucky someone like Heath Goddard didn't find it. He'd have pocketed it." Em had no love for Heath. He was one of the High Council's potion masters. But Em had discovered the hard way that Heath was also as powerful a psychic as she was, and a vicious person who took delight in invading others' mental privacy.

"It would have been just as bad if Morrell found it," Gar said flatly.

This surprised Chandler. Chancellor Morrell was generally well liked and politically very powerful. Sure, she didn't know him personally, but she'd gone to school with his son Salix. He'd seemed nice enough.

Em nudged Chandler's hand. "Put the ring on. I bet it'll fit you."

It had last been sized for Athena. But she and Athena had similarly large hands, despite Athena's smaller stature.

The ring slid onto her middle finger. As she tugged it to make sure it wouldn't come off easily, the dream she'd had last night rushed back to her. The dragons fighting. The ring biting into her skin. The coven and the sleeping witches. She felt herself pale.

"Are you okay?" Lionel asked.

"Last night, after—" She held his eyes for a second and then started again to avoid sharing their personal business. "I had a dream. In it, I was wearing this ring. The dream was intense, more of a nightmare—and related to a vision I had earlier this week after walking my labyrinth."

"Are you talking prophetic?" Devlin asked.

"I don't know. Not literally, at least."

Gar's voice hardened. "You are intuitive, right?

"Yes, but—"

Gar interrupted. "Devlin told me about the retrocognition everyone experienced. That could have left your intuition more open than usual."

"Except I had the vision before the retrocognition."

Gar clasped his hands behind his back. "Tell us what happened in both of them, blow for blow."

"Not that much, really." She gave an overview of the vision from the labyrinth, minus the sexy parts and the Great Fire Salamander's final words. Then she recounted what happened in the dream. When she was done, she confessed what bothered her the most. "I'm scared about what us standing apart from everyone else could mean for the coven and Peregrine."

"That's understandable," Em said softly.

Chandler hesitated, touching the signet ring as a forgotten detail from the dream came back to her. Not what had happened. It was a distinctive comparison that lingered in her mind. She gasped. "In the dream—the dragons: The black one was *'as dark as a demon's eyes'* and the red one was *'as glistening and crimson as a redcap's hat.'* The dragons symbolized the demons and fae, fighting for dominion over the witches. I'm certain of it now."

Gar looked at her steadily. "That makes total sense. It also mirrors why I used the excuse of the ring to come here instead of formulating our final plans on the phone." His voice deepened. "There has always been infighting at the Council. But the spying and duplicity is getting worse. Clearly, the demons have gained a foothold. It's at the root of our reason for doing the spell on Aidan ourselves, right?"

"That's true," Chandler said. "But why would the red fae dragon come from me? And, why would we side with the faeries? They are a danger to Peregrine."

She stopped talking as Brooklyn whisked into the room, bringing with her the scent of musty earth. Her purple cardigan and long black skirt looked as wrinkled as if she'd pulled them from the dirty laundry basket. She yawned and headed for the coffeepot. "Hey, all. Sorry I'm late."

"Late night?" Gar asked.

"You can say that again." She snagged a mug and started pouring. "So, have you figured out how to get into the infirmary yet?"

"We hadn't gotten that far," Chandler said. She gave Brooklyn a rundown about the dream and the vision, and everything else they'd discussed. Despite the fact that Brooklyn was acting nonchalant, she suspected there were more serious thoughts going on inside her head.

When Chandler was done, Brooklyn gripped her coffee cup in both hands and inhaled deeply. "I agree about the meaning of the dream, and I like the idea of Lionel going with you. But that only makes me more curious about how you plan on getting into the infirmary."

Gar nodded. "We really need to get those details hammered out while I'm here."

"All right then." Devlin's voice took on a more businesslike tone. "Here's what we've got so far. Midas doesn't think we should rely on picking locks with magic this time. He plans on deactivating select security wards, and some of the non-magical alarm systems and surveillance, just enough of them to safely take and return the summoner's bowl undetected. He recommended shutting down everything nonessential on the seventh floor where the palliative infirmary is, as well. We're also going to have to incapacitate the infirmary staff before they discover what we're up to."

Gar rubbed his hands gleefully, like this was the sort of planning he relished. "I've checked the staff schedules. Most of the Council guards will be stationed around the reception halls and main elevators. There will be three staff members on duty in the infirmary: one guard and two nurses."

The level of enthusiasm in his voice worried Chandler. "I'm assuming we're talking about a nonlethal way to deal with the staff?"

"Actually," Em said, louder than usual, glancing at Brooklyn, "the two of us and Chloe came up with an idea for that."

Brooklyn bit down on her bottom lip, looking sheepish. But eagerness gleamed in her eyes. "Chloe mentioned the powder that we—I—used to disorient her for the initiation at the quarry."

Chandler scowled. She'd known that Chloe had been forced to jump into a quarry as part of her coven initiation, but she had no idea Chloe had been drugged at the time. Once everything with Aidan was over, she'd have to sit down as high priestess and have a long talk with Brooklyn. Whether Brooklyn felt remorse over her prolonged relationship with Rhianna or not, it was important for the coven to know exactly what questionable magic she'd learned during that time.

As if she'd read Chandler's thoughts, Brooklyn grimaced apologetically. Then she went on, "We used a powder on Chloe that contained *Calvatia* spores. I was awake most of last night experimenting with ways to make it more powerful. What I ended up with can knock out several dozen people, like mass-induced twilight sleep. It only takes a handful. But it needs to be dispersed into the air and won't work unless it's in a contained space."

Gar grinned. "Like the infirmary's staff breakroom?"

"That would be perfect," Brooklyn said.

Gar rubbed his chin, thinking. "A food cart is scheduled to go up to the infirmary with a special dinner for the staff, on account of the gala. I'm betting the guard and the nurses will all be in the breakroom soon after that."

Chandler folded her arms across her chest and paced back to stand next to Lionel. There had to be a simple way to make this all come together. They were close. Very close.

"The powder is superfine," Brooklyn said. "Maybe Midas could inject it into the infirmary's air system?"

Devlin shook his head. "Midas has more than enough to do already. We need a simple dispersal method. Something foolproof enough that anyone could do it."

Chandler felt Lionel's touch on the small of her back. He leaned close and whispered, "Something old-school? Something Peregrine might think of and that Midas already invented?"

"You're thinking the camera-grenade launcher?" she asked quietly.

"Not the whole thing. Just the grenade part. Powder inside a balloon."

Gar's voice broke through their whispers. "Do you mind sharing with the rest of us?"

Chandler licked her lips, the plan forming as she spoke. "I visited the infirmary a few years ago. My mom passed away there. If I remember right, the main doors are automatic, glass sliding doors."

"They still are," Gar said.

"We could fill a small balloon with Brooklyn's twilight sleep powder. We'd just have to walk up to the doors, toss the balloon in and burst it before the doors shut. Then leave and come back once the staff were unconscious." She realized a flaw in her plan. "That doesn't confine it to the breakroom, does it?"

"Tossing it through the main doors wouldn't." Gar waggled his eyebrows. "But the staff entrance goes directly into the breakroom."

"A focused jolt of energy could be used to pop the balloon from a safe distance," Chandler suggested.

As everyone began to discuss the viability of using a balloon, the staff entrance, and an adjacent private employee stairwell, Lionel discreetly massaged the small of Chandler's back, a slow circular press of his fingers that made her body shiver with delight.

"We could use a condom for the grenade instead of a party balloon," Brooklyn suggested. "A condom in someone's purse would get past any security check. The spores look like face powder. Someone could stash that in a compact. The grenade could be assembled in a bathroom stall, no problem."

Gar chuckled. "You sure you don't want to come?"

"No way. Besides, you need someone in reserve in case you guys get caught."

Chandler leaned into Lionel's touch, listening and enjoying the sensation of his closeness. There were still lots of details to figure out, enough to keep them busy for the rest of the day and far into the night. But the plan was coming together. They just might succeed, if everything went right and they worked as a team like her dream had indicated.

Excitement seeped into Chandler's bones as her thoughts once again went to the future, a different branch of it this time, to Peregrine and what might happen if they succeeded.

Weeks, months from now… maybe next summer during school vacation, Peregrine could go to the Council's summer camp and meet Aidan. Aidan wouldn't remember Peregrine. If all went well, they'd be gone from the palliative infirmary before he recovered enough to be fully aware of his surroundings. Peregrine would have to keep what happened a secret. But, maybe, Peregrine could have the future he'd imagined. Maybe he and his half brother could come into their powers together, play and become friends.

Chapter 20

The first time Chandler saw the serpent in the fire,
we were in the backyard roasting marshmallows.
I didn't tell her mother about it that night or the next.
It was our secret for that short, blissful time.
—Cade Parrish

After working until almost 1:00 a.m. to get everything ready for Aidan's clandestine healing, Chandler was surprised to receive a text from Em at seven the next morning.

Can I come over? I need to talk to you about something. Privately.

Sure, Chandler replied. She rubbed her arms, uneasy about the message. Not only had they all worked hard and late yesterday, but why was Em out of bed so early with Gar around? And *privately*? That wasn't like Em at all.

I'll be right over, Em replied.

Chandler herded Peregrine off ahead of schedule for his self-defense lesson with Devlin. Despite—in fact, because of—tonight's plans, Devlin had wanted to extend rather than skip the lesson.

Two minutes later, Em knocked at her door.

Chandler rushed to open it. "Come in. What did you do, leave Gar to fend for himself?"

"He left for headquarters an hour ago. It's hard to believe, the next time we see him will be at the reception." She glanced over her shoulder at the sand dragon, crumbling slightly thanks to time and the elements. "Lionel made that? It's really good." Her gaze went to the duct tape-wrapped camera-grenade launcher. "I'm glad I knew about that. But it's more likely to catch a UPS driver in the shins than cover an invisible hellhound in flour, don't you think?"

"I'm just glad it helped us come up with an idea for tonight." Chandler motioned Em inside. "What's on your mind?"

Em pressed her lips together for a moment. "I almost didn't say anything to you. I haven't mentioned it to anyone else, including Chloe or Gar."

Chandler wasn't sure she liked the sound of this. "Is this something personal?"

"Not exactly. When Chloe and I were going through Merlin's Book, I found a spell." She hushed her voice, like she was afraid someone might overhear. "The night of the club fire, when everything went down with Merlin's Shade, I got scared and took off for an AA meeting. But before I left, I overheard the spell the Shade used to bring your flying monkeys to life. Do you remember that part?"

Scenes from that night flashed into Chandler's mind: Her discovering the Shade had chained Peregrine in the cellar. Fighting against the Shade's hypnotic magic to free Peregrine, then whisking him off and meeting up with Laura so she could take him to the safety of the vineyard. Then Chandler'd returned and helped everyone else force the Shade back into his otherworldly prison. Plus her flying monkeys, harmless scrap metal sculptures transformed by the Shade's spell into animated, zombielike weapons.

Chandler scrubbed her hands over her face, overwhelmed by the memories. "I vaguely remember the Shade doing the spell. I was mostly focused on getting Peregrine to safety."

Em hooked her hair behind her ears, hesitating. Her voice tensed. "I found the spell in Merlin's Book."

"Are you sure?" She'd seen the animated monkeys with her own eyes, but still it was hard to believe.

"It's illustrated with drawings and notations from Merlin about how he used it to bring a suit of armor to life one Christmas."

Chandler shook her head. Bringing inanimate objects to life was against the laws of nature. Dangerous and then some. But despite that, the thought of giving life to metal sent a tingle of excitement across her skin. And, in the back of her mind, the Great Salamander whispered that she needed the spell, that she had to have it. If she were Lionel, she would have called what she felt a hunger.

Em pulled her shoulders back. "I don't believe in anyone holding sovereignty over another being's body or soul. I'm not sure I even like it in the case of inanimate objects." Her spine straightened further, her resolve plain to see. "But I'm also afraid there may come a time when my beliefs are less important than the safety of others."

"You're right to believe it's wrong," Chandler said quickly. She'd always felt self-determination was vital. In Em's case it was even more important, after the years of abuse she'd suffered at the hands of her aunt and mother. "Everything contains a soul, or at least a form of one, in the case of inanimate things. Metal contains bits and pieces of its former incarnations as well as the intentions of the people who worked it. Art especially isn't something to be warped and tampered with, like the Shade did when he animated my monkeys."

Em smiled. "That's what made me decide to give the spell to you. I trust you and your intentions." She held out a scrap of paper. "When the Shade was working it, he acted like it was too complex for anyone else to perform. It's actually surprisingly simple."

Chandler willed her hand to not shake as she took the paper and unfolded it. The spell consisted of an incantation, a few dozen words in Archaic Welsh by the looks of it. The illustrations clarified the rest. Merlin had used his crystal to magnify his magic and connect the spell to the earth.

"It's not true dark magic," Chandler said, as much to make herself feel better as to alleviate Em's guilt for sharing it.

"That's what I thought. It doesn't require an exchange of souls or anything like that. I was thinking you could use it to create a guardian for Peregrine, if you had to."

Chandler nodded, then refolded the spell. "Hopefully, it'll never come to that." She lightened her tone to break the tension. "You want to come inside? We could talk some more over a coffee?"

"Thanks, but I should get back to the house. I promised to have breakfast with Brooklyn."

Chandler watched as Em made her way down the walk and across the parking lot. Once Em was out of sight, she pulled on her sweater jacket and headed into her storage area, to where a microwave-size iron plate was set into a wall.

She tucked the spell into one of the sweater's pockets so she wouldn't lose track of it, then drew her magic up into her fingers and pressed them against the iron plate.

A hum reverberated as the plate dilated like the pupil of an eye, revealing her personal safe.

Chandler removed her Book of Shadows from the safe, carried it back to the warmth of her workshop, and opened it to the first blank page. Then she took a deep breath to center herself, closed her eyes, and visualized the animation spell she'd seen only moments ago on the paper: The shape of the words and illustrations. The lines. The darkness. The bright negative spaces. She supposed her uncanny ability to visualize and remember was a form of eidetic memory. She hadn't and wouldn't ever ask a professional about that. She preferred to think of the ability as an extension of her artistic eye, her personal way of remembering things.

She picked up a pen and sketched the image in her head onto the book's blank page. Merlin's crystal. A few dozen unfamiliar words. Magic energy. The earth. Em was right, the animating spell was simple. It was the spell's consequences that were potentially enormous.

Chapter 21

You call yourself an inquisitor? Ridiculous.
You don't even know the correct question to ask.
It's not, how do I feel about spending eternity in your dungeons.
It is, how do you feel about your impending death?
—Transcript of interview with prisoner Magus Dux
Interrogation cell #5, EC-HWC headquarters

Chandler's flowing silk pants shushed against her legs as they walked from the hotel to the Eastern Coast High Council headquarters. She'd worn a sleeveless top with a tapestry of rich, dark colors and a draping neckline that revealed and framed her tattoos perfectly. She'd chosen her jewelry to reflect the color palette and enhance her magic: tourmaline, topaz, moonstone, copper, and gold, and most importantly, the amethyst of the signet ring gleaming on her middle finger. It was a show of power that couldn't be missed, any more than she expected her less visible displays to go unnoticed: the oils anointing her skin, the wand hidden at her waistline, and the braided herb talisman created by Brooklyn.

Excitement thrummed in her veins, even more than when she attended openings for exhibits of her art. She'd never have admitted it to anyone, but the high of walking into the gala reception as a high priestess and guest of honor reminded her of the way she felt the day she'd stood in as May Queen. The fact that she wasn't alone this time only added to the sense of power and prestige. Devlin—dressed in his black Brioni suit and amethyst-colored shirt with a narrow mandarin collar—gave off a vibe of sheer confidence, the sort that scoffed at formalities like ties. Chloe was fashion-model gorgeous: her blonde bob perfect, her swingy raspberry-pink dress short enough to show off her mile-long legs. Em had scavenged through Athena's closet and come out with a long black dress and shoes that were red enough to make the Wicked Witch of the West weep in envy.

Thanks to Brooklyn, Lionel now had a stylish short afro that matched the laid-back vibe of his tailored pants and shirt and the classy bow tie that he'd miraculously produced from the back of his VW. He certainly didn't look like a man who had spent his early childhood in the fae culture, a truth that, combined with the impending forgetting spell, had tipped the scales and convinced the High Chancellor into allowing him to attend.

Most importantly, there was Peregrine. His hair was tumbleweed wild. But there wasn't a speck of dirt on his dress pants or high-tops. He looked adorable, smart, and stylish.

She took Peregrine's hand, holding it and enjoying the eager jitter of energy radiating from his small fingers. Most likely a few other witches would bring their children too. She had no doubt that those parents, and the other witches, would be impressed by Peregrine. She lowered her voice to a whisper. "Remember, not a word if you see something otherworldly— black dogs, redcaps… just tell me about it, quietly."

He slipped his hand from hers and drew a finger across his lips, zipping them shut. "Don't worry, Mama. Not a word."

She smiled. "I'm not worried. I'm proud of you."

Actually, she was heart-burstingly proud of all of them. Evan Lewis might have been the youngest vice-chancellor ever, but the Northern Circle's entire entourage went against the norm of older witches heading covens and holding seats of power: Devlin, her, Chloe—and definitely Em, with her reputation as a medium dating back to when she was Peregrine's age, now striding along with Merlin's velvet-sheathed Book of Shadow and Light tucked under her arm. Even Lionel and his unique childhood made them stand out as exceptional, though his sight remained a secret.

She glanced at Lionel and found him already smiling at her.

He stepped closer and rested his hand on the small of her back. "You look amazing"—he revised that—"you are amazing, as blazing as a bonfire."

"A dragon," Peregrine corrected him.

Laughing, Chandler breezed into the historic headquarters building's brass and glass revolving door. Peregrine and Lionel were beside her. Devlin and Chloe followed. As she stepped out into the marble-floored lobby, she took a deep breath and pushed her giddiness aside. Perhaps her ego was on top of the world, but she wasn't as naive as she'd once been. An ego-fueled buzz could be dangerous. She needed to be smart. Careful. They all did, or tonight could end up worse than just having the coven disbanded. They could all have their ability to work magic stripped, lose their home… or even get locked away with other wayward witches and beings like Magus Dux.

"This place could use some up-lit planters or a decorative wall of water," Devlin murmured as they hiked deeper into the stark lobby.

"It is kind of plain, considering," Chandler said.

As they neared the rear, two beefy guards in black tuxes came into view, waiting at attention on either side of the arched frame of a metal detector. The whole idea of a metal detector seemed senseless; any witch capable of creating an energy blast could kill without the need of a knife or gun, not to mention using a murmured curse.

Chandler walked through the detector first. As she waited on the other side for Peregrine to remove his triskelion and take his turn, a third guard arrived with a normal-looking security wand in his hand. Even from a distance, the energy reverberating out of it told Chandler that in this case, *wand* was a more suitable term than usual.

She stood still as the guard fanned the wand up once side of her and down the other. Most likely it could spot unsanctioned, nonmetal weapons of a witchy nature, as well as check for biorhythms that might indicate the presence of fae or demonic glamour. Too bad Midas wasn't with them. He would have loved to check out the wand. Hopefully, though, he'd come nowhere near it or any of the Council guards.

Currently, Midas was back at the hotel room they'd rented as a central launching area. A few minutes before six o'clock, while the opening speeches were in full swing, he'd drive the coven van into the parking garage behind the headquarters building and remotely deactivate the select security systems and wards. Then he'd enter through the headquarters' back door. Once he reached the display that housed the summoner's bowl, he'd use various gadgets and his magic abilities to steal the bowl and temporarily replace it with a cheap Halloween version they'd picked up at Walmart. With the real bowl tucked into a gift bag, he'd blend in with the gala guests and work his way up to the infirmary on the seventh floor. There he'd meet up with the rest of them and assume the persona of the infirmary guard, who—along with the nurses—would already be unconscious due to the powder-filled condom that Em and Chloe would have detonated earlier.

"You're all set." The guard with the wand motioned Chandler on.

Peregrine stepped forward, raising his arms as the guard ran the wand over him. When they were done, she took his hand, pulling him aside so Chloe could take her turn. Neither guard had asked to look in Chloe's evening purse and it seemed like they weren't going to. If they did, the pair of foil wrapped condoms wouldn't raise any questions. But what about her compact filled with Brooklyn's twilight sleep powder? It didn't look unusual. It didn't contain any more magic energy than some witches' foundation powder. It didn't seem like it should set off the wand. Still...

Chandler's mouth went dry as the guard fanned Chloe a second time, pausing the wand over her purse. He motioned her on. "Next, please."

Em stepped forward. The guard glanced at the book beneath her arm. His brow furrowed. "Is that Merlin's Book of Shadow and Light?"

"Yes. And there are two ghosts attached to it. Athena Marsh and Saille Webster, past high priestesses of the Northern Circle," Em said nonchalantly, as if introducing two living people.

"Move along then, High Chancellor's orders." The guard waved for Em to proceed without the wand check, then turned to Devlin and Lionel and began to slowly track the device over every inch of them. Finally, the guard gestured for their entire party to advance to a set of glossy black doors. "Have a wonderful evening. Use the elevator to your right. The grand ballroom is on the second floor."

Once the black doors separated them and the guards, Em whispered, "Why do you think they let me and Merlin's Book through without checking us?"

Devlin slowed his steps. "I imagine the powers that be didn't want to chance that the wand's energy might damage the book. The question is: was it out of concern for a priceless artifact, or because they want Merlin's Book to stay pristine in case they can get their hands on it?"

"I imagine it's the latter," Chloe said.

Chandler noticed a man in a tux and a young red-haired woman in a cocktail dress about to get into the single elevator at the end of the hallway to their right. She wasn't worried that they might have overheard their conversation, they were too far away. But the elevator's indicator showed it was going up and the door was sliding open.

"Come on." Chandler snagged Peregrine's hand, rushing to catch it. They had a tight schedule to keep.

They all made it into the elevator just before the door slid shut. Chandler sidestepped the couple and situated herself and Peregrine at the rear.

"Second floor?" the woman asked.

"Yes, thank you," Peregrine said.

Chandler smiled, pleased that he'd taken a previous discussion they'd had about elevator manners and politeness to heart.

The drone of cheerful music filled the air.

"I hate this part," Chloe grumbled.

"Me too," Chandler said. She'd come here often when her mom had been in palliative care, but the elevator rides had never gotten less unsettling.

The redhead gave her a sidelong glance. "What do you mean?"

"We're being scanned to double-check our IDs," Chandler answered.

"Don't worry," Peregrine said. "You won't feel or see nothin'." He craned his neck, studying the walls and ceiling.

"How long does it take?" the woman asked.

"Not long," the man she was with said. His voice was sophisticated and oddly familiar to Chandler. But she couldn't fully see him from where she was standing.

Devlin wheeled toward the man. "Damian? Well, I'd say this was a surprise. But it isn't really."

"Nice to see you too, son," the man said.

Chandler pressed her fist against her mouth, smothering the urge to swear out loud. *Shit.* Damian Marsh, Devlin's father. It had been years since she'd seen or spoken to him.

"This is MJ." Devlin's father caressed the redhead's naked arm, making it clear they were a couple. Chandler couldn't deny that Devlin's father looked good for his age—a blond, older version of Devlin's sophisticated good looks. Still, he was easily three decades older than the twentysomething redhead.

Devlin introduced his dad to Chloe, Lionel, and Em. He paused when he got to Chandler. "You already know Chandler and her son, of course."

"Nice to see you again, Chandler," his dad said.

She forced a smile. "Are you going to be able to make Athena's service next week?"

His gaze returned to the redhead's arm, like he was steeling himself after a swell of emotion. He looked back up and nodded. "I may run a little late. But I wouldn't miss it. It's still hard to believe she's gone."

"I hope you plan on booking a hotel room," Devlin said, voice as cold as ice.

His father glared at him. "I wouldn't dream of imposing on you and your mother."

"She's not welcome to stay at the complex either," Devlin snapped.

His father wiped a hand over the back of his head. "Can't we get past this?"

"I don't think so," Devlin said. "Not considering Athena might be alive if you hadn't messed around with Rhianna."

"She and I were kids." Hot anger flared in his voice.

"Really? How about later? When you were married to my mother?"

"You know what your mother's like."

Devlin's magic crackled around him. His hands curled into fists. His father all but snarled.

Chandler pulled Peregrine against her, holding him by the shoulders and praying that the scan would hurry up and finish and the elevator doors would open. Devlin's father was a registered asshole. But Devlin normally was the poster child for cool and collected. Still, the death of a loved one could bring up all kinds of emotions, especially when family members despised each other. She was glad she had only good memories of her dad, even those last ones on the day he died.

The temperature in the elevator plummeted.

"What's going on?" Lionel said.

Chandler pulled Peregrine even closer. "I don't know."

"Athena's here." Em's voice echoed, hollow and distant like when she channeled the dead. "She wishes to speak to her father."

Devlin's father shuffled backward, retreating as far away from Em as he could. "Athena? Here?"

Em held out Merlin's Book, still in the velvet covering. "She wishes she'd made peace with you in life. She wants us to hold a séance after the service next week. She has asked to use my body to speak with you then, and to the rest of the coven as well."

He gaped at Em. "She really said that?"

"She is here." The energy in Em's voice vibrated like shuddering moth wings.

"I'd heard she was attached to... Merlin's Book. For the love of everything." He pressed a hand over his face, looking so much like Devlin that for a moment Chandler felt sorry for him, almost. "Of course we can do that, if it'll give her peace," he said.

"Good." Em lowered the book and the chill vanished from the air.

A *thunk* reverberated through the elevator. The music droning in the background silenced and a voice announced, "Welcome, guests of honor: High Priest Devlin Marsh, High Priestess Chandler Parrish, Initiate Chloe Winslow, Adept psychic medium Emily Adams. Guests: Peregrine Parrish, Lionel Parker. Welcome, party of two: Adept Damian Marsh and Acolyte MJ Green. Please proceed to the grand ballroom. Have a wonderful evening."

As the elevator door slid open, Chandler hurried Peregrine out and into what sounded, smelled, and looked like an autumn forest at twilight. The utterly realistic sense of endless nature and the whisper of energy in the air told Chandler the effect wasn't just the work of lighting and vast displays of potted plants, but rather those things combined with a healthy dose of magic.

Devlin glanced at his father. "See you next week, then." He hesitated. The hardness in his tone diminished. "Feel free to bring a guest."

"I'd already planned on doing that." His father rested his hand on MJ's arm, guiding her toward a line of columns that bordered where the autumn forest effect blended into a chandelier-lit ballroom. That room was already crowded with people, mingling with glasses in their hands around linen-draped tables. The lilt of music murmured in the background: a harp, piano, and violin.

"That was intense," Chloe said, once Devlin's father and his date were out of earshot.

Devlin grimaced apologetically to all of them. "I'm sorry about that. He pushes all my buttons."

Lionel shrugged. "No need to apologize to me."

"Heads-up," Em said sharply. She jutted her chin toward the ballroom.

A large black man with an impressive cleft chin and a gray stubble of beard was striding toward them. Instead of a tux, he had on a traditional black robe and the emerald-green stole of a Council member, etched with gold symbols. Rings studded with crystals encircled his fingers and thumbs.

"Nice to see you, Chancellor Jones," Devlin said as he neared.

The man dipped his head to Devlin and then Chandler. "Glad you could join us."

It took Chandler a second to respond. She'd been introduced to Ignatius Jones on several occasions over the years, but it felt strange to be singled out by such an influential man. "Glad to be here, Chancellor."

"Ignatius, please. No need for formality tonight." He smiled at Peregrine. "And who is this young gentleman? A young Parrish, if I were to guess."

Peregrine's face lit up. "You may call me Peregrine—like the falcon."

Chandler cringed as Peregrine's arms started to rise to give his traditional falcon-like wingspread and shriek. She let out a relieved breath as his arms lowered back to his sides.

"Well, Peregrine, how about if I show you to your table? Would you like that?" Ignatius's attention went to Devlin. "The High Chancellor wants you up front, near your grandfather's table."

Em slipped out from behind Chloe. "Ah, is Gar here?" She snapped her mouth shut and looked down, as if regretting having asked the question.

Ignatius chuckled. "Last I knew, he was meeting with some of the guards. He'll be free later."

"Thanks," Em murmured.

Chandler pressed her lips together, hiding a smile. Ignatius was not only Gar's mentor and supervisor, he also knew a lot about Em's participation in Magus Dux's capture and the recovery of the arcane books from his lair. It seemed he also was quite aware of her and Gar's private life.

As Ignatius led them toward the ballroom, Chandler hung back and walked with Lionel, letting Devlin and Chloe go first, then Em and Peregrine. She brushed Lionel's sleeve. "Are you doing okay?"

"Not totally. I've been getting flashbacks from when I was at the fae court."

"Shit. I wonder what's causing that?"

He laced his fingers with hers as they walked. "Probably the stress. I don't think it's all the magic in the air. That feels exhilarating to me, not upsetting."

Ignatius led them deeper into the room. He zigzagged between the round tables, pausing now and again to introduce them to someone. Eventually he came to an unoccupied table close to where the head table sat up on a low dais. A sign tented next to a centerpiece of orange roses and plum-colored candles read: RESERVED FOR NORTHERN CIRCLE.

He turned to Devlin. "The Vice-Chancellor is the master of ceremonies this evening. He'll introduce me. I'll give an abridged version of the events surrounding the recovery of the books and Magus Dux's incarceration, then the spotlight will fall on you. I suggest you keep your speech to perhaps three minutes max."

"Sounds good," Devlin said.

Ignatius dipped his head. "Then if you're all set, I need to go speak with Heath Goddard. He's all ruffled up about something, as usual." He tilted his head toward where a short, pasty-faced man in a black robe was flapping his arms and wagging his wand at a waiter. Chandler might have found the sight humorous, if Heath's psychic attacks against Em hadn't been so unwarranted and vicious.

As Ignatius walked off, Chandler pulled out a chair and nudged Peregrine into it. Though being in the limelight was exhilarating, she was glad Ignatius hadn't asked her to speak. It was easy to forget that sitting back and letting someone else take the lead was sometimes the wiser choice. It also didn't make her any less strong as a woman or witch. Devlin had taken an active part in the Magus Dux matter along with Em, Chloe, and Gar. Her limited involvement logically placed her in the background, despite her position as high priestess.

A sense of being exactly where she was meant to be settled over Chandler, and the Great Fire Salamander's words from the night of the vision came back to her: *"Be wise. Be strong. Listen to the quiver of your heart and the shiver of your soul. Be your dragon when you must."* As usual, the Salamander's wisdom was spot-on.

Devlin glanced at her and Chloe. "I'll be right back. I want to go say hello to Zeus."

He worked his way over to a table off to their left. Zeus was settling in at it with a group of older gentlemen. As always, Zeus was the most dapper of the bunch, with his styled white hair, trim beard, and impeccably fitted black tux. He defined *upper crust.*

As Devlin and Zeus began to talk, Chandler took a seat at their table between Peregrine and Lionel. Unfortunately, the chair she'd chosen left her facing away from the head table. She scooched her chair around until she had at least a partial view of it.

Ignatius was now behind the center of the long table, helping a small, humpbacked gentleman in a black robe and ornate gold stole into the center seat: the High Chancellor. Next to him was Chancellor Morrell, his silver-fox hair accented by his dark tux and glistening jewelry. Beside him, Salix Morrell was making himself comfortable. Though Salix's sleek black hair was going prematurely gray, she'd have recognized him anywhere from his high cheekbones and the set of his eyes, which reflected his mother's Japanese heritage. His place at the head table screamed that he was on his way to a position of power, not a huge surprise considering how influential his father was.

Chloe leaned across the table toward Chandler and lowered her voice to a whisper. "Don't look now, but directly behind you Evan Lewis and his wife are making their way toward the head table."

Peregrine wheeled around in his seat to look, then winged back and latched on to her arm. "Mom—the blond guy. He's my fa—"

My father. Chandler shut him up with a hard look before he could get the words out. "Remember what we talked about? You can ask anything you want about him on the way home. Okay?"

Peregrine's expression drooped, his bottom lip sticking out in a pout. "The lady with him doesn't look happy." A devious spark flashed in his eyes. "Maybe she'll be happier after we heal—"

Chandler raised a finger to quiet him. *Damn.* They should have figured out some way to get Peregrine up to the infirmary for the healing without bringing him to the reception.

He shrank down in his seat and grumbled. "She's really skinny. I bet she never eats."

Chandler had seen Yvonne Lewis over the years in fashion magazines, online, and on TV. Her long plaited brown hair and carefully crafted languorous poses had always reminded Chandler of oil paintings done by Russian artists like Marshennikov. But supposedly TV added pounds and magazine photos were touched up. Maybe Peregrine's impression was more accurate than hers.

She shifted her chair a couple of more inches, as if getting ready to listen to the upcoming speeches rather than steal a look at Evan and his wife. She swallowed dryly, her pulse jumping as she let her gaze glide past the High Chancellor and down the right-hand side of the head table.

Evan was about to sit. He was facing her direction, head slightly cocked as he stopped to chat with the High Chancellor's wife. His once wild blond hair was neatly styled, a little wavy on top and as close-cropped as hers on the sides. Diamonds and gold hoops studded his ears. His trim black tux enhanced his shoulders and arms, grown even more muscular and impressive with age.

Chandler swallowed again, harder this time as the memory of the forest and his naked body crept into her mind. She sucked in a breath, holding it and letting it out slowly to calm herself. But her body still tingled, and her mind went deeper into the memory, to the sound of him moaning her name and her orgasming a second later.

She gritted her teeth as her thoughts went back to her freshmen year at Greylock, to rushing out of class so she could "bump into" Evan in a hallway, and to her and Athena going to swim meets to gawk at him and the other older guys on the team. One time, Evan winked at her as he hoisted himself out of the pool, his wet suit hiding nothing.

She scooted her chair back around, facing their table. She'd been so stupid back then. So naïve. But it was even more ridiculous to let those memories and Evan's presence get to her now. Thank goodness no one at their table was a mind reader, especially Lionel.

A smiled pulled at the corners of her mouth. One good thing had come from checking out Evan. Now that she'd seen him in person, it was clear that Devlin was right. Peregrine's resemblance to his father wasn't as evident as she'd feared. Of course, there was still the similarity in their abilities, but that wasn't something she had to worry about tonight.

The music faded from the background. People rushed to their seats. Finally, everyone silenced, and a shimmering spotlight snapped on, brightening the head table.

Chandler pasted a calm expression on her face and swiveled around, knowing full well where the light would be focused. If she didn't watch

Evan speak, she'd look like an idiot. The trick was, she just had to avoid meeting his eyes.

Evan rose to his feet. "Good evening and welcome to you all—witches and guests."

The deep timbre of his rich, sophisticated voice sent a breath-stealing thrill rippling through her. She remembered the liquid warmth of that voice so well.

"I'm so glad you all could join us," Evan continued, "as we celebrate the Eastern Coast witches' momentous recovery and acquisition of the world's largest library of arcane books—not to mention the imprisonment of Magus Dux, a renowned thief and son of the demon Magna Drilgrath."

A waiter paused at their table, offering to fill their flutes with champagne. Chandler accepted, then sipped hers as Evan finished his speech. The spotlight moved onto Ignatius. He gave his version of the battle in Dux's lair, focusing the honor on the arrival of the Council Guard with a nod to Zeus for alerting them.

Chandler's gaze wandered back to Evan. His wife bent close to him, whispering something in his ear and clinging to him like caramel in a cat's fur. She was as bone-thin as Peregrine had said. Her dress was the color of cream and as filmy as a nightgown on a gothic-novel heroine, but her bloodred lips and fingernails looked like they belonged in a vampire movie.

Chandler bit down hard on her bottom lip and swiveled back around. What was she doing? Putting down Yvonne Lewis for being strikingly beautiful and hanging on her own husband? This wasn't prep school. They were adults. With adult lives. Yvonne and Evan's lives involved years of marriage she knew nothing about, a married life that would soon be even more joyful, if all went well and the spell healed Aidan.

She sat bolt upright, all thoughts of Yvonne fleeing as the spotlight swung away from the head table and landed on theirs, illuminating Devlin.

He stood and thanked the Council for the role they played in rescuing not only the books, but him, Chloe and Em. He totally downplayed their role in the whole event and didn't even mention Gar, who had been involved every step of the way.

Chandler scanned the ballroom, looking for Gar. He stood past the line of columns in the low light of the fake autumn forest, dressed in a sports coat and tie. He smiled at her and she nodded to say she'd noticed him.

". . . again, we owe our lives to the High Council," Devlin said, bringing his speech to an end. Applause rose. The spotlight returned to the head table.

Then, right on schedule, Chloe leaned forward and loudly announced, "I'm going to the restroom, anyone want to come with me?"

Em popped up onto her feet, leaving Merlin's Book behind on the table. "I do."

"I'm all set right now," Chandler said. She clamped her hand on Peregrine's forearm to keep him from getting up. He knew their plan, but better safe than sorry.

It was exactly six o'clock. Midas would be in the building by now. At any moment, the special dinner for the infirmary staff would be headed up from the basement level kitchen to the seventh-floor breakroom. All Em and Chloe needed to do was to put the grenade together in a stall in the ladies' room, then take it up the employee stairs to the infirmary's back entry. If everything went as planned, they'd reach the seventh floor moments after the food had been delivered and the kitchen worker had returned to the elevator and was headed back down to the basement.

Lionel rested his hand on her arm. "Everything's going to be fine."

"I hope so." She watched Em and Chloe as they worked their way to the columns, then turned away from where Gar stood and walked down a corridor toward the restrooms. The restrooms that—not so coincidentally—were on the way to the employee elevator and stairwell.

Everything's going like clockwork, she reassured herself as Em and Chloe vanished from her line of sight. The powder-grenade would take maybe two minutes to assemble. They'd be out of the bathroom in no time. Another two minutes and they'd be halfway up to the infirmary.

"Excuse me," a feminine voice snapped not far from her.

"Sorry," a man said.

Chandler pivoted to see what was going on. Yvonne Lewis had left her seat and was snaking her way between tables, fast-walking toward the columns. Yvonne stopped, craned her neck looking for someone, then flagged her arm to get the attention of two guards. They sprinted to her. She said something to them, then they all rushed off in the same direction as Em and Chloe had gone.

"Oh, shit," Chandler said under her breath.

Chapter 22

Tower of lies. Lightning of truth.
All crumbles. All tumbles down.
Chaos and crisis shatter illusion.
—The Tower
Tarot card drawn for Midas Reed, today.

Chandler turned to Peregrine. "Wait here. I'll be right back."

"Where you goin'?" he asked.

"Bathroom." She caught Devlin's gaze. He nodded crisply, to say he'd noticed Yvonne Lewis's hasty exit and agreed they needed to make sure it didn't mean trouble.

"I'll keep an eye on Peregrine," Lionel said.

"Thanks." Having him here certainly was a relief.

Chandler got to her feet.

In a second, she passed the columns. Gar was nowhere in sight—which was good and expected. Em and Chloe heading for the bathroom was the signal for him to take off in the opposite direction where he'd briefly play lookout for Midas.

The light around her dimmed as she hurried down the corridor, lined with the illusion of autumn trees and capped with a twilight sky. The scent of roast turkey and baked apples wafted out from a room on her left, most likely from a buffet waiting for the next phase of the reception to begin. The restroom signs glimmered to her right.

Quietly, she pushed the ladies' room door open and slipped inside. The place was dead silent. No voices. No click of high heels against the marble floor. No creak of stall doors opening.

She ventured farther inside, her footsteps echoing. She looked under the stall doors, checking for familiar shoes and legs. But no one was there. No Em. No Chloe. No guards or Yvonne, either. What the heck?

Chandler sped out of the bathroom and back into the corridor. Em and Chloe must have headed straight for the employee stairs. She would have seen them if they'd gone in any other direction, except for the buffet room. And it made no sense for them to go in there to make the grenade, not with the waitstaff coming and going.

Drawing up her magic, Chandler jogged toward a set of metal doors at the end of the corridor. The word "exit" shone overtop of them. The words "employees only" spanned their width. She opened one of the doors and stepped into the small, drab foyer. Ahead of her another door led to the employee stairwell.

"What are you doing here?" a woman's voice snapped. Yvonne Lewis.

Chandler wheeled to face her.

Yvonne and the two guards stood with their backs to a closed elevator. The guards glared at Chandler. Yvonne folded her gaunt arms across her chest, one red fingernail tapping impatiently on her sleeve. "Well? What are you doing?"

Chandler rested a hand on her hip. "You mean in this hallway?"

Behind Yvonne and the guards, the elevator's indicator showed it moving downward. Sixth floor. Fifth floor. The only person coming down in the employee elevator from the infirmary should have been the one delivering the food. And they should have been back in the kitchen long before now.

"This is a restricted area," Yvonne snarled.

Chandler leveled her eyes on the larger of the two guards. "Is she right? Is this area restricted?"

The guard bobbed his head. "Employees only, except for emergencies."

"Then how do you explain me entering?" she asked.

The guard went rigid. "I—"

Chandler didn't let him finish. "My coven has a priceless relic with them. We intended to reveal it later this evening, but it seems our concerns about security are justified. It's not up to its usual level."

"No, priestess," the guard said. "We've doubled our security measures for the gala."

"Really? It doesn't look like it to me."

Yvonne wet her lips, their vivid red glistening. "This priceless relic you're referring to, is it *his* book?"

"Why, yes. How did you know?" Chandler bit back a smile. Distraction complete.

Yvonne's voice sweetened, caramel-sugary and smooth, but there was a crafty gleam in her eyes. "I assume you've had a chance to review it?"

"Not yet. At least, not all of it. That will take years." Chandler felt bad for using Yvonne's weakness as a distraction. The woman only wanted to find a spell to heal her son, a spell she most likely thought was in Merlin's Book.

Tartness replaced the sugar in Yvonne's voice. "I'm not surprised you haven't finished, considering who you have on your team." Her lips curled into a sneer. "I can't believe you allowed that Chloe Winslow girl to join the Northern Circle, let alone be an interim priestess. She is a blight on the witching world."

Magic flared up Chandler's arms. She gritted her teeth and willed it back down. She couldn't blame Yvonne for hating Chloe. Chloe was responsible for Aidan's near drowning. Plus, it wasn't fair to forget that Yvonne had also walked in on Chloe's childish attempt at healing him with the spell she'd stolen from her father. She couldn't even blame Yvonne for getting tangled up with Magus Dux. He'd been her only hope for a cure. She certainly couldn't blame Yvonne for the fact that the High Council was covering up her connection to Dux. Everything was because of her love for her child, for Aidan.

Chandler hushed her voice and looked Yvonne square in the eyes. "You should be more careful in choosing your friends and assuming who your enemies are."

Yvonne scoffed. "The law of threefold justice will catch up with that Winslow bitch and the rest of your disgusting Northern Circle one of these days—and soon."

Chandler's hands longed to clench into fists. More than that, they wanted to strike. She pressed her hands flat against her pant legs, keeping them still. The truth was, she'd thought a similar thing about threefold justice the other day. Negative blowback ruining all their lives. At this point, who had started it and who was the victim of the universe's justice was becoming a moot point, other than Aidan, who clearly had gotten the brunt of it.

The larger guard coughed into his fist. "If you ladies don't mind, perhaps we should go back to the ballroom now?"

Yvonne lifted her chin and sniffed. "I suppose we should."

A loud *squeak* rang out as the door to the employee stairwell opened. Chloe and Em emerged.

Yvonne wrinkled her nose in disgust. "Speaking of the Devil."

Chandler walked quickly toward Em and Chloe. "There you are. Did you run into any guards? We were just discussing the lax security."

"Um—" Em glanced at Chloe as if confused and hoping she'd answer. Chloe lifted her chin. "We ran into someone from the kitchen. Plus, a security guard. They were quick to question what we were doing—just as we hoped." She looked toward Yvonne and the guards, then back at Chandler. "What's going on?"

"I had the same experience you did," Chandler said. "When I first left the ballroom and kept walking past the restrooms toward this restricted area, it seemed like no one was paying attention. But I've changed my mind. The security is tight down here. Apparently you discovered the same thing on the upper floors."

Yvonne narrowed her eyes on Em. "If this book of yours is so precious, then where is it right now? Aren't you its guardian?"

"Don't you worry," Em said. "It's in capable hands. But I do need to get back to it." She swished past Chandler and everyone else, her long skirt flying out behind her and the heels of her red shoes clicking as she made for the door to the ballroom corridor. Without hesitating, she flung it open and marched off.

The smaller guard whisked forward, grabbing the door before it could swing shut. Holding it open, he grinned hopefully. "Ladies first?"

Chloe breezed toward him. "Thank you very much. I'm sorry if we caused you any trouble."

Chandler started for the doorway as well. But she hesitated and turned back to Yvonne. Maybe she shouldn't have felt anything. Most likely her sympathy was because they were both mothers. But she did feel bad for Yvonne. "I meant what I said about friends and enemies. Be careful."

Yvonne rolled her eyes. "Like I'm going to take the advice of a woman who couldn't even attract a man to help raise her son."

White-hot anger roared into Chandler's veins. She ground her teeth, struggling to keep her thoughts hidden. She wanted to shout that men weren't a required ingredient when it came to raising children. She wanted to blurt out the truth about Peregrine's paternity and about how important his existence was for Yvonne's own child. But this wasn't about her pride or about putting Yvonne in her place. They were here for Aidan. Not his mother.

Chandler whirled away. She stormed out the door and down the corridor with Chloe keeping pace beside her. When they reached the restrooms, Chloe took her arm and whispered, "She's the Queen Mother of registered bitches."

"No," Chandler said, not slowing her pace. "She's worse than that. She's dangerous. More so than I thought."

Chloe gripped her arm. "I'm so sorry. I wish I could take back what happened that day at the pool. I was so stupid. I should have been keeping a closer watch on Aidan."

"You were a kid." Cold, hard, fear stole the energy from Chandler's legs. She slowed to a stop and faced Chloe. "What I'm afraid of is, even if the spell works on Aidan, I don't think Yvonne Lewis will ever stop hating us. I'm a hundred percent sure she left the ballroom to see where you were going. One wrong step and she'd have nailed your butt to the wall."

"Maybe we should tell Evan about the spell?" Chloe said.

The corridor darkened, the artificial twilight suddenly giving way to a star-studded night sky. Ahead of Chandler, a waning moon appeared behind a web of illusionary tree branches.

"You—we all were right before, about sabotage," Chandler said. "This isn't about us or being fair or unfair to Yvonne or Evan. This is about making sure Aidan is healed and not used as a game piece in some reprehensible play for power." She hardened her voice. "It's also about something else now. I won't go along with giving anyone else the spell and risk Peregrine becoming involved with the Lewis family. Can you imagine what Yvonne would do to Peregrine, if Evan gained custody?"

Chapter 23

My heart beats with joy. A child.
Something of my blood. For my power.
Something of my own choosing.
—Journal of Yvonne Demetri Lewis

By the time Chandler and Chloe caught up with Em at the columns, the spotlight had gone back to Evan and he was bringing the speeches to an end. ". . . dancing will begin at eight thirty. Until then, enjoy the buffet."

Applause rang out and everyone began to rise from their seats, readying to flood toward the buffet and restrooms.

"We might as well wait here," Chloe said. She waved to Devlin. He waved back, then picked up Merlin's Book from their table and headed toward them with Lionel and Peregrine.

Chandler stepped in closer to Em and Chloe. She lowered her voice to just under the clamor of the crowd, now swarming in every direction. "So, what really happened upstairs? Did you really run into someone from the kitchen and a guard?"

Em shuddered. "No. But it was effing close."

"We ducked back into the stairwell just before they saw us," Chloe clarified.

"But you set off the grenade, right? I looked for you in the bathroom, but you weren't there." Chandler didn't dare move as she waited for the answer. She didn't want to risk doing anything that might jinx the outcome.

"We decided to make it on the way up the stairs," Em said. "It was done by the time we got there. We opened the automatic door, tossed it in, waited until the door was almost closed again, and then…" She made an exploding gesture with her hands. *"Poof,* like a puffball. We were worried the door might not finish closing fast enough. But it did. Not even a trace of the powder escaped into the hallway."

Peregrine zinged up to them, a second ahead of Lionel and Devlin. He bounced from one foot to the other. "Mom, I've got to go pee."

"Sure, just give me a minute." Chandler should have expected this. But, *damn,* they were barely on schedule and she wanted to tell Devlin about her confrontation with Yvonne.

Lionel thumped Peregrine's upper arm playfully. "Come on, buddy. I'll take you."

"Thanks," she said. She gave Peregrine a mama-dragon glare. "In and out. No goofing around."

"Yes, Mama."

As she watched them make their way down the crowded corridor toward the men's room, she half listened to Chloe and Em tell Devlin what had happened. Though she'd wanted to be a part of the conversation only a moment ago, now she wished she'd gone with Peregrine. It wasn't that she didn't trust Lionel to take care of him. And it wasn't like she could go into the men's room herself. Still, there would be lots of strangers in the bathroom. Powerful men. Enemies of the Northern Circle.

Chandler folded her arms across her chest, her nervous impatience growing as Lionel and Peregrine swung away from the men's room and to a water fountain that was between it and the ladies' room. She shouldn't have been surprised. Peregrine loved messing around with water fountains.

Just as Peregrine jetted the water higher than necessary, the door to the ladies' room swung open. Yvonne stepped out, less than a yard away from him and Lionel. She stopped, pivoted, then stared directly at the two of them.

Chandler's arms fell to her sides. *Son of a bitch.*

Yvonne lifted her gaze, looking overtop the milling crowd and at Chandler. A slow smile crept across her lips, exposing a row of perfect teeth behind her bloodred lips.

Every muscle along Chandler's spine went taut. How had Yvonne zeroed in on her so fast?

Chandler swallowed hard. Now that she thought about it, she had no idea what abilities Yvonne had. But Evan wouldn't have accepted an arranged marriage to a witch whose powers were less than impressive.

Yvonne cocked her head at Peregrine and Lionel. Her nose wrinkled in disgust, then she pressed her hand over her mouth as if smothering a laugh.

Anger blistered inside Chandler, hot enough to melt steel and bend iron to her will. She could feel its heat burning in her cheeks and arms. Who did Yvonne think she was, anyway? She was a bitch. More than that, she was an ass, so much so that Chandler wasn't about to let her have the pleasure of knowing her needling had hit its target.

Chandler willed the heat from her body and plastered on a smile. She dipped her head, proudly acknowledging her son and lover—or her son and his father, if that's what Yvonne believed. To hell with her. Who cared what she thought?

Yvonne flipped a wisp of hair back from her face, then flounced away, across the corridor and into the buffet room.

"You sure she doesn't know about Evan?" Devlin's voice came from beside Chandler.

"Definitely not."

"By the looks of things, you'd be smart to keep it that way," he whispered.

As Peregrine and Lionel left the water fountain and vanished into the men's room, time slowed to an unbearable creep for Chandler. All she wanted was for them to get done and get back.

A woman stopped and congratulated her on being named high priestess. A couple asked Em if the rumors were true that ghosts were attached to the diamonds on the key that opened Merlin's Book... Chandler clenched her teeth. They were on a tight schedule. What could possibly be going on in the bathroom that was taking so long?

The men's room door opened, and Peregrine emerged with Lionel.

"Told you we'd be superfast," Peregrine said, once they reached her.

Her frustration drained away and she smiled. "And you were."

He took her hand, grasping it by the middle fingers, the way he'd done as a toddler. The first time she'd ever felt his grasp swept into her mind and an ache twisted in her chest. It had been in her bedroom at the apartment. Athena had been there, so had her mom and the midwife. Her newborn son. Peregrine. So small. So perfect. Her boy. Hers and hers alone, grasping her finger with his tiny hand.

Chandler squeezed her eyes shut. *Dear Goddess. Dear Great Salamander, Serpent of the Embers. Keep us safe. Grant us success and get us home safely. Protect us all. Help us heal Aidan. But most of all, protect Peregrine.*

Chapter 24

A two-year-old boy was hospitalized after nearly drowning in a private pool on Thursday. The child's current condition is unclear, as are the circumstances surrounding the incident. A babysitter was responsible for pulling the boy from the pool and starting CPR before paramedics arrived. No other information is available.

      —From *Connecticut Daily Cornet*

While everyone else headed to the employee stairwell to meet up with Gar and Midas, Chandler and Lionel took off for the main staircase with Peregrine. As they climbed the stairs toward the seventh floor, Chandler's confidence returned. Their plan was going to work. Everything was going to be fine.

When they reached the correct floor, she motioned for Peregrine and Lionel to wait, then she eased the door open and cautiously crept out. A bank of elevators spanned the wall to her left, but there were no other doors or rooms close by. Several dozen yards beyond the elevators, the corridor ended at the automatic doors that led into the small palliative care infirmary. On the other side of their glass, a guard slumped at the reception counter with his head on his folded arms as he slept, or more likely lay unconscious thanks to the magic of Brooklyn's twilight powder.

Chandler held still for a moment, checking to make sure nothing felt off. But there was no unexpected energy or magic in the air. No odors or tastes on her tongue. Not a single sound. The hall was as unnaturally scoured of all sensations as it had been the last time she'd come here.

She waved for Peregrine and Lionel to join her, and they hurried out, their footsteps surreally noiseless in the scrubbed atmosphere.

"Is this where Grammy died?" Peregrine whispered.

A heavy feeling settled in Chandler's chest. She'd wondered if he remembered those long days. Room number six. She could still see her mom lying there, as clearly as if it had happened yesterday. Chandler brushed her fingers across Peregrine's cheek. "Yes, it is."

He nibbled his lip. "Mom, is Aidan going to die like Grammy did?"

"Ah—" She took a breath. "If the spell works, he'll be as healthy as you are."

"But if it doesn't, he'll die?"

She swallowed dryly. "Everything's going to be fine."

"Um—Chandler?" Lionel's voice was full of worry. "We've got a problem."

Beyond the automatic doors, a short man in a black robe bolted across the reception room, past the unconscious guard and toward a panel of red buttons. Alarms. *Shit!*

"Stay put." Chandler motioned for Peregrine to hold still. Then she sprinted toward the doors. Supposedly, Midas had cut off the infirmary from outside help. No alarms. No phone services. No magical wards. Cameras set to repeat a harmless loop. But what if something had gone wrong? There wasn't supposed to be anyone up and walking around in the infirmary, either.

"Mama," Peregrine called after her.

Chandler blocked out his voice. Lionel would hold him back. She willed her magic into her tattoos and sheathed her hands in blinding-white sparks. She formed an energy ball. She didn't want to hurt anyone, especially a witch who had innocently stumbled into the middle of their plan. But they couldn't risk being caught.

The automatic doors *swooshed* open as she reached them. The robed man swung to face her: Heath Goddard. Pasty-white face. Nasty leer. The psychic who'd invaded Em's mind.

A black wand materialized in his grip, its tip glowing. Chandler hurled her energy. It *crackle-snapped* past his head, missing him by inches as he lunged sideways. The wall behind him exploded from the blast, plaster flying everywhere. He wheeled back to face her, wand ready—

He froze in midmotion, eyes bulging. He grabbed his neck, dropped to his knees and flopped forward onto the floor, out cold.

Gar strode out from a secondary hallway and into the reception area. His dart gun was gripped in his hand. Behind him Midas appeared, dressed in a white tux. He carried a gift bag in one hand and had a messenger bag slung over his shoulder. Em trailed them by a few steps, Merlin's Book still sheathed and tucked under her arm.

Gar slid the dart gun back into the sleeve of his sport coat. He turned to Midas. "Give me a hand. We'll get him and the guard out of sight, and you into the guard's uniform."

As the two of them dragged the unconscious Heath behind the reception counter, Chandler motioned for Lionel and Peregrine to join them.

"This shouldn't have happened," Midas said. "I did my part. No phone reception. Security cameras fucked up."

"No one's blaming you." Gar lowered the guard to the floor and began to undress him. "There was no reason for Heath to be up here."

"I hope whatever you put on the dart gives him an effing migraine," Em said.

Gar grinned at her. "He'll have one mother of a hangover when he comes to, complete with a blackout and the world's worst headache."

"Good. I'm sure he's given a lot of other witches worse than that," she said.

Chandler looked around. "Where's Chloe and Devlin?"

"They went to make sure there weren't any other surprise visitors." Midas stripped off his tux coat and took the guard's jacket from Gar.

The sliding glass doors *whooshed* open and Lionel and Peregrine rushed in, just as Devlin and Chloe emerged from the patient rooms hallway.

"All clear," Devlin said. "Nurses are passed out in the breakroom. Patients in their beds. No extra people."

"Can we go see Aiden now?" Peregrine asked.

Lionel took him by the hand. "Of course, buddy. That's what we're here for." He nodded at the gift bag Midas had set on the reception counter. "I'm assuming that's the summoner's bowl?"

"Sure is." Midas screwed the guard's cap on over his dreads and stood up military straight behind the reception desk. He fished out a walkie-talkie from his messenger bag. "No one's getting past me. But if they do, I'll give a shout out—old tech is the name of the game."

Gar pulled his sports coat open, revealing a matching walkie-talkie. "I've got it set to vibrate. Don't hesitate to call."

"Let's get started, then." Devlin turned, heading back down the patient hallway. Chloe snatched the gift bag and followed.

Chandler trailed after them with Em beside her and Peregrine and Lionel just ahead. Gar brought up the rear. This was it. *Dear Goddess,* she prayed, *please make the spell work. Please make all they were risking pay off.*

As they neared room number six, Chandler watched Peregrine to see if he'd remember it was the room his grandmother had been in. She exhaled when he kept walking without glancing toward it. Still, heavy sadness gathered inside her. She remembered every second she'd spent in that room: Her mom lying motionless under the twinkling pall of life-support magic, the crisp white sheets pulled tight under her arms, her labored breath, her hands so shrunken the skin hung loose, blue veins visible. She could still feel the featherweight of her mother's fingers on top of hers. She remembered the soft warmth of her mom's cheek, the last time she'd kissed it. But the worst was the fathomless silence after she'd passed on.

Chandler tucked her hands under her armpits and hurried her steps. She hated this place with its muted, sterile air and glossy floors. It wasn't a place for anyone to live. It was no place for a boy like Aidan to waste his childhood, lying under a pall of magic; to never feel the warmth of earth beneath his feet, build sandcastles, or toss wood onto bonfires and roast marshmallows with his father. To lie in a bed and never hunger or make mistakes.

Yvonne slipped into her mind. Despite how nasty she was, Chandler couldn't help feeling bad for her, spending not just days or nights here, but years holding Aidan's hand. Kissing his cheek.

Chandler's jaw tensed, determination bolstering her resolve. They had to succeed. There'd been enough heartache in this place. It was time for someone to walk away, time for a little boy to play in the fresh air, to grow up to fall in love and have his own children.

"Hey, everyone." Em's soft voice brought Chandler from her thoughts. "Look who's here. It's Athena."

Chandler followed Em's gaze. Ahead, by an opened door, Athena's shimmering form waited for them. Another woman materialized beside her: Saille Webster.

Chandler lengthened her strides. Two high priestesses even after death devoting themselves to helping the coven. And them, a small band of witches and friends putting their futures and magic on the line to right a wrong and help a child, to help without expecting anything in return. *This is what being a witch is all about,* she thought.

She marched through the open doorway and into Aidan's room. It was totally dark, except for the twinkle of the life-support pall that domed his bed and the glow of the two ghosts hovering around Em and Merlin's Book of Shadow and Light. There was no pulse and suck of a ventilator, no beeps or pulsations of other machines like in a mundane hospital room, only the faint vibration of the pall's magic hanging in the air.

Chloe hugged herself. "At least, this is better than the city hospital they had him in to start with—no IV needles or feeding tubes, no..." Her voice hitched, then trailed off.

Chandler stepped closer to the bed. Aidan's face was as pale as a winter moon. His hair was wispy and as blond as Peregrine's. His eyes stared straight ahead, open and unfocused.

"I'd rather be dead than preserved under one of those palls," Gar mumbled.

Peregrine beelined to the head of the bed. "Aidan, you don't know me. My name is Peregrine." He pulled a nearby footstool up close to the bed. Then he climbed onto it and pushed his fingers into the pall, penetrating the skin of the magic bubble. He touched the powder-blue cuff of Aidan's pajama sleeve. "Don't worry. We're here to fix you."

A sick feeling knotted in Chandler's throat. Dear Goddess, she hoped they could do just that.

Aiden's body didn't move, but his misty gaze drifted toward Peregrine.

"See, Mom"—Peregrine glanced over his shoulder at her—"he knows we're here."

"Of course he does." She liked to think it was true, though she suspected it was a meaningless reaction given Aidan's prolonged vegetative state.

"We need to get started." Chloe took the summoner's bowl from the gift bag and placed it on one side of a small food cart along with four beeswax votive candles. Then she pushed the cart to a spot between the room's curtained window and the foot of the bed. She turned to Devlin. "Can I have the wine, please?"

He produced a flask and a small bag of fresh herbs from his hip pocket and handed them to her. "All blessed and ready to go."

As Chloe poured the wine into the bowl and added the herbs, Chandler took off the braided herb talisman that Brooklyn had made. It was designed to look like a lucky charm. In truth, it was a braided combination of the specific incense and smudging herbs required by the spell.

Chandler drew up her magic, readying to light the talisman. She hesitated. "I know Midas has a walkie-talkie, but don't you think someone should still keep watch outside the room, just in case?"

"I agree," Em said. "We tried to make sure we weren't followed. But there were a lot of witches eying Merlin's Book and we already had an issue with Heath showing up."

Gar nodded. "There's no such thing as overdoing security."

"Sounds like a good job for me." Lionel headed for the door.

"Thanks," Chandler called after him. Once the door was shut, she added, "I'm really glad we took him up on his offer to help."

Chloe slid a smile her way. "I have the feeling Lionel would do anything you asked."

Heat washed Chandler's face. She pushed the comment aside and focused on the talisman. Drawing up her magic, she commanded, "Ignite."

Flames danced along its braided body, flaring for a moment then dulling into a pungent smoke. As the aroma of sage and cedar with an undertone of frankincense clouded the air, Chandler closed her eyes and sent out protective intentions with the smudge. Athena and Saille's otherworldly energies conjoined with hers, swirling through the room until the air buzzed with good energy.

Peregrine's hand wriggled into her grip. "Mama, I'm not sure I can get the bowl to Aidan's mouth without spilling."

She opened her eyes. "Don't worry. It doesn't matter if you spill some. As long as a little of the potion gets onto his lips. You remember what you need to say, right?"

He nodded. "I'm scared. I don't want to mess nothin' up."

Devlin ruffled Peregrine's hair. "You're going to do fine, kiddo. Now, if everyone's ready, let's get going."

"I'm ready," Chloe said. She stepped to one side, so Em could set Merlin's Book down on the cart in front of the summoner's bowl.

Em bowed her head and intoned, "Let us use the works and magic of Merlin. Grant us a channel to his wisdom to heal Aidan Lewis and restore his health."

The key and the purple crystal on Merlin's Book's cover shimmered. Saille's spirit placed her index finger on one of the diamonds that decorated the key. Athena rested a finger on the second diamond. Then they both chanted, "To restore. To use his wisdom to heal."

Em placed her fingertip on the corner of the key that lacked a diamond and joined the chant, "Crone. Mother. Maiden. The three aspects of the Goddess. Open to us, Book of Merlin. Grant us your wisdom."

Chandler took a breath, then joined in. "Grant us power. Grant us wisdom from the root of the tree of knowledge…"

As Devlin began to echo the words, light shot out from the crystal. It illuminated the ceiling, then fountained down all around them like purple rain. The book shuddered, mist waterfalling out from inside it as Em and the ghosts withdrew their hands and the book fell open to the page Em had bookmarked with a sprig of rosemary.

Em splayed her hands on the page. Her eyes rolled back into their sockets until only the whites showed. Her voice became deep and masculine as if she were channeling Merlin himself as she intoned in what Chandler recognized as Archaic Welsh, "From the level of the sea, element of air lend me your power. Heal this child. Element of earth ground his soul that it remains with his body. Element of fire burn away the damage..."

Chandler pushed her magic out from her body, into Em and out again into the summoner's bowl. She could sense everyone else doing the same, their magic energies conjoining and undulating into the bowl's wine and herbs. Mist and the bitter tang of tansy rose from the liquid, wafting into the air. A sense of vertigo crashed over Chandler and then receded as the air pressure in the room climbed.

She touched Peregrine's shoulder to tell him it was time, then she stepped forward, took the summoner's bowl from the cart and placed it into his waiting hands.

One step at a time, Peregrine crept carefully toward the head of the bed with the bowl cradled in both hands. When he reached it, he glanced back at her to make sure he was doing it right.

She nodded for him to go on.

He bit his lip, then climbed onto the stool and held the bowl out toward the life-support pall. The potion's mist fogged the pall's exterior like breath hazing a mirror. The scent of burning leaves and hot sun on earth flooded the room.

"I offer this to you, dear brother. For your health. To heal you." Peregrine enunciated each word with great care, the way they'd practiced.

As he pushed the bowl through the pall, the dragon tattoo on Chandler's chest clawed at her skin. A shiver of warning prickled across the nape of her neck. Something was wrong.

"Do you hear that?" Gar said.

Muffled voices. Shouts. More shouts, coming from outside the room, distant but getting closer. Footsteps running.

"Fuck!" Lionel's voice shouted. A *thump* resounded as if something or one hit a wall.

The door to Aidan's room flung open.

Chapter 25

Summoner's Bowl
Ca. 1500–1569 AD
Human calvaria
Ritual bowl attributed to Aradia di Toscano
Donated by Honorable Rafael Mastroianni
—Exhibit Label. Eastern Coast Headquarters Museum

Evan stormed into the room, followed by Yvonne and Chancellor Morrell. There were other witches behind them. Lots of women, men, and guards. Two dozen. Maybe three. All talking and shouting at once.

Yvonne streaked straight toward Peregrine. "What are you doing to my baby!"

Chandler threw herself in Yvonne's path, blocking her from getting to Peregrine. "Stay away from my son!"

Yvonne shoved past her and Peregrine and up to the bed. Her arms and body seeped through the pall until her fingers reached her son's cheek. "My baby. They didn't hurt you, did they?"

Spittle bubbled from between Aiden's lips. He groaned, a long, unbearably pain-filled sound that went straight to Chandler's heart. The only thing more painful was the fact that they'd interrupted the spell before Peregrine could finish.

Evan rushed forward, eyes widened in fear. "Was that Aiden? Is he all right?"

"He's fine," Chandler said softly, hoping to calm Evan. "We were just trying to help him."

Evan wheeled away from the bed, his gaze ice-hard. "Help him? Are you crazy? I know you, Chandler—and you aren't a healer." He pivoted back and bent into the pall, touching his son's forehead as if checking for a fever.

"Mama, I'm scared." Peregrine rushed to her side, huddling against her with the summoner's bowl now gripped by one edge. Its contents drizzled down and onto the floor.

Chandler trembled as she propelled him toward the foot of the bed. There was no way to escape, not with the crowd of witches blocking the door and pushing into the small room.

"What's going on here?" Ignatius's voice boomed over the din. He appeared a moment later, shoving his way forward. Gar and Devlin rushed to him and began to talk low. That was good. Not so good was Chancellor Morrell leaning in to whisper in Evan's ear.

Something damp touched Chandler's pant leg. She looked down. Peregrine had rested the bowl against her leg. The summoner's bowl. The stolen bowl. *Shit.* She needed to get rid of it before someone noticed, which would have happened before now if the crowd hadn't been so focused on Aidan and the weeping Yvonne.

Chandler gently gripped Peregrine's shoulder, towing him farther along the foot of the bed to where he was partially hidden from the crowd's view. The only people behind them were Chloe and Em, standing near the small food cart with the candles arranged on its top.

She glanced over her shoulder at Chloe and widened her eyes, silently asking for help. She tilted her head to indicate the bowl in Peregrine's hand. With a quick nod, Chloe said she understood, then she crept forward. Chandler slid the bowl from Peregrine's grip and held it behind her back. After a moment, she felt Chloe take it from her hand.

"Got any ideas?" Chloe whispered.

"Just that we should let Ignatius and the guys do the talking, for now at least." She might have been high priestess, but Devlin had been high priest for years and had the benefit of being Zeus's grandson. Gar would know what to say and, more importantly, what not to say.

"I agree." Chloe lowered her voice even more. "There are dish towels on the food cart's bottom shelf. I'm going to stash the bowl under them."

Chandler nodded, then listened to Chloe's retreating footsteps. At the thought of footsteps, she remembered hearing running steps just before the door to the room had flown open. Had that been Lionel? Where was he now? And where was Midas?

"Stand aside." An imperious voice echoed in from the hallway. The crowd scurried to make way as the High Chancellor shuffled in. An inch behind him, Heath tottered along, swaying as if drunk.

The High Chancellor scanned the room with grave intensity. "Does anyone care to explain what's going on?"

"That odious boy"—Yvonne waggled a finger at Peregrine. She pointed at Chloe—"and her. And the rest of their detestable coven, they were doing black magic. On my son! On Aiden."

The High Chancellor stroked a hand over a gold skull emblem that hung at this throat, as if he were consulting it. Then he turned toward where Devlin stood with Ignatius and Gar. "Is this true, Devlin?"

Devlin's jaw tightened. "Yvonne has no idea what was going on. She's lying because she has a grudge against the Northern Circle."

"I saw what you were doing to my child, to my poor, defenseless baby." Her voice went even higher. "I want to press charges. Endangering the life of a child. Performing a spell on a minor without permission!"

Evan took a firm grip on Yvonne's arm. "Quiet. Let me deal with this."

Patches of bright red colored her cheekbones. She screeched, "Be quiet? That Winslow girl has been out to get us for years and you know it."

Evan scowled at Yvonne. He turned to the High Chancellor. "Can we take this out to the hallway? Loud noises disturb Aidan."

"I agree," Devlin said. "Seriously, we had no intention of hurting your son. We found a spell that can help him. We didn't tell you because we didn't think you'd believe us."

Chandler pulled Peregrine closer and bit her tongue to keep herself silent. Maybe that was one of their reasons. But she was surprised Devlin had said so much, so fast. It wasn't like Evan was going to swap sides and defend them against his wife.

Yvonne raked her hands down her face and sobbed. "My poor baby. I want them charged: attempted murder, using illegal spells…"

The High Chancellor cut her off. "Enough already. Everyone in the hallway, now!"

Heath clutched the High Chancellor's cloaked arm. "S-s-someone needs to stay and make sure the boy's okay." He nodded, agreeing with himself as he continued, "I'll do it. I don't mind, really. Until a doctor gets here."

Fear rushed through Chandler. Aidan was fine. After all, the spell hadn't had time to affect him. But sabotage? That could still happen. Besides, what had Heath been doing in the infirmary in the middle of the gala to start with? What if he found the hidden bowl and took it for himself? It would be less stressful for Peregrine if he and she stayed behind, away from the center of the fray. She squared her shoulders. "I'll stay, too. Someone else needs to be in the room."

"Are you saying I'm not trussstworth?" Heath slurred.

An older man with white hair pushed his way forward. Zeus. *Thank goodness*. He had far more seniority and friends than any of the Northern Circle members did.

Zeus's gaze met hers. "You don't need to stay. I'll keep Adept Goddard company." He turned to the High Chancellor. "Legally, there should be two witnesses who can swear any potential evidence in this room wasn't tampered with, in the event that the charges are formally leveled, which hopefully will be deemed unnecessary after further discussion. Wouldn't you agree, High Chancellor?"

The High Chancellor touched the gold skull again. "Hmm… yes, that could prevent unpleasant complications. Thank you, Zeus." He nodded his thanks once more, then tottered toward the doorway.

With Peregrine held tight in front of her, Chandler filed out of the room at the rear of the crowd. Em kept step with them. Her expression and grip on Merlin's Book were as fierce and determined as a Swiss Guard protecting the pope. And rightly so; unlike the summoner's bowl, there wasn't a chance that Merlin's Book had gone unnoticed.

As the door to Aidan's room closed, Chandler propelled Peregrine to an empty spot behind everyone else. Devlin and Chloe were in the middle of the hallway with the bulk of the crowd, gathered in front of the High Chancellor with Evan and Yvonne.

Chandler glanced down the hall toward the distant reception desk. As high priestess she had no intention of deserting her coven, but her motherly instincts demanded she at least check for a viable escape route.

Lionel crouched halfway between where she stood and the desk. He had his hand pressed against his cheek and was wincing in pain, as if he'd been hurt. Midas was with him, also crouching but uninjured. It was a relief to know they were alive. But not far from them a Council guard stood watch, eliminating the possibility of any of them slipping away unseen if the need arose.

"I don't know how we're going to get out of this," Em whispered, as she came to stand next to Chandler.

"Neither do I," Chandler said.

"High Chancellor," Chloe's voice rose above the clamor of the crowd, "with all respect, we were just trying to heal Aidan. It would have worked if we hadn't been interrupted."

Yvonne snorted. "Like the last time? You almost killed him with that spell you stole from your father. Do you think everyone forgot about that? You're a menace to the witching world."

"You're one to talk." Chloe's voice edged higher. "What about your dealings with Magus Dux? And don't tell me you didn't go to him looking for the same spell."

Yvonne growled, "I don't need to explain myself to you." She spun to face the High Chancellor. "I don't want them charged with just this crime. I want to know why the Northern Circle hasn't already been disbanded. They should all be stripped of their magic. Locked up for good!"

The energy in the air climbed, crackling like wildfire.

"I'd like to know that too!" someone shouted.

"Yeah, why hasn't that happened?" another person snarled.

Peregrine trembled against Chandler. "I want to go home. Please, Mama."

"Shh... It's going to be fine," she said, sending out a wave of calming magic to ease his fear. But inside she was shaking just as badly. They were in serious trouble. But they'd known the risks when they decided to do this. Now they had to deal with the consequences.

"Silence!" The High Chancellor's voice echoed. He whipped his wand from his cloak and sent a blast of energy into the air. *Boom!*

Everyone hushed and fell motionless, even Chloe and Yvonne.

"That's better." The High Chancellor wiped the glow of residual magic off the tip of his wand, then shoved it back into the folds of his robe. "Now, who wants to tell me about this alleged healing spell?"

"The spell is from Merlin's Book of Shadow and Light," Devlin said quickly. "We're ninety-nine percent sure it'll work. We are also sure it will not cause harm if it fails."

Yvonne sniffed disdainfully. "Why would anyone believe you? You're even ignorant enough to involve one of your coven's children. To corrupt an innocent child."

Peregrine stiffened. He looked up at her. "You have to tell them, Mama—"

She frowned a stern warning down at him. If he didn't say anything else, their secret was safe. Chloe, Devlin... even Gar wouldn't breathe a word.

Unfortunately, every set of eyes in the hallway were already on them. And the hardest glare belonged to Evan. He pinned her with nothing but disgust. "I'm not surprised Chloe Winslow is involved in something this unpleasant. But I always thought you were... I never would have believed you'd risk your child this way."

The dragon inside Chandler blazed to life. Her fearful trembling transformed in an instant into shuddering anger. She clenched her teeth.

She couldn't—she wouldn't give him the full truth. But she wouldn't let anyone accuse her of being a bad mother. "Peregrine is here because it is a requirement of the spell. He was in no danger, except what the Council and you represent."

Yvonne sneered. "What kind of spell requires a child? This stinks of necromancy."

Chancellor Morrell's deep voice came from the far side of the crowd. "They were using a summoner's bowl. A *human* skullcap. That's more than worrisome when combined with the presence of an underage child." He hesitated. "The bowl is still in the room, on a cart hidden under a towel."

Icy sweat slicked the length of Chandler's spine. Why couldn't he have missed that? She closed her eyes. *Dear Serpent of the Embers, guide me, help me to find a way through this.*

A hand brushed her shoulder, Lionel's touch as he crept in to stand next to her. One of his cheekbones was swollen and spiderwebbed with blue, typical of a glancing blow from an energy ball. He whispered, "Do what feels right."

Chandler could barely breathe. The trouble was, right was too dangerous to chance. She couldn't risk Peregrine becoming involved with Evan, especially with Yvonne in the picture. There had to be another way out. There had to be.

Gar stepped out of the crowd. "High Chancellor, maybe we should take this someplace private?"

The High Chancellor's hand went to his throat, stroking the skull emblem. He studied Devlin, then Peregrine. Lastly, Chandler felt the grim intensity of his gaze on her. "Perhaps. A private chat is a good idea. I'd prefer to get to the bottom of this now, rather than being forced to remove all of them to interrogation cells, including the child. Though I suppose Magus Dux would enjoy the company."

"Mama?" Peregrine swiveled under Chandler's grip, once more looking up at her with wide eyes. "Please. I don't wanna go to jail. I wanna help Aidan."

Chandler smoothed her hand down his cheek. Then she met the High Chancellor's gaze. "I agree, we need to talk, in private."

Chapter 26

Most often things don't end the way I expect,
so I've learned to expect very little.
—*Musings of a Hedge-Hare* by Isobel Lapin

Chandler kept Peregrine close as they walked across the hallway toward
an empty doctor's office for the private meeting. But when they reached
the room's doorway, she gave Peregrine a hug and left him behind with
Lionel and Em. The meeting wasn't something she wanted him to witness
and he'd be safe with them. Perhaps Lionel's presence wouldn't intimidate
many of the witches, but she'd seen more than a few sidestep Em. Besides,
Gar was standing watch only a few yards away.

She took a deep breath, marched into the office and closed the door
behind her. Though there were only six people in the room, a dizzying
sense of claustrophobia pressed in around her. She felt sick to her stomach
and her legs trembled.

On the other hand, the High Chancellor's steps were light, and his eyes
glistened as he took a seat behind the office's executive-style desk.

Yvonne collapsed into a wing chair and moaned, "This is so upsetting."

Chandler eyed her suspiciously. Oddly enough, Yvonne's pose resembled
a photo Chandler had seen of her in a magazine: the flush on her cheeks,
the purse of her red lips, even the way her pale dress poured over the chair's
dark upholstery, everything right down to how Evan stood sentinel beside
her, his expression grim as he talked with Morrell.

Chandler pushed Yvonne's affected pose from her mind and walked
forward to join Devlin and Chloe in front of the desk with Ignatius.

"If everyone's all set, I'd like to cut to the chase," the High Chancellor said. His gaze swept to Devlin, then Chandler. "I'm going to assume you two and your cohorts were performing a spell on Aidan Lewis."

Yvonne straightened, sitting bolt upright in the chair. "Assume? What else could they have been doing?"

The High Chancellor ignored her, his focus remaining on Chandler and Devlin. "As I was saying—assuming you were performing a healing spell, then for the love of all the Gods, why didn't you simply give the spell to Evan and Yvonne? And why was a child involved?"

Devlin shifted uneasily. He cleared his throat. "We wanted to do the spell ourselves to avoid the chance of sabotage." His jaw tensed, a nerve twitching in his cheek.

Chandler swallowed back the taste of bile. He'd answered one of the High Chancellor's questions. But the more terrifying one remained. The one with the answer that would change everything.

"We were only trying to help Aidan," Chloe said meekly.

"Is that so?" The High Chancellor's eyes narrowed in disbelief.

Chandler gritted her teeth. Part of her wished Chloe would just blurt out the truth about Peregrine and get it over with... but it wasn't Chloe's or Devlin's, or anyone else's truth to tell. It was hers. If she told, she could keep Peregrine, Lionel, and her coven family from being thrown in an interrogation cell. Peregrine would get the chance to help his brother. Aidan could be healed. Could live. She could waste time by lying and saying the spell required only a boy. But the second anyone else read the spell, they'd know the truth.

As if caught in a nightmare, Chandler stepped forward. She couldn't feel her body. She couldn't see anything, other than the High Chancellor and the gold skull glistening at his throat. She straightened her spine, standing up tall. "The spell requires a male sibling. Aidan's brother had to present the potion to him."

The High Chancellor stiffened. Then he gave her an unbearably slow once-over. He looked at Evan, then back at her.

"Fuck," Devlin said.

"For the love of Hecate," Ignatius murmured.

Sweat dampened Chandler's sides as she turned to face Evan.

He stood frozen, his face caught in a wide-eyed look that teetered between utter shock and unmitigated rage. She let go of her defensive magic, opening herself up to him. His hands fisted at his side. But he kept himself under control and didn't take her up on her offer to sense the truthfulness in her energy.

"This is an interesting development," the High Chancellor mused. "Very interesting."

Yvonne sprung from her chair. "Interesting? It's a flat-out lie!"

"Sit down, Yvonne," Chloe snarled. "Let Chandler have her say."

Chandler pressed her lips together. Chloe was wrong. She'd actually already taken her turn. Now it was time to stay quiet, like Devlin and Ignatius were doing. Time to let the High Chancellor take the lead. And, most of all, time to resist the urge to shout back at Yvonne.

The sleeves of the High Chancellor's robe shimmered like raven wings as he rested his hands on the desk and leaned toward Yvonne. "What makes you so certain this isn't the truth? It wouldn't be the first time a handsome man like your husband strayed. Paternity would be easy to test."

Yvonne scoffed. "She's trying to gain fame for her little bastard. Even if the spell is a cure, she's lying about the fraternal part. All the spell requires is a boy, not a brother."

Anger seethed in Chandler's blood. She'd always prided herself on not hating anyone, but she detested this woman. If Yvonne said one more word, she'd—

"Shut up, Yvonne," Evan growled, bringing Chandler back to her senses in time to see his razor-sharp gaze slice toward her. "Is she right about the spell? Does it just require a boy?"

"Evan," Devlin said, "we were friends in school. Chandler isn't lying about anything and we can prove it. The spell is in Merlin's Book."

Morrell stepped forward. "We should call that Emily Adams girl in here and take a look."

Ignatius nodded. "It would be solid proof."

"Are you all insane." Yvonne wheeled on Evan, her fury going icy. "You didn't sleep with that bitch, did you?"

Evan raised a hand to silence her. "We'll talk about that later." He turned to the High Chancellor. "I believe them. I want to perform the spell on Aidan."

Yvonne flung herself on Evan, hands clutching at his lapels. "How dare you humiliate me like this? This isn't true. They're out to kill Aidan. They have been for years, and you know it." She stopped screaming at him and spun to glare at Chloe. "That murderous bitch is behind all of it."

"Why would I want such a thing?" Chloe snapped.

"Because you're a ladder-climbing bitch. Destroy my family and yours has a better chance of gaining power. Don't think others aren't wise to you."

Heat roared into Chandler's arms, her anger flaring into rage. "Chloe was nothing but a child when Aidan's accident happened. She's lived every day regretting it. She's anything but your enemy."

"Shut up!" Evan shouted, his voice shaking in frustration. "All of you just fucking shut up."

Chandler clamped her lips together, teeth grinding.

Yvonne folded her arms across her chest. "This is ridiculous. Lies, all of it." She scowled at the High Chancellor. "I want them all thrown in a cell immediately."

A strange chill came over the room as Evan stepped toward Yvonne. His expression had change to something darker, colder than simple frustration and anger. He seized Yvonne by the arm and yanked her toward him. "For years we've been searching for a spell to help Aidan. It's all you've wanted. Why are you so convinced this one won't work?"

"Why are you trying to turn this on me? It's their doing. Only theirs," she said.

His voice deepened, icy and fathomless, the very heart of wrath. "Is there something you need to tell me? What did you do, Yvonne?"

Her voice shrank to a squeak. "They're trying to destroy you. Devlin's like his parents, and his grandfather. They'll do anything to gain a spot on the Council."

"I'm not stupid, Yvonne."

She yanked free from him, the flush on her cheekbones deepening. The squeak in her voice gave way to a defensive huff. "I don't need this—any of this... I'm going to see my son." She turned her back on him and started for the door.

He caught her by the shoulder, a powerful grip. "Tell me the truth."

Her eyes flashed. "What's wrong with you? Have you lost your mind? Am I the only sane one here? They're playing you for a fool, Evan."

"This isn't about Peregrine, is it?" he said.

Only then did Chandler realize she hadn't moved. She and everyone else were watching Yvonne and Evan's fight unwind before their eyes, like the final scene in a horror movie, when the ax is about to fall and everyone wants to look away but they can't.

Her mind raced. *This isn't about Peregrine, is it?* What was Evan thinking? What wasn't Yvonne saying?

A possibility took root in her mind and her breath stalled. If it wasn't about Peregrine, then was it about Aidan?

Yvonne stepped closer to Evan, her flushed face mottled white with rage. Her magic whipped in the air around her, a tornado of energy. "All right.

You want the truth? You want everyone to know? Maybe this Peregrine brat is yours. But my son—my Aidan—doesn't have a drop of your blood in him. He's mine. All mine."

Evan's eyes went dark. His magic rumbled. "I raised Aidan. I came here every day to see him. You—you—"

"That's enough, Evan!" Morrell interrupted, loud and firm.

"I agree," the High Chancellor said.

"I want everyone to hear," Evan snarled. He took a firm grip on Yvonne's upper arm, then fisted his free hand in a threat to strike her. "Who was it? Who were you with? When? On our wedding night? A week later. A day later? On our honeymoon?"

Yvonne laughed, high and haughty. "Wouldn't you like to know." Her voice went sweet. "I want Merlin's Book. If this spell is so wonderful, then I'll perform it myself. Without your bastard who isn't related in any manner or form to my Aidan. And without that detestable Northern Circle that you seem to be in bed with, literally."

"I was with Chandler once, and only once. Years ago," he said.

She laughed again. "I can't even bear to think about you sleeping with that bitch."

What she'd said registered in the back of Chandler's mind. But it didn't mean anything compared to the shock of what Yvonne had revealed.

"Tell me who Aidan's father is."

"Never." She wriggled from his grip, fled to the door and went out, slamming it shut behind her.

"Shit," Devlin mumbled under his breath.

Chandler nodded. "You can say that again."

Morrell coughed into his fist. "This is an ugly mess. But we need to find a resolution. Since Yvonne did press charges against the Northern Circle members, I believe they should be detained."

Ignatius spoke up, lawyer firm. "They aren't a flight risk. I suggest we give everyone time to cool down. The Northern Circle was wrong. But their fear of sabotage is understandable."

"What do you think, Evan?" The High Chancellor walked around the desk and over to where Evan stood staring blankly at the closed door. "It's your move."

Chandler reached out blindly, searching for the comfort of Chloe or Devlin's hand. She found Devlin's. He gave her hand a squeeze and whispered, "It's going to be okay."

She swallowed hard. If only she could believe that.

Slowly, Evan's gaze left the door and went to the High Chancellor. His voice was low and mechanical, devoid of emotion. "I don't care what we do. I need to go see Aidan. I don't want Yvonne to be alone with him." That said, he strode to the door, leaving it open as he vanished into the hallway.

Noise from the hallway flooded the room, breaking the sense of isolation and stealing a measure of the tension.

Devlin let go of Chandler's hand. He approached the High Chancellor and dipped his head respectfully. "Does this mean we're free to go?"

The High Chancellor stroked his throat. "For now. We'll schedule a hearing for right after Samhain. If I'm not mistaken, that's when your sister's service is?"

"Yes, sir. Thank you, High Chancellor," Devlin said.

"Thank you." Chloe stepped toward the door.

Chandler mirrored her, eager to escape. "Yes, thank you so much."

The High Chancellor held up his hand. "One more thing, as a matter of nipping grievances in the bud. There will be an adjustment to our prior agreement. The man you brought with you? The one who lived with the fae? The one you've agreed to sever all ties with?"

A chill raised goose bumps on Chandler's arms. "You mean Lionel?"

"I agreed to allow him to attend the reception based on the impending use of an experimental PTSD forgetting spell. I'll freely admit, I let my personal interests and curiosity cloud my judgement. However, I think it's best to rectify that misstep before it becomes a point of argument in the Council chamber. For expediency, the spell will be postponed for now, and performed before witnesses at the hearing. However, I won't risk an untried spell."

Chandler's mind reeled. What was he saying? There was only one spell the Council traditionally used on problematic non-witches. But it was worse than experimental. There was even the possibility of Lionel reverting to an infantile state. "You're not suggesting using the amnesia spell?"

"Yes, my dear, I am. We can't have him remain a threat to the witching world's anonymity. Loss of all memories seems far better than the assassination pledge he made, wouldn't you agree?"

Her mouth dried. Dear Goddess. It was. Except, Lionel would still hunger for magic and have the sight. But he wouldn't be aware of the danger the fae represented. He wouldn't know to pretend he couldn't see them and to refuse their offers and gifts… He wouldn't remember the rules of the otherworld—or about witches, either. This was no less a death sentence than the pledge; it was more so.

Chapter 27

Killing doesn't help much with the already dead.
—Gar Remillard
Thoughts on poison-tipped darts and wraiths.

Once Chandler and the rest of their group had gathered in the hallway, Devlin told Lionel about the amnesia spell.

"Shit. That really sucks," Lionel said. His voice held no anger or fear, not much emotion at all, other than resignation. Chandler suspected his lifeless reaction was a matter of shock. It was overwhelming, everything was. She felt catatonic herself, her thoughts dulled and her body as heavy as if her bones were made of lead pipe.

"You all need to get out of here before someone drums up a reason you shouldn't be released." Gar herded them down the hallway toward the infirmary's front door. When they got to the elevators, he steered them past and to the stairs.

Chandler held Peregrine's hand as they started downward. A few voices and footsteps echoed up the stairwell from below. But they were essentially alone. Much better than being trapped in an elevator under the eye of the Council scanners.

When they reached the fifth floor, Chandler released Peregrine's hand and glanced at Lionel. His shoulders were slumped, his face grim. "Sure you're all right?"

He shook his head. "Truthfully? I'm scared shitless about this amnesia thing."

"Maybe Devlin could talk to Zeus," Chloe said. "There have to be ways to minimize its effects."

"Maybe. But you"—he gestured, indicating all of them, including Gar and Em, who'd moved ahead and were almost a flight of steps below them now—"you've got bigger worries than me. Yvonne's charges could lead to the coven's disbandment, right?"

Devlin nodded. "Among other things. But not a death sentence, which is essentially what they've given you. It's not right."

"Shh." Midas put a finger to his lips. "The surveillance and security are still deactivated in this stairwell, but I should reactivate them now. Everyone will want to stay quiet after that."

As Midas slid the messenger bag off his shoulder, Chandler glanced over the railing. Em and Gar had made it down to the fourth-floor landing and were kissing goodbye before he headed back to work. She was glad Gar wasn't going with them, not for Em's sake, but because Gar would be able to report back what happened after they left. There had to be a way out of this. For the coven and Lionel.

Chandler turned back to see what Midas was up to. His dreadlocks partly screened her view of the contraption he'd taken out of the messenger bag. It was wrapped in camo-colored duct tape, she could tell that much.

The *snap-crackle* of magic emanated out around Midas, prickling against Chandler's skin. The magic subsided. "That's weird," he said. He looked back at his contraption and shook his head. "I don't get it. I've got all the other security systems back online. But I can't get the one in this stairwell to do anything."

A look of concern slipped over Devlin's face. But he clapped Midas lightly on the back. "I thought your plan was infallible?"

"It was—is. It's like someone else was dicking around with the alarm systems." Midas shoved the contraption back into the bag. "Let's get out of this place."

Peregrine tugged on Chandler's arm. "Did you hear that?"

Everyone stood still, listening. More distinct voices echoed from lower in the stairwell. A door opened and closed. "It's just Gar and Em, and people leaving the gala."

Peregrine scowled. "Not that. The rumbly noise."

Chandler cocked her head. He was right. There was a faint grumble, a sound like far-off thunder. But it didn't come from outside the building. It was below them. Way below.

"What the heck was that?" Lionel said.

The stairs started to vibrate, subtly at first, growing stronger quickly, as if a train were approaching from beneath the building.

Gar shouted up to them, "You need to get out of the building! Hurry!"

Chandler went to grab Peregrine's hand. Lionel stopped her. "I've got an idea." He squatted down. "Hop on, buddy. You're going to get a piggyback ride out of here."

"Thank you. That's a great help," Chandler said.

They caught up with Em and Gar and headed down all together.

"What's going on?" Devlin asked.

Gar shook his head. "I don't know. But it's happening below ground level."

"Fuck. That's where the interrogation cells are," Midas said.

"Dux," Em gasped.

"Could be." Gar took hold of Em's arm, helping her lengthen her strides.

Bang! Bang!

Adrenaline jolted into Chandler's blood. "That was an explosion for sure."

She glanced at Peregrine, his arms clenched tight around Lionel's neck. She drew up her magic, pushing it into her tattoos until they reverberated with power. They were going to get out. No matter what was happening.

Bang! Crack, crack, crack. Rapid-fire blasts thundered in the distance. The walls rattled. Sickly green haze belched up the stairwell.

A stomach-turning odor of rotting flesh filled the air.

"Wraiths!" Em screamed.

Chloe's voice shuddered. "You're right."

Smoke billowed upward, darkening the haze. The shriek of alarm bells echoed all around them. "Evacuate!" came a shout from below.

"Jesus Christ," Midas mumbled as they flew down the stairs.

"Hold tight, buddy," Lionel said.

Peregrine buried his face against Lionel's back. "I'm scared."

"It's okay." Chandler swept her hand across his back. "We'll be out of here and on our way home in a minute."

Her father's voice echoed in the back of her head: a fireman's instructions, drilled into her over and over when she was tiny. *Crawl on your belly to avoid the smoke. Touch doors before you open them. If cool, open. If hot, leave alone.*

But that advice wasn't going to help them. They had to stay on their feet. They had to keep moving downward, toward the explosions and into the smoke, down and out of the building.

The air grew thicker, darker. Bursts of energy rumbled up the stairwell. Howls. Shrieks.

"Keep your heads down. Cover your mouth and nose," Chandler called out.

On the second-floor landing they joined a sea of witches in tuxes and gowns, all pushing downward. "It's not just wraiths," someone shouted. "I sense higher demons."

Gar worked his way ahead of everyone, vanishing into the smoke and haze. His voice rang out. "Keep moving. Everyone out!"

As they reached the first floor, the crowd slowed to a crawl, everyone funneling forward through the throat-burning stench and eye-burning haze. Chandler had come this way sometimes when she'd visited her mom. There was a single door for everyone to get through, then a narrow entry room, and finally a single exit that led out into an alleyway dotted with shops and cafés.

She let her magic subside and latched on to Lionel's sleeve. No matter what, she had to keep track of him and Peregrine.

"This way." Gar's voice came from just ahead. "Single file. Keep moving!"

Chloe appeared beside her. Devlin was there, too. In front of them, she could make out people moving aside as Em passed through the doorway, Athena's and Saille's ghosts brightening the haze on either side of her.

Chandler reached the doorway into the entry room, Lionel and Peregrine with her. Gar waved them through. "Get out. I'll call later," he said as they passed.

The air on the far side of the door was less acrid. Easier to breathe.

"Look out!" a woman shrieked.

A yard ahead, a wraith swooped out of nowhere, flying low. Gar vaulted into its path. He aimed his gun and fired. The wraith exploded, misting the air with stench.

"Em, behind you!" Midas shouted.

A wolf-size praying mantis sprung out of the haze and toward Em. It was the color of bacon—

"Dear Goddess!" Chandler screamed. The praying mantis had the face of a human. Giant eyes. Heart-shaped mouth. A Barbie doll face!

Devlin hurled an energy ball, magic sizzling. The Barbie mantis wheeled, too late. The energy blast hit it in the chest, sending it cartwheeling backward into the crowd. A woman in a purple robe pulled a knife and plunged it into the creature's eye. It hissed and took off, streaking into an open elevator.

Everyone started shoving forward, faster, more chaotic.

"Go! Go!" Chandler felt the pressure of Devlin's hand against her back as he hurried her and Lionel toward a distant exit sign, glowing red in the haze.

"Mama." Peregrine's voice quavered.

"We're going to be fine," she said, glancing up at him.

He waved toward the exit. "Look, Mama! Look!"

Through the haze and crowd, she caught the flash of glowing red eyes. A howl resounded, high and otherworldly. Then the eyes were gone. *Shit.* The black dog.

"Told you, he's on our side," Peregrine said.

Chandler wasn't sure about that and this wasn't the place to debate it. She brought up her magic again, pulling it into her arms as they pushed toward the exit. But what Peregrine had said lingered in her mind. *Their side.* The black dog was fae. Her vision and the dream. The black and red dragons. Demons and fae fighting over witches. Their small team standing apart. Was this part of that?

Chandler followed Lionel and Peregrine through the exit and into the alley. The haze and smoke hung close to the ground, spreading out and dissipating into the open air. Instead of following the crowd toward the parking garage, Lionel led Chandler toward a folding café sign that sat next to a display of mums. Peregrine scrambled down and raced over to her. She crouched, taking deep breaths of fresh air as she hugged him close.

Em and Midas jogged over. Devlin and Chloe joined them.

Chandler released Peregrine and looked back toward the building. Haze curled along its foundation. But the rumble of explosions had stopped. There were no other unusual sounds coming from inside, either. The escaping crowd had thinned to a trickle. No wraiths. No giant praying mantises with Barbie faces.

"Oh my God." Chloe pointed toward the far end of the alleyway. "Is that Magus Dux?"

In the distance, a man with disproportionately long legs and crooked shoulders sprinted through a lingering trail of haze. He reached the mouth of the alley and leapt into a waiting SUV.

"That's him," Em said. "The bastard's escaped."

Chloe looked at Devlin. "Shouldn't we go after him?"

Chandler rested her hands on her hips. "No. We need to get home." She thought of her vision and the upcoming hearing. "This is just the beginning."

Chapter 28

Reconnect with nature. Healing. Safe for the whole family.
Ingredients: calendula oil, beeswax, coconut oil, lavender flowers, rose
geranium oil.
—Label on the back of a bottle:
Brooklyn Borgella's Calendula Lotion

It was long after midnight. Chandler sat on the couch in her apartment with Lionel. They'd finally gotten Peregrine to bed. He'd claimed he wasn't tired, but he'd fallen asleep as soon as his head had hit the pillow. His snores drifted out to them from his room.

"I wish I could sleep like that." Chandler set her beer on the coffee table. She wiped her hands over her face. "My body's so drained it's numb, but I can't stop thinking about everything. The hearing. The wraiths. Aidan..."

"And telling Evan about Peregrine?" Lionel asked.

She pressed her hands over her face. Yes, that. And, the amnesia spell.

Chandler picked up her beer and finished the last sip. On the way home, Em had received a text from Gar. The Council guards had killed a good number of wraiths and other demons, including a Barbie mantis. A couple of guards were in rough shape and an interrogator had been killed. There was no structural damage to the building. However, rumors were flying that Dux's escape was connected to the Circle's unsanctioned healing attempt. A connection drawn because select security systems had been taken down throughout the building.

Stick close to home. Don't say anything to anyone. I'm going in for debriefing with Ignatius right now. I'll call in the morning, was how Gar had ended his message.

"I hope Gar's okay," Chandler said. "They aren't accusing him of being involved with the healing, but his relationship with Em and the Circle isn't much of a secret."

"I'm sure Gar can take care of himself." Lionel shifted around on the couch so his back was against the arm and his legs were splayed on the seat cushions. He patted his chest, inviting her to come lean her back against him. "How about a shoulder massage? I'm pretty good at it."

She smiled, a sense of happiness radiating inside her. Her thoughts went back to Lionel crouching to give Peregrine a piggyback ride when they'd escaped. Him, helping her and Peregrine when his own life was shattering and falling to pieces.

Deep sadness tangled with her joy. She had to talk to the coven about finding a way out of this for him. Faking the amnesia spell wasn't an option, not with it being performed at the hearing. Still, she couldn't bear to think of Lionel being left on his own, seeing things out of the corners of his eyes and hungering to be near magic, but with no memories to protect him from the fae or anything else. Or worse, him reverting to an infantile state and being totally vulnerable.

Chandler slipped to her feet. She also couldn't stand the idea of Lionel not being a part of her and Peregrine's lives. But they had tonight with him, and she didn't want to waste it talking about depressing things. "I've got a better idea. Instead of a back rub out here, how about we go to my room?"

"You sure?" Lionel glanced toward Peregrine's open door.

"Don't worry. I have a special solution for that." She focused her intentions on Peregrine, sent a veil of magic toward his room, and then intoned, "Circum silentium. Vigilate. Moneo."

"Latin, huh?" Lionel grinned, then translated the spell. "Surround with silence. Watch and warn."

"You know Latin?"

He nodded. "A little. I've always enjoyed exploring the roots of words."

Chandler smiled. "Actually, it's the intentions and focus that are important with spells, not the words or language. I use Latin sometimes as a tribute to my adoptive mom. This is a spell she used on my room when I was little." Chandler tugged on Lionel's hand, pulling him up from the couch. "If you want, we can make that back rub extra special. I've got some calendula lotion in my room. Brooklyn makes it. Smells—and tastes—nice. I use it a lot."

He willingly followed her, but his grip was not as firm as she'd expected and the slight downcast look on his face made her wonder if he'd misinterpreted what she'd said.

She laughed. "I use it all the time to soften my hands, not on my hundreds of gentlemen callers."

His face brightened. She stepped closer to him, looking up into his eyes. She gingerly touched where the energy blast had bruised his cheekbone, feeling the slight puffiness as well as the heat of his embarrassment from assuming she had lots of lovers.

He bent down, his lips meeting hers in a warm, closed-mouth kiss. Unhurried. Kind. His long fingers curved around her waist, holding her tight as they backed through her bedroom doorway and toward the king-size bed. The bed was the one piece of metalwork she'd created purely for herself. Its headboard resembled an arbor entwined with wild roses, arching up and transforming into stars. It was draped with a deep burgundy quilt and was home to far more pillows than necessary. She'd never invited any man to share it with her before now.

She closed her eyes, relaxing against one of Lionel's arms as his free hand moved up to cup the back of her head. The kiss deepened, lips opening, tongues caressing teeth. As her legs began to weaken, she broke free and danced away.

"I thought I was getting an extra special back rub?" she said playfully.

He grinned. "Sorry. I got distracted."

"Why don't you make yourself comfortable. I'll get the lotion."

As she headed for the bath attached to her bedroom, she heard the bed creak under his weight. "This bed is incredible," he said. "You made it?"

"A long time ago." She stripped off her clothes and put on her favorite hand-painted kimono-style robe. Opening the medicine cabinet, she took out a couple of condoms and tucked them into the robe's pocket. She'd swiped them this morning from the main house's supply room, in hopes this might eventually happen.

Lionel was waiting for her under the covers. His clothes were on a chair, neatly folded with the triskelion lying on top. The smile of approval on his face as she walked toward him sent a flush across her skin and kindled an even hotter fire down low in her body.

She pressed her hands around the lotion bottle, focused her intention on heating the contents, and murmured, "Calefac sursum." Under her touch, the bottle warmed to body temperature, then a few degrees more. She set it on the bedside table. "It should be perfect, but we might want to let it cool for a second to be sure."

"Nice trick," he said. His gaze went to her robe. His eyebrows lifted suggestively. "You don't happen to know a spell that goes something like, 'robe disappearum'?"

She cuffed his arm, lean and all muscle. "I thought you knew Latin. That sounded more like Harry Potter magic."

He scooted over to make room on the bed and held the covers up as an invitation to her. "How about 'please'? That's a magic word, right?"

She pulled the robe slowly from her shoulders and let it fall to the ground. Goose bumps peppered her skin as the cool air hit it. She slid onto the bed and under the covers, face-to-face with him. The warmth of his body soothed away every hint of a chill. He cradled her face in his hands and looked into her eyes. She ran her toes up his feet, long and narrow like his body.

His lips brushed hers. She let him lead, rolling onto her back as the kiss deepened. He caressed her lips with his tongue. Gentle. Moistening the kiss, his lips parted slightly, easing hers open. Moving ever so tenderly, slowly.

His lips withdrew. He reached over her and got the lotion off the stand. "Roll over," he said. "Close your eyes. Relax."

She did as he asked. And as the warm lotion trailed down her spine, the scent of calendulas and rose geranium wafted into the air. His hand stopped the warm trickle at the end of her spine. Then he massaged it slowly over her butt cheeks before returning to her back. His fingers easily spanned her rib cage, pressing, rubbing.

She turned her head to the side and breathed in the wonderful smell. Her muscles relaxed under his touch, her tension and worries fading. He added lotion to his hands, rubbing them together to coat his fingers and palms before he started on her shoulders. Her head moved with the ebb and flow of his caresses. Her body tingled from the pleasure. He worked down her arms, pushing the lingering tautness from her muscles and the spent magic from her tattoos.

He rubbed more lotion onto his hands, then did her arms again, even slower than before. He worked from her shoulders, to her elbows, her forearms, massaging each hand, each finger. He whispered, "Is that better or do you want more?"

"That's perfect," she murmured, because it was. She'd often rubbed her arms herself after stressing them with magic. Athena had done it for her sometimes, when she worked too long on a project. It was wonderful to have someone do it for her again. It had been a long time. "Beyond perfect, in fact."

She rolled over, smiling up at him. "Your turn now."

He shook his head. "I'm not finished."

The husky timber of his voice and the impish smile on his face sent tight shivers of anticipation rolling through her.

He tipped the bottle, releasing a warm pool at the base of her throat. For a second, he blocked the lotion's flow with his hands. Then, with one sweep of his fingers, he smoothed it down over her breasts. He leaned in, tickling her nipples with his tongue and sucking them as he caressed the lotion into her skin.

Her toes curled, her entire body arching upward. She pulled his head up to her mouth, kissing him deep and hard. He nipped her lip and murmured, "Enough massage?"

She nibbled his earlobe. "If you don't fuck me now, I'm going to die."

"Aren't we missing something, like protection?" he said.

Every inch of her body trembled with readiness and desire for him, but she forced her attention away from him and onto one of the condoms in the pocket of her robe. "Veni ad me."

Her robe rose up, tumbling toward the bed like a drunken ghost as the condom escaped from the pocket and packaging, then flew to her hand.

"An even better trick." Lionel laughed.

"That's not the best part." His laugh transformed into a groan as she sent a thrum of magic into her fingers and slowly unrolled the condom over his cock.

He slid his hand between her legs, stroking gently. "Ready?"

She nodded and he wriggled up her body, kissing her shoulders. Her throat. Her chin. Her body ached for him. She raked her hands down his back, then splayed them against his sides. The pulse between her legs quickened, a hard, fast throb crying for satisfaction.

His hands parted her legs, unhurried. The tip of his cock brushed her. She closed her eyes, holding her breath, waiting. He entered her slowly, giving her just an inch.

"Quit teasing," she moaned.

He rested his hands on either side of her shoulders, thrusting just as slowly, but deeper, farther. Harder. His pace picked up and her body responded, pushing back against him, matching his rhythm. His mouth found hers. Lips wide apart, tongues exploring. Sweat joined the lotion, slicking their bodies.

She pushed him onto his back and straddled him, pleasuring him with the same slow torture he'd used on her. To her surprise, he easily tossed her back onto the bottom. Intent now, he thrust into her, driving her pleasure higher until a climax coiled inside her. He kept pace, not relenting as her entire body went taut. His lips found her nipples, sucking hard. He pushed into her. Long, smooth, strokes. The tension erupted from her body, shock wave after shock wave.

He kissed her lips, thrust again and came, the tension draining from his body.

She pressed her face against his chest, taking in the soothing calendula scent and the warmth of his arms around her.

"That was amazing," he said.

"Perfect," she murmured.

Chandler woke to the distant chime of her phone. Foggy with sleep, she stumbled out of bed and into the bathroom. She fumbled through her cast-off clothes and located the phone. Hopefully, the ringing hadn't woken Lionel.

"Hello?" she whispered. Who was it? Devlin? Chloe? Worry stirred inside her. Why was someone calling this early?

"Chandler." The voice on the other end was smooth, masculine and very cultured.

She jolted fully awake. "Evan?"

"I need to talk to you."

Dread froze her in place. She glanced toward the bed. Lionel slept on his side, facing away from her. She swallowed dryly. "Give me a second."

"Okay."

She tiptoed across the bedroom, snagging her robe off the floor and pulling it on as she headed into the living room. She needed more than a bathroom or bedroom door between her and anyone else before she talked to him.

Chandler crept out to the workshop, pulling the apartment door closed behind her. The air was cool. Moonlight hazed the windows. It was five o'clock, according to her phone.

"It's awfully early," she said.

"I couldn't sleep." His voice was brusque.

Her throat squeezed. He had a right to be angry. More than angry, in fact. "I understand how hard this must be for you. But I tried to tell you about Peregrine. I called—I called a lot. When you told me you were getting married, it seemed better to just let it go."

He didn't answer.

She walked to the workbench and slumped down on her stool. The flying monkey watched her from its oil drum perch, as seemingly alive in the half-light as if she'd taken Em's spell from her sweater pocket and used it to bring the creature to life.

"I don't blame you for being upset," she said.

"Upset isn't exactly the word for it."

She bowed her head, looking down at her hands, fingernails clipped short, skin burn-scarred from her work. The moonlight brightened for a moment, reflecting off the high priestess ring. Would things have turned out differently back then if Evan had known she'd become a high priestess? What if her abilities had been stronger when she was at Greylock—or if her mom had served as Greylock's headmaster instead of the school's guidance director? Would Evan have seen her as more than a fling that Beltane night? Would she have tried harder to tell him the truth?

"Chandler." His voice rasped. "I know who Aidan's father is."

She sat up taller. "Yvonne told you?"

"Eventually."

Cold sweat chilled her spine. Her heart hammered hard against her rib cage, each passing heartbeat pushing more fear into her veins.

"Chandler," he said after a long moment, "you have Merlin's Book. Chloe wants Aidan healed. The entire Northern Circle seems willing to risk a great deal for the same end. I'd like to see Aidan cured as well. But—"

"Yes?" she said, urging him to go on.

"Before I'm willing to do anything, I want something."

A sick feeling coiled in her stomach. She knew what he was going to say.

"Peregrine."

Chapter 29

Like love letters in a bonfire,
our night of moonlight and flame
turned to ash at the break of dawn.
—Journal of Chandler Parrish. 4 months pregnant.

"Are you crazy? I'm not giving you my son. Never."

"That's not what I meant." Evan's voice lowered, demanding rather than asking. "I'm going to spend time with Peregrine. I want him to get to know me."

The workshop seemed to spin around Chandler, then everything became surreally clear. She could feel the hot prickle of her sweaty palm against the phone, hear the hectic *thump-thump* of her heart, and smell the lingering sweet scent of calendulas and Lionel on her skin. She could also see the future stretching before her, like links of a hand-forged chain leading toward a bloodred horizon.

Evan had rights. He could demand a paternity test in the mundane or Council courts. He had money. Lawyers. He could back up Yvonne's charges against the coven. Or he could choose to speak on the Northern Circle's behalf, if she relented to his demands. He might even be able to help Lionel. He had all the control. He had all the power. He could step into Peregrine's life and then cast him aside later if he changed his mind for whatever reason. She didn't want Peregrine to go through that kind of hurt. She wouldn't let it happen.

"I can't think about this right now," she said. "I'm exhausted. We're all exhausted."

Without waiting for him to reply, she shut off the phone and tossed it onto the workbench. Then she crossed the room to the front door, flung it open, and sank down on the top step. She should have been able to keep her cool with him. She was better than that.

She rocked forward, hugging herself. There was a sharp chill in the air. The moonlight, so bright moments ago, now faded behind gathering clouds. A few yards away the baby dragon lay, eroded by time and wind. She pressed her hands over her face. Tears burned in her eyes. She shouldn't have told anyone her secret. But if she hadn't, she wouldn't have been able to live with herself. Attempting to heal Aidan had been the right thing to do. Still, she'd risked her own baby. Dear Goddess, if Evan didn't divorce Yvonne, the woman would be Peregrine's stepmother.

The pad of bare feet came up behind her.

"You okay?" Lionel sat down on the step. "Was that Evan on the phone?"

She nodded. For a non-witch he was disturbingly perceptive.

"I'm guessing he wants to see Peregrine."

Another nod. She hooked her hands behind her head, looked skyward and closed her eyes. "What am I going to do if he decides to take Peregrine away from me?"

Lionel cupped his hand over her knee, giving it a squeeze. "*If* that happens, you'll fight back. You have powerful friends too. But you need to remember, Peregrine needs Evan in his life."

Her eyes flashed open. She glared at him. "I'm not even going to debate whether Evan or I have more powerful friends. We both know it's him. As for the other part—Peregrine and I have done fine without Evan for years. Why would we need him now?"

"The *sight*."

Her anger dropped away, leaving her smack-dab in the middle of the hard, rational truth. "Dear Goddess," she murmured. Evan didn't know Peregrine had the sight, but he would as soon as he spent any time with him.

"Evan could teach Peregrine how to defend himself against the fae." Lionel touched his chest. "Horseshoe nails and your magic help. But do you really think that's enough?"

Chandler shook her head. It wasn't and she knew it. Not for Peregrine or Lionel.

"Evan's the Council's envoy to the fae, right? Maybe he can get them to sign an agreement not to go after Peregrine."

A thought prickled in the back of Chandler's mind, but she couldn't quite put her finger on it. *Special Envoy. Fae. Treaties.* "Way back, the Northern Circle used to work with the fae," she said, thinking aloud. "In my vision and the dream, the Circle was aligned with the red dragon, my dragon. It represented the fae, or at least it seemed like it did. But the Circle stood alone."

"Are you thinking the Circle should attempt to negotiate a no-harm treaty without Evan's help? My memories of the fae may be from a child's perspective, but the codes they live by are nothing like ours. They're devious. Dangerous."

Chandler leapt to her feet. She paced down the steps, then swiveled back to face Lionel. "The fae are all of those things. But perhaps they aren't quite so perplexing and dangerous to someone who knows them well. Someone who has lived with them. Someone who can see them and would benefit from a no-harm agreement himself."

Lionel held his hands out, fending off her words. "I know where you're going with this and it's a bad idea. Have you forgotten about the amnesia spell?"

She licked her lips. Sure, someone like Evan might be able to convince the High Chancellor to not do the amnesia spell. But even the possibility of what that would cost made her sick to her stomach.

She quieted her voice. "If you were the Northern Circle's sworn envoy to the fae, then technically you'd not only be a satellite member of the witching community, you'd also be a Northern Circle coven member. Between that and you having the sight, you'd fall into the gray area between witch and non-witch. The legal argument and even the logic for using the amnesia spell on you would be gone, or at a minimum the situation would be so complicated that the argument would be nearly impossible to defend. You'd be around magic. You wouldn't have to hide your sight."

"Envoy to the fae? I wouldn't know where to begin. Why would they even want to make an agreement with the Northern Circle?"

As if she'd been studying a pile of scrap metal and suddenly saw how it could become an army of flying monkeys, Chandler's thoughts came together. "We know for a fact that Yvonne was tangled up with that half-demon, Dux. Marriage issues or not, Evan must be aligned with the same legion of demons or cambions. If we suspect this, then the fae have most likely figured it out."

"So, you think the fae would jump at the chance to renew an alliance with the Northern Circle, out of fear that Evan might convince you to align with the demons for Peregrine's safety?"

"It makes sense. If they and the demons are vying to gain dominion over the witching world, they'd both want to be in bed with as many chancellors and covens as possible." What she'd just said repeated in her head. Forming alliances, perhaps literally—not metaphorically—*in bed* with witches. She felt herself pale. No. It couldn't be.

"What are you thinking?" Lionel asked.

"You don't suppose Yvonne's lover was—"

His eyes widened. "You're thinking a demon?"

"I'm thinking Magus Dux."

Chapter 30

I see wild geese from the window of a train,
a lake at evening with autumn coming on.
The ice is thin, cattails blanched as gold
as the sunset when I was with you.
—"Never Forget" by E. A.
Memory. Johnny. 16 years old.

A few hours later, Chandler sat on a barstool at the kitchen island in the main house. Lionel, Chloe, and Devlin were there as well. She'd just sent Peregrine off with Em to feed the kittens. Midas had left for the university and Brooklyn was taking a late-morning shower. Chandler was about to tell Chloe and Devlin that Evan had called, when Devlin's phone buzzed.

He snatched the phone from where it lay beside his coffee, answering before it could ring a second time. "Hello. Is that you, Gar?"

He put the phone on speaker and Gar's voice flooded the room. "I would have called sooner, but I just got out of that damn debriefing."

"Last night, you said something about rumors connecting the attack and Dux's escape to the attempted healing?" Devlin said.

"Several of the chancellors and the chief of security contend that Midas taking down various systems to steal the summoner's bowl allowed Dux's minions to infiltrate and free him."

Devlin scoffed. "The interrogation cells are on the lowest levels, right? Midas pinpointed security and wards on part of the third floor where the bowl was, the seventh floor, and the stairwells between the two. Nothing other than those floors."

Chandler rested an elbow on the island and leaned closer to the phone. "Midas did say there was something screwy about the stairwell security system. If I had to guess, I'd say someone else simply had the same idea as we did. Namely to use the reception as a cover." She was dying to mention the possibility of Heath Goddard being involved. But Gar had warned them against saying too much over the phone and she had absolutely no proof other than distrust.

"I should tell you." Gar's tone became cool, businesslike. "As far as the attempted healing goes, the Council has given Evan Lewis a free hand in deciding what actions will be taken against the Northern Circle. So far, he's not saying a word."

Chandler closed her eyes. She'd pretty much seen this coming. "I spoke to him earlier," she said. Gar was perceptive. He'd know Evan's holding off on deciding the coven's fate was a bargaining chip in his move to get what he wanted from her, namely Peregrine.

Gar was silent for a moment. "I've got to run. I'll call later if I hear anything else."

"Thanks for keeping us in the loop," Devlin said, then he hung up.

Chloe gawked at Chandler. "You talked to Evan. Today?"

"I was about to tell you when the phone rang. I didn't say anything before because I didn't want Peregrine to know..." She told Chloe and Devlin everything Evan had said on the phone. "You don't think Dux could be Aidan's father, do you?"

Chloe shuddered. "That's plain creepy. Wouldn't the Council doctors have figured it out if Aidan was part demon?"

"The idea of Dux being his father is hard to believe," Devlin said. "But doctors can be bribed or threatened to keep their mouths shut."

Chandler wiped her hands down her pant legs, working up her nerve. "There's something else." She glanced at Lionel, then she told Devlin and Chloe their idea about protecting Peregrine by forming an alliance with the fae and having Lionel act as the coven envoy. About the no-harm agreement, and how an alliance would also make it difficult for the High Chancellor to proceed with the amnesia spell. "... I'd rather the coven stay neutral and not side with either the demons or the fae. But I really think we can't afford that option anymore."

"I agree," Chloe said. "My parents work with some of the garden faeries, the same as Brooklyn. They're very careful, but the relationship benefits everyone."

Devlin sat back on his stool, thinking for a moment. "We'd have to run the idea past the rest of the coven members. But I'm for the idea, and I think it's important to get everything in place and done before Samhain." He turned to Lionel. "Are you sure you want to do this?"

Lionel nodded. "As long as it's not going to make things worse for all of you at the hearing. Are you sure this won't give the Council another excuse to disband the coven, strip your powers… or whatever else they can do?"

Fear at those very real possibilities knotted inside Chandler. She pressed her hand against her upper chest, gathering strength from her dragon. "We've had those threats hanging over our heads for too long. We can't let them intimidate us anymore. We're not guilty of causing or failing to cover up a breach in the witching world's anonymity. We're not responsible for things Rhianna did. We are guilty of attempting to heal a child without permission, and that was justified. We need to stop being afraid of the Council and start protecting ourselves, even if we have to do it one member at a time. Even if it means restoring the Circle's ancient relationship with the fae."

"I'm with you there," Chloe said.

"All right then, it's settled." Devlin brought the subject to a close. "I'll get in touch with all the coven members."

Chloe's eyes brightened. "I've got an idea where we could start. From what I've heard, the fae like negotiations to be super formal. Lionel can't simply ask one of Brooklyn's lowly faeries to initiate this or give a note to the black dog and tell him to take it to his queen."

"What are you thinking?" Chandler asked.

"I believe Lionel and I share an otherworldly acquaintance who might be willing to help."

Chandler caught her drift. "You're suggesting Lionel ask Nimue, the Lady of the Lake, to deliver a message?"

Lionel nodded. "That makes total sense. Sibile may have raised me. But it was Nimue who played go-between and answered my adoptive mom's prayers by putting me on the ferry, right here in Burlington."

"There's one problem," Devlin said. "I bet Nimue hasn't forgotten that the coven was responsible for releasing Merlin's Shade from her imprisonment."

"But she returned my charm bracelet after we forced the Shade back into the otherworld." Chloe picked up her mug and started for the coffeepot. She stopped and turned back like something had just occurred to her. "Before I offered Nimue my charm bracelet as a sacrifice, she wouldn't speak to me or Keshari. This time the offering will have to be personal to you, Lionel. Or Peregrine, since this alliance is largely about him."

Defensive anger bristled inside Chandler. "Peregrine's not going to be involved with this, at least not physically. Last night was bad enough."

Sympathy shone in Lionel's eyes. "I agree. We need to keep this focused on an alliance and me as a potential envoy. Once that's in the works, I'll insist on a no-harm clause for all the Northern Circle coven members. That will include Peregrine without drawing him into the limelight."

"We can't assume they haven't figured out that Peregrine has the sight," Devlin said. "It also doesn't solve how we're going to attract Nimue's attention."

Lionel grinned. "Silver coins."

Since none of them had silver coins lying around, Lionel took off to check at the local pawn shops and precious metal dealers. Chandler vividly remembered from the retrocognition that Nimue had lifted Lionel from the lake after hearing his adoptive mom's prayers and seeing three silver coins drift downward. If they were lucky, the coins had stuck in Nimue's memory as well.

"I hope this works," Chandler said, as she put a bottle of jasmine oil on the kitchen island next to the other items she and Chloe were gathering in preparation for going to the park to call Nimue. Along with the cream there were blue votives, a bottle of May wine, an apple, and an assortment of small crystals, all the things they'd previously used to attract her.

"Last time, Keshari and I mixed the crystals with mandala sand," Chloe said. "That might not have been part of Nimue's culture, but I'm a little worried our entreaty won't feel familiar to her if we don't include some of that same sand this time. Should I call Keshari and ask what she thinks?"

Chandler shook her head. "I've got a different idea." In swift strides, she crossed the room, opened the cupboard over the sink and took out an empty jelly jar. "There's a certain sand sculpture by my doorway. It's full of Lionel's good intentions and creative fire."

Chloe's face lit up. "That's perfect. It should work even better than mandala sand." Her expression went serious. "I didn't want to bring it up in front of the guys, but I'm worried about your and Lionel's relationship. I'm not wrong about there being one, am I?"

Chandler shrugged, then nodded. "I think there is. I haven't really known him that long."

"The guy threw himself over you and Peregrine to save you from a supernatural dog attack. He risked a lot for you again last night. He's offered to be an envoy to the fae. And don't tell me that's just so he can avoid the amnesia spell."

"I know. Being with him feels right. Easy. Natural." She wasn't sure where Chloe was going with this. She looked worried. "You don't think this whole thing is some kind of journalistic scam, do you? That's a crazy idea."

"It's not that at all. I'm worried about what could happen if he becomes the Circle's envoy and we all get through the hearing unscathed, and then you close yourself off to him. It's a weird thing to say, but Lionel wears his heart on his sleeve. You're..."

Chandler laughed. "Are you trying to say I'm cold?"

"Not exactly. You're a wonderful friend. You're a wildfire when it comes to Peregrine. But it always feels like there's a part of your heart that you keep to yourself. Love—falling in love is taking a risk, opening yourself up."

Chandler lowered her gaze and nodded. "I suppose I am scared. Lionel's the first guy who's made me want to take that kind of chance." Even as she said it, she realized that wasn't true. There had been another guy she'd taken that risk with. A guy she'd opened her heart to. Evan Lewis. Her logical brain had known Beltane night was nothing more than a fling. But when he'd moved on to marry Yvonne and forgotten her so easily, it had hurt—and, stupidly, it still did.

The door to the kitchen swung open and Lionel and Devlin walked in. "I hate to wait until after dark," Devlin was saying.

"Don't other people do ceremonies at the park?" Lionel asked. "I thought pagans and Wiccans held rituals at the Earth Clock."

"They do for special occasions, like solstices."

"Will the average person know today isn't one of those occasions?"

"Good point," Devlin said.

Lionel took a trio of silver quarters from his pocket and held them out to Chandler. "Do you think these will work?"

As she took them, their eyes met and her body melted, and the room seemed to fade all around them. She opened herself up to Lionel, caressing him with her magic and taking strength from his sweet energy.

Chloe's voice came as if at a distance. "If I were an average person and I saw people chanting and a mystical woman rising from a lake, I'd assume I'd stumbled onto a movie set. Didn't some famous Bollywood singer film a video at Oakledge Park a few years back?"

"I think so," Devlin said, equally distant.

Lionel's gaze left hers and the room came back into focus as he said, "A journalist could always write a fake gossip article about a movie shoot. He could even make sure the article went viral. That is, if someone happened to see something strange."

Chandler set the quarters on the island. "As long as it wasn't an article that raised a red flag in the Council's eyes."

The excitement vanished from Lionel's face. His stance, his voice, even the energy in the air around him filled with utter candor. "I meant what I said; other than it leading to me meeting all of you, I can't tell you how much I regret my attempt to infiltrate the coven. I was blind to the danger my actions posed to the very things I wanted to find."

Chandler cringed. "I wasn't referring to the witching world's anonymity. I meant, we don't want to raise any red flags that might make the Council more determined to do an amnesia spell on you. You've more than made up for anything you ever did."

He pressed his fingers against his chest. Perhaps close to the triskelion. Perhaps closer to his heart. "It feels like nothing compared to the problems I caused for you."

The scrape of chair legs against tile sounded as Devlin pulled out a stool and sat down at the island. "What's done is done. What we need to focus on now is calling Nimue. What if there are other people around? Do you think she'll still come?"

"What if she doesn't?" Lionel said. "Then we'll simply try again after dark. If she does come, we'll have saved a lot of time."

Chandler moved closer to Lionel and rested a hand on his shoulder. The other night, when she'd shook his hand and felt his energy for the first time, she'd liked him and been attracted to him physically. But she hadn't noticed how sensible as well as sensitive he was—or perhaps she had, but it had taken the conversation with Chloe for it to sink in.

He reached up, closing his fingers around hers.

She really did want to have more time with him. Lots more.

Chapter 31

Such wondrous gifts each court has offered:
Sweet milk in a ruby bowl, crystal chimes, elfin bells...
Do not call me fickle that I turned them down.
Perhaps in time, I will choose to leave my solitude.
Meanwhile, more gifts would be most welcome.
—Nimue, Lady of the Lake

Chandler pulled her Subaru into Oakledge's parking area. It was almost three o'clock, overcast, windy, and cool. Two older men were playing bocce. A woman rode past on a bicycle. But, by and large, they couldn't have asked for the park to be less busy.

She slung the messenger bag packed with their supplies over her shoulder, then turned to Chloe. "You should lead the way. You're the one who knows exactly where you and Keshari contacted Nimue the last time."

"Sure. It's not far."

As Chloe headed away from the car, Chandler strode beside her. Devlin and Lionel stayed a few steps behind. They went past the park restrooms, down a short path, and out onto a rocky section of shore just south of the beach.

The rocks were an earthy red, flattened into sharp shelves and dampened by the windblown spray. Normally, the view would have revealed Burlington's downtown and the ferry docks straight ahead, and New York's Adirondack Mountains to the west. But today, the view was blocked by fog, rolling toward them overtop the rise and fall of choppy waves.

Chandler tucked her hands into the pockets of her sweater jacket and let her magic rise enough to warm her fingers. The chill and fog seemed oddly appropriate, with all their futures so precariously on edge.

"I should have put on a winter coat," Chloe said over a gust of wind.

"Here. Take this." Devlin peeled off the wool vest he wore over a thick sweater and handed it to her. "Don't worry. I'm feeling better."

Not sure she'd heard right, Chandler frowned. "You're sick?'

Devlin shrugged. "I started having chills back when we were in Aidan's room. I couldn't get warm all night. But I'm fine now."

"You sure?" Her mama-dragon instincts didn't like the sound of that.

"Totally." The wind rose again, whistling overhead. Devlin leaned close to her. "I bruised a couple of ribs during the fight in Dux's lair. Brooklyn used some sort of salve to heal them. I think it gave me a fever." He shuddered. "Don't tell Brooklyn."

"My lips are sealed," she said. Most of Brooklyn's salves were great, but sometimes they were excessively potent.

Brushing that worry aside, Chandler headed away from him, down onto a larger flat area where the waves thrust up and over the edge of the rocks.

Lionel joined her. "It's not going to be easy to keep the votives lit."

"I've got an idea about that." She turned back to Devlin and Chloe. "Should we try to calm the wind?"

Lionel gawked at her. "You can do that?"

"The chance of success would be higher if one of us were a witch with an affinity for weather. We don't have that. But when Rhianna was disguised as Athena, she showed us how to call wind from a calm sky. I'm crossing my fingers that our conjoined magics might be strong enough to do the reverse."

"I think we should try," Devlin said.

Chandler set the messenger bag on the rocks away from the waves, then faced the wind. Doing the reverse of what they'd done under Rhianna's charge might well be impossible, especially without more coven members. But at least there were three of them. The magic number.

Chloe made her way down to them and settled on the rocks cross-legged, looking much warmer in Devlin's oversized vest. Devlin took a spot beside her.

"I'll go keep watch to make sure no one disturbs you," Lionel said.

As he retreated to the height of the rocks, Chandler lowered herself, so she sat facing Chloe and Devlin, completing their small circle. Dampness seeped through her jeans. Both Devlin and Chloe's fingers felt icy-cold as they joined hands. She thought about using her magic to dry and warm the stone beneath them. Earth and fire were her elements. But it wasn't smart to use her magic for anything extra, not when they needed to accomplish something so monumental.

"I call the element of air," Devlin intoned. "Grant us your calm that we may call the Lady Nimue to us."

Chandler drew up her magic and sent it out into the universe. "Grant us calm," she repeated.

"Element air," Chloe murmured. "Grant us your calm."

Chandler focused on the sensation of the air around her, her magic reaching out to join with Chloe and Devlin's. The dampness and cold, the crash of the nearby waves faded under the rush of the wind against her skin and its voice in her ear.

"Air hear us. Grant us calm," Chandler said.

The wind surged, sending lake mist swirling over them.

"Please," Chloe implored.

Voices reached Chandler's ears, whispers, or maybe they were only the sound of the wind-lashed waves. The voices melded into one. It coiled, a wave of energy circling them, closer and closer. She shivered as the voice whistled in her ear and stroked her neck. It raked a chill across her scalp.

"Grant us your calm." Devlin's voice sounded in the background, beyond the stroke of the wind's energy and the dizzying mist.

"Calm. Calm. Grant calm…" the airy voice repeated Devlin's words, murmuring, whispering—

Then it fell silent.

The wind was gone. Not even a breeze remained.

Without warning, the voice returned, stern and rigid. "Speak with the Lady if that's your intent. Speak now. Speak while I rest."

Chandler jolted from her daze and scrambled to her feet. They didn't have much time.

"Lionel," she shouted to get his attention. But he was already rushing back from his lookout point. "Can you pour the wine?"

He retrieved the chalice from the messenger bag, pausing to hand Devlin the votive candles before taking out a bottle of wine. As everyone moved with swift purpose, Chandler's confidence grew. Maybe this was going to work.

Chloe lit the votive candles with a flick of her fingers, then all four of them gathered on the edge of the rocks. The waves ebbed and flowed, pushing against the stones and falling back in a soft cloak of retreating foam, totally different than the wind-driven waves of only a moment ago.

The waves calmed even further, the water turning as gray and smooth as polished steel. Fog blotted out the world beyond them, muffling every trace of sound.

Lionel's teeth chattered, as if he were frozen to the bone or petrified with fear. "We should have brought insulated jackets."

"It's going to be fine," Chandler said. She was certain it would be, down to her very soul. If not now, at least in the end.

Devlin drew his athame from a sheath at his waist and pricked the end of his finger. As his blood welled, Chandler took the knife from him and cut her fingertip. Momentary pain zinged across her skin. She pushed the twinge aside and held her hand out, letting droplets of her blood fall into the water in unison with Devlin's. High priest and priestess, doubling their power by acting as one.

Lionel passed Chandler the jar of sand from the sculpture. She poured half of the contents into the water, then gave the jar to Devlin. As he emptied the remaining sand, they chanted, "We call upon you, Lady Nimue. Hear our entreaty."

Chloe sliced the apple they'd brought into four pieces and anointed them with jasmine oil. Carefully kneeling on the edge of the rocks, she set the slices into the water. "Lady Nimue. We offer these gifts."

The wind remained calm, but the waves picked up, foam increasing as they slapped the rocks harder. Chandler glanced at Devlin. He nodded. He'd noticed the change too. No more wind, but more waves. Definitely not natural.

"Nimue. Lady of the Lake," Lionel called out. "I offer these gifts." He knelt and poured the chalice of wine into the water. He leaned farther forward, resting one hand on the rock to steady himself as he placed the three silver quarters one at a time onto the water's surface. They floated outward, shimmering against the dark slick of wine for a moment, before sinking out of sight.

Chandler held her breath as the seconds ticked past. One. Two...

Mist dampened her hair and slid down over her shoulders. The waves whispered and lapped. The slices of apple bobbed farther away from them, into the fog and out of sight.

Chandler drew up her magic and sent it into the water. "We call the Lady of the Lake. We seek your aid. Come to us, Lady Nimue. Hear our plea."

Devlin repeated her words and then all four of them chanted, "We call the Lady of the Lake. Come to us. Hear our plea. Come to us."

An ache knotted in Chandler's chest. "Please, Lady. The air has given us respite, will you?"

Only an arm's length ahead of her, a geyser of water shot up from the lake and whirled back down like a cyclone. Chandler grabbed Lionel's arm, hauling him back as whitecaps crashed over the rocks, foam spraying everywhere.

"Shit," Chloe said, as she scurried to escape but slipped on the wet rocks. Devlin scooped her up by the armpits, bringing her back to her feet.

A haughty laugh filled the air. Nimue stood on top of the swaying water less than five feet from shore. Symbols of the Craft gleamed on her skin. Her seaweed-entwined hair curled around her like solar flares. Her eyes shone with fury. Three silver coins hung like glistening tassels from her waistline.

"It's her," Lionel whispered.

Chandler nodded, unable to form even one word. Still, she couldn't let awe make her foolish. They'd all agreed not to trust Nimue until Chloe had a chance to sense her energy and make certain it was what she'd felt the last time. Like faeries, some demons could use glamour to imitate the appearance of someone or something else. And demon glamour was something that could fool even Lionel's eyes.

"My Lady Nimue," Chloe greeted her.

Nimue snorted. "Were you expecting someone else?"

"No, My Lady." Chloe dipped her head respectfully. She glanced toward Chandler and nodded to say she was sure it was Nimue.

Nimue spun away from Chloe, her eyes glistening as she cast a coy smile at Lionel.

He stepped forward with his head bowed. "As a Child of the Lake, I ask a favor of you. Will you carry a message from the Northern Circle to the courts of the Good Folk?"

Nimue plucked a coin from her waistline and placed it in her hair, like a rosebud. Her gaze swept over Lionel. "I know you. When my fair Sibile first brought you home, I thought she'd mistaken an eel for a newborn babe." Lines fanned out from her eyes, glowing with stars. She licked her lips. "Sibile was wrong to give you up. You have grown into a handsome mink, Lionel of the Lake."

"Will you take the message?" Devlin asked.

Nimue's eyes flashed toward him. "Quiet, witch. I wish to talk to the handsome man." Her gaze returned to Lionel, her voice sly. "You *see* me—is this not true?"

Fear jolted through Chandler. She leapt in front of Lionel, blocking him from Nimue's sight. Nimue's voice was becoming disturbingly warm, and this wasn't supposed to be just about the two of them. "We *all* came here to ask for a favor, on behalf of the entire Northern Circle—not just Lionel."

"But you brought *him* here. Where I could see him. And I do *see*—I see many things." Nimue's eyes flashed again, gold and red like coals in a fire—or like the eyes of the red dragon in Chandler's vision. And Chandler understood at a soul-deep level that the flash of dragon-eye brightness was intended as a message for her. *You see too,* it said.

"Yes," she answered Nimue's question, the same question she'd only recently started asking herself more seriously. "I do *see*. Not as Lionel does. I see in dreams and in the fire. A war has begun. A rising battle between demons and the Good Folk, a battle for dominion over my kind." She met Nimue's eyes. "The Northern Circle will not bow before either dragon. But we wish to renew our alliance with your kind. We would like to have Lionel act as our envoy to your courts. That is the message we ask you to carry."

A smile crested Nimue's lips. She wet them with a long, slow caress of her tongue, tasting the idea. Her fingers toyed with the coins at her waistline, touching them both, then the one in her hair. She dipped her head, ever so slightly. "High Priestess Chandler. Sister-witch—follower of the Serpent of the Embers. I will respect your vision. I will carry this message for you." She nodded at Lionel. "And for you—Lionel of the Lake, chosen boy-child of Sibile, I will carry it to the court of my sister."

Chapter 32

When the dark times came and we went forth,
armed with our Craft and abilities,
it was not war or treaties or alliances that stopped the bloodshed.
It was one coven. One decision. One act of defiance.
—From *A Witch's Study of History* by Zeus Marsh

Chandler stepped on the gas, speeding away from the park and toward home. As she turned into the complex's driveway, a large brown rabbit bolted across in front of the car. She braked in time to miss it, but her thoughts flashed to the hedge-hare shapeshifter who'd posed as *The Thinker* on Church Street.

Her grip tightened on the steering wheel. She glanced toward where the rabbit had vanished into the weeds. If that hedge-hare was Isobel Lapin, it wouldn't be out of the question for her to stop by to give her condolences. She had been a friend of Athena's. But right now, a surprise visitor was the last thing they needed.

She rolled her shoulders, forcing herself to relax. After seeing Nimue and agreeing to let her choose the time and place for Lionel's first meeting with the fae envoys, Chandler's nerves and imagination were working overtime. The rabbit hadn't really been that big. Most likely it was just fat from sneaking into the coven's gardens. Perhaps it was the greenhouse invader that Brooklyn had photographed with the camera-grenade contraption.

As Chandler drove under the complex's gateway, the shadows of the winged monkeys on its arch flickered over the car's windshield. She pulled into the main parking area—

Her breath sucked from her lungs.

A silver Porsche sat next to Lionel's VW. A well-proportioned blond man in a sports coat and jeans put one foot up on the Porsche's bumper and began dusting something white off his pant leg.

Evan. The flour grenade.

Dread rolled over Chandler. Dear Goddess, she shouldn't have hung up on him earlier. But she never dreamed he'd show up at the complex without even attempting to call again.

He put his leg back down and turned to watch their approach. His arms hung calmly at his sides. But his feet were planted like a general readying to face an adversary.

"Damn it." Devlin's voice came from the back where he and Chloe sat. "This is the last thing we need."

"I should have expected it." Chandler gritted her teeth and willed the dread from her body. This was her territory. She had her coven to back her up.

"I know this isn't easy for you," Chloe said. Her tone lightened. "But I'd be lying if I said I wasn't excited about the possibility of discovering who Aidan's father is. Think about it. We still might be able to heal Aidan. If there is a brother."

Chandler nodded. "I hope so."

As she parked her Subaru next to Evan's car, Lionel touched her shoulder. "I'll go inside and make sure Peregrine doesn't come out."

"I'd appreciate that." She took a deep breath and opened the car door.

Devlin was out a second ahead of her, striding toward Evan. "This is quite the surprise. You should have told us you were coming."

Evan looked right past him and at Chandler. "I'm not going to beat around the bush. You know why I'm here. I want to see Peregrine." He jerked his head toward where Lionel was disappearing into the main house. "I assume that's where he's going?"

Chandler swallowed dryly. This would have been so much easier if the Circle already had a no-harm agreement with the fae in place, covering the entire coven including Peregrine. Once that happened, she wouldn't be as worried about Evan discovering that Peregrine had the sight. But, without the agreement in place, Evan could use his knowledge and personal experience with protecting himself against the fae as leverage to gain access to Peregrine—or, worse yet, custody.

Evan sidestepped Devlin and strode up to her, so close she could feel the rumble of his magic against her skin. "I'm not going to ask for a paternity test. I have no doubt that Peregrine is my child. I also believe you told the truth about why you risked bringing him to Aidan's room. The High

Chancellor, Chancellor Morrell… everyone who was there believes those things."

Chloe stepped up next to Chandler. "Speaking of Aidan, Chandler said you know who his father is?"

Evan knifed her with a cold look. "If you want to know that, then I suggest you convince Chandler that she needs to let me see my son, now. Alone. Behind closed doors." His voice lowered to a growl. "The Northern Circle is in deep trouble. There are those who think you were responsible for Magus Dux's escape."

Chandler's hands went to her hips. "That's bullshit and you know it."

"Is it?" He smiled, a slow snaking upcurve of his lips. "What I want is for our son to not end up on the wrong side of this. That may not be easy with so many working toward their own goals. Evidence can appear or vanish in the blink of an eye. Tell me, what are the Northern Circle's goals?"

Anger prickled Chandler's arms. She deepened her tone. "You and your wife are aligned with Magus Dux and the demons, aren't you?"

He frowned. "Are you insane? Why would I become involved with those creatures, particularly that disgusting cambion, Dux? Are you forgetting I'm the vice-chancellor—and Special Envoy to the Good Courts?" His voice sounded sincere, but she didn't trust it.

"My assumption is that Magus Dux offered your wife the cure for Aidan in exchange for a partnership, and she sweet-talked you into it." Chandler bit her tongue to keep from giving voice to her thoughts on exactly how close Dux and Yvonne's relationship was, or about Evan's well-known ambition, including having his eye on the high chancellorship.

Evan's tone hardened. "I'd never let anyone talk me into something like that. Especially not my wife." The rumble of his magic increased, the air vibrating with its power. The driveway gravel around his feet began to tremble. It pulsed up from the ground, rattling faster and faster as if it might explode. He locked his gaze on hers. "Believe me, you don't want to turn this into a battle, Chandler."

She thrust her anger and magic into her tattoos until the dragons and monkeys quivered with pent-up energy. "Neither should you."

The corners of his lips twitched into a smile, so wicked that it sent a chill across her skin. "Back in school, I thought you had potential. I see I was right."

Heat washed her face. Back then she would have been flattered by such a comment. Now it was nothing but dangerous.

He flicked his fingers and the gravel hovering around his legs burst into dust and drifted to the ground. He cocked his head. "My wife may have made a mistake by allowing herself to become pregnant by another man. But our mistake could be a cloud with a silver lining for you. Everyone knows your son is mine, or they will shortly. Your coven is in deep trouble."

"Be careful, Evan." Devlin's magic reverberated. "I won't tolerate threats, veiled or otherwise. This is my home. Chandler is our high priestess."

Evan wheeled to face him. "I'm aware of those things. In point of fact, it pleases me greatly that she occupies that position and that you are willing to protect her and my child. However, the Northern Circle's current reputation concerns me. I won't have my son raised by a bunch of miscreants."

Sparks burned at Chandler's fingertips, aching to be shed. She fisted her hands, her body shaking as her emotions teetered between anger and fear. "Get out of here!"

Evan's voice remained firm. "Don't you want your son to have a relationship with his father?"

"We've done fine so far without you," she snarled.

But under the fire of her anger other emotions flared to life. Doubt. Regret. Deep sadness. Was *fine* really good enough? What about the future? What about Peregrine's life? Would it really be better if he grew up without the chance to know his father?

A voice reached out from her past. *"Love you, sweetheart. You and me forever."*

Chandler inhaled sharply. Her father. Her dad.

In an instant, she was transported back to the last time she'd heard his voice. It was third grade. As she'd dashed down the school bus steps, he'd come out of the garage dressed in his fireman's coat and hat. The biggest, best man in the world, gathering her up in his arms.

"I love you, sweetheart," he'd said, squeezing her hard. *"You and me, forever."*

Tears welled in Chandler's eyes. Later that same day, her dad had burned to death saving another family. The best man in the world. The man who'd showed her how to build a bonfire and call the Serpent of the Embers. The man who'd roasted marshmallows with her and taught her the difference between maple and hawthorn wood. The man she'd do anything to spend one more second with. Her father. Her dad.

She pressed her fingertips against her eyes, forcing back the tears. She didn't want Peregrine to have anything to do with Yvonne. But the painful truth was, she wouldn't be able to live with herself if she didn't give him a chance to know his father, even if it didn't work out. This wasn't about her. Not about power. Not about control or the *sight*. Not about alliances or even the Northern Circle. This was about Peregrine and his father. The other truth was, Peregrine would never forgive her if she tried to prevent it.

Chandler lifted her gaze to Evan. "All right. I'd like you to meet Peregrine, officially, as his father. But not alone, not behind closed doors, and not now. Can you come back"—she thought for a second—"in two hours? Give us all time to calm down."

Evan nodded. "Fair enough."

The tension eased from her body. She forced a laugh. "Peregrine's all boy. He'll probably need a shower and clean clothes before you meet him."

She expected Evan to crack a smile or make a comment about the flour grenade that had dusted his pant leg. Instead he turned to Chloe. "I'll tell you who Aidan's father is, when I return—in one hour and fifty-nine minutes."

Chapter 33

Happy 6th birthday to my little sweetheart.
Burn bright always.
—Love, Dad
Gift tag on stuffed red dragon

At exactly six thirty, Chandler met Evan in the front parking lot. As she walked him around the outside of the main house, she explained, "I thought the teahouse would be a good place for you and Peregrine to meet. It's out back in the gardens."

"Fine by me," he said, then he fell into weighty silence.

She lengthened her strides, hurrying them past the coven garage and Devlin's apartment and to the garden's main path. Twilight had fallen. Mist drifted low to the ground, but the heavier fog had retreated.

Chandler tucked a hand into the pocket of her sweater jacket, fiddling with a sharp corner of the folded spell Em had given her. She should have burned the paper once she'd finished copying the spell into her Book of Shadows. She also should have let Devlin escort Evan to the teahouse. He'd offered to do it. It would have been more comfortable for everyone.

When they reached the footbridge, she slowed her steps and broke the silence. There were things that had to be said. "I was serious about not leaving you alone with Peregrine."

Evan stopped. His gaze went to her. Finally, he spoke, his tone distant, perhaps even bittersweet. "I'm not surprised. If I were you, I wouldn't let me be alone with him either. Believe me, I respect you for it."

She looked past him, down at the stream and mist. That Beltane night it had been the white blooms from the shadberry trees that had glimmered in the nearby stream. Tonight, it was the glimmer of autumn cattails, reflecting gold in the water. Still, and despite all the reasons she had to dislike and not trust Evan, she couldn't escape the fantasy of *what could have been*. Even now—after years of life and other men, after becoming a mother, even after what was kindling between her and Lionel—Evan's mere presence made her want to open up to him, to risk rejection. His energy enticed her. The layers of his voice burned into her soul, like compliments murmured from an upperclassman's lips into the ear of a lonely outsider. Or like him, glancing over his shoulder to smile at her in the rush between classes. His lips and hands worshiping her body in the moonlight. The moist, warm forest floor against her back. Fleeting moments in time when their paths intersected, then separated. Sparks in the darkness of their pasts. It all made her wonder about destiny. She firmly believed people made their own. But there were times when her soul whispered, "meant to be."

She felt the warmth of his hand on her arm. "You can trust me. I want you to know that."

"I don't want Peregrine hurt," she said.

His voice deepened. "My intention isn't to take him from you or harm him. I want to know my son. He would benefit from having a relationship with me, you know that."

Chandler pressed her lips together. Evan was powerful and clever. And, as much as a small part of her wanted to do the easy thing and surrender, the dragon side of her didn't trust how Evan affected her. The workings of physical chemistry and magic were complex and in large part a mystery even to witches. He could have even been plying her emotions with his magic right now, more than her heart wanted to believe.

She glanced back at the reflection of the cattails and took a deep breath. Only a few nights ago, she'd watched Chloe's burning scrap of birch settle into those reeds. Chloe had chosen to cast aside self-doubt. On her own birch, Chandler had scratched the words fear, sorrow, and guilt. Perhaps self-doubt should have been on there as well.

And secrets.

As much as she hated it, she had to surrender another secret to Evan. She had to tell him about Peregrine's sight before he discovered it on his own and accused her of withholding something else from him. Evan knowing would add a huge amount of weight to his argument for gaining custody over Peregrine, in the form of vital protection. But she'd have to tolerate the weight of that argument only briefly. Once the Circle's alliance and no-harm agreement was in place with the fae, that reason would evaporate.

Chandler faced him and steadied her voice. "There's something else you should know. Peregrine has the sight."

Evan's mouth fell open. He shuffled back a step. "How do you know? When? He's barely old enough."

"A few days ago, he saw a black dog." Her voice was meeker than she'd have preferred, lost in the open air of the garden.

"Plenty of children imagine things," he countered. But his chest rose and fell, his breath coming faster, fueled by excitement.

"I saw the dog after it materialized."

He frowned. "This changes things. Peregrine needs protection immediately. He can't be alone. Even for a minute. You haven't experienced the things I have, Chandler. The diminutive fae are as deadly as the ones that look like us. There's darkness in them, true darkness."

A surge of adrenaline put fire back in her tone. "I may not know as much as you, but I'm no fool."

"When the fae came after me the first time, I wasn't much older than Peregrine. They trapped me in the woods. Dozens of them held me down, readying to gouge out my eyes with thorns. You might have heard that they killed my grandfather. But I bet you didn't know that he offered himself to save me. I saw him, blood spurting from his empty eye sockets. But that wasn't the last time they attacked me." He reflexively touched his forehead and the remains of the deep scar.

Her adrenaline drained. "But you agreed to be the Council envoy to the fae?"

"I understand them better than any other Council employee. The job also comes with a no-harm agreement, for me and my family. I can protect Peregrine—and, frankly, you can't."

She nodded. There was no point arguing with that. It was true, for now.

She took a deep breath, calming herself. "We need to talk about this. But can we put it aside for the time being? Peregrine and everyone else are waiting for us."

"Fine," he said. "But before I leave, this will be settled."

Chandler started down the other side of the bridge, lengthening her strides to put distance between the two of them. He caught up with her in a second. And, in another heartbeat, they were up the teahouse steps and walking inside.

Peregrine sat at the low table on a floor cushion, casting rune bones with Devlin. The light from the candles in front of them gleamed in his wild blond hair. He looked up at Evan with dark, falcon-sharp eyes. His lips parted in awe.

Chandler sensed Evan stiffen beside her, then his magic tentatively reached out toward Peregrine, warm, inviting—

Time seemed to slow, as if the Goddess of Autumn had taken hold of the Wheel of Time and was keeping it from moving toward Winter. At the low table, Devlin glanced over his shoulder at them. Chloe crouched beside him, studying the runes. Nearby, Em stood at the brazier with one hand on the handle of a steaming kettle. At the rear of the room, Lionel held a tray with three handleless teacups on it: one for Evan, the others for her and Peregrine.

Evan's magic reached Peregrine's cheek, brushing it gently. Chandler could feel the caress in the silence of the moment, like the uncanny toll of a bell at midnight.

Peregrine's energy shrank in close around him. He flinched away, his lips tightening.

Chandler let out her breath. *Good boy,* she thought. But then worry took root in her chest as Peregrine's energy loosened. His eyes widened. A smile crossed his lips.

In swift strides, Evan crossed the distance to the table and lowered himself onto a cushion that sat at the head of the table, next to Peregrine. "Bone runes," he said. "Whose fortune are we reading?"

Peregrine bit his lip and pointed to a *V* marked onto one of the bones. "I'm trying to read Devlin's, but I can't remember what this one means."

"You don't need to remember their meaning." Evan cupped his hand over the bone. "Close your eyes. Release your energy and see the symbol in your mind. Let your instincts tell you their significance. It takes practice. If your gift for reading is weak, the results will be unreliable. But the symbols and meaning lives inside every witch." He glanced at Devlin. "Right?"

"Exactly." Devlin brushed his hands together. "It looks to me like it's time to put this lesson away for now." He leaned to one side so Lionel could set the teacups on the table.

Chandler longed to join them immediately, preferably by sitting down between Evan and Peregrine. Instead she made herself walk to where Em had finished pouring the hot water into the teapot. Steam rose from its spout, scenting the air with a hint of sweetness.

"Jasmine tea?" Chandler asked.

Em nodded. She handed the pot to Chandler, then picked up a plate of almond crescent cookies. "I didn't dare put the sweets on the table until you two got here."

Peregrine sat up taller. "I wouldn't have eaten them."

"You mean, you wouldn't have eaten *all* of them." Chloe laughed.

But beneath Chloe's laughter and everyone's else casual friendliness, tension sang, breaking only as Devlin got to his feet so Chandler could set the teapot down and take his place at the table.

Chloe readied to leave as well. "We'll be outside, if you need anything," she said.

"Right outside," Lionel repeated, sweeping his hand across Chandler's shoulder on his way to the door.

A moment later, they were gone, and Chandler sat alone with Evan and Peregrine.

Peregrine snagged a cookie, as fast as anything. Then he pulled it close to keep it safe. "Brooklyn makes the best cookies. But jasmine tea is kind of yucky."

Evan chuckled. "Maybe I should only have half a cup?"

Chandler poured him a full cup and did the same for Peregrine, then herself.

"I'm really glad to meet you," Evan said quietly.

Peregrine eyed him. He dunked his cookie in his tea, sucked off the wet part, then wiped his mouth. "Me too. Can I ask you somethin'?"

"Anything. I'm your father. Even if I haven't been a part of your life, I want you to feel free to call me any time. Ask anything. Is that a deal?"

Peregrine nodded, then his eyes went to Chandler, asking for approval.

She gritted her teeth, then reluctantly returned his nod. Dear Goddess, this wasn't easy.

"Well"—Peregrine slurped down the rest of his cookie—"Mom says you have the *sight*. If you do, then tell me: what do redcaps look like? Not the *Dungeon & Dragons* kind, the real ones."

He smiled. "*Dungeons & Dragons* isn't that far off, except they have the height and iron boot part wrong. Redcaps can be short and squatty or as tall and skinny as an average man. They have sharp, beaklike noses. They're wrinkled and bearded, even when they're young—" He stopped and raised an eyebrow, holding on to an especially juicy detail.

Peregrine leaned forward, staring at him. "And?"

"Most important, they always wear a red stocking cap—greasy with blood, animal or human. But they don't wear iron boots nowadays. They prefer metal cleats and high-tops. Makes them more dangerous. Faster."

"I thought I saw one out front. He was hanging around Lionel's car."

Evan glared at Chandler. "Really? I thought you'd only seen a black dog."

She grimaced. "*He* believed he saw a redcap at the time. Peregrine might exaggerate just a little, but he doesn't lie."

Evan's gaze returned to Peregrine. "Not lying is something you should be proud of. It takes skill and makes a man more powerful." He smiled slyly. "There are other ways to manipulate situations."

"That's enough," Chandler interrupted him. That was the sort of thing she didn't want Peregrine to learn from anyone, especially not from Evan.

"Um—" Peregrine's mouth worked, as if he were deciding whether to say what was on his mind or not. Then he blurted, "I want Aidan to get better."

Evan's face remained calm, but his hold on the teacup tightened. "I do too. Your mother and I are going to talk about that shortly, along with some other important things."

"I wanna be friends with Aidan," Peregrine said. A frown wrinkled his forehead. He looked first at Evan, then Chandler received the full force of his serious glare. "You guys aren't making all the rules. I want to be friends with Aidan, and I want to keep the black dog."

Chandler matched his glare with a serious look of her own. "We'll discuss those things some more later," she said. But now that healing Aidan had been brought up, she didn't want to let the subject drop. She turned to Evan.

He spoke first. "We can do the healing tonight. Yvonne is *gone* right now. I'll get you into headquarters and the infirmary. I've already had the summoner's bowl moved to my office. There won't be any questions."

Chandler blinked, surprised by the suggestion. It sounded wonderful, but there was a huge issue. "It's one thing to know who Aidan's genetic father is. It's quite another to talk that man into letting us use another of his children in a ritual. I'm assuming there is another boy?"

"Not exactly a boy."

The teahouse door whisked open.

Chloe stuck her head inside, then motioned emphatically at something behind her. "We've got trouble. Serious trouble."

Chandler scrambled to her feet and sprinted to the doorway.

"Over there." Chloe gestured past where Devlin, Lionel, and Em stood on the top of the teahouse steps, staring down toward the gardens.

At first all she saw was what looked like mist rising from between the clumps of cattails. It rapidly thickened and transformed into the shape of two hunched creatures with long, shaggy hair and possum-like faces. They were no taller than Peregrine and each carried a torch, flaming brighter as they emerged from the reeds. Behind them, two short men materialized. Ripped jeans. Scraggly beards. Huge noses that looked like they belonged on prehistoric birds. Beady black eyes set close together.

Chandler didn't know what the first beings were, but the second ones fit Evan's description of redcaps right down to the bloody sheen on their hats.

"A faery entourage," Chloe murmured. "The envoys are coming."

Terror surged into Chandler's veins, sending her pulse pounding. The last thing they needed was for Evan to realize what they were up to—or for the fae to see a Council representative lurking in their teahouse.

She swiveled back, hand rising to stop Evan from getting up—

He already stood an inch behind her with a dark look on his face. "What's going on?"

Chapter 34

First and foremost, the fae are uncannily skilled at manipulating language.
They are devotees of the unsaid and masters of loopholes.
—*WHC Special Envoy Handbook.* New Haven, CT. 2019. Print edition.

Chandler stepped toward Evan, forcing him back away from the door. "I wanna see!" Peregrine was on his feet.

She narrowed her eyes on him. "Sit. Now." And then, to Evan. "I'll explain later. If you care about Peregrine, keep him in here." She toughened her tone further. "I'm trusting you won't try to pull anything."

"Just what do you mean by that?" Evan snapped.

"Nothing. I just expect to find you both here when I get back." There, she'd said it. He knew she wouldn't put anything past him.

Chloe came up behind her. "I'll stay with them. You need to get down there with Devlin."

"I really appreciate that," Chandler said. As high priestess, her place was beside Devlin. But fulfilling her duty would be easier knowing Chloe was making sure Evan didn't do anything unwarranted.

Chandler let Chloe slip past her and into the teahouse, then she headed outside and closed the door.

Down by the stream, a taller shape was emerging from the clumps of cattails. It materialized into a woman. In the flickering light of the torches and the blue glow of the path, she looked to be made from oak bark and ferns as much as flesh and bone. Great horns coiled from her head, thick as an ancient ram's. The plaits of her midnight-black hair twined with a wreath of thorn branches. *Regal* was the only word Chandler could think of as the woman strolled between the torchbearers and redcaps, away from the reeds and stream and onto the path.

Behind her, a man emerged. He was dressed in black leathers with gold knives and chakra-like throwing circles holstered across his chest and back. With his long straight hair and forbidding expression, he looked like a shadowy Lord of the Rings elf. He paused for a moment, waiting as a lithe woman in white emerged. Chandler recognized her immediately. Sibile.

Though years had passed since Lionel's childhood, Sibile looked exactly as Chandler had seen her in the retrocognition. Willow-gold skin. Tiny waist. Tiny rosebud mouth. Her hip-length blonde hair floated around her like an aura. Close on either side of her, gigantic black dogs kept time with her steps. A staff was strapped to her back and a knife hung at her waist.

Chandler hurried to join Devlin, Lionel, and Em on the top of the steps. She bent close. "I didn't expect them to just show up, did you?"

"Definitely not." Devlin kept his posture dignitary-straight and his eyes on the approaching fae.

Em hushed her voice. "I know some of the rules for communicating with them: Don't tell them your full name. Don't say 'thank you' or use the word 'faery.'"

Lionel rested his hand on Em's arm. "You and I should let Devlin and Chandler go first and do the talking. We also shouldn't say anything unless asked."

"Sounds good," Em said.

Chandler took a deep breath. "Let's get this done."

With Devlin beside her, Chandler strode down the teahouse steps. The horned woman, elf, and Sibile continued up the glowing path toward them. The redcaps and torchbearers hung back, standing at attention and watching their progress with steely gazes.

When there was no more than twelve feet between them, Chandler felt Lionel's hand on her shoulder. "Stop here. Let them come closer and introduce themselves if they want."

The horned woman continued a few more feet, then she dipped her head in a restrained greeting. Chandler mirrored her action, nodding first to the woman and then to the elf, and lastly to Sibile. She and Devlin might have been the elected leaders of the coven, but right now she wished Brooklyn was outside with them instead of somewhere in the main house with Midas. Other than Lionel, Brooklyn had the most firsthand experience with the fae. Of course, there was Evan. But he undoubtedly symbolized the High Council to them, and that wasn't even taking into account his possible alliance with the demons.

Devlin bowed his head politely. "We're pleased to see you, though it is unexpected. We had anticipated a message would arrive first—or perhaps that you would knock on our front door."

A glint of amber flashed in the woman's goatlike eyes. "Why would one knock? When you called down the moon, you left the door open. Granted, the entry was as slender as a reed. But we have friends—*nay,* we have sisters and brothers among the cattails and lily pads. They were more than glad to open their arms and let us pass."

The elf stepped up next to her. "You should take care, witches. If the ashes and sparks of your wishes and prayers can flow into the otherworld and into that of the Gods and Goddesses, then why can we not in turn follow their path back to you?"

The woman took over again, as smoothly as if they were reciting lines from a play. "If you bid us to come, do you not bid us enter? What do you expect of us?"

Devlin swept into a low bow, then rose. "The witches of the Northern Circle Coven wish to discuss a possible alliance."

Her lips pursed, holding back a smile. "You wish to bind yourselves to us?"

"We wish an alliance of equal measure. No binding vow. Only mutual respect, good wishes, and a pledge to do no harm to each other."

Chandler pushed the sleeves of her sweater up, nonchalantly and just far enough that the fae could catch a glimpse of her monkeys and dragons. If the woman and elf were going to double-team Devlin, then an extra show of power couldn't hurt.

She rested her hand on Devlin's wrist and smoothly took over the lead, "As high priestess, I agree that is our intention." She glanced over her shoulder. "Lionel—a Child of the Lake—has agreed to serve as envoy between your courts and the Northern Circle coven."

The horned woman hissed. "Do you think me a fool? He is not one of you. He is no witch."

"But he lived in your realm." Chandler clamped her lips shut, going quiet as Sibile stepped forward. If there was one thing she'd learned in the retrocognition, it was that Sibile cared about Lionel, deeply enough that she'd risked a great deal to help him return to his kind.

"Lady," Sibile addressed the horned woman. "I swear he is the child that suckled from my breast. He slept in my arms in the otherworld and at the court beneath the waves. I gifted him with sight. I paid for his freedom."

The woman stroked her hand along one of her horns, slowly considering Sibile's words. "I suppose he is."

The elf nodded. "I smell no lie in it."

Chandler's gaze went past them to where the redcaps were inching closer. What were they up to? According to Evan, they could move as fast as wildfire when they wanted to.

The horned woman eyed Lionel again. "These things being true, we will grant Lionel of the Lake the privilege of representing the Northern Circle and promise no harm will come to him." The amber gleam in her eyes brightened. "In exchange for this we ask for one thing." She lifted her gaze, indicating the teahouse. "The boy-child."

Anger blazed into Chandler's blood. "Never!"

"Be careful," Em whispered close behind her.

"There will be nothing offered"—Devlin folded his arms across his chest—"or given or taken on either side of this agreement. Lionel will serve as our envoy. We will exchange ideas and extend protection to all on both sides. You may assign one of your kind to speak as your representative. But what you are suggesting will not happen."

The elf ran his fingers along his belted weapons. "The boy. The child with the *sight*. We want him."

Chandler released her magic into her fingertips, sparks snapping. No elf with a few knives was going to intimidate her.

A sharp pain prickled her chest. Her dragon, warning of something.

Chandler withdrew her magic, focusing instead on the air around her. It was colder than before. It smelled... horrible.

"Wraiths!" Em shouted, just as she'd done last night in the stairwell.

Dark shapes jetted upward from between the cattails, demonic wraiths. They swooped into the air, circling in the dark sky like vultures at midnight.

The horned woman wheeled to glare at the wraiths. She pulled a silver rapier from the folds of her skirt, swiveled back, and snarled at Chandler and Devlin. "You dare lure us into an ambush?"

"They aren't our allies," Devlin growled. He cupped his hands, forming a spark of magic, growing it rapidly into a gyrating ball.

More wraiths surged from the cattails, dozens of dark shapes rising upward. Behind them, enormous hyena-like demons with furless skin and glistening fangs seeped from the muck. Hunger shone in their eyes. Saliva trailed from their muzzles.

"This isn't the time to debate our trustworthiness." Chandler yanked her wand from her waistline. "Watch out! Behind you!"

As the horned woman glanced back, the hyena-demons sprang onto their hind legs and launched themselves at the fae torchbearers. The redcaps rushed to intercept the demons, sickle-claws ready to rip. Screeches and howls rang out.

"You do realize we're fucked," the elf said, sliding a knife from his belt. Lionel muttered, "I'd say, seriously outnumbered and fucked."

"Shut up, both of you." Sibile swung away from the witches, ready for battle with her staff gripped in two hands and the dogs snarling at her sides.

"Screw waiting," Em said. "I'm going to put a dent in their numbers." Chandler turned to Em. "We need to work together. Conjoin our magic." But she'd spoken too late. Em rushed past her and past the fae envoys. She stopped midstride. Her face contorted and her entire focus centered on the circling wraiths as she shouted, "Be gone! Be gone!"

Two of the wraiths exploded, howling as they burst into green haze.

The elf ran to Em's side, hurling his knife at an oncoming hyena-demon. Explosions of energy flashed. The haze thickened. Fog closed in.

A wraith swooped at Devlin.

Chandler thrust energy into her wand and pointed at the wraith. "Ignite!"

The wraith burst into flames and tumbled to the ground, sparks gyrating across the path as it dissolved into haze. More wraiths materialized. She put her wand away, drew her energy into her hands, and thrust a wall of white-hot heat at them. They recoiled, but more surged forward, endless wraiths.

Through the haze and fog Chandler caught sight of Sibile, running to drive a demon away from Lionel. Given the ferocity of the battle, she was surprised neither Chloe nor Evan had rushed out to help. But mostly she was grateful they were keeping Peregrine safe and out of the way.

"Midas is coming. There's Brooklyn!" Devlin shouted.

Fantastic, Chandler thought. Her arms ached. Her head swam from the stench of the wraiths. The haze stung her eyes. She couldn't keep this up much longer.

Em appeared beside her. "I've tried calling up orbs to help us, but something's interfering. I can't get Athena or Saille's help either."

Chandler peered through the haze, looking for anyone or anything that might be focused on hindering Em. At the end of the footbridge, a woman with a gigantic afro and hips as narrow as a Barbie doll's stood scowling at them. Beside her was a man in snakeskin tight pants: crooked shoulders, disproportionately long legs, long wizard beard. His gaze was pinpointed on them. His lips were moving as if repeating a spell. Magus Dux.

She elbowed Em and nodded toward Dux. "You mean, someone like him?"

"That bastard. If I had Merlin's Book with me, I'd..." A dangerous look came over Em's face, devious and slightly smug. "You didn't happen to memorize that spell I gave you—the one for the monkeys?"

Chandler slid a hand into her sweater pocket, clutching the paper the way Evan had cupped his hand over the rune. She hadn't looked at the spell long enough to translate it. But a glimpse was all she really needed, and she had the added benefit of having copied it into her Book of Shadows.

Em lowered her voice. "I'd bet anything that Evan is in on this attack with Dux."

"Could be," Chandler said. But she couldn't afford to think about Evan right now, especially not about him in the teahouse with Peregrine. Chloe was with them. Chloe would protect Peregrine. One thing at a time.

She squeezed her eyes shut and concentrated on the paper. The illustrations and lines of the untranslated words became clear in her head. In her mind, she enlarged the centermost illustration. The most vital detail. The staff crystal.

A sinking feeling dropped into her stomach. The crystal was in the coven vault, attached to Merlin's Book. "Shit."

"What's wrong?" Em asked.

"The staff crystal. The spell requires it."

"We're toast," Em said.

Chandler let go of the paper and rubbed her arms, stealing strength from the protective magic in her tattoos. There had to be a way around this. There had to be... She followed the train of her thoughts. "The staff crystal is a stone. An amethyst. A blessed amethyst." Hope rushed into her. "The high priestess ring, its signet stone is a blessed amethyst."

"Try it," Em said. "The fog is getting thicker. I don't think Dux can see what you're doing."

Chandler clenched the paper again. She pushed all her magic into her right arm, through the tattoos and down into the finger that was encircled by the ring. She focused on her visual memory of the spell. Then she took her hand from her pocket, stepped off the path and planted her feet on the grass. The spell required grounding to the earth. It also required the energy level of a witch like Merlin.

"I need all the power I can get," she said to Em. "Put your hand over my fist."

As soon as Em's hand embraced hers, the surge of their conjoined energy electrified Chandler's skin and jolted into her bones. She closed her eyes, refocusing on the spell, the ring—and on her flying monkeys, the one in her workshop and the others on the gateway.

The spell's words and illustrations flashed in the darkness behind Chandler's eyelids. Lines. Contours. Boldness. Lightness. Negative space… The physical shape of the words tumbled into deeper meaning and sounds. Sounds became songs. The trill of flutes. The rhythm of drumbeats. The voices of ancient witches. Voices from early times and otherworlds. The rhythm of blood in veins. Of sap in roots. Fae and humankind. Trees and earth.

The blank spaces between the spell's words transformed into specifics. Chandler's intuition superimposed spaces and the voices on top of images of her flying monkeys. She released her magic into the ring and shouted, "Roots of trees. Blood in veins. Life comes. Life goes. Stone of earth. Metal of the ground. Earth. Air. Fire. Water. What are we? What is essence? Roots of trees. Blood in veins. Stone of earth. Fire. Air. Water…"

She opened her eyes and pointed with the ring in the direction of the flying monkeys, beyond what her eyes could see, but firmly set in her mind. Light flared from the ring's stone, a purple beacon cutting a path through the fog toward the spell's target.

Drumbeats and flutes sang in her head. The ancient witches echoed her chant in languages she didn't know. "Decay. Earth. Fire. Blood in earth. Blood in metal. By my will. Mine alone. Live. Do my will. Protect. Defend, from foes demonic. Come to me. Drive the wraiths and all other demons from this garden. Do my will!"

Power like she'd never felt before raged up from deep within her. Her nerves twitched. Her muscles spasmed. A sharp pain clawed her chest.

She fell to her knees, head in her hands as the voices and drums drew her deeper into their primordial song. Earth. Air. Fire. Water. What is essence? Roots of trees. Blood in veins—

Someone was shaking her.

"Snap out of it, Chandler," Em's voice shouted. "They're coming!"

Chandler jerked from the trance. She blinked against the fog, looking across the garden. Flashes of energy flared through the haze. Screams of redcaps and wraiths echoed. Above it all, in the distance, the outlines of winged monkeys lined up across the roofline of the main house, backlit by the even more distant lights of the city.

"The odds just got a whole lot better," Em said, as the monkeys folded their sheet-metal wings and jetted toward the demons.

Chandler shuddered. She agreed with that. But she wondered what the magical blowback of this would be. What costs would she pay for violating one of the most fundamental laws of nature?

"Chandler! Em!" Chloe's screams echoed in the air. She staggered out of the fog. Her hand was clamped against her forehead. Blood oozed through her fingers and dripped down her temples.

Chandler rushed to her. "What happened? Where's Peregrine?"

"Evan took him," Chloe gasped.

Chapter 35

She sees a dark shape on the bloodred horizon,
the outline of a dragon rising fast,
razor wings spread, tail lashing as it turns to face her dragon.
—Chandler's vision

"Where did they go?" Chandler screeched at Chloe.

"Teahouse. Back door."

Chandler took off at a dead run. She rocketed up the teahouse steps. The teahouse door was smashed, blown apart by an energy blast by the looks of it. She leapt through the gap, raced across the main room and out the back door.

The motion sensor floodlights blazed brightness down a trail that went to the compost area and toolsheds. There was no one in sight. But there was only one way they could have gone without her seeing them—down the shortcut that led out of the gardens and into the rear parking area.

Chandler flew down the trail, fueled by fury. Light from the battle flashed through the trees. Shouts and howls echoed. Haze misted the ground beneath her feet. She darted around the compost bins. She veered into the shortcut, between the toolshed and the outside of Devlin's apartment. Evan had to have forced Peregrine to show him the way. He couldn't have found this trail on his own. She now also suspected where Evan was taking Peregrine: To the front parking area where his Porsche waited.

She careened down the shortcut and into the coven's back parking area. She pumped her arms, racing up the driveway, heading for the front of the main house. She hadn't heard a car engine yet. If she got there soon enough, she'd throw herself on top of the Porsche or in front of it if she had to. Evan wasn't taking Peregrine. Never!

She rounded the corner of the main house.

Lionel's VW was there. Her Subaru was where she'd left it— Her heart stopped.

Evan's Porsche was there too. Dark and still. Unoccupied. No one anywhere around it.

She spun in a circle. Where were they? They couldn't have just disappeared!

Crack, crack, crack! The sounds reverberated from the back garden. Flashes of light strobed the sky over the main house. Shouts and screams rang out. But the light and sounds were more erratic now.

The outline of a winged monkey skittered across the main house rooftop, fists raised in a victory dance. The battle was waning. But where were Evan and Peregrine?

Chandler raked her hands over her head. Evan could have dragged or carried him out to the main road. Evan could have called someone to meet him there. But that didn't make sense when he had his car.

Boom! An explosion echoed behind her workshop. A blast of red energy brightened the sky above it. A yowl rang out.

Chandler shot toward her yard. The labyrinth. Of course! Peregrine's safe place. She'd told him to go there and build a fire if he ever needed protection. He'd escaped from Evan. She wasn't too late.

She tore around the outside of her workshop, plowing through the hip-high spires of goldenrod and asters. She passed the terrace. Her feet barely touched the ground as she flew by the scrap-metal griffins and dragons. Another energy blast lit her way. A hot orange flash. Evan's magic, lighting the sky and a mass of circling wraiths. No wonder the main battle had waned. The wraiths had come here to help Evan catch Peregrine.

Magic throbbed in her arms. Her pulse thundered in her ears. She could see outlines of people near the faintly glowing firepit. Not Evan. Not Peregrine.

Magnus Dux. And Lionel.

Lionel had the fire poker in his hands, brandishing it like Sibile had done with her staff. Magus Dux was closing in on him, an icicle-shaped dagger in his hand. Chandler had heard about Dux's daggers. Rhianna had been killed with one, her blood spraying the room as her body exploded into a gelatinous mass.

She spotted Evan, not far from Lionel. A praying mantis Barbie with bacon-colored limbs and a hairy thorax was prowling toward him, her needlelike teeth bared. Evan stumbled backward toward the stones that edged the heart of the labyrinth. Why was the mantis demon attacking Evan? And where was Peregrine?

She flew toward them and the labyrinth's heart, leaping over the stones that edged the path and ignoring the well-worn trail. Long ago she'd created every inch of the labyrinth, laid every stone with Peregrine strapped to her chest. Peregrine was smart. There was no safer place on earth for him. No place where she was stronger than here.

She panted for breath. She could feel Peregrine's energy. He had to be close by.

He came into view near the woodpile, stumbling under the weight of an armload of firewood. He was carrying them to the pit, readying to call the Great Fire Salamander. The Serpent of the Embers. Like he'd been told to do.

Chandler clenched her teeth and drew up more magic, holding back nothing. Her bones could break and reform. Her skin could become scales. She could become something wilder, something sharp-toothed and less human than who she'd been. She'd become a dragon if she must and stay that way forever, be banished from the human realm. She didn't care. No one was going to hurt Peregrine.

"Peregrine!" Evan screeched. "Get out of here."

The mantis Barbie dove on Evan, sending him to the ground. Its jaws clamped Evan's shoulder. He howled in agony. His energy faltered, snapping weakly from his hands as he kicked. The creature grabbed for Evan's leg—

A black dog leapt out from the darkness. Its eyes glowed like live coals as it landed on the mantis's back, biting and ripping at the creature's thorax.

The mantis threw Evan aside and whirled to face the dog. The dog snarled. Saliva trailed down the mantis's blood-crusted lips. It crouched, readying to spring. The dog launched itself forward. It seized the mantis behind the head, fangs sinking in. Yowls filled the air. Black sludge spurted from the mantis's neck... Snarling and screaming, they rolled into the darkness, out of sight.

"Get the boy!" Dux's command ripped through the air.

Chandler reached the heart of the labyrinth and streaked toward Peregrine.

A team of wraiths dove from the sky.

But she reached Peregrine first. She wheeled to face the wraiths, welding-bright magic blazing in her hands. The wraiths recoiled and hurtled back into the darkness.

"Mama," Peregrine said. "I started a fire. But it's little."

She let her magic ebb and took the firewood from his arms. "Now I need you to call the Great Salamander. Do you remember the words?"

He nodded.

"Stay by the fire. No matter what happens. Promise?"

"Yes, Mama."

With him close beside her, Chandler sprinted to the firepit and threw the wood on top of the glowing kindling. She sent energy at the kindling and shouted, "Ignis ignite!"

Flames erupted, licking skyward. The wraiths screamed and circled higher, away from the light as they waited for Dux's next command.

"Call the Salamander now," she said to Peregrine. She whipped her wand from her waistband. Peregrine had never used one, but he'd seen it done a million times. "Use this to focus your energy."

His hand shook as he accepted the wand. He pointed it at the flames and commanded, "Evigilare faciatis!" *Awaken*. His voice strengthened. "Great spirit, Serpent of the Embers, Great Fire Salamander. Come to us. Protect us…"

Renewed energy surged inside Chandler. He had it right. He knew what to do.

She pushed the world around her aside: Peregrine's voice. The haze and stench of the wraiths. The *snap-crack* of magic. The snarls. Lionel's grunts. Dux's laughter. She focused her entire being on the flying monkeys and pointed the high priestess ring toward the roofline of the main house and gardens beyond. "Protect. Defend. Come to me. Do my will. Drive the wraiths back into the otherworld."

Light flared from the ring's stone and a sharp tug pulled in her chest as her command connected with them, like a cable suddenly drawn tight. The flying monkeys were coming. She was certain of it.

"Mama," Peregrine whimpered. "Help Lionel and my daddy, please."

She glanced toward Evan. He lay curled on the ground, twitching. His eyes were wide open. A dark stain spread across his shoulder. Demon venom, as lethal as a cobra's. Not all demons had it. But clearly the Barbie mantis did. Evan didn't have much time. And no matter what his original intent had been, he had protected Peregrine.

She turned to Peregrine. "Use your phone. Call Devlin. Brooklyn. Everyone. Tell them we need help. Tell them someone's demon-bit." It was their best choice, their only choice. With the battle in the garden waning, maybe one of them would answer.

A *snap-hiss* of magic rang out, like the sound of a lit firecracker being thrown.

Lionel yelped.

She whirled. Lionel was moving backward, away from the firelight, closer to the darkness with the fire poker still gripped in both hands. Dux slithered toward him, black sparks hissing from his icicle-shaped dagger.

As if he'd sensed her watching, Dux glanced over his crooked shoulder at her. His eyes narrowed as he leered. "You'll like this next part."

Lionel hurtled forward, swinging the poker at Dux's head. Dux ducked and dodged, his long legs surprisingly agile. Lionel swung again. Dux slashed with his dagger, sparks arcing in its wake. They circled each other, moving close to the firepit. Nearer to Chandler.

She pulled magic into her hands. If she could hit Dux, it would buy Lionel time to strike him. But if she didn't aim perfectly, she'd hit Lionel by mistake.

Dux's dagger whined with magic. It shimmered like liquid silver. "I'm going to kill you, then skin the sculptress. With all that ink, she'll make a pretty pair of slippers."

"We've never done anything to you," Lionel said. His focus never left Dux's eyes. His movements were deliberate, but his ineffectual swings revealed he was far from a master of the staff.

Dux snorted. "Don't think so highly of yourself. You're just an appetizer. It's the Vice-Chancellor and the boy I want. My coffers are empty after the raid on my lair. The two of them are worth a fortune. One dead. The other alive."

A shriek ricocheted overhead as a team of monkeys streaked past and arced upward toward the wraiths.

"Enough of this," Dux snarled. He twirled like a ballet dancer and one hand sent a blast of energy at Lionel's chest. Lionel staggered sideways, the wind knocked out of him. Dux's other hand hurled the dagger at Chandler, blindingly fast.

"Calor!" Chandler shouted. *Heat.*

The blade melted in midair.

But Dux already had another blade in his hand, readying to throw.

"Veni ad me," Chandler shouted. A rock flew from the edge of the labyrinth to her hand, only long enough for her to hurl it. A *crack* resounded as the rock hit Dux's chest at the same moment as he threw the blade. She dodged but felt a burn as the icicle-shaped blade nicked her upper arm.

Numbness streaked up her muscles, paralyzing them and spreading across her shoulder. She tightened her shoulders to stanch the flow of the poison, then sent a wave of magic to drive it back into her arms and her tattoos. Her head throbbed from the effort. Darkness and flashes of light swam before her eyes. Her consciousness wavered. She had to do something fast. Peregrine needed her.

She thrust what energy she had left into her legs and ran straight at Dux, like a crazy person playing chicken with a bull. But what she had in mind was something slyer. Something she'd have preferred Peregrine not witness.

Dux dodge jubilantly out of her path, one boot brushing the edge of the firepit as he pirouetted and laughed.

"Serpent of the Embers!" she shouted. "Take him!"

Light and flames roared upward from the firepit. Heat washed her skin. The smell of scalding magic erupted in the air. Blinding gold light illuminated the heart of the labyrinth, the surrounding field, the sky, flashing light as strong as a thousand torches. The Great Fire Salamander rose, twenty feet tall and hissing with anger. His eyes were amber. Enormous red wings that Chandler had never before seen unfolded along his spine.

"Jesus Christ!" Lionel scuttled back.

Dux stood frozen, staring up at the serpent with his mouth open.

"Cambion," the serpent addressed Magus Dux, "half brother to Merlin, son of Magna Drilgrath, pater daemonium. You have violated the sanctity of this place. You sought to harm those I protect. Your punishment is death."

Dux unfroze. His hand winged toward his waistline and another icicle dagger. As fast as a whip, the serpent lunged and seized Dux in its clawed fingers, squeezing him tight. Flames spewed from the serpent's hand, surrounding Dux in an incinerator of fire. Dux howled, his voice escalating as the skin on his face blistered and burned. His hair and clothes caught fire. The stench of his cooking flesh exploded into the air.

"Mama!" Peregrine ran to her and threw his arms around her waist.

She crouched, wrapped her arms around him, covering his ears and pressing his head against her chest. She couldn't shield him from the smell or from what he'd already seen and heard. She couldn't protect him from reality. Not now. Not ever.

Dux's eyes popped out. Liquid sizzled from the hollows left behind. His head fell forward. The black char of his skin peeled off. His meat turned molten, scorching into stench. His bones *snap-cracked...* Tears boiled from Chandler's eyes. She wouldn't have wished this fate—her father's fate—on anyone.

"Fire. Air. Water. Earth. Everything rides the Wheel of Life," the serpent intoned. "So it ends. So it is renewed."

He opened his fist and the sparking gray ash that had once been Dux floated downward into the firepit's bed of embers, like petals from a shadberry tree on Beltane night falling through moonlight and into a stream.

Chapter 36

Who am I? Mother. High priestess. Artist.
I suppose I am still a daughter, despite my mothers and father being gone.
Lionel is right, too. I am a lover,
a part of me I've cast aside for far too long.
And I am a part of a community beyond my coven,
or I aim to be, at least.
—Journal of Chandler Parrish

Chandler grabbed Peregrine's hand. The Great Salamander would have to forgive her for not thanking him. She needed to help Evan. The last time she'd looked his body had been twitching. Now he lay motionless.

"Do you think he's still alive?" Lionel asked, as they rushed to where he lay.

She didn't answer. She hoped so. Evan wasn't all light. But he wasn't all darkness, either.

"Chandler! Peregrine! Where are you!" Brooklyn's shouts came from somewhere near the workshop.

"Over here!" Lionel waved both hands.

Chandler dropped down beside Evan. His breathing was labored. But he was still alive. "Lie still. Help's on the way."

"Demon. Poisoned," he groaned.

Peregrine sobbed, "Don't die. Please."

Lionel took Peregrine by the shoulders, pulling him back from Evan and making room for Brooklyn to slide in. Sibile arrived with a bowl of supplies. Devlin and the horned woman were with them.

"Remove his jacket," Sibile commanded.

Chandler did as she asked, tugging it off with Devlin's help. Evan lay limp and heavy, unable to assist.

"Do you have your knife?" Chandler said to Devlin.

He handed it to her, and she began cutting the shirt. Blood saturated his shoulder and arm. The fabric stank of sulfur and urine.

"If you feel numbness in your hands, stop working," the horned woman said. "That will mean the demon venom wasn't confined to the bites."

Sweat soaked Chandler's back. The horned woman's advice wasn't exactly comforting, considering the numbness she'd felt earlier when Dux's knife had nicked her. But her arm felt fine now. Perhaps the magic in her tattoos had neutralized the poison.

Chandler peeled back the fabric, exposing Evan's naked shoulder. Six gaping puncture wounds spanned its length. They were deep, black, and as swollen as erupting volcanoes. Orange sweat beaded on the skin around them. But when she touched his shoulder, it felt ice-cold.

"That's good enough," the horned woman said.

Chandler scooted back and the woman moved into her place. She might have thought the woman looked regal when she'd first arrived. But now her horns looked disturbingly dark and wet, like they'd been polished with blood. Plus, the thorns on her wreath had grown longer and sharper, as deadly as the spindle that pricked Sleeping Beauty's finger. It was like the battle had brought out another side of her.

The woman leaned close to Evan's face and hissed, "I'm going to enjoy this, *Special Envoy Lewis.*"

He groaned and shook his head, as if to object to having the woman tend to him.

Worry thrummed inside Chandler. She nudged Brooklyn, hoping she'd been privy to what was about to happen. "You sure this is a good idea?"

"Don't worry," Brooklyn said. "*If* it works, we'll know right away."

The woman smiled at Chandler, a slow, spreading smirk that showed off a row of thornlike teeth hidden behind thin lips. "I'd be glad to administer the antidote later. We could discuss politics over a cup of milk and honey instead. The delay would be excruciating for him, but he might survive until sunrise."

"The man is suffering. Do it now," Sibile commanded, her voice shrill.

"If you insist, dear Lady." The horned woman sighed, then she made a hawking noise deep in her throat. She leaned even closer to Evan, working her mouth. Finally, she spit a thick chunk of phlegm on one of the fang marks.

Black worms of foam fizzed from the wound. Yellow vapor and an even stronger stench of sulfur and urine belched into the air.

An urge to vomit heaved in Chandler's stomach. She hurriedly fanned the stench away from her face and swallowed back the taste of bile. "Is that good?"

"Depends on your point of view," the woman said. She hawked and spit again on the next puncture. More foam boiled up from it. More vapor. More stench.

By the time all the wounds glistened with the woman's phlegm, Chandler's eyes burned from the smell and her mouth tasted like she'd eaten spoiled meat.

"Is that it?" Devlin asked.

"Almost." The woman hawked even harder and spat on Evan's face. She snickered. "Oops, I missed the wound. I don't know how that could have happened."

"Like hell you don't," Chandler snapped. Doing something like that to someone who couldn't even defend himself was vile. She clenched her teeth to keep the rest of her thoughts inside. The woman wasn't human. The fae had different morals, different rules. Besides, Evan might have protected Peregrine, but judging by the way he threatened and manipulated people, it wasn't hard to believe he'd earned the contempt.

The horned woman moved aside, letting Sibile and Brooklyn take over. As they packed Evan's wounds with moss, Chandler took a minute to sort back through everything that had happened. Dux's praying mantis Barbie had attacked Evan. But before that he'd tried to make off with Peregrine. And Chloe... Evan had attacked her.

Chandler swiveled toward Devlin. "Where's Chloe? Is she okay?"

"She took an awful blow to the head when the teahouse door exploded. But mostly she was glad Peregrine and Evan escaped the blast. Midas carried her to the house."

"The door hit Chloe? Are you sure?" Chandler glanced back at Evan. Brooklyn was now wrapping bandages over the moss.

"That's why Evan and Peregrine left," Devlin explained. "Peregrine said they needed to go to his safe place."

She didn't know what to say. She could hardly believe it. Evan hadn't been trying to kidnap Peregrine. He'd been helping him.

A hooting sound filled the air. *Hoo, hoo, hoo! Owah, hoo!*

Chandler squinted against the darkness to see where it was coming from.

Along the workshop roofline, winged monkeys were chattering and bouncing up and down, like bored children waiting to be given something to do. But they weren't going to get their wish. Em was right. No one had a right to hold sovereignty over another being whether they were flesh and blood or created from metal and spells. On top of that, the longer they stayed animated, the more likely it was that an outsider would spot them.

Chandler closed her eyes, reached into her pocket and clutched the paper. As she focused on the spell, the ancient rhythms and voices that had initiated the animation poured back into her consciousness. She pointed the high priestess ring at the monkeys and intoned, "Roots of trees. Blood in veins. Life comes. Life goes. Stone of earth. Metal of the ground. Earth. Air. Fire. Water. Return to *as-you-were*. Be metal. Be earth. Be *as-you-were*..."

She could feel the surge of the magic and heat of the light flaring from the ring, and the tug when they connected with the monkeys. The hooting silenced. So did the conversations of everyone around her. When she opened her eyes, she wasn't surprised to find everyone staring at her. She'd actually stunned herself with the whole animating metal and returning it to *as-you-were* thing. The spell had seemed impossible when Merlin's Shade had done it. Even more so to have done it herself, plus reversed it.

The horned woman dipped her head to Chandler. "You impress us. A talent for art and metalwork combined with a remarkable gift for magic. It leaves a sour taste on our tongue to say it, but without your flying creatures of iron, we likely would have perished."

Chandler bit her tongue to keep from reflexively saying *thank you*. She nodded. "You're most kind."

The woman tilted her head, indicating Lionel. "We didn't fail to notice the iron pendant he wears. It thrums with your magic. It is impressive as well, witch-artisan, high priestess, and mother of a boy—"

Evan curled forward, coughing loud and painfully hard.

The woman huffed. "Such a rude interruption."

Chandler cringed. The cough didn't sound good. She looked at Sibile. "Evan's going to be all right, isn't he?"

"Perfectly fine, he just needs to finish expelling the nasties."

Yellow vapor spewed from between Evan's lips. His chest heaved, then he hawked and vomited a wad of soupy phlegm the shape of a rat. He hawked again, and out came something shaped like a leathery tail.

"Gross," Peregrine whimpered.

Brooklyn scuttled backward. "Yeah, that is nasty."

Chandler wasn't sure her stomach could take much more. "Is that the end of it?"

"Most likely." Sibile looked at Lionel, smiled and changed the subject like a butterfly flitting to a fresh flower. "If I am not mistaken—and I rarely am about such things—I see a glimmer in your aura, bright as starshine, or new love?" Her gaze glided to Chandler. "Aha. I am not mistaken."

The horned woman scoffed. "Enough frivolity. As I was saying, before I was interrupted." Her gaze went to Chandler. "Because of your impressive magic and your monkey creatures' aid in protecting us, we have decided to grant your son a no-harm agreement which will also extend to the rest of the Northern Circle members."

Chandler nodded to show she'd heard. But she didn't smile. She didn't trust the ease of the woman's offer and was certain the conversation was about to veer down the same dark path that it had taken earlier. Next, the woman would add an unacceptable contingency, like that they would agree to not harm Peregrine as long as he lived in the otherworld with them.

Evan pulled himself up onto one elbow. His voice shook, but it was nonetheless determined. "Northern Circle can't decide now. Won't do it. We need time to discuss."

The woman harrumphed. "We never cared for that one. He stinks of demon. This"—she gestured, indicating the fight that had occurred around the firepit, then toward the distance to include the garden—"all this disturbance smells of his work. We should have killed him long ago. Now one of my torchbearers is dead. Others are wounded."

"The attack wasn't his doing," Chandler said. No matter what she'd thought earlier, she was now convinced that all the evidence pointed away from Evan. "It was Magus Dux's work, not his."

She hissed. "We're supposed to believe that?"

"It's the truth," Devlin said.

Brooklyn got to her feet. "He's not lying."

"Is that so?" A pleased look passed between the woman and Sibile, as if the conversation had gone exactly where they intended all along.

Wary, Chandler sidestepped to Peregrine and draped a protective arm around him. What were they up to?

The horned woman licked her lips. "I smell a lie in this." She looked at Lionel, a smile building. "However, earlier my Lady Sibile put an idea into my head that I believe would transform this lie into the truth."

Evan staggered to his feet, gripping his bandaged shoulder. "I have always acted as a just and honest envoy between the Council and the Good Folk. I was not responsible for this attack."

The woman snorted. "As usual, your eager denial presents a condemning argument."

As Evan swayed unsteadily, Sibile scrambled to her feet and took his arm, steadying him. "Hush. Listen to her offer before you end up in flames like the magus."

Peregrine shuddered against Chandler. "She's not going to kill my dad, is she?"

"Shh," Chandler said. She hoped not, but at this point she wasn't sure of anything.

The horned woman waited until everyone was quiet. She took a deep breath. "The path forward that Sibile and I propose would please my kind and serve the witching world as well." She leered at Evan.

Sweat beaded on his temples. "Go on."

Her tone sharpened. "As representatives of our kind, we break our ties with you for violations against our safety. You are no longer welcome in our realm, Evan of the Eastern Coast High Council of Witches." Her gaze swept to Lionel. "But we wish to extend an offer to you, Lionel of the Lake, to replace the disgraced special envoy as the representative of the Eastern Coast portion of the witching world. In exchange, we will agree to your previous terms: a no-harm agreement and open exchange with the Northern Circle. And a no-harm agreement with you, Lionel."

"I'll do it," Lionel said.

Too late, Chandler held up her hand to stop him. "You can't, Lionel. She's not talking about you just representing the Northern Circle. She means all the Eastern Coast witches."

"I know. I want to do it for all of you." A gleam shone in his eyes. "I also have a selfish motive, right?"

Her breath stalled in her throat. *Of course.* They'd hoped Lionel representing the Northern Circle would be an argument against the amnesia spell being performed. But this... this defense was watertight. The High Chancellor, none of the chancellors, no matter what their bias, would want a mentally compromised non-witch to represent them. They also wouldn't want to upset the fae by turning down their proposal.

She bit down on a smile and nodded. She didn't want the fae seeing how happy the idea made her. Still, her body quivered from the implications. Peregrine would be safe. So would Lionel.

Evan pulled free from Sibile's stabilizing grip, looking much better now. His magic reverberated in the air around him, not at full force, but a force to be reckoned with nonetheless. "This can't be decided here and now. There's more to it. The idea must be presented to the High Council. The Northern Circle must vote on it."

Chandler squared her shoulders. "But you do think the Council would agree to something like this?"

Evan lowered his voice, speaking to Devlin as well as her. "This agreement would make it clear that the Northern Circle is not neutral. Your link with the Good Folk would be public knowledge, while other witches' allegiance would remain hidden. It's a hazardous move."

Chandler pressed again, "But the Council would agree?"

"I don't see as they'd have any other option, given the current situation and the Good Folk's insistence."

"And it will protect Peregrine, right?" She knew the answer, but she wanted to make sure Evan got the implication. A no-harm agreement with the fae would make it impossible for him to contend that he should have custody of Peregrine because he was better equipped to protect him than she was.

"I believe so." Evan smiled, but there was a clear twinge of resentment in his tone.

"It will protect the boy," Sibile clarified.

The horned woman cleared her throat. "One more thing."

Brooklyn laughed. "It's always one more thing with you guys, isn't it?"

"Quiet," Evan said sharply.

Chandler looked at Devlin. He shrugged as if to say he had no idea what this additional point could be.

The woman folded her arms across her chest. "If you're all done interrupting, I have something additional to say to Lionel."

Lionel dipped his head. "Yes?"

Her eyes shone, then darkened. "You, Lionel of the Lake, must pledge to never reveal the existence of our realms and kind. If you do, you will pay by never being allowed to return. You will be left without the sight. But your hunger for the sensation of our magic—for its slightest smell, sound, taste, and feel—will grow stronger instead of fading with each passing day. You will die of this hunger. But you will live to be the eldest of men."

"I agree," Lionel said.

"Are you sure?" Chandler shuddered. One misstep could cost him everything.

He pressed his fingers over his heart and smiled at her. "I won't ever breathe a word. I have too much to lose, now."

The glisten in his eyes told her he was referring to what was growing between them. Warmth flushed her body. "I know how you feel."

Sibile broke into the conversation. "This is pleasant. But my Lady and I should depart before the court fears harm has come to us. We have our own explanations to make."

"And pledges to present at the court," the horned woman added as smoothly as if she and Sibile shared one voice.

"Wait a minute." Evan touched his shoulder, indicating the bandaged bites. "I'm going to be driving home by myself tonight. Should I be worried about aftereffects? Sleepiness. Hallucinations."

Peregrine wiggled away from Chandler. "You can't go home. You said we could heal Aidan tonight. You said you knew who his father was."

Evan shook his head. "It's late. Everyone's exhausted."

"But you said we could do it." Peregrine's voice filled with horror. "He does have a brother, right?"

A sick feeling crawled up Chandler's throat as she remembered exactly what Evan had been saying when the fae envoys' arrival interrupted their meeting in the teahouse. She'd asked him if he knew who the boy was. Evan had said, *not exactly a boy.*

Shit. What was Aidan's brother?

Dear Goddess, not a cambion.

Not Dux's son, like she'd suspected.

Chapter 37

Son, this is about power, pure and simple:
a strong lineage of magic, wealth and position,
not to mention physical attractiveness, a pleasant bonus.
—Note to Evan A. Lewis from John E. Lewis
on proposed engagement to Yvonne Alexa Demetri

Chandler was grateful that Evan suggested they finish saying goodbye to the envoys, then continue the conversation about Aidan's father in the main house. She suspected the news was something he preferred the fae not hear. No doubt it was also something better revealed when everyone was sitting down with a beer or something stronger in their hands.

When they got to the lounge, they found Chloe on the couch with an ice pack pressed against her forehead. Em and Midas were sitting at the bar. Em looked the same as she had when Chandler had last seen her in the garden, but Midas was a wreck. His usually impeccable dreads were frizzed out like a wild man's. His pink button-down shirt hung open and torn. His lip was swollen. He and Brooklyn might have arrived late to the fight, but clearly, they hadn't missed all the action.

Em swept down from her barstool. "What took you so long? Peregrine texted to say everything was okay, but we were starting to worry." She came to an abrupt stop and wrinkled her nose at Evan. "You smell like the kittens' litter box."

"It's not me." Evan glared. He pressed his hand against his bandaged shoulder. "It's this foul thing."

Brooklyn propelled him into an upholstered chair. "I'll change the bandage and put ointment on it before you leave. It won't be so bad then."

"I'll need a clean shirt as well," he said.

A headache pinched behind Chandler's eyes. Enough delaying. "Earlier, you said Aidan's brother isn't a *boy*. What did you mean by that?"

Chloe gasped. "So, it's true?"

"Is what true?" Evan winced as he sat up taller.

Devlin took over. "When Em and I were in Dux's lair with Gar, we overheard Dux admit he'd promised to give your wife the spell to heal Aidan. He was blackmailing her with it, we know that much. But was there a reason Dux knew he could work the spell? Were your wife and Dux... more than a little close?"

Evan's lips curled in disgust. "I wouldn't put it past her. But that's not what I meant. Neither Aidan or his brother have demon blood. His brother isn't a *boy* because he is a *man*."

"What?" Lionel said.

"You mean, he's older?" Chandler thought back. Yvonne was what? Maybe a year or two older than she was. How old could her lover have been back when she was twenty?

Evan steadied his voice. "My wife—our marriage was arranged, that's no secret. Her lover was a man well-known for his preference for much younger women. One of whom was Rhianna."

"Fuck." Devlin covered his mouth with his hand. But Chandler could tell by the horrified look on his face that his reaction had nothing to do with swearing in front of Peregrine and everything to do with the mention of Rhianna. Devlin shook his head. "You're not saying... it can't be."

Evan nodded. "Aidan's your brother, Devlin. Your father slept with my wife. From what I gather it went on for some time." Anger corded his neck. "The bitch resisted telling me. But in the end, she took pleasure in throwing it in my face. I suspect it's public knowledge already."

Devlin pressed his hands over his eyes. "It makes sense now. When we were in Aidan's room, performing the spell, I felt chilled to the bone. The spell must have been trying to tell me that the summoner's bowl belonged in my hands, not Peregrine's."

For a long moment, no one moved. Finally, Midas got up from his stool and went around the bar. "Anybody want a drink?"

Lionel waved his hand. "I'll take a whiskey."

"I'll have a grapefruit juice," Em said.

Chandler slumped down at the end of the bar, too overwhelmed to speak. She couldn't believe it. Not that beautiful young women didn't ever have affairs with older men. But Yvonne had been newly wed to Evan. He was smart and rich. Attractive. Was Yvonne that soured by the arranged marriage that she acted out of spite—or did Devlin's father have a special ability when it came to seduction? Witch sex by nature was somewhat addictive, but there were those that honed it to a fine art.

"Can we help Aidan now?" Peregrine asked.

Devlin nodded. "Tomorrow, maybe. If that works for Evan?"

"It can't come soon enough for me," Evan said. His jaw worked, then he added, "Afterward, I'll talk to the High Chancellor about having Yvonne's charges dropped. I don't foresee an easy future ahead for the Northern Circle. But if my son is going to be a member, then at least I can make sure you start with a clean slate."

Midas opened a Switchback and slid it down the bar to Chandler. The bottle was cool against her lips, the liquid refreshing as the first sip went down. The tension drained from her body and she took a deep breath. Finally, there was nothing standing between them and helping Aidan.

Late the next afternoon, Chandler and everyone else involved with the healing gathered in Aidan's room. It was warm and dark, except for the twinkle of the life-support pall and the flicker of beeswax candles. The air was rich with the scent of the rosemary and sage smudge.

A sense of peace settled over Chandler. This was so much better than the last time. There was no fear that they'd be interrupted, even though the Council was keeping the healing under wraps. If they succeeded, then how Aidan had recovered would become public knowledge. If the spell failed... she bowed her head. If it failed, then nothing would change, and Aiden would remain under the pall until eventually his body and soul gave up.

"It's time," Em said. Merlin's Book of Shadow and Light sat open on the table in front of her. Athena and Saille's spirits hovered on either side.

Evan looked up from where he sat beside the bed, holding Aidan's hand. He nodded. "We're ready."

Across the bed from him, Peregrine squeezed Aidan's other hand. "It's going to be all right. I promise."

Chandler sent out a prayer to the universe, "Make it so. Please, make it so."

But even though everything else felt better than before, Aidan looked no different than the last time. His face was as pale as a winter moon. His eyes stared straight ahead. Tonight. his pajamas were as white as a fading spirit.

Gar moved up behind Em and rested his hands on her shoulders, his voice low. "Don't worry. This is going to work."

"It's got to," Em said.

Chloe set the summoner's bowl on the table in front of Merlin's Book. Devlin poured wine into it. As Chandler stepped forward and sprinkled herbs on top of the wine, a surreal feeling came over her. The spell was already coming to life. It was going to work. The Gods and Goddesses were with them.

Midas and Brooklyn each lit an incense burner. Smoke and a heady aroma wafted into the air. Cedar. Frankincense. Myrrh.

Em bowed her head and intoned, "Let us use the works and magic of Merlin. Grant us a channel to his wisdom to heal Aidan Lewis and restore his health."

The gold triangle and the purple crystal on the book's cover shimmered. Their brightness grew stronger as Saille and Athena placed their index fingers on the diamonds and chanted, "To restore. To use his wisdom to heal."

Em's voice joined theirs as she touched the last diamond. "Crone. Mother. Maiden. The three aspects of the Goddess. Open to us, Book of Merlin. Grant us your wisdom."

Chandler drew up her magic, pushing it out into the air with her voice. "Grant us power. Grant us wisdom from the root of the tree of knowledge…"

Devlin, Chloe, Gar, Evan… all echoed the words.

Light flared up from the crystal, illuminating the ceiling and fountaining down like purple rain. Merlin's Book shuddered, mist waterfalling out from inside it. Em and the ghosts withdrew their hands and it fell open to the page Em had bookmarked with rosemary.

Em's eyes rolled back into their sockets. Her voice became husky and masculine, as if she were channeling Merlin himself as she intoned in Archaic Welsh, "From the level of the sea, element of air lend me your power. Heal this child. Element of earth ground his soul that it remains with his body. Element of fire burn away the damage…"

Chandler sensed everyone's magic rippling and conjoining and undulating toward the summoner's bowl. The bowl shimmered. Mist and the bitter tang of tansy rose from the liquid and wafted into the air. A sense of vertigo crashed over Chandler, then receded as the air pressure climbed.

Devlin took the bowl from the cart. He bowed his head, lips moving in a silent prayer as he carried it to the head of the bed where Peregrine stood. Peregrine released Aidan's hand and moved aside, making room for Devlin to lean through the pall.

The scent of burning leaves and hot sun on earth flooded the room. Devlin's voice echoed in the air. "I offer this to you, dear brother. For your health. To heal you."

He held the bowl up to Aidan's lips.

One drop needed to touch them, not even a sip.

Just a drop.

The drop glistened on Aidan's pale lips, as dark as a child's tiny body lying motionless in a pool of water. Lying there, the way Chloe had described what she'd seen in the swimming pool all those years ago.

Devlin retreated from the pall.

Em whispered, "So it is done. So mote it be. Power of goodness, let this child awaken."

The air hung silent, simmering with magic. Purple light swirled like mist.

Chandler held her breath, waiting for something.

Anything.

Aidan blinked. His lips quivered, forming a breathy word. "Daddy?"

"Aidan!" Evan dove forward, through the pall, embracing Aidan, holding him, rocking him. His voice choked with tears. "Baby. My baby. It's going to be all right. I promise."

Aidan looked over Evan's shoulder, staring at all of them.

Not long after that, the Council nurses and doctor rushed in. As they took over tending to Aidan, Chandler followed the rest of the coven toward the door. But just as she reached it, she felt a touch on her arm.

"Wait a minute," Evan said.

She turned, letting everyone else go ahead into the hallway.

Evan's eyes sparkled with happiness, but his jaw was set. He bent close to her, his voice hushed. "I do intend to see Peregrine, you understand that?"

She met his eyes with the unyielding strength of a dragon. "It's only right. But for now, you'll see him at the complex. You and Aidan are welcome to stay with us. However, Peregrine will not go anywhere alone with you. I'm sorry. I don't trust you that much."

She braced herself for his anger; instead, a slow smiled flicked across his lips. "Hopefully, I'll regain that trust with time." His voice went husky, seductively so. "I haven't forgotten that night. I've wondered sometimes about you—us."

For a second, Chandler stared at him, dumbfounded. She laughed. "Are you crazy?"

His voice didn't change. "You have a lover, for now. But the fae otherworld is a tempting place. What if he doesn't return to you? Then what?"

She scowled. "I don't foresee that happening. If it did? I wouldn't suddenly become desperate, if that's what you're insinuating. I have Peregrine and my coven, and my profession and community. It's not the family or the life I envisioned when I was a lonely child or a lovesick teenager or even that night with you. But it's my dream now—and it's perfect."

Chapter 38

There was a symbol at the bottom of Chandler's teacup.
A heart. Perfectly rendered in moist leaves,
waiting for her. After the sadness. And the baby.
After the isolation and amid the battling dragons.
—Tasseography reading for Chandler by Athena Marsh

"Love you, Mama," Peregrine said as she tucked the blankets under his chin.

Chandler kissed his forehead. "Love you too, sweetheart."

"Can I have a black dog?" he asked.

"Sneaky, aren't you. But, *no.*" She kissed him again. "You can ask Em about a kitten."

"Really? Two kittens?"

"Sure. Two, but not three."

She turned off the bedroom light and left the room. As she closed the door, she murmured, "Circum silentium. Vigilate. Moneo." *Surround with silence. Watch and warn.*

She padded across the living room to the kitchen. It was almost one o'clock. Aidan's healing and even the drive home from headquarters felt like it had happened years ago instead of hours, surreally so.

Lionel hunched at the table with his laptop open. He looked up at her. "You must be dead on your feet."

"Beyond tired, actually." She brushed a hand across his shoulder and looked down at the laptop's screen. "What are you working on?"

"I wanted to get a few ideas down before I forgot them."

"Using a movie as a cover-up for all the noise and flashes of light in the sky is going to work brilliantly," she said.

Lionel nodded. "Zeus messaged me while you were in with Peregrine. He's got a friend who makes art films."

She laughed. "I swear Zeus has connections everywhere."

"Sounds like it." He rested one elbow on the edge of the table. "Anyway, Zeus's friend is going to stop by tomorrow and leave some production equipment on the terrace. The theory is that when the non-witches show up for Athena's service on Tuesday, the equipment will back up the movie rumor I'm starting online."

Athena's service. Chandler sighed. She'd almost forgotten about it with everything going on. Sadness gathered inside her and for a moment she stared at the laptop screen, looking but not seeing. Athena's service would happen the morning before Samhain eve. That evening, the entire coven—including Laura and the other outlying members—would take part in their regular Samhain rituals, plus the ceremony to officially name her as high priestess. Life continuing, despite all the changes.

She took another deep breath, thinking some more about the service. One thing she needed to do was be on the lookout for Isobel Lapin. It was possible she might come, and there were things that needed to be asked and resolved if necessary—such as, was she The Thinker?

Lionel brought up an image on the computer screen. It was a photo of an old, derelict motel. A child stood in one of the open doorways, strong and defiant despite the peeling paint and rotted wood all around her. She was backlit. Her face hidden by shadows.

The photo tugged Chandler from her thoughts. It had to be for the article he'd been working on. "Is that the motel where you were staying?"

He nodded. "On the way back from headquarters, when you guys were talking about the cover-up and everything, I was thinking about people finding their strength and rising up, driven by need and their hungers. I've been searching for something to center my article around. I want it to be a story of survival and empowerment, not defeat. I just remembered this photo."

"Is she the girl you were getting the sand for?"

He nodded. "I still owe her a castle."

Chandler looked again at the image of the girl and her defiant strength. She bent down and kissed Lionel's cheek. "It's going to be an amazing article. You're amazing."

He smiled. "How about giving me a few minutes to finish up, then I'll meet you in the bedroom?"

She skimmed her hand down his arm. "I've actually got something I need to do, too. Make it twenty minutes?"

His smile spread into a grin. "Perfect."

Leaving him behind, Chandler went out to her workshop.

The flying monkey silently watched her arrival from its perch on the rusty oil drum.

She smiled at it. "Don't worry, I haven't forgotten you."

She put on a pair of safety glasses and shoved a pair of pliers into her hip pocket. Then she took the heart from the box she'd stashed it in and carried it over to the monkey.

"Don't tell your friends on the roof, but you're my favorite," Chandler whispered, as she opened the door in its chest and set the heart into its housing.

She brought up her magic and drew a focused line of heat along one of the arteries. The metal glowed red, then edged toward salmon, then yellow. Using the pliers, she bent the glowing wire into position, then applied more heat. Her hands and magic worked in unison, shaping and securing everything into position. Harp string arteries and veins attached to the metal body, gripping like roots, like a source of life. More sparks. More heat...

Once everything was how she'd envisioned, she closed the door and stepped back. Warmth spread through her body, satisfaction at a job well done.

She gave the monkey a thumbs-up. "I'd love to stay and chat, but I've got someone waiting. And you know what? He's smart and kind. He's one fine man—and Peregrine likes him, too."

Chandler rubbed her fingers across her upper chest, feeling the stir of the red dragon as she thought about her bed and sheets and the man who'd soon be waiting for her.

She smiled. She could almost smell the sweetness of the calendula lotion already.

Be wise. Be strong.
Listen to the quiver of your heart and the shiver of your soul.
Be your dragon when you must.
—Wisdom of the Great Fire Salamander, Serpent of the Embers

Also by Pat Esden
DON'T MISS THE DARK HEART SERIES

A Hold On Me

Annie Freemont grew up on the road, immersed in the romance of rare things, cultivating an eye for artifacts and a spirit for bargaining. It's a freewheeling life she loves and plans to continue—until her dad's illness forces her return to Moonhill, their ancestral home on the coast of Maine. There she meets Chase, the dangerously seductive young groundskeeper. With his dark good looks and powerful presence, Chase has an air of mystery that Annie is irresistibly drawn to. But she also senses that behind his penetrating eyes are secrets she can't even begin to imagine. Secrets that hold the key to the past, to Annie's own longings—and to all of their futures…

Beyond Your Touch

Annie Freemont knows this isn't the right time to get involved with a man like Chase. After years of distrust, she's finally drawing close to her estranged family, and he's an employee on their estate in Maine. But there's something about the enigmatic Chase that she can't resist. And she's not the only woman. Annie fears a seductive stranger who is key to safely freeing her mother is also obsessed with him. As plans transform into action and time for a treacherous journey into a strange world draws near, every move Annie makes will test the one bond she's trusted with her secrets, her desires—and her heart.

Reach for You

A world of deception and danger separates Annie Freemont from her mother—and from Chase, the enigmatic half ifrit with whom Annie's fallen in love. But she vows to find her way back to them, before Chase succumbs to the madness that threatens his freedom. The only person who can help is the magical seductress, Lotli, a beautiful, manipulative woman… a woman who has disappeared…

Available where books are sold.

Printed in the United States
by Baker & Taylor Publisher Services